KAM

Anuja Chandramouli graduated from Women's Christian College, Chennai, and was the college topper in Abnormal Psychology. She also holds a Master's degree in English. Currently she is studying classical dance and working on her next book. Her critically acclaimed debut novel, *Arjuna: Saga of a Pandava Warrior-Prince*, was named in a poll conducted by Amazon India as one of the top 5 books in the Indian Writing category for the year 2013. She is the mother of two little girls and lives in Sivakasi.

Email: anujamouli@gmail.com
Website: www.anujachandramouli.com
Twitter handle: @anujamouli

KAMADEVA

KAMADEVA

The God of Desire

Anuja Chandramouli

RUPA

Published by
Rupa Publications India Pvt. Ltd 2014
7/16, Ansari Road, Daryaganj
New Delhi 110002

Sales Centres:

Allahabad Bengaluru Chennai
Hyderabad Jaipur Kathmandu
Kolkata Mumbai

ISBN: 978-81-291-3459-2

First impression 2014

10 9 8 7 6 5 4 3 2 1

The moral right of the author has been asserted.

Printed by Thomson Press India Ltd, Faridabad

For
Meekster, Gassy Goosey and Stinky Monkey

Contents

The Song of Kama*

I cannot be destroyed by any creature by any means.
He who tries to destroy me by attacking my strength with knowledge;
in this very attack of his, I will appear again and again.
He who tries to destroy me with sacrifices and offerings;
I will appear like a man of action in the essence of these actions, among all
the mobile creatures of the world.
He who tries to destroy me with the Vedas
and sadhanas of the Vedanta;
I will appear like the essence of stillness among all the immobile creatures.
He whose attack is truth, who tries to destroy me with firmness;
I will be the essence of him and he will not be aware of me.
He who firmly adheres to his vow, who tries to destroy me
with the heat of tapas;
I will appear again and again in that very tapas of his.
He who is a man of learning, who tries to destroy me
by being intent on moksha;
I will dance and laugh at the intentness of his resolution to
gain moksha. I am eternal. I am the only one among all creatures
who is indestructible.

The Birth and the Curse

*B*rahma, the Creator of the Universe, had been known on many an occasion to err on a truly grandiose scale. He had granted boons of power to villains who had a pronounced predilection for megalomania, thereby throwing the delicate balance of power between good and evil out of whack. He had lied to Vishnu, the second in the holy Trinity credited with being the Protector of the Universe, while they were engaged in an argument, only to get cursed in return by Shiva, the foremost of the Trinity, going by the sinister cognomen of The Destroyer. Brahma had even blown up his painfully accumulated store of ascetic merit several times by injudiciously indulging his coarser passions in a manner that ill befits someone of his revered stature.

Yet, his saving grace was that he did take his task of creation very seriously and indeed, few could fault him on his labours in this noble cause. He performed the severest austerities known to the Gods and mankind in order to better perform his divinely appointed duties unhindered. Through a combination of willpower and penance—neither of which came easy to him given his history—he ensured that his mind, body and soul had been purified before embarking upon the process of creation. And it was thanks to his efforts, knowledge and inherent genius that the cosmos emerged, in all its magnificent glory.

Having completed this onerous task, Brahma calmed his mind with more meditation in a sylvan spot somewhere in Brahmaloka, his chosen abode. Joining him were the Prajapatis, sons of his mind that he had willed into being. They were ten in number and to them had he entrusted the task of populating the world and serving as the guardians of all creation. The Prajapatis were named–Marichi, Atri, Angiras, Pulastya, Pulaha, Kratu, Bhrigu, Vasishta, Daksha and Narada. Made in the image of their creator and possessing more of his vaunted strengths than lampooned weaknesses, the Prajapatis were exalted beings and embodiments of purity. They combined within themselves the agelessness of immortals with the vitality and virility of youth and the wisdom of ancient rishis.

The Prajapatis applied themselves to the task set by their father with due diligence. However, their efforts were stymied when each realized that the task was too daunting to perform on their own, since none had the unique gift of the divine Progenitor. A solution was gradually arrived at. They each concentrated their efforts towards creating a vessel, which was the bounteous female form, into which they could pour their seed, rendered potent by their ascetic merit, so that they could bring forth the multitudes needed to populate the world. And thus emerged every manner of living creature their mind could conceive, borne by the sanctified vessels—the mothers they had partnered with. Having completed their mission, they returned to Brahma. In his company, they also devoted themselves in earnest to prayer and penance, to better recuperate from their labours.

Brahma gazed at this august gathering and was pleased with their combined efforts. Even his worst detractors wouldn't be able to ridicule him for being an example of too much knowledge failing to compensate for want of common sense, which was their preferred jibe. Yet, he felt his contentment to be incomplete for there was a niggling sensation of resentment that gnawed away at him. He pondered over it and realized that perhaps his sons had done too good a job and may have just supplanted him by devising an ingenious and far more pleasurable shortcut to bring about creation. Terror gripped him as he realized that there was a very distinct possibility that he had outlived his usefulness and may be done away with by his enemies who had boldly suggested that he was not worth the trouble he caused.

The sudden onslaught of volatile emotion that tore apart his hard-earned tranquillity made him feel the full extent of his terrible loneliness. Dissatisfaction and unhappiness congealed in his breast, and his dormant powers stirred recklessly to life. Powerful feelings emanated unbidden from his soul, or perhaps his loins, where life's struggle to assert itself over death usually emerged, and exploded over the assembly, shattering the collective calm like so much glass. The very air was rendered pregnant with the physical manifestation of the Creator's need to reassert his mastery. A female of unequalled beauty, thus emerged from the sudden chaos in the previously unsullied mind of the God.

In all of creation, there was nothing as exquisite as her. She was the product of primordial desire, every inch of her seeming to cater to that tender yet terrible emotion. Her name was Sandhya. Brahma gazed on his masterpiece with pride and adoration—and rightfully so—for nobody in the past, present or future could ever hope to equal the damsel in terms of sheer beauty. With her by his side, he could create the world and fill it to overflowing with their children and do away entirely with the irksome Prajapatis who had dared make him feel insecure.

Overpowering lust filled the Creator even as he cautioned himself that the damsel was his daughter since he was the father of all creation and she had emerged from him literally. In fact, he was her mother as well. But knowledge of the nature of their relationship, far from quenching his desire, only served to inflame him further as the idea of the forbidden dalliance worked up the originator of the Vedas into such a sweat, that even the risk of eternal damnation couldn't hold him back.

Even the Prajapatis, that uber respectable gathering of superior beings, discovered to their horror the inner lecher in them as they ogled their sister to their heart's content, wondering if they would be able to stop themselves from staking first claim on her. Their understanding of universal truths or the purity of purpose which had united them in the cause of creation vanished into thin air as they looked on at Sandhya like gluttons at a buffet.

Brahma, meanwhile, had started to rack his brains for a way out of this conundrum. Knowing fully well that it would be a sin to lie with his daughter and yet wanting her with a passion that threatened to split him asunder, Brahma's mind offered him an ingenious alternative. Out of the wellspring of forbidden passion that emanated from his loins and bubbled over into his heart, rose a golden youth who rivalled the beauty of the exquisite damsel who had so thoroughly thrown that gathering of exalted beings into riotous confusion.

His countenance reflected the brilliance of a billion suns. Rich waves of blue-black hair skimmed his forehead sensuously and fell down to his magnificently sculpted shoulders. Supple, slender and strong was his form. And in a face more handsome than anyone had ever seen, rested a pair of beautiful eyes that were easily his most captivating feature—lit up as they were by the promise of mischief and secret adventures that held the promise of unlimited joy. The youth was clad in blue and he seemed to exude a deliciously provoking odour of concentrated sex.

Good looks he had in abundance, for Brahma and the Prajapatis, despite having been driven to distraction by the diverting Sandhya, found themselves staring at the impossibly good-looking youth who stood before them. His spectacular looks aside, there was a certain aura about the boy that set him apart. All who looked upon him in that gathering knew at once that he was unique and unparalleled, and that there would never be another like him.

When the lad spoke, his voice was deep and mellifluous, 'Creator! Father! Allow me to offer you my deepest gratitude for bringing me into being and for the abundant gifts that you have showered on me. A billion lifetimes spread out over eternity will be insufficient to repay the kindness you have done me. Therefore, it is my humble request that you assign an honourable station for me so that I may be of service to you and the rest of creation.'

Brahma smiled down at his marvellous creation and said, 'It was desire that gave you life and hence desire shall be the domain where you will reign supreme. In this form, and with the bow and flower arrows which shall be my gift to you, the power to penetrate and captivate minds shall be yours. Through this power, the noble tradition of creation will be carried on for all of eternity. None will be able to withstand your might, not even Vishnu and Shiva, and certainly not men—nor I. You will be known, henceforth, as Kamadeva, the God of Desire!'

Brahma and the Prajapatis blessed the newly anointed God with his wonderful power, and flowers rained down on his head. Pleased with the show of approbation, Kama now held the bow in his hand and decided to bestow the gift of pleasure that he had been given upon all present. Anxious to please, he shot his arrows indiscriminately and soon, even the air around them began to turn muggy with the scent of arousal.

Sandhya was not exempt and she too began to respond to the sexual energy that had pervaded the air around her, demanding acknowledgement and indulgence. With everyone present slowly but surely surrendering their last vestiges of self-control, the scene would most certainly have culminated in an orgy of unparalleled depravity—the hallowed beings desecrating the grounds they stood on, by their debauchery. Brahma himself was well on his way to losing his privileged status, thanks to the misdeed he was dangerously close to committing—when, all of a sudden, there appeared on the scene, Shiva, the Destroyer. Famed for his ascetic merit, it was his intervention that stopped the orgy before it could get underway and proceed to its messy conclusion.

Some of the Prajapatis themselves had prayed to him for help as they felt control slipping away from them, leaving them vulnerable to the addictive call of desire. They did not wish to commit the dreaded sin of incest and bring down perpetual infamy upon their heads, especially as they had worked hard to become respectable pillars of the universe. Shiva responded to their plea for help and arrived on the scene. He took in the signs of extreme moral lassitude in motion and the faces of the would-be participants, contorted as they were with bestial passion, and he was repulsed. His enormous eyes smouldered with ill-concealed fury and disgust, striking fear in the hearts of all present.

The presence of the Destroyer and his magnificent contempt had the effect of a cold shower, and the flames of passion kindled by Kama were doused all at once. Shiva rounded on Brahma in contempt, 'What is the matter with you? It should not be this hard for someone of your learning, wisdom and stature to behave with a modicum of decency! This is not the first time you have allowed lust to blind your better judgement, leading to dire consequences both for yourself and the rest of this world. During my wedding to my beloved Sati, which you were supposed to be officiating, you looked at her with your lecherous gaze and proceeded to spill your seed, thus profaning the sacred occasion and guaranteeing a short-lived marriage for me on account of your perfidy.

For all intents and purposes, I wanted to strike you down then and there, but Vishnu made me desist by pointing out that it was in the best interests of the cosmos that the three of us stay united and in harmony with each other. Paying heed to his counsel, I thus contented myself by making you wander the earth with my image branded on your head so that others may laugh at you and learn a valuable lesson about the imprudence of coveting another's wife. But it appears that you have failed to learn and now seek to bring further infamy upon yourself by lusting after your own daughter!

It amazes me that the being from whose mouth the precious

Vedas emerged could be capable of such sickeningly degenerate behaviour. Don't the laws laid out in the Vedas clearly state that a man shall not look upon his mother, sister, or daughter with anything even close to desire? This is because incest is a damnable sin and offensive to God and man alike. And here you have felt free to come up with a nefarious scheme that will give you the license to copulate with your daughter and have created for that purpose this indecent creature with his ridiculous bow and flowery arrows!

What manner of creature is this Kama? Ignoring more deserving souls, you have bestowed unlimited powers on him, even though it is evident that he has roots in the basest dregs of your immorality. His behaviour also reflects on the complete lack of self-control and utmost stupidity that resulted in his being. Without the least amount of responsibility or the tiniest shred of decency, he has carelessly wielded the power given to him as if he were a child with a toy—which in effect is what he is. A foolish, silly child who has no business using the so-called weapons you have bestowed on him in a carnally charged moment to play such dangerous adult games.

If his foolishness is sufficient to make even the Creator and his Brahmarishis forget themselves so completely, can you begin to imagine the chaos he is capable of wreaking in the world of man that you have so lovingly forged? I have spared you in the past because my beloved Hari spoke to me in your defence and he is the reason the lot of you have not been incinerated right now, as I am wont to do, viewing such perversion. Sensing my rage, I can feel him making his way towards us. I will, therefore, leave him to talk some sense into this sorry lot while I myself depart before I forget myself and turn you all into a smoking pile of ash, which is truly more than you deserve!'

Having said his piece, Shiva stalked off, his matted locks (which housed numerous reptilian creatures) lashing Brahma across his face—leaving him, the Prajapatis, Kama and Sandhya quivering with shame and quailing in the face of his wrath and scorn. Brahma felt the desire for Sandhya still roiling within him and this time he was repelled by it. With Herculean effort, he fought to subdue his baser instincts; the sweat poured down his body as he struggled to expunge that desire which had made Shiva heap such virulent contempt upon him in front of all his progeny. Slowly but surely, he succeeded and once again became the master of his senses.

Anxious to save face, the Creator now espied Kama who, in his original plan, was supposed to have absolved Brahma of blame for cavorting with his own daughter. Instead, Brahma had been hauled up and chastised by Shiva—and not having dared to take on the Destroyer; he now turned his wrath on the far less formidable Kama: 'You have shamed me in front of my equal and rendered me inferior. I have been made a laughing stock and have lost all respectability in the eyes of my own creation. For bringing about the infamy of the beloved father who gave you life and such powers as had never before been heard of, I curse you! When you use your powers against Shiva, he will open his third eye and burn you to cinders—but not before you have triumphed over him, leaving him an abject slave of ardent desire. And then I will be avenged upon the pair of you.

Does the three–eyed God think himself above the baser emotions? I will show him! And the world will know that he is as fallible as the rest of us, if not more so. You will bring about his downfall and then you shall be obliterated!' So saying, Brahma bade his audience to be gone and then left the place blindly, shame burning away inside him. Exhausted with the effort that it had taken to bring his desire under control, coupled with the encounter with Shiva which had left him bruised and battered inside, as well as the cursing of Kama, he realized that he had expended all the ascetic merit that he had gathered so painstakingly over the eons. Unwilling to go on in the world which he had so lovingly created, but which had suddenly become anathema to him on account of his disgrace, he gave up his life in an abrupt moment of morbid recklessness.

Sandhya, who had inadvertently caused so much pain, had also been feeling thoroughly ashamed of herself. Kama's arrows had inflamed her thoroughly and she blushed to think of the wanton woman she had been merely a few moments ago, who had been more than willing to participate in an orgy with her brothers and her own dear father. While Shiva had been verbally lambasting Brahma and Kama, he had not even deigned to look at her as if she were nothing but a whore and did not even deserve his attention, let alone censure. Unable to withstand the thought that she would be remembered by future generations as the lustful lady who had brought destruction upon her own father, Sandhya also gave up her life.

Watching all this, Kama was shell-shocked. His life, which had begun with such promise, appeared to be over even before it had begun. He had been doubly blessed by the Creator and had been given power by him that was comparable with that of the divine Trinity. It had given him intense pleasure to think of exactly how fortunate he had been. His status and the admiration of all gathered had intoxicated his senses and had gone straight to his head in a mad rush that had proved to be his undoing. Carried away, he had used his power imprudently without exercising his better judgement, and as a result, between Shiva and Brahma, they had cut him down to size. Bewildered and suddenly bereft of the joy for life which he had been feeling only a few moments before, he fell to the ground in a dead swoon.

When he came to, Kama found himself looking at none other than Vishnu himself. He got to his feet, wondering if another verbal lambasting was in store for him and if he could take it, especially after the bruising encounter with the Creator and the Destroyer which had had such unhappy consequences for him. As if reading his thoughts, Vishnu smiled at him gently, and the compassion in that beatific smile brought tears to Kama's eyes.

Vishnu put his arm around Kama as if he were a brother or

an equal and said, 'Quite an eventful day you are having, aren't you? Brahma has outdone himself by creating you, for, like him, you appear to be a trouble-maker par excellence. But unlike him, you have barely exerted yourself or your powers, and already we have an end-of-the-world sort of crisis on our hands with two divine beings no more, and the Brahmarishis scurrying from the place, tails between their legs, terrified of the sudden catastrophe that has befallen them. Let us walk a bit, shall we? Perhaps we can figure a way out of this unholy mess?'

Completely flabbergasted, Kama allowed himself to be led onwards by Vishnu who continued to address him, 'No sooner did you come into being than you caught the attention of none other than Shiva himself and got Brahma into trouble with the three-eyed God who seems to have barely restrained himself from destroying the whole lot of you! And Brahma's unprecedented kindness to you seems to be equalled only by his unkindness. You have been blessed with more than your fair share of good looks and bestowed with the power to agitate minds that puts you on an equal footing with the greatest Gods in the pantheon. And yet, as if to counter your good fortune, fickle fate has spat in your face and prompted Brahma to curse you with a premature death at the hands of the Destroyer.

Now he has gone and forfeited his life, as has that dazzling damsel. But fear not, for as always, I will restore order in a world that has suddenly gone completely haywire. Brahma and Sandhya must be revived, for the world needs a Creator and he clearly has some pressing issues that need to be urgently addressed. And don't worry about what will become of you…I have taken a great liking to you, so trust me when I say that there will be plenty of good things in store for you just around the corner, even though it may hardly seem likely to you at this low point in your existence.'

Kama laughed aloud for Vishnu had restored his good cheer by simply putting his arm around him in that brotherly fashion of his. He felt rejuvenated on hearing the comforting words and he carelessly shrugged away the sorrow that had wrapped itself around him. Deciding to be a little reckless himself, he put his own arm around the Protector and declared, 'You are my favourite by far! My father, with his repressed sexuality and anger issues, behaved like a complete cretin by first using me to fulfil his deranged fantasy and then cursing me for doing exactly what he created me to do. As for Shiva, he is a great one for brandishing his authority and scaring us poor souls senseless. He was so severe. And he made me feel worse than death warmed over.

You, on the other hand, are absolutely amazing. Your very presence is so soothing and I feel like everything is going to turn out just swimmingly—even though for the life of me, I can't imagine how that will happen right now!'

Vishnu smiled at him fondly before cautioning him, 'I find your irreverence diverting. But in my opinion, it would be prudent for you to take a more respectful tone and avoid name-calling. Brahma will be revived by my Grace, but his wounded pride will remain and I doubt he will be in the mood to take any more flak from you. Plead your case with him and I am sure he will be reasonable enough.

As for Shiva, he is a dear friend of mine and without doubt the greatest of the Gods. The loss of his beloved Sati has left him bereft and until the time they are reunited, I am afraid, he will continue to remain somewhat on edge and be an even more foreboding personage than is usually his wont. Now I have said enough about my fellow divinities, so stand back and let me do my job.'

So saying, Vishnu closed his eyes and meditated briefly. And before Kama's astonished eyes, Brahma and Sandhya re-emerged from the dark passage on which their souls had embarked, as though they had never departed in the first place. All his dignity forgotten, Brahma hugged Vishnu and wept in misery and relief. He said, 'I knew you would bring me back, but I can't say that there is any joy left to me in this miserable existence of mine. They say there is no fool like an old fool and I will be reviled in the Three Worlds for my horrendous lapse of judgement. Shiva has already decreed that no worship shall be offered to me on earth, on account of the falsehood I uttered during our battle of wills—and now I have been disgraced even further. There seems to be little purpose for me to go on. And sinner that I am, despite everything, I still yearn to be with yonder maiden who is my...daughter!'

'Such self-pity is most unbecoming of the Creator of the Universe,' admonished Vishnu. 'Dry your tears. Despite this sorry episode, the respect the Gods and man have for you on account of your sterling achievements will be undiminished. You said it yourself...desire cannot be withstood by the Gods themselves, even if they are forewarned that such indulgence can lead to trouble and strife. Simply having knowledge doesn't arm one against the caprices of the soul.

As for Sandhya, it is past time you took a wife. She will be a worthy consort for you, since she is no longer your daughter. It was I who brought her back into the world of the living. Therefore, she is my daughter and willingly do I give her to you. This noble lady will be venerated as the Goddess Saraswati. She will have the ability to kindle the power within and give it the impetus to express itself. If your knowledge is unequalled then hers will be the gift of channelling this knowledge so that it enlightens and benefits both humanity and the Gods. Her domain will be the realms of intellect, music and the creative arts. She will reside in the tongue so that she may preside over language and the expression of inspired ideas. In this way, she will truly be your better half. Thanks to her, you will be able to fulfil the demands of creation, quench your appetites in a healthy manner, and she will also assuage the restlessness within you which has proved so detrimental in the past. What do you say? Will you accept the Goddess Saraswati as your consort?'

Brahma smiled, for he had been given a fresh lease of life and he was filled with hope for himself. 'I have often thought it unfair that everybody, including Shiva, loves you so much, but now I realize that it is because of your boundless capacity for compassion and your commitment towards preserving everything that is good and truly pure. If Saraswati is willing, I will be delighted to accept her as my wife and together, we can perform great things that will restore my honour.'

Saraswati smiled her acceptance but spoke up tremulously, 'It is a great blessing for me to be chosen as the consort of the Creator and I accept with a glad heart. But I have a boon to beg of you, Lord Vishnu! My heart still aches to think of my disgraceful behaviour which played a part in my Lord giving up his life and that made me follow suit. I do not wish to be remembered as a woman of loose morals and hence beg you to offer me a chance to redeem myself in the eyes of the world.'

'So be it!' Vishnu replied with a smile, 'You will be reborn as Arundhati, the wife of the great sage Vashishtha, and your chastity and honour will be held up as a lesson for all women of future generations. Your name will become synonymous with virtue and your story will be told and retold to inspire the same good conduct in others. Goddess Saraswati will also be revered as the patron Goddess of Knowledge and the Arts, and all in pursuit of excellence will offer their prayers to you. The Gods will also come to you in times of duress, for you will have the power, courage and wisdom to help them out of sticky situations.'

On hearing Vishnu's words, which can never be false, Brahma and Saraswati prostrated themselves at his feet and washed them clean with their grateful tears. Raising them to face him, Vishnu addressed Brahma one last time: 'Before you go off to enjoy your newfound marital status and begin creating new worlds, allow me to congratulate you on the remarkable creation of the God of Desire. It was sheer genius on your part, for Kama will prove instrumental to the processes of life by using his gift to ensure procreation, sacrifice, and timely death—depending on the need of the hour. There will always be balance in the cosmos, thanks to him. I firmly believe that he is more than up to the great task appointed to him and we can all expect wonderful things from him. Before I depart, it is my wish to effect reconciliation between father and son. Kama, don't you have something to say to Brahma?'

Kama approached his father and bowed deeply before him. 'Father!' he said. 'Allow me to offer my congratulations on your new wife. I am certain that she will be a never-ending source of happiness for you and I pray that you will always find delight in each other.

As for me, I am sorry that I brought you grief, but I beg you to undo the curse you pronounced over my head. For it was never my intention to cause you hurt or bring infamy to you. I was merely using my power in the manner you instructed me to and thought that I would be able to repay you this way for all the gifts you had bestowed upon me.'

Brahma sighed deeply, 'My words cannot be undone. But I can make a few amendments to it. Shiva, once he is reunited with his consort, will restore you to his favour. The power which I have bestowed upon you can never be destroyed and while it endures, so will you!'

Kama was immeasurably relieved and he smiled gratefully at Vishnu before addressing his father once again, 'Oh Lord! Your mercy is boundless and I will never forget your kindness to me. And I will prove myself worthy of the gift you have given me and do you proud.'

Pleased with all that had come to pass and the damage control carried out by Vishnu, which had allowed him to get his heart's desire and once more hold his head high, Brahma departed with Goddess Saraswati. Vishnu addressed Kama again before departing himself, 'Since you have undergone more in a single day than most people do during the course of several lifetimes, I sense a newfound maturity in you and I am pleased with what I see. Shiva was right to chastise you for playing with your power and treating it like a child's toy. Never use it the same way again. Let Shiva's displeasure and Brahma's curse serve as a warning to you. Employ your skills to further the cause of all that is noble and worth preserving in the Three Worlds, and I will consider it as sufficient payment for the service I have done you today. And there is no need to look so solemn for as I told you sometime back, a most fortuitous union awaits you and you will find that the happiness which was your lot at the time of your birth has been fully restored to you.'

On that charming note, Vishnu vanished, leaving Kama filled with wonderment and a heady anticipation of what lay waiting for him. Already his sense of well-being had returned in full measure and he felt more than ready to take on the world with his trusty bow and arrows by his side.

When Desire Met Sexual Delight

The Prajapati, Daksha, had been entrusted with the weighty task of populating the world with creatures in his own image. For the purpose of efficiency he decided that copulation was the most suitable technique to ensure the rapid multiplication of the species. He and his wife, Asaikani, turned to the task at hand with due diligence and gusto. Soon they had successfully produced entire legions of progeny that included great Rishis, Devas, Gandharvas, Asuras and Nagas, among others.

Pleased with himself for the successful manner in which he had carried out his duties, Daksha reported to the abode of his father to meditate and purify himself before undertaking any further tasks the Creator may have in mind for him. And so it came to be that he was present when Brahma created the enchanting Sandhya. To his surprise, he was not immune to her prodigious charms, though he had long fancied that he was above the vulgar sensations that were the bane of mere mortals. The sidelong glances he imagined she threw at him coyly from beneath her lovely, long lashes proved to be his undoing, and the Prajapati found himself not unlike an adolescent male in the first throes of hormone-fuelled lust. The subsequent creation of Kama and the loosening of the latter's arrows only served to titillate him further, and if Shiva had not intervened, Daksha was certain that he would have become guilty of the sin of incest.

Goaded by the withering contempt of the Destroyer into

subduing his forbidden passion for his sister, D
most strenuously—and the unwanted desire
through droplets of sweat that fell to the gr
downpour. And from this telltale evidence of lust, ...
embodiment of sexual delight—was born. Daksha himself may
have seen his desire as ugly and unworthy, but the maiden born
from his less savoury attributes was so lovely that her father was
proud that something so divinely splendid had been salvaged from
his great shame.

Later, when the dust had settled on the tumultuous events
of the day, which had already seen instances of taboo passion, a
curse that promised death, two actual deaths and resuscitations,
Vishnu persuaded the Prajapati to offer Rati in marriage to Kama,
the God of Desire, who, he believed, was ideally suited for her.
Daksha decided that the Protector was right and lost no time in
approaching Kama with the offer of marriage, confident that the
God of Desire would consider it his great good fortune to have
for a wife such a winsome damsel as his daughter.

The Prajapati had been correct in his conjecture, for when
Kama first laid eyes upon Rati, he did not need his arrows to lose
his heart completely and utterly to her. One look at those fawn
eyes and luscious blue-black hair so like his own and he knew
with a certainty that sprang from deep within the core of his
being, that he had found his true mate for all of eternity. After a
day in which he had already started to doubt the veracity of his
existence, bemoaned the death of his father and regretted his own
rash actions, he had perhaps needed something like this to cheer
him up—to make him remember the power of love at making
things right. A love that filled him with hope, even in the face of
his impending death that he now had foreknowledge of.

Rati felt exactly the same way, unburdened as her ebullient
spirit was about the trauma of widowhood that was to be her lot,
and she was deliriously happy to have found such a wonderful

band. The happy couple realized intuitively that they were meant to be, and felt themselves to be the luckiest creatures in all Three Worlds. They proceeded to get married hastily in the Gandharva style which calls for nothing more than mutual consent. Exchanging garlands and consummating their union without bothering to stand on ritualistic requirements, the couple bypassed the conventional route to respectability, thrilled as they were to embark on a new journey together as husband and wife. Ensconced in this newfound marital bliss, the couple began making plans for their future. Kama decided that they should repair to the fabled city of Amaravathi, the city of the Gods, and make it their home. Rati raised no objections, so they began their journey thither.

Shiva's unmasked disgust for him and his powers had wounded Kama badly, and as he recalled the events that had occurred, a shadow fell over his proud brow. Vishnu had also admonished him for being frivolous regarding the use of his gift and had warned him not to repeat his mistakes if he did not want to risk being cursed again. Kama had decided that before Shiva burnt him to death, as was ordained, he would build a decent legacy for himself that Vishnu himself would approve of and that even his arrogant father could take pride in. Linking his fingers through his beloved wife's, he now outlined some of his ideas for the future to her as they journeyed to Indra's abode. Rati listened in rapt attention.

'I have no wish to be branded as the good-looking lord who only goes about toying with hearts and messing up other people's lives for sport with his bow and arrow,' Kama began. 'It is my fervent desire to make my powers amount to something worthwhile and emulate Vishnu in the process. He is tireless when it comes to his responsibility in preserving life and well-being, while promoting happiness wherever he can. His ability to appear in times of crisis is extraordinary. Without him, life on the cosmos would deteriorate past all recognition before being extinguished altogether. It was his wish that I employ my skills towards a good cause, and so I have decided to offer my services to Indra and do my part towards maintaining balance in the Three Worlds. All this sounds somewhat pompous when I say it aloud, but I do mean every word, and so they have the merit of being truthful at least.'

Rati responded excitedly, 'It is a noble thought indeed and not at all pompous! I shall help you every step of the way for I would also like to contribute towards a worthwhile cause. Unlike you, however, I will not complain for being known as the most ravishing woman to ever walk the Three Worlds. After all, a woman cannot be burdened with too much of that particular commodity called beauty! But how come you have opted to help Indra? Everybody says that his appetites are borderline gluttonous and he is something of an ego maniac… I have heard that he is jealous of anyone with power comparable to his own and to compound these shortcomings, he is a Brahmin killer and an adulterous philanderer to boot. What if he makes you the engineer of unlimited orgies in heaven or anything else that his kinky tastes can come up with? It is the sort of thing you wish to avoid, is that not right?'

Kama interjected: 'It was Vishnu's suggestion that I forge an alliance with him and he can never be wrong. Besides, Indra's reputation for perfidy is largely undeserved, I am sure. He has long proved his commitment towards upholding all that is good and righteous in the Three Worlds. Besides, being the Lord of Heaven cannot be easy, I am sure. I bet it is the demands of the job that have forced him to take some decisions that may not always pass muster in terms of morality.'

Rati nodded agreeably, 'That sounds about right, I suppose. When you are under a lot of pressure, sleeping with the wives of your subjects is the best possible way to take the edge off all that stress! Be that as it may, he will not have any justifiable cause to be jealous of you, if you place your services at his disposal—especially since you are determined to be virtuous, as opposed to devoting your life to a senseless pursuit of sybaritical pleasure. Unless of course, he decides that your devastating good looks are a threat to him and decides to seduce me in order to feel better about himself!'

Kama grinned in response to the lascivious wink his wife threw his way before replying, 'Everybody knows that he is remarkably good-looking in his own right, so I doubt he is going to feel threatened. And as regards any designs Indra might have towards seducing you, I am just going to console myself with the thought that you would rather kill yourself than sacrifice your modesty to him.'

'You can keep telling yourself that if it makes you feel more comfortable, although I'd like to go on record to say that illicit sex trumps a violent self-inflicted death any given day of the week,' Rati said solemnly before bursting into peals of laughter. Kama laughed along, thinking how fortunate he was to have a wife who was not only beautiful, but also someone who could make him laugh hard enough to make everything else seem irrelevant, including the future.

In Rati's company, Kama enjoyed their trip to Amaravathi. They saw many wondrous sights along the way and they kept a running commentary on all their observations to entertain themselves. Narada, one of the Prajapatis and famed devotee of Vishnu, acted as their guide for part of the journey and he told them many enthralling tales about the Gods and their way of life. He told them about the famed battle between the Devas and the Asuras involving the churning of the Ocean of Milk and Vishnu's role that tipped the balance of power in favour of the Devas—a story he was happy to tell Kama who, he sensed, was a fellow devotee like himself.

Pleased to have such a receptive audience, Narada began his tale, 'Once Durvasa, the famed ascetic and son of the Prajapati Atri and his wife, Anusaya, well-known for his fierce temper and potent curses, met an Apsara who was carrying a lovely garland made entirely of flowers that would never wilt. Requesting the heavenly garland from her, he made a gift of it to Indra. Now Indra, acclimatized as he already was to seeing all things beautiful in the Three Worlds (especially celestial flowers since they were grown in his garden, Nandana) and being at the moment preoccupied in the tender embrace of an Apsara on the back of his mount, was somewhat underwhelmed with Durvasa's well-meaning gift. Rather injudiciously, the thousand-eyed God placed the garland on his elephant, which flung it to the ground in irritation as the incessant buzzing of the bees attracted by the garland maddened the poor beast. Infuriated with this cavalier treatment of a precious gift, Durvasa cursed Indra saying that he would lose his vitality, powers and Kingdom for his hubris.

This was more than Indra had bargained for and he was entirely unhappy with the sudden turn of events. When Durvasa flung aside his belated apologies with the same careless air with which his pachyderm had dashed the garland to the ground, Indra appealed to Brahma for help, who in turn directed him towards Vishnu. Accompanied by the rest of the Devas, who all felt the loss of their vitality acutely since they could no longer hold their own against the Asuras (who were definitely not above taking advantage of their predicament), Indra led the way to Vaikunta, the abode of Vishnu. He knew that the great God would somehow rescue them from their sorry situation, the way he had so many times in the past.

Vishnu was reclining on his serpent, Sesha. He listened patiently as to how they had allowed the Asuras to gain the upper hand and drive them away from their Kingdom. He then proceeded to offer words of comfort and advised them to churn the Ocean of Milk in order to procure the divine nectar of immortality called Amrita which would help restore them to their former glory and even surpass it. As per his instructions, the Devas collected herbs of great medicinal value and other properties, and emptied it into the Ocean of Milk. Then they made peace with their sworn enemies and half-brothers, the Asuras, to enlist their help in the gargantuan task they had undertaken.

The ancient Mount Mandara was to act as a stick for churning and the great serpent Vasuki would be the rope. Mount Mandara consented to take part in this epic endeavour, but the Devas and Asuras ran into a problem of logistics when they attempted to uproot and carry the mighty Mount to the appointed venue. Many of them were crushed to death as they collapsed underneath its bulk. Vishnu came to their aid and revived the fallen Devas and Asuras before lifting the mountain with ease and placing it on his own mount, Garuda, bidding the great eagle to carry it to the designated spot.

Once there, with Vasuki in place, the Devas and Asuras began the monumental task of churning. But without support, the Mount kept sinking into the fathomless depths of the Ocean, frustrating their combined efforts. So Vishnu had to take the form of a giant tortoise to bear the weight of Mandara in order to allow the warring brothers to go on churning. And still the problems continued to pile up for the intrepid warriors.

A deadly poison arose from all the aggressive churning and the fumes began killing all those who inhaled it in droves. To compound its effects, Vasuki, whose body was horribly battered from the ill-usage it was being subjected to, began bellowing in pain, and now its poisonous breath began killing those present in great numbers. This time, Shiva responded to their prayers for help and scooping up all the poison, he swallowed it, imprisoning it within his windpipe with no discernible ill-effects to his health. His throat, however, turned blue from the poison and, thus, he was given the moniker, Neelakantan.

Many were the marvellous things that were churned up from the Ocean of Milk. Kamadhenu, the cow of plenty, emerged from the ocean and was quickly claimed by the sages. It was followed by the divine horse, Uchaishravas—which Bali, the King of the Asuras, took for his own; and the elephant, Airavata, which would become Indra's mount. The Kaustubh Mani, a diamond with a brilliant blue hue, also rose to the surface. It was believed to bless its owner with prosperity and the gift of invincibility and everyone agreed that it should be presented to Vishnu, who graciously accepted it. The fabled Parijitha flowers emerged during the churning. These had the power to bestow riches and glory upon the home that housed them and ensure the fidelity of the husband when a wife adorned her hair with them. Later, Indra would plant it prominently in his Kingdom of Amaravathi. Lakshmi, the Goddess of Prosperity, arrived seated on a lotus and became the consort of Vishnu and she was followed by Varuni, the Goddess of Wine. Heavenly maidens of incomparable beauty rose from the depths as well. And finally, it was the turn of the divine physician, Danvantri, founder of Ayurveda, who arrived on the scene, bearing the gift that their hearts most desired—the nectar of immortality.

No sooner did Danvantri come forth bearing the gift of immortality, than the greedy Asuras with scant respect for all that is holy and with complete lack of decorum, snatched it right out of his hand in a brute display of vulgar strength. And then to compound the error of their ways, they began to fight with each other over who deserved the largest share—like starving dogs at a dumpster outside a wedding feast where they were most unwelcome.

Vishnu, using the brief respite their fighting allowed him, took the form of the beguiling enchantress, Mohini, and seduced the Asuras into allowing her to distribute their ill-gotten goods among them. And while they gazed upon her greedily, their beady eyes bulging with lust, Mohini kept them under her spell with bewitching smiles that held out the promise of so much more, while proceeding adroitly to distribute the nectar among the Devas, who, to their credit, had shown great restraint and decency even as their half-brothers disgraced themselves with a disgusting display of greed.

An astute Asura by the name of Rahu got wise to Mohini's

scheme and, disguised as a Deva, he stood awaiting his share with the other brethren. However, the Sun God, Surya, and Soma, the Moon God, became wise to the deception even as Rahu was in the process of gulping down the nectar and they shouted a timely warning. Mohini, immediately reverting to Vishnu's form, severed the Asura's neck with his famed Sudharshana chakra, sending the decapitated head hurtling through the cosmos. Legend has it that it is on account of the demon's animosity towards the Sun and the Moon that we experience Solar and Lunar eclipses—when Rahu's head, which had managed to become immortal, attempts to swallow them up for depriving the rest of his body of the same gift.

In the cataclysmic battle that followed, the Asuras were vanquished and the Devas returned to heaven in triumph as the proud possessors of the nectar of immortality, along with other treasures that the ocean had put forth in its generosity. As promised by Vishnu, their vitality and powers were fully restored and Indra made a mental note to himself not to antagonize any more bad-tempered sages in the future—a resolution which delighted his loyal subjects. Meanwhile, the defeated Asuras had to slink away and seek refuge in the bottom of the ocean or deep within the rocky underbelly of the world until such time as they would find themselves in a stronger position to make more mischief for the Devas,' Narada concluded.

Kama and Rati cheered raucously on hearing this marvellous tale and whole-heartedly agreed that Vishnu's service on behalf of the Three Worlds was truly remarkable. Narada then taught them hymns to propitiate and please the Protector, which they sang lustily for many leagues. The ancient sage was pleased with this delightful couple who shared his devotion to Vishnu and had been so welcoming of his company. Narada was usually hailed as a meddlesome harbinger of trouble, his presence barely tolerated and mostly shunned. Promising them that he would repay their kindness in the future when they would be in need of his services, the sage made his exit.

The couple was nearing their destination and had to traverse the Milky Way to reach Indra's bastion of power. The countless stars they had to pass by on their way fascinated and enthralled them. Narada had already informed them that each of these stars denoted the souls of the individuals who had led the most blameless lives during the time allotted to them on earth. They paused to examine the stars and decided it was the most charming sight they had seen so far and that it was definitely a worthy way to honour those who lived right.

The legendary city of Amaravathi that they had heard so much about, was located on the side of Mount Meru past the Milky Way. It extended about 15 miles high, was 450 miles wide and 300 miles long. It was guarded by the Guardians of the Universe known as the Lokapalas. Indra–the Thunder God, Agni–God of Fire, Yama–God of Death, Varuna–Lord of the Waters, Kubera–God of Wealth, Surya, Vayu–the Wind God and Soma, guarded the city at every vantage point, rendering it impregnable. Constructed by Vishwakarma, the architect of the Devas, the city that stood before them was unimaginably beautiful and Kama and Rati gazed at it with speechless wonder for a long time before proceeding to enter its hallowed portals.

Palaces built only from the finest materials were visible as far as the eye could see. The pillars were flecked with diamonds that twinkled merrily as Surya smiled down benignly on the city of the Gods. Furniture of all kinds, whether in the palaces or numerous parks, were made entirely of gold, as were the cutlery of the Gods which served up the choicest viands cooked to perfection. Varuni, the Goddess of Wine, also made her home in the city and she made sure that the cups of the residents literally runneth over. Numerous gardens and parks adorned the city, most notable of which was Indra's personal garden, Nandana, making the great city even more pleasing to the eye.

Amaravathi also housed all the known wonders in the Three Worlds. Having been victors in the great battle between the forces of good and evil, the Devas were entitled to treasures like the divine horse, Uchaishravas; the cow of plenty, Kamadhenu; the Parijatha blossoms; Kapataru, the tree that never withered and bore on its branches all the fruits that one could wish for; the remarkable gem Parasmani that could fulfil the wishes of the user; the Akshaya Patra that never ran out of food, and many other miraculous things.

The city was also blessed with an abundance of beauty as it was also the abode of the heavenly nymphs—Rambha, Menaka and Urvashi. Well-versed in the sixty-four arts, they shared the bounties of their beauty liberally with the inhabitants of the city and kept them well-entertained and sated with pleasure. The Gandharvas made sure that sweet music wafted over the city at all hours, soothing the listeners and keeping them in a constant state of bliss, far removed from the niggling cares of daily existence.

The climate was deliciously moderate as the wind God Vayu and the Maruts, who were the storm lords, ensured that cool and refreshing breezes always blew across the city. Indra's Sabha, in terms of its physical stature, was undoubtedly the best in the Three Worlds which, in addition to being an architectural marvel and Vishwakarma's crowning achievement, was capable of housing thirty-three crore Devas, forty-eight thousand rishis and all their attendants. It was a city where its denizens felt blessed to live, as there was no room for sorrow or misery; only a plethora of pleasure, prosperity and lack of want.

Kama and Rati fell in love with Amaravathi at once and were pleased to discover that Indra had already been informed of their arrival, thanks to the munificence of Vishnu. Celestial attendants personally escorted them to the Sabha of Indra where they were warmly welcomed by the God of Heaven and the rest of his court. He gave them a sterling introduction before all the dignitaries assembled. Kama was particularly grateful when Indra, in a stirring monologue, praised him as someone blessed, who had the power of bringing happiness and pleasure into their lives and who was the newest warrior in the eternal struggle to ensure that good triumphed over its nemesis. Indra also announced that he was inducting Kama as a trusted member of his court. Rati, for her part, was pleased with him for pronouncing her as the most beauteous creature in all of creation right in front of the famed apsaras of Amaravathi. Indra's signs of favour to them were not limited to words alone and he had them escorted to the beautiful palace that had been readied for them as an unprecedented sign of his goodwill. Vishwakarma had taken care of the construction personally and the palace stood as a towering symbol of his prodigious skill. It was a magnificent edifice of white marble and crystal with pillars crusted with diamonds and furniture wrought in white gold, embellished with dozens of unique enhancements that were suited to the domain of the God of Desire and his lovely consort. Flawless sculptures and exquisite paintings, devoted to themes of love, desire and passion, adorned the walls and palace grounds sending Rati into paroxysms of delight, over their aesthetic merits and erotic appeal.

Luxurious baths, comfortable rooms and hot food awaited them as they entered the palace. Several attendants had been allotted to take care of their every need. Rati promptly pronounced herself as over the moon with their new house and she insisted that Kama accompany her so that they could personally thank Indra for his generosity and thoughtfulness. The Lord of Heaven was charmed, as was Vishwakarma when he was also made the recipient of their profuse gratitude.

In what felt like no time at all, Kama and Rati settled into their new home and seamlessly blended into the fabric of life in Amaravathi. Timeless denizens of the city came to accept the charming couple as one of their own and most felt that they had known them forever. At the clever suggestion of Indra, Kama and Rati allied themselves with the Gandharvas and the Apsaras to better carry out the dictates of their divine duties.

The Gandharvas, creatures of air and water, were the Lords of music and the sixty-four performing arts. Their female counterparts were the Apsaras led by Rambha and they were the celestial dancers. These heavenly creatures moved about the Three Worlds like clouds appearing and dissolving at will. They were capable of changing their forms and could incite desire by taking on the forms of apparitions from the realms of fantasy. As is to be expected of creatures capable of fanning the flames of desire, they were incredibly good-looking as well.

Under their expert tutelage, Kama and Rati together began their education pertaining to the fine arts as well as the curricula of sensual delights and the assorted secrets of love. Right at the outset, they were schooled in singing as well as playing all manner of instruments before being taught the exquisite art of dance. Long were the hours they spent mastering the nuances of music as well as dance, and great was their combined talent—so much so that the Gandharvas and Apsaras, purveyors of perfection in these very fields, were spellbound when they watched the God and Goddess of Desire perform. They moved as a single entity, and it was obvious to all who watched them that the impossible synchronicity which they achieved was the result of the deep love they shared that had them so finely attuned to each other's thoughts and feelings. Even when they sang or practised on their instruments, the birds would stop singing and gather in the courtyard to listen to the divine couple who complemented each other so perfectly. Later, their concerts would go on to become so famous in the Three Worlds, that Brihaspati, the preceptor of the Gods, would declare them the finest examples of spousal devotion and the greatest performers he had seen. Indra went one step further and pronounced them as the pride of Amaravathi.

Singing, music and dance were only the beginning of the many skills they would go on to master, before surpassing even their teachers with their expertise. They learned how to paint and used their new skill to add to the paintings that already adorned their palace—with sweet memories of their fervent and often frenzied lovemaking during the long watches of the night.

The duo was also trained in the art of rangoli, the traditional floor art, meant to entice the Gods into entering the home so that the residence may grow blessed in their presence. Together they waded throught the science of aesthetics, finding out new and beautiful ways to enhance the simple things that nature had already provided. Hence, they wove garlands, created beds made entirely of flowers that would heighten the pleasures of sex, learned to paint their nails, polish the teeth, to enhance physical appearance, the art of jewellery making, the skilful application of cosmetics and fixing hair in a manner that was most flattering. They mastered the fine art of wearing clothes, the creation of scents, perfumes and unguents that would drive the severest Rishi into distraction with the sweetness of its appeal, as also the mechanics behind the perfect massage which would leave the body saturated with a feeling of well-being. These were amongst the plethora of secrets they uncovered with the help of the Gandharvas and Apsaras. They also added to the extant knowledge of aesthetics with the discoveries they themselves made.

The next step was to be inducted into the fine arts of conversation, poetry, verse and writing. Soon they could discourse at length with the most learned scholars on any topic under the sun and compose pithy poems and prose with ease. Posing intricate riddles, solving complicated puzzles and debating with dexterity became second nature to the enchanting couple and they cut fine figures in Indra's Sabha with their combined beauty, eloquence and wit, which set them apart even in that gathering of glorious beings.

Kama and Rati learned swimming and a host of other water activities, becoming practically amphibian in nature, as the water became a second home to them. Kama was invited by the warlike

Gods to learn martial arts, the lore of weapons and martial strategies for waging and winning wars. Rati insisted on being allowed to learn with him, and when the Gods merely looked askance at the unladylike tendencies of the pretty slip of a woman in front of them, she appealed directly to Indra, who was somewhat taken aback but gave in eventually to her impassioned argument.

Much to the pride of Kama, Rati went on to become one of the finest warriors in the Three Worlds and her skills were comparable to his, even as he went on to impress the Gods with his own skills in the warlike arts which were as good as his astuteness in the amorous arts. Both Kama and Rati could pacify the fiercest horses and elephants with a single look or touch and train them to respond to their very thoughts. They became experts with every weapon their fingers grasped and soon became the envy of their fellow immortals.

More arcane lore beckoned them and they trained their sights towards unearthing the mysteries of magic and enchantment. They discovered spells that could bewitch or bend individuals to their will and carry out their commands, tricks of illusion that would enable them to make themselves invisible, and spells that would allow them to travel faster than thought. All of these they added to their remarkable arsenal. Kama and Rati conducted experiments of their own and created love potions that were imbued with their own essence and, therefore, entirely potent. Gifts of these potions of love were purveyed across the length and breadth of the Three Worlds, so that the deserving or lucky ones could experience the joy of love. Spells and charms to enhance fecundity and vitality, to capture a heart and hold it imprisoned, to ward off a jealous rival and to stop the husband from straying were included in their repertoire. They also combined their expertise with divine physicians to find cures for ailments like impotence or low sex drive and other conditions that would rob the afflicted of the pleasure they were entitled to experience.

Communication with animals and birds was another useful skill they were taught. Kama proved particularly adept in this department and had a special gift with parrots, so much so that it was not uncommon for him to use them as his preferred vehicles while traversing the Three Worlds. He also trained them to repeat messages and deliver those using codes and ciphers. Indra made use of Kama's birds on many occasions and the chatty birds became firm favourites with the Gods.

Kama and Rati, not surprisingly, had a natural proclivity for the sixty-four arts of love. They quickly established their expertise in all forms of sexual congress and were happy to share with the Gandharvas and Apsaras their combined knowledge towards giving and receiving pleasure. They explored every conceivable and inconceivable kind of sexual union in addition to honing the skills of kissing, embracing and the oral arts.

Rati suggested they start a school of lovemaking so that all manner of celestial beings, and a few privileged mortals, could benefit from the pearls of wisdom they had so pleasurably gathered over eons devoted to this express purpose. It would offer instruction on the finer points of lovemaking so that men and women would learn how best to please each other in bed, as well as pick up the tricks of sexual etiquette, the art of seduction and personal grooming. Needless to say, the instruction offered was a huge success among the celestials.

The couple also spent a lot of time in consultation with the greatest sages who were familiar with the mysteries of the universes in Brahma's creation, and compiled prodigious notes on all aspects of life which would prove invaluable to future generations. They employed scribes to meticulously record particulars on methods for successful conception and childbirth, prevention of premature births and attacks by minions of evil on pregnant women, recipes for a happy marriage, successful ways to win spouses and secure their affection, means to acquire virile power and prolong fertility, among other things of a related nature.

It was at this time that Indra and Kama became very good friends. Indra dispensed with formality and ceremony and was known to drop in on Kama and Rati at all hours. He was very pleased with the work done by Kama along with the Gandharvas and Apsaras. On one occasion, Indra asked him where he had got the charming notion to provide instruction on love, to which Kama replied, 'In my experience, of all the human emotions, happiness is by far the most elusive. Even for the Gods. It can be sampled only in a fleeting moment before it vanishes, giving only a small taste of what life could be like, leaving those thus deprived in despair and tottering on the brink of a spiritual death. Such is the case with most individuals, who are allowed only a dip in the pool of happiness before it once again disappears from their sight, and they spend most of their lives pining away in hope of its reappearance.

So I was explaining to Rati that my mission through the endless corridors of eternity will be to help people squeeze every little drop of happiness they possibly can out of their existences. And she suggested that desire as well as pleasure, when incorporated into the routine of life in judicious doses, will prove to be the key towards happiness and fulfilment. It is important that these emotional elements be included in moderation, for too much becomes destructive to the self and others—whereas, too little desire leads to a juiceless existence. Rati felt that people ought to be taught how to get the most out of desire and passion by developing a healthy attitude towards them, as well as pick up other techniques which would be inculcated in them by experts in the arts of love.'

Indra said: 'Let me guess...she has gone and befriended Rambha! That irrepressible nymph is sure to have shared with Rati all her experiences with the male of the species in the Three Worlds and their stunning lack of ability to help her climax. The original plan would have been to teach clumsy males how to pleasure females but they decided to modify it before pitching it to you and threw in all that pseudo philosophical jargon!'

Laughing heartily, the two men had begun a spirited discussion on the capricious nature of the fairer sex, before they were interrupted by Rambha and Rati, and they hurriedly switched to a lengthy discourse on how Kama's new skills could best be employed in a manner most profitable to the Gods.

Indra often opted to employ the charms of Kama and his assistants, both together and separately, against all who chased power greedily—whether they were Asuras or purer-minded sages. The demons had on many occasions managed to accumulate power by performing the severest penances to propitiate the Gods, and having succeeded thus, would ask for boons that would make them invincible. What had traditionally followed was them making pests of themselves and creating havoc for both Gods and humans alike.

It was Indra's strategy to send Kama and Rati, as well as their celestial companions, to these demons, either when they were engaged in penance or later, so as to bring about their downfall by stimulating in them all sorts of excessive desires and an irresistible need to indulge them, knowing that it was the surest path to self-destruction. Similarly, sages who gathered far too much ascetic merit by practicing tapas, tended to lay waste to their surroundings with the scorching intensity of their intent and hence they had to be distracted as well, before they ended up destroying all creation.

In this manner, Kama and Rati made themselves thoroughly at home in Amaravathi. It gave them great happiness to successfully carry out the tasks they had been divinely appointed to do and to perform it so well. Rati was an able partner in these tasks, as she was entrancing and could use her charms to suitably captivate their targets.

Kama also delighted in spreading happiness through the Three Worlds in whichever way he could. He firmly believed in helping people discover pleasure in the arms of their better halves and was fully committed to this cause, so that through the magic of love, a dull existence would become transformed into a beautiful one. And so it came to be that Kama and Rati, with a little help from the celestials, engineered the ideal existence for themselves.

Spring, Pus-Filled Boils and Another Wife

*E*very once in a while, Kama liked to visit his father, Brahma, at Brahmaloka—his abode in Mount Meru—and pay his respects. Father and son shared a loving, if prickly, relationship, for Kama had never entirely forgiven his father for cursing him and Brahma still tended to look on his son with a touch of acrimony as it was his belief that Kama had made him disgrace himself in front of Shiva by infecting him with forbidden desire for his daughter. Their differences notwithstanding, their lines of work were aligned, hence both were passionate about what they did and utterly devoted to their respective causes, which was why a visit, though not pleasant, was not entirely unbearable either.

Yet another thing father and son had in common was a pernicious tendency to annoy each other with barbed critiques on how one felt about the other's performance of his job. Kama would make it a point to congratulate his father on the extraordinarily good judgement he had exhibited on numerous occasions by granting boons of power to various demons and men with particularly pronounced sociopathic tendencies. Brahma had thus given their despotic and tyrannical natures a dangerous edge. Kama would point out and put them in a virtually unassailable position from where they could make unholy nuisances of themselves. He would stress the untold hardships and suffering that had sprung forth from the depths of his father's folly with relish. As a dutiful son, Kama would feel the need to inform his father about the juicier epithets that had become attached to his august name by some of the Gods, as well as the nastier jokes that were being circulated in Amaravathi about the Creator's singular aptitude for creating a stink.

Brahma would then feign nonchalance while suppressing his anger and tell himself that petty rejoinders were beneath him even if they weren't for his obnoxious offspring. Having regained his composure, he would then launch into a lengthy homily about how it was impossible for sons who had treated their fathers with disrespect to achieve any sort of prosperity or well-being, at the same time predicting the most violent of deaths for them. Kama meanwhile would annoy him further by making elaborate gestures as if to ward off the sleep that seemed determined to overwhelm him and prevent him from listening to the rest of his father's lecture.

On one particular occasion, Kama found only Saraswati at Brahma's residence. He was happy to see her as he was genuinely fond of his stepmother and respected her immensely. The Goddess loved him as well and thought of him as a dear friend and an equal. Kama greeted her enthusiastically, 'You look very well indeed! I take it as a sign that my father is taking good care of you.'

Saraswati smiled at him warmly, 'Your father is a good husband but I am perfectly capable of looking after myself. As always, you are looking very handsome indeed. I have been hearing good things about you and that wife of yours. A number of Gods and great sages have come to your father and told him glowing tales of your achievements. It is the common consensus that the services you have been performing for the Gods will earn you unparalleled respect and fame and will be sung about for the rest of eternity. Your father will never admit it, but he gets puffed up with pride whenever people praise you to him. I am also proud of you and am sorry you are not from my womb. Anybody would love to have such a great son!'

'That is so kind of you!' Kama said, touched with her sincerity and fully aware of the power of her words and the generous blessings she was heaping on him, 'But I have not really been thinking about fame or glory. Ever since Shiva spat on me and my powers, a certain stigma has attached itself to me. There are all kinds of power and mine will be considered somewhat frivolous especially when compared to Shiva, Vishnu, and some of the other Gods. It is also highly unlikely that in future, people will build temples in my honour or compose beautiful songs for me. I will be lucky if I am remembered enough to be featured prominently in pornographic material; worse still is the distinct possibility that the God, Kama, will be lampooned as the divine pimp!

I am not really concerned about that sort of thing though. Hopefully, I'll do my divine duties without causing any major foul ups or getting cursed into oblivion for as long as I am allowed. At the risk of sounding like a puffed up popinjay, perhaps I'll be able to make a difference or even spread a touch of happiness—barring which, I may at the most manage to help a few achieve sexual nirvana, if not moksha. If I can pull that off, then I will be content and may just allow myself a small pat on the back.'

The Goddess smiled a little but she did not respond in the same light vein, 'You will not be forgotten and I will personally make sure of that for as long as I preside over the creative arts. Kama will be a familiar figure in literature of the highest water, for romance makes a great muse as does sex, wouldn't you agree? This self-deprecating attitude of yours is surprising! Extraordinary good looks are almost always the surest indicator of arrogance... And in any case, even if all you do is become a permanent fixture in pornography, there is always comfort to be had from the fact that not everybody has what it takes to be a successful porn star!'

Brahma walked in just then as his wife and son were laughing up a storm over a joke he was absolutely certain was objectionable and more than a little inappropriate for a stepmother and stepson. As always, Kama filled him with mixed emotions. He was a worthy son and had exceeded his expectations on many occasions. But seeing him engaged in animated conversation with his lovely wife, Brahma felt a frisson of disquiet and could not help thinking that perhaps he should have been less generous while endowing Kama with such exceedingly handsome features and such a winsome personality. Brahma himself may bring out his son's inner jackanapes, but Kama had a wonderful way about him with everybody else and they all thought him too amazing for words. Moreover, he had a reputation for being kind, gentle and generous as well.

Sensing his presence, Kama and Saraswati stood up to greet him, palms joined together in the ageless symbol of respect and devotion. Brahma was ridiculously pleased to note that they did not freeze in a tableau of guilt. 'To what do I owe the pleasure of this unexpected visit?' he enquired, surprised at the affectionate note in his own voice.

'Can't a son visit his beloved father and stepmother for no other reason than the fact that he loves them?'

'A son can but this son never does... Are you in some sort of trouble? I am surprised you came to me, for I would have expected you to go running to Lord Vishnu.'

Kama was ready with a barbed retort but Saraswati intervened smoothly knowing that they could keep at their bantering till the end of time. 'It is touching as always to know that males, even when they are great Gods, behave no differently from bickering adolescents, though they should know better! How long do you intend to keep this up? Kama, it is your duty as a son to forgive your father for all the real and imagined hurts done to you and be nice to him, the way you are to everyone else. As for you, dear husband of mine, you should really put aside your resentment as he has done nothing to deserve it. In fact, I insist you give him a gift to take home—something special to make up for your unfair treatment of him all this time and for beginning your nonsense with him within moments of greeting him. That is no way to treat a guest in our home who happens to be your son and one who is exceedingly dear to me. Do make sure that you present him with something truly worthwhile that he will treasure forever.'

'My father has proved that his skills in creating beautiful women are unmatched as the fruit of his labours is standing right before me, uttering words that are music to my ears—but I feel that I must warn you that Rati has sworn to me that if I dared to return with a wife, she would scratch her rival's eyes out before poisoning the both of us.' Kama piped up laughingly, clearly amused by his wife's possessiveness. Saraswati smiled a little at the off-colour joke but Brahma remained serious.

'Saraswati is right about many things... You certainly put the Gods to shame with your infantile behaviour at times. Even so, I will overlook your proclivity for highly galling behaviour and present you with something that will be of immeasurable worth to you!' Brahma took a deep breath to ready himself to comply with his wife's wishes, then closed his eyes. He mused over the relationship he shared with Kama. Often he found his son bewildering but his name—Manmatha—was fitting as nobody could agitate minds like him. It was not his habit to dwell on the events that had led to Kama emerging from his heart, but he found himself thinking about the day of his disgrace. He noted with pleasure that he had managed to win himself a consort such as Saraswati and a noble son, whom many insisted was the best gift he had given the Gods and men—even at a time, when his mind had slipped past the restraints he had put in place and wandered away from his steady grasp.

It saddened him to think that the youth who stood before him would soon be devoured by the wrath of Shiva. He himself had guaranteed such a fate for him. Kama's anger towards him was perfectly justified; Brahma had been generous in granting boons even to demons who had perceptibly wanted to annihilate the

Vedic way of life, and yet he had found it in him to curse a son that was so dear to him. Powerful feelings rushed through him while he ruminated thus, and a sigh of co-mingled anxiety and despair escaped his lips like a gust of wind. And it was from this audible exhalation that Vasanta, the God of Spring and the King of Seasons, appeared.

Like his predecessor, the youth was most pleasing to look upon and extremely well-endowed. He was as tall as Kama but dark complexioned and equally radiant. Dark ringlets of hair swept down his well-shaped head, like Ganga—as she flowed down from her prison in Shiva's matted locks. Strong limbs and magnificent shoulders rounded out his assets and Vasanta bloomed before them bedecked in the loveliest flowers that bespoke the arrival of Spring.

Brahma raised his hand and addressed Kama, 'I give to you, the gift of friendship. Vasanta will be your constant companion and helper. Like wind is to fire, he will complement your efforts. Spring, which brings with it fragrant blooms and cool breezes carrying the promise of fresh beginnings and lasting love, will provide the ideal atmosphere for your arrows to do their work and soften the objects targeted by your bow, making them more responsive to your advances.

Vasanta will also be a brother to you and stay loyal forever. It is my hope that with Rati and Vasanta by your side, the journeys you are destined to undertake will be pleasurable and fulfilling ones. I am also confident that your good wife will be delighted to welcome him into your family.'

Kama and Vasanta bowed their heads in gratitude; Saraswati thought she saw tears in the former's eyes even though he had clearly taken pains to conceal his emotions behinds a curtain of civility, as he said: 'Thank you so much for giving me a friend and brother. I am grateful to the Goddess and you, father, for doing so much for me and providing me with the most suitable tools I would require to carry out my duties.'

Seeking and receiving the blessings of Brahma and Saraswati, the newly minted duo left the abode of the Creator and started to make their way homewards.

Watching them go, Brahma felt the uneasiness stir within him again, even though Kama had departed his presence leaving no trace of any negative emotions behind. Even Saraswati seemed pleased that they had more or less resolved their differences, thanks to her resourcefulness. Brahma sighed again and this time there was a feral intensity to his breathing which had grown increasingly rapid. Out of this there now rose completely different beings than the cheerful one that had risen a while ago, like a breath of fresh air. These were smoke—like apparitions of myriad shapes and varying degrees of weirdness, who gave every intention of being bloodthirsty brutes. They had fiery eyes and protruding lips that were bared open in a perpetual snarl with red tongues rolling out. Terrifying to behold, they began to charge about, disrupting every ounce of spirituality that had always distinguished Brahmaloka, nestled as it was within the protective confines of Mount Meru. The rolling slopes which had only recently been illuminated with the presence of Kama and Vasanta had now transformed into a scene of utter horror and chaos. All of a sudden, these horrific creatures chased after the departing twosome, chanting in feral screams, a gut-wrenching mantra of death.

Saraswati grew pale with apprehension at the sight of the apparitions that had suddenly marred the beauty of the tranquil hillside. Watching helplessly as they charged after Kama, she turned to Brahma in distress and asked him who they were and what truck they had with his son. She wanted to know if they ought not to appeal to Vishnu to keep the God of Desire safe. Brahma's voice was tinged with sorrow when he replied, 'They will not harm him for they were created with the intention of helping him shoulder the great burden he bears with so much élan. Those creatures will be called maras and they are the heralds of death and invisible to most. Their task is to eradicate any and everything that will serve to deter the arrows of the God of Desire. As he approaches his target, they will accompany him, and bring with them not merely the clammy touch of death, but also images of the impending journey of the soul after it departs from the body. They will never be far from him, for when death draws close life will fight to assert itself and Kama's mark at that time will be all the more effective because of their presence.

The maras will also represent the harsh reality of the power of desire which Kama wields. For, his peculiar gift is capable of creation as well as destruction. My son walks a tightrope across these equally potent forces that are the two faces of desire and it is only through his grace, innate goodness and sincere efforts that a delicate balance is achieved which protects the interests of both life and death without either ever gaining the upper hand.'

The Goddess wiped the lone tear that was meandering down her cheek and she swore, 'My prayers and blessings will also accompany him wherever he goes and they will keep him safe even when your curse takes effect. Mark my words! With the help of the other Goddesses, I will do my utmost to save him from being torn to pieces, caught as he is in the ego clash between Shiva and you!' Brahma said nothing but he hoped with all his heart that his wife would succeed where he himself had failed.

While this emotionally charged drama was unfolding between his father and Goddess Saraswati, Kama and Vasanta were journeying back to Amaravathi, thoroughly enjoying each other's company. Despite his firm belief that any gift from Brahma ought to be treated with the same caution that one would exhibit while unwrapping an explosive missile, Kama felt more at ease with Vasanta than he had with anybody else. It was as if they had known each other forever. Vasanta spoke little, but there was comfort to be gleaned from his silence and Kama had no cause for complaint. He confided in him the story of his own origins telling him almost all of the events that had transpired then. Finding him to be an attentive and sympathetic listener, Kama told him about his beloved Vishnu, Rati and other friends in Amaravathi.

The sage Narada, whom Kama had befriended earlier, once again caught up with them. Kama welcomed him warmly and performed the introductions. Once the pleasantries were dispensed with, Narada explained the purpose of his visit to Kama and Vasanta. 'As you know, I am the messenger of the Gods,' he said. 'I have been sent to bring Kama before the Goddess Gauri with due haste as she has some urgent assignments for you. We must go to her at once. Vasanta can come along for I am sure Kama will need your assistance soon.'

Mystified, Kama and Vasanta obediently followed the great sage as he took them on a meandering journey across the abode of the Gods. He explained that Mount Meru was located in the centre of the earth, and was shaped like a banyan tree. Unlike a regular mountain, its base was small and narrow like the trunk of a tree and widened upwards, with ascending height, to better accommodate the homes of all the Gods. These abodes were named for the Gods in question, like Brahmaloka or Indraloka, which was another name for Amaravathi. The uppermost branches housed the Preserver and Destroyer. Vaikunta was the name given to Vishnu's home and Kailasha was where Shiva chose to retire.

As the geography lesson wound up, Kama and Vasanta eagerly quizzed the sage about the Goddess Gauri and he proceeded to furnish them with details, 'The Goddess Gauri was Shiva's former wife when she was born to Daksha and went by the name of Sati. She will be his wife again when she takes rebirth so that she can be reunited with Shiva. As the personification of feminine energy, she is also worshipped as Shakthi and she is the actual ruler of all the universes stretched out across the cosmos as it is her power that keeps them all from exploding into fragments. It is she who ensures the health and happiness of all that are living, for it is through her munificence that the hard earth yields good and nourishing food to eat, the trees grow in abundance, flowers bloom and the birds sing on earth. All the Gods defer to her, for they rely on her protection.

On earth she is worshipped as Durga, the ten-armed Goddess. In each of these arms she carries weapons that were presented to her by the Gods while she roams the Three Worlds on a lion, and the arsenal gifted to her helps her rid the world of its scum who surface regularly with alarming persistence, such as Asuras and other demons. Mercilessly, she hunts down and exterminates those purveyors of evil who prey on the weak and helpless. She is the Divine Mother who feeds her children with the milk of her kindness and is ever ready to bail them out of trouble when they call out to her in prayer—or oftentimes, even when they don't. Her offspring run into copious multitudes, and when the safety of any of them is endangered, there is none in the Three Worlds or even among the Gods who can withstand her fierceness. In her wrath she is capable of annihilating everything in existence. If Shiva is known as Rudra when his fearsome anger is provoked, then the Goddess strikes terror in the hearts of evildoers everywhere as she takes the form of Kali, the dark Goddess with her red eyes, lolling tongue, killing instruments and garland of grinning skulls.

It is the Supreme Mother who has summoned you to her presence and Vishnu suggested that I carry the message to you. It is his wish that you place yourself at her disposal without being too inquisitive and serve her with devotion. By doing this you will reap manifold benefits through her grace which will help you when the darkness descends on your world.'

Kama and Vasanta decided that they were about to have a grand adventure and were in high spirits as they accompanied Narada. They surmised that the Goddess would receive them in her palace of unmatched splendour seated on a throne encrusted with precious stones, her beauty overpowering their own, her luminous face wreathed in smiles of benevolence. Kama remarked that they would find her adorned from head to toe in dazzling jewellery, the magnificence of which would outshine the brilliance of the Sun God, and that he must take careful note of her ethereal raiment and the rest of her ornaments for Rati would definitely want to know every single detail. Narada, however, only smiled when they voiced their thoughts on the Goddess and said that she would show to them of herself only what she really wanted to.

With those enigmatic words, Narada led them into the thick of a jungle. It appeared to be a blasted ruin of a place, with gnarled trees, stinking bogs that belched out gas and muddy streams. It was as if Mother Nature had fashioned such a place only out of a rebellious desire to wallow in ugliness. Even Vasanta, whose aesthetic sensibilities were deeply offended, could not work his magic on the place which persisted in being stubbornly and uniformly unattractive despite his best efforts.

In the middle of that jungle, there stood a simple wooden hut which was mercifully clean and tidy. A young girl could be spotted on the premises arranging logs of wood in a sturdy pile. Possessed of short cropped hair, medium height, a boyish chest, and a slight build, she cut quite an impressive figure on account of her rippling musculature. Perhaps it was because of the way she hefted her axe or the ease with which she stacked up thick logs of wood, as though their weight was immaterial to her. But something about her seemed to intone a warning that it might not be the smartest thing to pick a fight with her.

Kama and Vasanta had carefully controlled their features to betray no sign that they were thoroughly baffled, but truth be told, Goddess Gauri did not look anything like Saraswati or Lakshmi or any of the other Goddesses Kama had previously been acquainted with. Privately, Kama told himself to be grateful that it was not worse, for Narada could have led them to a pool of red blood and the Goddess may have decided to appear before them in her fiercest guise, with the unhappy result that they would have walked in on Kali bathing, adorned in nothing but her garland made entirely of skulls, pausing in the performance of her ablutions only to chug the contents of the pool.

The young woman snapped around just then and addressed Kama directly, 'If you had seen me like that in a pool of blood with lolling tongue and adorned in nothing but a garland made entirely of skulls, pausing in the performance of my ablutions only to chug greedily from the contents of the pool, two fine youths such as yourselves would have lost control of your nether sphincter muscle and then even the delicious aroma of spring would not have been able to mask the stench!'

This time their cool composure snapped like dry twigs and the Goddess Gauri laughed merrily, clearly pleased with herself for having shocked them senseless. As the tinkling sound of her laughter reverberated around the jungle, it vanished entirely along with Narada. Kama and Vasanta found themselves seated on a tiny rock with nothing but water as far as the eye could see. The remarkable lady was seated beside them, her feet dangling in the water while little fish nibbled on her toes which showed up pinkly against the turquoise blue of the water. 'Chopping up wood is hard work and I really needed to cool off; hence this change of scene. I bid the sun to stay away and asked Vayu to send his coolest breezes this way so that we can converse in some quiet and comfort.'

Realizing that her shell-shocked companions needed a little more time to regain their equanimity, Goddess Gauri continued speaking, 'I am indeed the Goddess Gauri you were instructed to see, so you can set your panicked minds at ease on that score at least. Forgive me, but it is too much trouble to get decked out in the yards of fabric, endless accoutrements and other paraphernalia a Goddess is expected to sport. I find that one can get along splendidly without the rigours of extreme grooming and it is a firm belief of mine that personal comfort is the first step towards achieving whatever it is one wants to.

In addition to that, the expressions on your faces were entirely priceless and it was great fun to rattle you out of that supremely prepossessing air the two of you were born with. Now that you no longer look like you have swallowed a porcupine or have one stuck up your behind, perhaps we may begin to discuss the reasons for my summons?'

Kama smiled gallantly at the Goddess, whom he decided was intensely likeable, and offered his services to her. Vasanta went one up on him and made her a present of a lovely bouquet of flowers which he conjured up especially for her. Exclaiming prettily over the flowers, Goddess Gauri proceeded to explain why she had brought them to her, 'A devotee of mine, Apala, has been praying to me for many years, requesting release from her troubled existence on earth. The time has come for me to repay her unwavering faith and grant her the innermost desires of her heart. This is where the two of you come in...what I need is for you to convince Indra to take her as his lover.'

Kama and Vasanta exchanged uneasy looks and the former could not help thinking about the self-deprecating joke he had recently made to Goddess Saraswati about his becoming known as the divine pimp. The Goddess interrupted his thoughts immediately and said, 'Kama, you will be performing for me a great service, one that will add lustre to your reputation—as opposed to getting you confused with a mere solicitor for prostitutes. Let me tell you a little more about Apala. She was the daughter of Atri. Fated to lead a mortal's life, she was soon married. And though she loved her husband dearly, she was chafing a little at the tedium of marital life.

It was a restful life even if it was lacking in terms of excitement. But all that changed when a poor Brahmin came to their doorstep begging for alms. Apala's husband had just finished his midday meal and told her to join him in bed. Long years of marriage had taken the zing out of their sex life and Apala had to admit that her looks did not entice her husband as much as it used to and was delighted with the rare initiative he had shown. Feverish with impatience, she hurriedly tidied up the remnants of their meal and was en route to hopping into bed for a rare afternoon of pleasure—when she heard the Brahmin call out.

Apala was not entirely pleased with his timing as the couple had been going through a dry spell and she had no intention of prolonging the drought which had been hard on her rather active libido. Yet she realized that it behoved her to do her duty by the Brahmin, so she dumped some food into a sack and thrust it into the Brahmin's hand before wishing him well—her urgency robbing the gesture of all merit and the needed sentiment of sincerity. Reminding herself not to slam the door in his face—for that would have been considered rude—she shut it gently in his face before rushing off to embrace her husband, praying that he had not fallen asleep.

The Brahmin had sensed her sexual arousal and was infuriated that she seemed to give more precedence to her sex life than to the rules of hospitality. He scattered the grains she had given him on the sand in front of their residence and then cursed her for not giving due respect to one who deserved her hospitality and charity. The curse issued forth from his lips with a hissing sound, like a serpent poised to strike: 'The lady of this house has not only been negligent of her duties as a hostess, but, with her wanton behaviour, has robbed her husband of his judgement as well, making her doubly guilty. As punishment, she will henceforth be afflicted with a skin ailment that will cause her to appear repugnant in the eyes of the world so that nobody else will ever fall victim to her overflowing sexual desires that would cause them to stray from the path of righteousness!'

Apala's judge and punisher walked on, hoping he could find more hospitable people further on, and wishing he could curse her all over again—for his stomach had started rumbling and if not for her friskiness, he could have been dining at that very moment! The object of his curse meanwhile was oblivious to the noose tightening around her throat as she was otherwise occupied. It was her husband who noticed the pus-filled boils that were erupting all over her body, bulging grotesquely with greenish pus. He jumped back in shock at the terrible metamorphosis of his lovely wife which was taking place before his very eyes. The ineluctable contact between them caused a few of the bulbous boils, swollen with the effluent they carried, to burst and empty the discharge over them like a foul fountain. Apala cried out in pain and shock, hurting more from the look of loathing she saw in his eyes than from the acute physical discomfort she was suffering.

Unable to look into those eyes or to bear her shame, she fled from the room. Running to the well behind her house, she emptied countless buckets of water over her head to wash away the pus, but her efforts did no good for new boils replaced the old ones and on and on it went. Far too proud to beg her husband not to reject her, but terrified that the odds of his rejecting her in favour of a younger woman who did not come with pus-filled baggage was too high, she struggled to come up with a solution to keep him tied to her. Trying to keep the desperation out of her voice, she told him that she would practice the highest forms of austerities, which were also wish fulfilling endeavours, to find a cure for herself and also win a boon from the Gods that would allow her to bear him worthy sons. Having made up her mind, she bid farewell to her husband, and forgiving him for the relief she saw stamped large on his features, she ran away and disappeared into the woods.

Apala has spent long years in isolation since then. It is to her credit that she did not let bitterness, anger or resentment get the better of her. Instead, she placed all her faith in me and has waited patiently for a way out of this entrapment. The Brahmin who cursed her said that it will be lifted if Indra accepts her as his lover. He thought that since the Lord of Heaven is known to be a connoisseur of beauty, he will never take a pox-addled wretch into his bed and Apala will be trapped for all of eternity—but he did not reckon with Kama, the God of Desire, with his unstoppable arrows, which carry on their tips the chance to win happiness and a fresh shot at life. Will you go to Indra and help out this girl?'

Kama ruminated briefly on the most plausible response Indra was likely to give if he was propositioned with the offer of bedding a 'pox-addled wretch' before making up his mind. 'Vishnu told me to carry out your wishes unstintingly and I can never disobey him or you,' said Kama. 'But I hope you will forgive me when I say that what you wish of me will be done not because of him or even you but for Apala herself. It will be an honour for me to render whatever assistance I can to throw off the dreadful curse and free that brave girl.'

'I am so proud of Kama. It is just like him to care so much for those downtrodden souls!' Vasanta added quietly, 'This will be our first assignment together and I could not have asked for a worthier one. It is my good fortune to support Kama and do whatever I can to ensure success for him and Apala!'

The Goddess had expected them to comply and she was happy that she had not been let down. 'Very good! The Brahmin was not too far off the mark about Indra but he is certainly no match for Kama, with Vasanta by his side. Now that we have completed the discussion on one of the reasons I summoned you, let us begin on the next. I trust you will not find it too trying, for it is actually a gift! It is my wish for Kama to take as his wife the noble Karnotpala who is unmatched in the Three Worlds for her affectionate and caring nature.'

The groom-to-be had not seen this coming and he was gobsmacked to say the least. Despite himself, he recoiled from the command of the Goddess, as if one of Apala's boils had exploded and hit him in the eye. He looked at Vasanta hoping he could magically figure out a way from the quandary he found himself in. Yet, although his friend was looking horror-struck for his sake, Vasanta at the time was mostly relieved that he himself had not been called upon to wed a devotee of the Goddess, who was in all likelihood suffering from yet another unsavoury ailment. But it was Goddess Gauri who responded again, 'If you have something to say, do speak up Kama! I will not force you to carry out my will by threatening to add your well-shaped skull to my collection, nor do I expect you to fall in line simply because it was Vishnu's desire that you obey me. Just do me the courtesy of paying her a visit. You have my assurance that she does not suffer from any unseemly condition. Listen to what she has to say for herself and then decide if you want to marry her.'

'Forgive me Goddess, I will certainly marry Karnotpala. My mind is made up on that score for I realize now that she is meant for me. I do not need to hear her story nor am I concerned with her appearance, for we can all agree that my good looks are probably enough for the both of us. It was Rati whom I was thinking about. She is the great love of my life and I would hate to cause her grief.'

'You are right, Karnotpala is meant for you. It pleases me that you became cognizant of that truism with only the slightest prompting from my side. Loving Karnotpala and marrying her does not mean that your love for Rati will be diminished in any way. She will come to realize that herself, provided you do whatever it takes to keep both your wives happy. Nobody said that it would be an easy feat to walk a tightrope between two women, but though your stress levels are bound to double, so will your pleasure! Your little family will be better off in the long run with the addition of Karnotpala for she is a wonderful person!

It was clever of you to figure out that your marriage to Karnotpala has been preordained and to accept it so graciously. Vishnu will be so proud! But for now, you will have to forget about the impending nuptials and focus on rescuing Apala. Keep your wits sharp, your arrows sharper and success will be yours! Now you will have to excuse me for I do hate protracted farewells!'

And just like that, Kama and Vasanta found themselves back on the path where they had run into Narada. There was no trace of the Goddess who did not look like one. Kama shook off his daze, 'Let us go to Indra…it is high time somebody put an end to Apala's suffering. What is it about these self-righteous holier-than-thou types that makes them run around cursing all and sundry or granting stupid boons to goons? If they have ascetic merit to spare, then they could use it to end poverty, misery, crime, rape and whatever newest outrage the humans have come up with to destroy themselves. But no…the best they can do is punish a poor girl for the unforgiveable crime of wanting to get laid!'

'It is rich that a beggar should have such attitude,' Vasanta replied, 'What are you going to do about Indra though? Are you going to tell him Apala's story with a graphic description of her condition like the Goddess did with us, hoping to galvanize him into action? Or would you prefer to blindfold him, point him in Apala's general direction and shoot him in the heart?'

'Not exactly… He is my friend, after all.' Kama said absent-mindedly. 'I have not yet decided the surest way to persuade him to do the right thing by Apala, for whichever way I phrase it, Indra is far more likely to take a vow of celibacy! Moreover, I am reluctant to use my arrows on him just to coerce him into doing what I want. For now, I have decided to just go with the flow.'

Kama and Vasanta made discreet enquiries to find out the whereabouts of Indra. They learned that the God of Heaven had been holed up with his preceptor Brihaspathi. The session had taken a toll on him and he had opted to relax and unwind in his pleasure garden in the company of his favourite Apsaras and Gandharvas. Having spotted him atop his magnificent mount Airavata, the dashing twosome hastened to intercept Indra's retinue.

From his lofty position atop Airavata, Indra saw his dear friend, and commandeering a horse from one of his attendants, he dashed off to catch up with Kama. 'Well met Kama and Vasanta! It is my business to acquaint myself with the sordid details involving the private affairs of my subjects. This is why I know for a fact that Goddess Saraswati stepped in to stop Brahma and Kama from exchanging blows, following yet another infamous altercation. In fact, she even managed to finagle a favour from her dear husband for your sake, which is how you now have a faithful companion to assist you, Kama! Now the two of you can feel free to shower me with compliments about how brilliant my powers of perception are and I will listen humbly.'

'If you want compliments, I suggest you go to mother Aditi instead of badgering your so-called humble subjects who can correctly surmise that Sage Narada has paid you a visit!' Kama retorted, with a knowing smirk.

'Whatever happened to the innocent young lad I knew who took everybody at their word? Now he is bent over with the burden of keeping the Three Worlds free from strife by waging fierce battles against those who are trying to swear off sex, and is barely able to bear the weight of his sugarcane bow!'

Kama said: 'If you are done making lame jokes at my expense and forcing Vasanta to force his facial muscles into a simulacrum of a smile out of respect to you, perhaps you would let me know if Narada told you anything else about my travels?'

Indra replied, 'Actually, that is what I wanted to talk to you about... Narada told me about your latest visit to Brahma, and in response to my query as to whether there was anything else I should know, he looked fit to bursting but said nothing else. When I started digging for dirt, he muttered something about a Goddess who had promised to feed him his genitals if he dared to let his big mouth run away with him and he found excuses to make a hasty departure. I could have forced him to spill his guts of course, but since it clearly concerned you, I held my hand and decided to wait for you to come to me and here you are! Something tells me that there is a juicy tale to be heard and I command you to tell me everything! But first, let us find a comfortable place to sit and talk, for though riding on Airavata befits the King of the Gods, it is extremely hard on my backside.'

Indra's retinue hastened to set up a comfortable pavilion for him and his friends. Soon they were all taking delicious sips of mango sherbet, seated comfortably on cushions that were actually clouds—except that they were stuffed with petals and feathers instead of ice crystals and water droplets, which would not have done any favours for the aching backside of the Lord of Heaven.

Kama, with a little help from Vasanta, told Indra about Apala, leaving out the details of her skin condition and the little fact that Indra himself was her sole hope. Pleased that Indra was listening intently, Kama ploughed on, 'The problem is that the Brahmin decreed that the best among the Gods, one who is unmatched in looks and valour should accept her for a lover for the curse to be lifted. Apala has been offering her prayers to this God, begging him to come to her rescue. So I have come to you, to ask if you know this God and if he will have the magnanimity to ignore her physical imperfections and take her to bed.' Looking directly into Indra's eyes, Kama paused and tried to gauge his reaction.

Indra's face was inscrutable when he answered his friend, 'I find it amusing that even when you are in dire need of my help, it is still not possible for you to compose elaborate paeans in praise of me and the best you can manage is an obscure reference to the best of the Gods and the rest of that jazz. The good news is that your quest for this peerless God has ended for it is to me that Apala has been crying out for help. She got pushed to the back of my mind for I was busy with Sage Brihaspathi, and now I am sensing that Goddess Gauri herself sent you along to speed up the process.

Now, getting back to this Apala, I am guessing that her skin
ailment is a serious concern, given that you took pains to make it
sound like nothing more than a rash on a baby's bottom. Which
would make her as pretty as an Asura's hairy arse, I suppose…
But I am curious, why are you talking me into this when all you
had to do was lead me to her with the promise that she was the
most exquisite creature in the Three Worlds and then fire all your
arrows into my heart?'

'It should be obvious, should it not?' Kama said. 'You have
been good to me and I consider you a dear friend, albeit one
with an appalling sense of humour. And it could never be in
the best interests of friendship to stick something into the other's
heart—especially if it is pointy! In addition to that, you know as
well as I do, that despite all the jokes doing the rounds about the
effectiveness of a sugarcane bow in fighting the war against the bad
guys, there is no denying its powers in matters of the heart. If I
were to employ my arrows you will fall in love with Apala—make
no mistake about that, but she is a married woman. All her efforts
have been solely directed to winning her husband back and once
her beauty is restored to her, she will fall at your feet, wash them
clean with her tears, declare herself your greatest devotee and then
she will return to her husband.

I don't want you to become the victim of unrequited love.
Which is why I decided to let you have all the facts before requesting
your assistance and appealing to the goodness of your heart.'

'Well, notwithstanding my famed nobility, what if I was to
deny you? What if I told you to bugger off? Maybe I expect the
Goddess to come to me herself when she wants something done.'

'You won't.'

'And pray do tell what makes you so damn sure?'

'For one thing, despite all your pretensions to the contrary,
you are one of the good guys! And second, you are secretly afraid
of the Goddess even though you would rather hand over your

crown jewels to your half-brothers, the Asuras, than admit to it!'

'Damn you and your friendship!' Indra roared at him, pretending not to have heard the last part but Kama was secretly relieved to note that he was not getting ready to impale him with his thunderbolt. Keeping silent, he waited for Indra to decide how best they should deal with the Apala situation.

'Alright! This is how we'll do it,' said Indra. 'I will personally slough off the repellent hide of this Apala. Maybe I'll do it three times just to make sure. And when I am done, you have my permission to use your arrows on me, just to see me through it, you understand? You will have to use all the powers at your disposal to help me through the entire process of bedding this girl who is apparently so ugly that her husband has chosen celibacy over co-habiting with her. After all, one cannot afford any mistakes that are likely to anger Goddess Gauri! As for those annoying buggers who feel the need to punish every lusty lady they encounter, you would think my reputation for being a Brahmin killer would deter them from involving me!

Anyway, I am glad that we have settled the issue. Now let us go do this thing before I change my mind. Perhaps this affair will be good for me, for, after all, it is high time that the Lord of Heaven rid himself of the unflattering reputation he has earned for being superficial.'

'Stop treating this whole thing as a joke,' replied Kama. 'I need you to go into this knowing exactly what it is you are getting into. You are committing yourself to becoming besotted with a married woman who cares only about using you to get her looks and her husband back. Your position has ensured that you don't know what it is like to be spurned or suffer rejection at the hands of someone you care for. Are you sure that you will be able to handle the idea of a mortal choosing to go back to her husband over you—even a husband who was able to satisfy her only sporadically and who even abandoned her when she became physically repellent to him?

Indra lost his good humour at this point and his reply was chilling, 'Since we are being brutally honest here, let me tell you a few things which are bound to be unpalatable to you. You have been handed a mission by the Goddess and so far you have done a thorough hash job. Your limited powers of comprehension and lack of faith are the greatest handicaps in your way. By professing to believe while being a disbeliever, you jeopardize your chances of success and risk the fates of all whose lives are linked to the outcome of your actions.

Narada told me that you will be taking another wife. Have you seen her? Do you love her? And yet you are fully committed to marrying her for you realized that it was meant to be. This clearly indicates that you are not fully ignorant of the natural progression of mysterious rhythms that govern the universe to which all creatures, high and low, are bound in life and death. You act as though by laying the naked truth at my feet, for my understanding, somehow the both of us will be able to exercise some degree of control over that which has been preordained. I refuse to be as childish as you! Now why don't you just shut up, so that we can both get on with our bloody jobs?'

There was nothing more to be said. Accompanied by Kama and Vasanta, Indra wasted no time in going to Apala. The trio was driven to her by Matali, Indra's charioteer. Once there, Indra saw that Apala was deep in penance, her entire being calling out to him. An army of ants had built their home around her and she was barely visible. Sensing his presence, she broke free from her imprisonment. On seeing the Lord of Heaven, her eyes which had been closed to the world all this time, opened up and flared to life overflowing with great love and gratitude. Seeing those incandescent eyes with the powerful feelings they carried for him, Indra was deeply moved. Touched by the simple faith she had in him, Indra felt slightly ashamed for treating Kama's request like an odious chore. The distaste he had felt about bedding her, faded away to be replaced by immense respect for this woman who had borne the horrors fate had meted out to her with such dignity and grace.

Taking her in his arms, Indra promised Apala that her suffering was drawing to a close. With those soothing words—meant to take the edge off the brutal force he was about to employ—Indra dragged her through the large hole of his chariot, the smaller hole of his cart, and the smallest hole of the yoke. Thrice the blighted woman shed her skin. The first discarded layer became a porcupine, the second became an alligator and the third became a chameleon. When the ritual scouring was completed, Apala looked resplendent like the Sun. The effect was enhanced by Kama with his tricks of illusion and Vasanta who rendered her formerly barren scalp fertile again and her crowning glory was returned to her, its splendour magnified by the power of Spring.

Indra looked into the loving, grateful eyes that were raised to him in naked adoration and the final traces of the clinical detachment he had brought to this task slipped away like one of Apala's moulted skins, and his heart softened towards her. When Kama's arrows struck, he was ready to give her all his love.

The final vestiges of her hideous skin ailment vanished when they consummated their relationship as lovers and Apala was truly liberated. She touched Indra's feet with devotion for she was unable to meet his eyes and said, 'Bless me my Lord, so that I may bear mighty sons like you for my husband!'

Indra placed his hands on her shoulders and gently raised her to her feet. 'You will be a proud mother of many fine sons and your husband will thank the Gods for reuniting you with him,' he said. 'He is a lucky man to have a woman like you in his life and he owes it to every good thing he has done over a billion lifetimes! Go to him now and promise me that you will be happy!'

Apala did not trust herself to speak. Joining her palms together in prayer, she thanked him and walked away to her husband, without looking back even once. Indra was sorry about that, among other things. He realized he had been hoping that Apala would say she would rather be his whore than her husband's wife. But she had not said that, nor had she even thought it. He could have cried, but he did not. For the Lord of the Heavens was a lot of things, but a colossal fool he was not!

With that thought to sustain him, Indra hardened his heart and returned to his chariot. To Kama and Vasanta who had withdrawn to a discreet distance and only just re-emerged, he gave a sardonic wave. As Matali made ready to leave, Indra told him to tarry a bit before addressing Kama, 'The next time anyone pokes fun of your sugarcane bow, he will have to answer to me. And the next time I make fun of your sugarcane bow, I want you to do me a favour and punch me in the face.' And with that, Indra left Kama and Vasanta alone in the spot where his heart had been broken and buried, and was gone.

By silent mutual consent, Kama and Vasanta decided not to discuss Apala's relation to Indra ever again. Kama also felt it was best to pay heed to Indra's words. So he shut up and went off in search of the stranger who was meant to be his wife. He also decided it was best not to dwell too much on what Rati would have to say about his new wife.

While journeying over to the Ashram where Karnotpala was engaged in the performance of penances, Kama and Vasanta disguised themselves as beggars and entered a kingdom which appeared not to have a ruler and consequently, the subjects were in a state of great agitation. Having recently decided to simply take a leap of faith, Kama was determined not to scavenge for every scrap of information he could unearth about his mystery wife-to-be.

Unfortunately for Kama, there appeared to be no getting away from the subject, for Karnotpala was a princess of the land and it was her father who had absconded from the throne to take up the ascetic way of life. Everywhere he went, people were keen to inform him about the particulars behind the father and daughter's decision to turn to tapas which had in turn left them bereft of an authority figure. Her father had been wracked with guilt, for he had prevaricated endlessly about finding a suitable groom for his only daughter. She was precious to him and he wanted nothing but the best for her. Hundreds of hopeful suitors had been summarily dismissed on account of the monarch deciding that they did not measure up to his exacting standards. Grooms who came highly recommended, were dismissed by the pernickety patriarch for being too fat, too thin, too stupid, possessed of bad manners, or in one case, for having a pronounced case of flatulence. Those proud men left the kingdom, smarting from the insult, and vowing vengeance.

In the early days, the king was spoiled for choice as men came from far and wide, hoping to win themselves a winsome bride who also came with ruling rights to a prosperous kingdom. But as the days wore on, the stream of suitors slowed to a trickle and suddenly, there were no takers. Nobody wanted to face rejection seeking the hand of an ageing princess—even if her old man was the epitome of filthy lucre. Karnotpala had reached that age when, those with an obsessive predilection for harsh truths over any kind of diplomacy, would easily have declared her to be long in the tooth. Her smooth skin had grown lined with worry and a few straggly, graying remains were all that were left of what had once been a luxurious mane of glossy, black hair. Out of habit, she still braided her hair but whereas once they had looked like thick coils of rope, now they were closer in appearance to a rat's tail. Age had robbed her body of its slimness as well as suppleness and left her with a heavyset frame that favoured waddling over gliding. Those two dead giveaways of age—the hands and chest, betrayed the sorry state of their owner, with the former growing gnarled and the latter sagging to within an inch of its life.

Karnotpala could not help but notice the telltale signs of her age, and she was saddened. Determined not to dwell on her physical deterioration, she told herself to be happy that she was not tripping over her sagging breasts, laughed a little at that mental image and immediately felt better. It was a joke she was known to make often and those who heard her almost wept every time they heard it. The king could not get over his inability to find a suitable match for his daughter and grew sick with worry for he refused to lower the bar and persisted in searching for the perfect specimen of manhood. By then, even the most avaricious of potential suitors chose to reject emissaries for Karnotpala's hand as the kingdom had been largely reduced in size.

Neighbouring rulers who had once been crushed with an iron fist grew increasingly aggressive, while the old king's hand started to stray from the reins of kingship, obsessed as he had become with his need to get his daughter married. Others derived a mean-spirited sense of satisfaction from the proud old man's grief and they rejected his offer of marriage outright.

Finally, things came to a head when the king decided to seek a miracle, and abandoning his kingdom, he disappeared into the wilderness to seek divine intervention by dint of religious fervour at its most extreme. In this state, he wasted away slowly and still there was no surcease to his suffering as he was simply not able to make the sacrifices of body and mind required by such ritualistic practices.

Karnotpala had for long reconciled herself to loneliness and a loveless life as She had found inner fulfilment by dedicating her life to the well-being of her subjects whom she had adopted as her children—since she herself would not be able to experience the joys of motherhood—and taking care of her beloved father. Not in the least bit concerned about her own future, she grieved because her father grieved so and wished there was some way she could give him comfort in the little time left to him. While he rotted away in his hermetic retreat, she decided to follow in his footsteps and achieve by ascetic merit the means to fulfil his heart's desire.

Staying close to her father, so that she could care for him,

Karnotpala began praying in earnest to Goddess Gauri to grant her father peace of mind. She begged the Goddess to make possible the impossible, and help her regain her youth and beauty so that she might be a worthy mate to the kind of man her father had dreamed of finding for her. Having seen his daughter well-settled in life and having shut up his detractors for good, she knew her father would be able to find the happiness that had eluded him for so long.

Pleased with her selflessness and determination, the Goddess appeared before her and granted her the boon she had requested. Certain secret instructions had been imparted to the fortunate princess by the Goddess and having followed them precisely, Karnotpala had retained the first flush of her beauty and was waiting patiently for the husband she had been promised.

Kama had become fascinated with the princess by then. The love her subjects bore her had to be seen to be believed and he found her story truly inspiring. Guided by the hand of the Goddess, he went to her as quickly as he could, the sudden urgency in his heart spurring him on. When he beheld the princess who had managed to do what none before her had achieved, Kama was speechless, for her beauty which borrowed its radiance from the inate goodness that was her distinguishing feature, exceeded his wildest expectations and Kama fell madly in love with the girl who had been meant for him.

Karnotpala could not believe her good fortune as she had finally found the ideal man her father had insisted she marry. When Kama proposed to her, she requested him to seek her father's permission for her hand. The old king was only too happy to give his consent for even his keen eye could find no fault in Kama.

Soon Kama was married to Karnotpala—whom he named Priti for the affectionate pleasure he felt for her and which she had given him back a hundred fold. Vasanta was in attendance for the nuptials, after which he decided to find his way back to Amaravathi on his own in order to give the newly-weds some privacy—and, at Kama's request, to soften Rati for their homecoming, just in case she was planning to welcome them with cauldrons of boiling oil.

The couple propitiated Goddess Gauri and thanked her for bringing them together, before making their way homeward. What greeted them on their arrival was completely and utterly unexpected. Rati had planned lavish celebrations in honour of her truant husband and his new wife. She had even turned over a portion of the palace entirely for Priti's use. Priti in turn, presented her new sister with a magnificent collection of jewellery which had belonged to her ancestors. Kama decided that under the circumstances, the meeting between his wives had gone very well indeed and he was determined to make sure that they were both happy.

After the celebrations had wound down and Priti had diplomatically retired, Kama and Rati found themselves alone. Kama was searching for words to fill the awkward silence when Rati got the first word in, 'Don't tell me you are sorry, because then my self-control will snap and I will definitely pour boiling oil over your empty head. Just listen to me rave and rant for the next couple of minutes and then we won't have to discuss this ever again. Vasanta told me all about Priti and I know that she is not a husband-stealing whore, which is why I have decided not to murder her as she sleeps. According to your new best friend, if I give her a chance, she will soon be like the sister I never had, and he is probably right, but at this precise moment I am not too concerned about all that.

It is important for you to realize that when it comes to your affections I cannot and *will not* take second place to anyone— not your hot stepmother, not the Apsaras who come to you for extra classes on love, not any daughters you may have in future and certainly not the reincarnated old hag you took for a wife. It is my belief that you love me more than any or all of them put together. That may or may not be true, but if the day were to come when I cease to believe this, I will walk out of your life and never come back...'

'You will never leave me! For without you, I cannot go on and will die of a broken heart!' Kama cried.

'I warned you to shut up! Don't you dare interrupt me again!' Rati snarled at him, but the tears she had fought so long to contain, finally burst free and she struggled to stem the flow as she continued, 'Sometimes you are such a moron!' she finished with a sob as she finally allowed him to take her in his arms.

'For the record you were right. I do love you more than any or all of them put together. And that is the truth!' Kama whispered to her.

'Oh shut up, Kama! There is no need for any clarification and you know that I hate it when you state the obvious...' Rati retorted sharply, but this time she was smiling, and Kama was glad.

The Stone Women

$\mathcal{K}$ama was a blissfully wedded man to two wives—Rati and Priti, who thought the world of him and literally worshipped the ground he walked on. The former was his friend as well as his lover and she kept him satisfied in the marital bed as well as out of it. Though she challenged him and kept him on his toes, he was well aware that her fierce loyalty towards him would always be unmatched. Priti also adored him and seemed to want to devote her entire life to taking care of his every need and keeping him emotionally sated. To his surprise, when his two wives discovered that they were united in their all-encompassing love and devotion to their husband, they put aside the natural antipathy that would arise from such a relation and became good friends and allies. It helped that they were as different from each other as it was possible to be and neither considered the other a threat.

Therefore, it was not surprising that although his work required him to interact closely with the Apsaras, Kama was for the most part not in the least bit interested in having romantic dalliances with any of them. These Apsaras were famed for their beauty, renowned for their prodigious skill in the arts of love, and notorious for their libertine lifestyles which saw them hop blithely from bed to bed in the Three Worlds. Every single one of them who floated in and out of his palace (clad in diaphanous garments that left little to the imagination), made it abundantly clear to him that they would not object too strenuously towards becoming his lover. Yet

Kama knew how to let them down gently and would do as much, without provoking an inordinately angry reaction from them.

Indra was impressed with this particular ability of his and sounded him out on the subject, 'So how is it that none of the delectable Apsaras you have taken under your wing have made their way into your bed? I have noticed the admiring glances they keep throwing your way, even though you are fond of pretending to be blind in their presence. Tell me honestly, have you never considered using your arrows on those nymphs—or does Rati keep you on too tight a leash?'

'Rati does not consider them a threat. In fact, it was her idea to start the school of lovemaking so that proper instruction could be disseminated on the most effective ways to pleasure your partner. And since, in the early days at least, all of us were teachers as well as students in the school, we employed certain novel techniques of study. It was common to hold demonstrations featuring just Rati and me, or sometimes the Gandharvas and Apsaras as well, when words proved insufficient to illuminate the points we were making. So now you can tell why I have refrained from taking any of them as lovers; it would definitely compound an already complicated situation.'

The Lord of Heaven patted his friend on his shoulder jovially before quipping, 'Let me get this straight…you and Rati, along with the Gandharvas and Apsaras, study sex as a subject with practical classes? Therefore, you get to be exhibitionists without actually being exhibitionists, voyeurs without actually being voyeurs and willing partners in exploring the limits of your libido, while genuinely believing yourselves above that sort of depravity? And then you have the unmitigated gall to use that matter-of-fact tone with me! As to my question, I believe I already have the answer: you don't have to use your arrows here because there is no need.'

Kama wagged his finger at Indra before replying, 'I knew you would find a way to make it seem a lot more salacious than it actually is. Experiments or lessons conducted with the sole objective of gaining knowledge render the participants mostly immune to passion, love or even lust. There is a certain clinical detachment to the proceedings which precludes desire completely. If you don't believe me, Rati and I will be happy to give you personalized instruction on the subject.'

'As befitting the Lord of Heaven, I try to refrain as much as I can from participating in any kind of debauchery, so that I may be a worthy role model for all who strive to reach the highest echelons of virtue and goodness...' Indra said piously. The moment was ruined with Kama laughing raucously and scaring the birds from the trees. Undeterred by the mockery Indra continued, 'You are a clever one indeed! But have you ever considered using your famed arrows on yourself? I always wondered about your lack of curiosity when it comes to your own formidable powers. Surely you should know exactly what it is they are capable of?'

'I don't play with my weapons because they almost always lead to terrible consequences,' said Kama. 'Besides you don't have to embrace fire to know that it will burn you! That is something which is just obvious. And even you don't use your thunderbolt on yourself or your loved ones because you are fully aware of its destructive power, do you? You have already observed the unmatched success that your Vajra has enjoyed in vanquishing demons. Similarly, I know full well about the power of my arrows to enslave minds with desire, and I have no intention of misusing them!'

'Then you are more responsible than I,' Indra intoned solemnly and Kama diffused the situation by assuring him that he had always known it for a fact but was delighted that Indra was now aware of the same. The thousand-eyed God responded by shoving him playfully, but their forced jocularity could not shake off the premonition that suddenly dawned upon Kama. He felt their conversation was an ill-omen, and that somehow, a sequence of events with unhappy results for him had been set inexorably in motion. Unfortunately for him, he was right.

One day Kama accompanied by Rati and Priti decided to offer worship at the famous Kamesvara linga, where devotees of Shiva often went to pour out their hearts' deepest desires, confident that their faith would be rewarded by the mercy of the three-eyed God. Rati and Priti had been eager to visit the spot as they had heard wonderful things about the place but Kama had been unwilling for reasons he could not fathom. He had capitulated when his wives berated him on his inauspicious behaviour.

The linga was to be found at the bank of a river in the middle of a forest which was also home to the ashram of the great sage, Harita and his wife, Purnakala. The latter was a simple woman blessed with beauty so serene that although she herself seemed oblivious of it, her looks had the potential to stir up the Gods themselves.

Even as his wives were lost in religious fervour, Kama responded to the mysterious workings of fate and opened his eyes. On doing so, he saw a wondrous damsel undressing herself, completely unaware of the God of Desire who could not take his eyes off of her on the opposite bank of the river. Naked as the day she was born, she entered the water and her flesh goose-pimpled from the icy cold. Kama shook violently in response. He had been holding his arrows in his hand and at that precise moment an insect landed near his heart. Unthinkingly, and enamoured as he was by the sight in front of him, Kama plunged his arrows into his heart in a reflexive motion meant to kill the pest. However, not only did he impale the little insect, he also managed to lose his heart completely and utterly to the bathing beauty.

Using his statuesque proportions to shield the object of his desire from his wives, he bade them to wait for him elsewhere, before making a hasty departure. Rati offered to accompany him, but he waved her away before walking over to a solitary spot that allowed him a better view of the unknown woman who had won him over. There, he continued his solitary vigil, worshipping her with his eyes—until he was so flooded with desire that he felt the hair on his body stand up. Knowing that he could have no happiness till he possessed her, Kama raised his bow and fired his arrows in quick succession towards her and sighed with satisfaction when they found their mark.

Responding to his scorching gaze and the potency of his arrows, the simple Purnakala—who knew nothing of the world outside the ashram—suddenly found her heart filled with powerful feelings that defied comprehension, yet demanded satisfaction nevertheless. The blood rushed to her face and she found herself paralyzed with various nameless emotions that besieged her, as Kama held her transfixed with his gaze. So inflamed was she that she wanted to throw caution, upbringing and virtue to the wind and run to him immediately to put them both out of the exquisite misery they were experiencing.

Reminded painfully of her nudity, Purnakala dragged herself out of the water in a slow, sinuous movement and clutched her garments to her chest while she stared fixedly at the ground even as her toe furrowed the earth, refusing to take her away from the line of his vision. At that moment, she belonged body and soul to Kama and he revelled in the pleasure the knowledge brought him. Gently, he addressed her and his words, coated in honey, wafted across the water and was irresistible to her ears: 'I don't know who you are and yet, life will have no meaning for me if you are not a part of it. Beautiful one! I am known as Manmatha because of my ability to agitate the mind—and yet having beheld you, there is not a soul in the Three Worlds whose mind is as frenzied as mine. There is nobody in all of Brahma's vast creation as skilled as I am in the art of love and seduction, and yet, when it comes to pouring out my heart to you, my legendary prowess and powers of articulation have abandoned me and I stand before you not as the God of Desire whose power even Brahma, Vishnu and Shiva cannot withstand, but merely as a mad fool in love. If you deny me the gift of your person and the sweet pleasure to be found within your embrace, I will wither away and die on this very spot of a broken heart!'

On hearing the poignant words of Kama, which were all the more moving because they were infused with honesty, Purnakala felt desire course through her veins, snuffing out all other thoughts. Filled with longing that would brook no suppression, she forgot who she was and would have been hard-pressed to remember her name, let alone the fact that she was a married woman who had previously devoted her whole being to the well-being of her husband as befitting the best of wives. But her virtue, which was so deeply ingrained within her, refused to be cast aside and stood as the final barrier between the two smitten souls.

And so they stood for long moments with Purnakala refusing to look Kama in the eye, knowing that the passion she would see there would prove to be her undoing, and continuing to stare determinedly at her feet as they drew circles on the wet earth. Meanwhile Kama continued to murmur gentle words of endearment to her, sensing that something held her back despite her great love for him, loving and wanting her all the more for the admirable restraint she was displaying, wracked as she was by passion.

In the meantime, Harita had returned to the Ashram and was surprised to find for the first time in his married life that Purnakala was not waiting to greet him and the evening meal had not been prepared. Deciding that something terrible must have happened to her, he began searching frantically for her. Nightmarish images flooded his mind and he kept seeing her broken body in his head, torn apart by wild animals or violated by a horde of bloodthirsty demons. And then he discovered her—standing on the bank of the river, half-nude and listening with complete attention to a handsome youth whose voice throbbed with such ardent passion that she could not even sense the presence of an enraged husband.

Taking the sight in, he almost wished that he had found her corpse instead—ruined beyond recognition by beasts or demons.

Senseless anger and jealousy filled the sage as he became painfully aware of his own shortcomings next to the impossibly good-looking person who was his rival for his wife's affections. The creature who had usurped his rightful place was everything he was not. Where he was old and venerable, this stranger was young, virile and a hundred times more comely to look upon. As he walked towards them, his rage consumed him and he hurled his kamandala at her feet with such ferocity that it shattered. Purnakala cried out in terror as the spell that had kept her so attuned to her beloved broke, much like the vessel that now lay in pieces at her feet.

Harita rounded on Kama first and spat out a curse that was designed to strip his adversary of his unfair advantages over all other men, 'Bloody pretty boy and filthy wretch that you are, who has robbed my wife of her innocence, you will lose your damnable good looks and become afflicted with leprosy. Your healthy body will be ravaged by your illness and it will become suppurated with noxious sores. You will be shunned by all who have the misfortune to look upon you, and they will hurl stones at you in revulsion. The hideousness of your visage will be enough to frighten children, cause flowers to wither and fresh milk to curdle. Your wives will be unable to tolerate your presence and they will spit on you. Abandoning their virtue, they will run away with the first thing they come across with genitals who is ready, willing and able to elope with them!'

An involuntary groan escaped Kama's lips, not because of the terrible curse that had been pronounced on him by a wronged husband but because he sensed that the beautiful Purnakala had slipped out of his grasp forever. Whereas earlier he had been able to sense her love and longing for him like a tangible presence that struggled to escape the repressive prison of her virtue, now there was nothing but overwhelming shame and guilt that held her captive and completely out of his reach. The sense of bereavement that he experienced at the moment was so profound that it eclipsed even the enormous implications of the curse that hung over his head. In fact it was already working its way into his system like slow poison. Rati sensed the trauma that was lacerating her better half and without a word of explanation to Priti, she ran to be with Kama in his grief.

Meanwhile, ignoring him and leaving him to his pain and sorrow, Harita rounded on his errant wife, and let loose his anger upon her as well, 'As for my wife, who stands before her wedded husband unable to look him in the eye, bowed with shame like a harlot caught in flagrante delicto, she will be turned to stone, and it is my fond desire that her new avatar will help her withstand temptation better as she is clearly easily susceptible to the charms of every stranger traversing this way. As an unthinking stone, perhaps she will find it easier not to betray her husband again.'

Purnakala still would not look up and stood so still that it was almost as if she had become a stone already. It was Kama—wracked with guilt for the horrible fate he had helped bring upon the woman he loved so dearly—who spoke up on her behalf: 'Great sage! I beg of you to pay heed to my words! Your wife is ill-deserving of the curse you uttered. It is I who am to blame for this state of affairs. I saw her bathing in the river and accidentally wounded myself with my own arrows, thus losing my heart to her. Driven to despair with the depth of my feelings towards her, I shot my arrows at her as well. My father, Brahma, decreed that even the Gods will be helpless in the face of my power and if they themselves cannot armour themselves against me, then what chance did your hapless wife have—unschooled as she is in the ways of this wicked world?

At the moment of my conception, I tested my powers and Brahma and the Prajapatis lost control of their senses entirely and gave themselves over completely to incestuous desire, bringing down the wrath of Shiva on themselves. They were great beings, some among them the most venerated in all of creation, and yet they were reduced to ravening beasts of lust. But this noble soul who you were so quick to disparage—bewitched though she was by the power of my arrows—held firm against me and stayed faithful to you in body, if not in mind. I beseech you! Punish me as you see fit, but spare this blameless woman who has done nothing wrong nor committed any act worthy of upbraiding.

According to the wise men, there are three kinds of sins: each of which have their roots in the mind, speech and action. The effects of mental sins can be expiated by the performance of severe austerities; sins of speech can be exonerated by making gifts to the needy as a form of atonement; and sins of action can be expunged by embarking on certain ritualistic procedures which are prescribed for this purpose. As a wise man yourself, I am sure you are well aware of this. Your noble wife is guilty of only mental sin and even that was entirely on account of my instigation. If you show mercy and spare her, the store of ascetic merit you have just depleted on account of your anger, will be restored and you need have no fears for your next life.'

This impassioned outburst—that was yet another indicator of the great love borne by another man for his wife—infuriated the sage and he dug in his heels becoming all the more intractable as regards the punishment he had decreed for the offending duo, 'It is truly touching that my wife can incite such strong feelings in a God even as she has debased herself and besmirched her honour by betraying a husband who has loved her, stayed true to her, kept her free from want and spared her ill-usage.

That impressive account you just gave to me of the different types of sin just proves to me beyond a doubt that you are well-versed in all things evil and, hence, truly deserving of becoming a scabrous leper. My wife is also not as exempt from sin as you would like the world to believe. All sins have their origin in the inner sanctum of the mind and therefore, it behoves us to ensure that our thoughts are kept pure in order to prevent evil from gaining a foothold in our lives. Once evil has firmly taken root, damnation is inevitable and, therefore, it is imperative that we safeguard our thoughts and our mind first from such evil, so as to prevent censure. Since Purnakala betrayed me, her husband, by allowing thoughts of lust unhindered into her mind, it would have been inevitable that she eventually surrendered to her desire and cavorted with you like a bitch in heat. And therefore, it is fitting that she pays for her adultery even though you choose to quibble over whether it took place mentally or physically. She will be known henceforth as Khandasila, for, like a broken stone she is damaged goods and of no use to anybody. In this fitting guise for a sinner, she will serve as a lesson for all members of the weaker sex and act as a warning if they decide that virtue is a cheap price to pay for a few moments of cheap passion. Both of you are base sinners and hence I am perfectly within my rights to damn the two of you with my curse and make sure that it is binding!'

-Rati arrived on the spot just as Kama sank to his knees in abject despair, as the sage walked away leaving them to their fate. Purnakala transformed into a stone before their horrified eyes. Dignified as she had always been in life, she surrendered to her fate with a calm acceptance and did not deign to plead with her husband, nor did she seem to harbour any resentment towards the two men who were responsible for her fate. She smiled sadly at Kama, hoping to offer him what comfort and succour she could before she was shut forever behind her prison of stone.

Kama wept shamelessly to see Purnakala go beyond his reach and continued to sob even as Rati cradled him in her arms like the mother he had never had. The curse was taking effect for Kama as well, and Rati joined her tears to his, when she saw the handsomest among the Gods and man vanish to be replaced with a parody of what he had once been. His blemishless skin blackened and erupted in thousands of smelly, pus-filled sores, while his limbs withered, robbing him of his great vitality. The beauty of his features disappeared as they were marred beyond recognition; his once boundless energy dissipated leaving him robbed of all essence. When Priti finally caught up to them, she saw Rati holding on to an abominable creature, both weeping and utterly inconsolable. Watching the couple who had formerly lit up the very heavens with their radiant presence, the tears ran unchecked down her cheeks as well.

In the midst of his horrifying transformation, Rati never once let go of her husband and she focused all her energy towards offering him whatever meagre comfort she could. As she spoke soothing words, Rati rocked Kama gently, trying her utmost to ease him past the terrible trauma he was undergoing. Priti joined in and embraced them both. Held in the reassuring grip of their great love for him, Kama bestirred himself enough to put the worst of his sadness behind him and regained sufficient control over himself.

Kama then told his wives all that had occurred, sparing no detail. Rati and Priti listened without interrupting, sensing that it was a cathartic experience for him, one that would lance the worst of his pain and help him gain a measure of acceptance that was crucial for his healing to begin.

Having reached the end of his sorrowful narrative, Kama addressed them once again—this time more calmly: 'I should have been content to have not one, but two amazing wives. That alone should have been enough to restrain me from pursuing another man's wife. Now, on account of my covetousness, I have destroyed a family and brought misery to our doorstep. And yet, I am not even completely sorry that this entire episode took place for I experienced love like never before and even now it makes me feel truly fortunate. All too briefly, the lovely and virtuous Purnakala loved me back before she was snatched away from me. And now

I am unfit to rejoin the Three Worlds and so I shall remain here with Purnakala and draw what comfort is possible to be derived from my memories of her.

The two of you need not pay the price for my mistakes. Willingly do I offer you your freedom and you shall have no trouble finding new husbands for yourselves among the scores of men who would gladly welcome you into their homes. Leave me and try to find happiness elsewhere for it was never my desire to cause you sorrow, and I cannot have the two of you—who are my dearest possessions—suffer on my account.'

For the first time Rati spoke up, 'You are thinking of that stupid sage's poisonous words aren't you? That self-righteous old fool dared to say that your wives will abandon you? As far as I am concerned, from the time we left you, to this moment, this is the first time you have behaved in a manner unworthy of you. I am the product of my father's unholy passion and I emerged from the perspiration that was evidence of his shame; therefore I would have been reviled as a polluted creature anywhere in polite society. But when you saw me and fell in love with me, without the benefit of your infallible arrows, I was reborn, and by virtue of our marriage became not just an auspicious woman but a Goddess fit to be welcomed by Indra himself into his celestial abode. For that, among other things, you have always had my love and gratitude and nothing has happened to change that.

A dried up old sage's senseless words will never prove true for either Priti or me. We did not wrong him in any way, so he was not within his rights to include us in his curse. Besides, curse or not, no force will ever entice me to abandon you while there is life left in me. I am just grateful that you are still with us! Your being a leper makes no difference to me for it is you who are responsible for the beautiful life I have enjoyed so far and it is an honour for me to take care of you when you need me the most. I will not walk away like an ungrateful cur. Even you cannot make me leave, and I shall stay here with you and together we will find a way to work our way around the sage's curse.'

Priti also spoke up at that point, 'Everything Rati said is true. I also prayed for long years to get a husband like you and have since considered myself the luckiest woman for having won you through the grace of the Goddess. And it will take more than a jealous sage's curse to separate me from you. I will also share your fate and continue to serve you!'

Kama had no words with which to thank his wives for their unwavering loyalty and so he said nothing. The three then took up residence near Khandasila and spent long years in prayer and penance, hoping for a way out of their predicament. Kama was steadfast in his belief that the Gods would come to his rescue, as were his wives, and they were not mistaken.

In the absence of desire and pleasure, a pall of darkness had descended on the denizens of the Three Worlds and all happiness was leached out of their lives. The Gods and men alike were plunged into a deep gloom and could no longer derive comfort from an existence bereft of joy. Trees withered and died and flowers ceased to bloom. Cattle refused to yield milk and the fields lay fallow. Husbands and wives could not bear to look upon each other and procreation ceased all together. The world was dying, and worst of all, there was no promise of fresh life. The happy cries of children could no longer be heard and there were no pregnant women to be seen anywhere. Even the Gods began to feel the ill effects of the terrible miasma that had gripped the world—all in the absence of the gentle God of Desire and his consorts.

Accompanied by Indra, the Gods went to the Kamesvara Linga where they knew Kama could be found. His shrouded and wasted form confronted them like an apparition from hell, and he bowed his head in shame, unable to look upon his visitors when he saw the horror reflected on their faces. Offering their condolences to the God of Desire who had been brought so low, only because he had fallen in love, the Gods added their voices to his and together they all meditated upon Lord Vishnu, begging him to intervene and lift the curse inflicted by Harita. Life, as they had known it before the dreaded curse, had come to a complete standstill and now they needed Vishnu's help desparately in order to bring about a fresh beginning. Almost immediately, the Preserver appeared before them. Kama and his wives threw themselves at his feet. With infinite compassion, he lifted Kama to his feet without showing the slightest trace of revulsion and promised him that his troubles were at an end. He then went on to exclaim: 'Kama! I am surprised at you. You should have more faith in the power of love. What you experienced was pure and uplifting and there is no reason for you to be ashamed. You dishonour Khandasila by feeling as you do.

Propitiate her and you will be cured of your leprosy and your former glory will be restored to you. Her love for you was tremendous and it will always protect you. Believe in it and so it shall be. This place is blessed for henceforth it shall bear testimony to the power of love that preserves all that is good and beautiful in this world. The waters here will be called Saubhagya Kupa, the Well of Good Fortune. People will come from far and wide to bathe here and worship Khandasila and they will be cured of their bodily ailments, physical deformity as well as afflictions of the heart that are brought about by forbidden love. I have also devised a way to spare other lovers (who are deemed illicit by a heartless society) the same fate. For, those who are guilty of the sin of adultery will be forgiven simply if they perform a puja on the thirteenth of any month to Khandasila and the linga which witnessed the fate of the star-crossed lovers. They will also be absolved of all the guilt and shame that had attached to them when they fall at Khandasila's feet and offer her their heartfelt homage for the great sacrifice she has made!'

Grateful to Vishnu beyond all expression, Kama sought his blessings again, thinking how this was the second time that the great Lord had come to his rescue when he had been close to giving up all hope. Gladness began to fill him again, and he bid his benefactor farewell before turning to obey the instructions he had been given. He spent long months propitiating Khandasila, and just as Vishnu had promised, his sin was expiated and his leprosy left him. Once again, he was devastatingly good-looking and filled with vigour. Kama and his wives, who had prayed to Khandasila with equal devotion and come to love her almost as much as he did, prostrated themselves before the stone and thanked her profusely. Then, leaving a piece of his heart with Khandasila, Kama prepared to return to Amaravathi and take up his duties again.

On hearing the good news, the Gods themselves began celebrating in earnest, delighted to welcome the God of Desire and his wives back into their midst. Since his essence and great generosity of spirit had been repaired, the world came back to life through his grace and was greener and more beautiful than before. Trees sprang up all over the place and flowers bloomed in riotous colour. Wells and springs that had gone dry, bubbled over with water and the fields gave rich yields again. Husbands and wives rediscovered themselves in each other's arms and the wondrous process of procreation was once again set in motion.

Most importantly, there was peace, happiness and contentment in the world again and great was the rejoicing among Gods and men. Even Shiva looked down and smiled, pleased with the selflessness of the God of Desire that enabled him to do such good work with his powers; he began to reminisce fondly about his own beloved consort whom he had also dearly loved and lost. Brahma was proud of his son and decided he was worthy of his name—while Vishnu was also happy with his devotee who had repeatedly proved that his trust in him was not misplaced.

All was as well as could be hoped for given the circumstances, and the Gods heaved a collective sigh of relief, glad to have normalcy returned. Kama, Rati and Priti were comfortably ensconced within their crystal palace and none of them showed any ill effects from their ordeal outwardly, though their hearts continued to ache for Purnakala who was doomed to remain a stone.

It was business as usual for the God of Desire but in the innermost reaches of his mind, where even Rati had no access, Kama continued to mourn for his Purnakala. He bemoaned his fate for not being given enough time with her, though in all fairness a billion lifetimes with his beloved would still seem too short a while.

Rati also found herself dwelling on the fate of her rival and was aggrieved whenever she remembered that sage's deadly curse which had left her as a broken rock. She confided her thoughts in Kama, Indra and Rambha one day, 'I can't stop thinking about Khandasila. It was immeasurably kind of Vishnu to offer a way out for Kama and free him from that nasty old man's foul curse. But it saddens me deeply to think about that poor woman who will remain trapped as a stone for all eternity. It is too cruel a fate and one she did not deserve in the least.

There are people who have sinned simultaneously in thought, word and deed and they are free to roam about happily—whereas, Khandasila was only a hapless victim to my husband's arrows. It is horribly unfair!'

Kama nodded sadly, 'I am happy that through the grace of Vishnu, the entire world came to know of her virtue and goodness. It pleases me to think that she will now serve as a sanctuary for lovers and those afflicted with physical ailments with the power to heal them. Ideally, I would have preferred that she be freed of her curse as well, but this was a decision made by Vishnu and it is not in me to question his will...'

Rati was pleased to note that Kama had at last found his acceptance of a hard situation, but was even more surprised to realize that there was a deep sense of resentment in her against him and all males. Giving voice to her heated thoughts, she said, 'You may not be able to question Vishnu, but I have no such qualms. The

Preserver could and should have lifted the curse from Khandasila as well but it is so typical that a woman should have to suffer far more terrible consequences than a man for the same crime. I can cite so many examples of men getting off lightly when they behave stupidly, whereas a woman has to go through hell and back—or, as in Khandasila's case, stay put in that hell even when they are guilty of nothing more than a small error in judgement. Why, Rambha here was forced to spend a thousand years as a stone only because she followed the instructions given to her by the Lord of Heaven! She, of course, was bound to adhere to his word, while the said Lord and the irascible sage who had formerly exhibited an inability to practise celibacy, certainly suffered no such painful and uncomfortable transformation. And Ahalya's fate was worse. She merely gave in to the will of the Lord of Heaven and she was also transformed into a stone, whereas her partner in crime merely held on to his status of being one of the greatest lovers of all time, which was further brought to light by certain quirky physical manifestations.'

Kama had the grace to look shamefaced, but Indra merely shrugged and started to say something—when Rambha plunged headlong into the conversation: 'The world has always been and always will be unfair to women! The time has come for me to tell you all the circumstances that led to my downfall and don't you dare roll your eyes at me, your Majesty or I will dump this jug with its entire contents on your royal head! Rati was right when she suggested that you were more to blame than I for what had happened, and the least you can do is listen while I indulge in a little whining about a story that you are already much too familiar with.'

Well pleased with herself for having successfully won over a somewhat unwilling audience to listen to her, Rambha plunged into her tale: 'The events that led to my personal tragedy were set in motion when King Vishwamitra strayed into the hermitage of sage

Vasishtha in the middle of a military campaign. He was amazed at the ability of the great sage to feed his entire army at such short notice and discovered that it was only possible through the grace of Nandini—the calf of the cow of plenty, Kamadhenu, which belonged to the great sage. Deciding that such a wonderful creature ought to belong by rights to a king, he requested Vasishtha to sell it to him for a princely sum. When the Brahmarishi refused to part with the calf even in exchange for half the kingdom, Vishwamitra became enraged that his great generosity and famed recalcitrance were wasted on Vasishtha and he tried to take the divine calf by force. But he was no match for Vasishtha—especially since Nandini herself rose in defence of her noble master.

Humiliated in front of his army, Vishwamitra realized (to the detriment of his king-sized ego) that Brahmins wielded powers that Kshatriyas dare not dream about, and he decided to become a Brahmarishi himself by practising penances with a vengeance. He could not be dissuaded from this foolhardy endeavour which had hitherto never been attempted in history. Soon he was performing tapas, the likes of which had not been seen before and it must be accepted that his determination and ability to withstand hardships, if not his motives, were entirely commendable. It appeared that all of creation would explode…so terrible was the heat he generated through his single-minded purpose. Brahma went to him and begged him to stop as it was impossible for him to convert a Kshatriya into a Brahmin, but Vishwamitra refused to give up and began performing even more extreme austerities, that gave the mighty wielder of the thunderbolt, sleepless nights.

Indra realized that the hot-headed king-turned-ascetic was becoming formidable as he had now successfully gained enough ascetic merit to emulate Brahma and even create his own world. And so he sent Menaka, who is considered by some to be the most beautiful of the Apsaras, to the great sage. Taking no chances where the great Vishwamitra was concerned, she begged Kama and

Vayu to help her carry out Indra's wishes. They executed their plan to perfection. Even as Menaka strutted in front of Vishwamitra, displaying her redoubtable assets, Vayu blew away her clothes and revealed her magnificent nudity to Vishwamitra. At that opportune moment, Kama struck home with his arrows and their victim became completely smitten.

Vishwamitra and Menaka became lovers and he forgot himself completely, so enamoured was he with her flawless beauty. Long years passed in a happy deluge of carnal delights. The spell was broken when Menaka became pregnant with his daughter, Shakuntala. Flighty Apsaras are not made for child-bearing and motherhood, and she became increasingly petulant and he, increasingly disillusioned with the shallow creature that had so entranced him. And so he threw her out and she was not exactly heartbroken for she had grown tired of pleasing the cantankerous sage. Abandoning her child outside the Ashram of the merciful sage Kanva, correctly anticipating that he would provide the best care for their little girl, Menaka returned to Amaravathi, glad to have completed the onerous task she had been given and relieved to be back where she belonged.

Filled with regret for the events that had transpired—which had not only undone several years of hard work, but also added his name to that ignoble list of men who slept with comely Apsaras and made fools of themselves—Vishwamitra hardened his resolve once again. He decided to return to prayer and penance in order to achieve his original desire, except that this time he was determined to reach a higher plane of existence where he would be free from succumbing to such temptations. This time, there was no shaking him and it seemed that nothing would stop him from succeeding. In desperation, Indra asked me to try and seduce him again.

Foolishly, I accepted the dangerous assignment, believing in my arrogance that I would surely succeed. After all, I was more beautiful and accomplished than Menaka! When Kama offered to come along, I turned him down and went to Vishwamitra all by myself. Concerned that I was determined to embark on such a precarious mission on my own, he went to Indra who convinced him that I would be perfectly fine. Needless to say, Vishwamitra would not be swayed so easily a second time and he was furious with me for confirming his secret fear that everybody believed him to be a lusty old fool. Consequently, he cursed me but not before telling me off for being a woman with no moral integrity. His words had the effect of a billion lashings and the tears that I shed in abject shame formed little pools at my feet when he announced my punishment: I was to spend the next thousand years as a stone.

The only thing to be said about this miserable incident is that without realizing it, I had succeeded in the task entrusted to me—for, by causing him to lose his temper and formulating a terrible curse, he once again lost all the ascetic merit he had gained. This time around, his downfall was not on account of his unpredictable libido, but for giving free rein to the equally destructive emotion of anger. Indra, with all his cunning, had foreseen just such an outcome and had barely hesitated before proceeding to sacrifice me on the altar of his grandiose plans.

And so, while I languished as a rock, Indra went back to his restful nights filled with pleasure in the arms of one or more of my companions, having successfully thwarted the sage again. As for Vishwamitra, he did find a way past this setback as well and finally became a truly enlightened soul, reconciled himself with Vasishtha and succeeded in becoming a Brahmarishi. After a thousand long years, the curse was lifted and I was free to return to Amaravathi.

I consider myself fortunate—now more than ever—because fate decreed that it was not my lot to spend an eternity as a rock, where pilgrims would come to relieve themselves of their heartaches. But even now, when I dwell on the events of the past, I am more angry than sad that I was reduced to the role of a lousy pawn, while men gone mad in their quest for power, grappled savagely with each other—not caring about the unfortunate souls who got caught in the crossfire.

The sad tale of Purnakala has disturbed my equilibrium again and I keep thinking of that poor girl. Harita behaved like a complete moron and a typical male. If he had been the one guilty of adultery, it would have been expected of Purnakala to grin and bear it as it is a wife's duty to love her husband unconditionally even when he is behaving like an unmitigated jerk. But if she were to fall in love with another due to forces beyond her control, it is decreed that she be cursed. No one expects her sexually incompetent husband to love and accept her unconditionally.

At this point, I would like to add that Kama behaved with a grace and magnanimity that is rare among males. Most men are content to get laid and escape, leaving their partner for the nonce, with nothing more than stained sheets and regret—but Kama was different. He genuinely cared for her even though she held firm against his advances and did all in his power to divert Harita's wrath away from the object of his adulterous affection. It was truly worthy behaviour and Kama, in my opinion, should be emulated by the rest of his ilk. This is to thank him for restoring my faith in bloody males and convincing me that that not all of them deserve to be flung off a cliff at birth!' So saying, Rambha hugged Kama, in the genuine spirit of friendship and admiration.

Kama hugged her back affectionately in response. It still hurt him to think of Purnakala, but he was able to draw solace from the sacrifice she had made for him as it was evidence of her love for him—and it both gladdened and saddened him simultaneously. For the longest time, he found himself unable to shake off the tidal wave of despair that threatened to drown him even after his affliction had been cured and his wonderful form returned to him. Unable to come to terms with all that had transpired or even make sense of it, he had gone to see Vishnu without telling even Rati. The Preserver, with his divine omniscience, had known he would come and was waiting to receive him. Goddess Lakshmi herself had kind words for him on the services he had done for the Three Worlds and commiserated with him on the tragic loss he had suffered. Not only that but she waited on them while they conversed.

Vishnu had explained to Kama that the Gods themselves needed to have faith, for it was what sustained them in a way that not even the nectar of immortality could manage. He had explained this, amongst other things, to him on that day of divine healing, 'It is not beneath you to feel such profound sorrow over Purnakala's fate. The Gods are not above emotions that are generally considered to be the bane of human experience. Even Shiva is unable to reconcile himself to the loss of his beloved Sati and will not be the same till he is reunited with her. It is supreme faith that helps him hold it all together and endure unchanging over the eons. You would do well to emulate the three-eyed God, who is the greatest of us all.'

Kama sighed and replied, 'It is not the grief alone that has incapacitated me so. The guilt is far harder to bear, for it is I who must be held responsible for what happened to her. If I had not gone and lured her away from her husband she may still be alive and at peace.'

'She is at peace at this very moment and you were responsible neither for her predicament nor her salvation,' Vishnu informed him gently, and since it was he who had uttered the words, Kama realized that it could not be false. It was what he needed to hear, and the redemption that he had been craving for so long was finally granted to him by Vishnu. Tears sprang into his eyes as the Preserver continued, 'Every little thing in creation, from a humble speck of dust to the Gods themselves, come into being for a certain inherent purpose. Actions that are performed keeping this duty in mind and without investing too emotionally in them, helps the said actions to retain their purity and also keeps the performer free from censure. To surrender wholly to the will of God with simple devotion is the only way towards finding salvation.

Let go of the questions that are plaguing you day and night and robbing you of your tranquillity. Why did I fall in love with a married woman? Why did her husband refuse to listen to reason? Why was I spared and she doomed even though she was by far the more blameless? Why? Why? Why? The answers to these questions—if they do exist—are highly irrelevant and it is fruitless for you to chase after them. If you persist, you will have reduced yourself to the level of a cur chasing its own tail, unable to stop even to eat, drink or relieve itself.

As the God of intoxicating emotions like love and desire—both of which have a dual nature—it is simply imperative that you discover your inner balance. It is through your grace that beauty and flavour can be found on earth, and without it—as was demonstrated in the period of your disgrace—there is no hope for the Gods or mortals as it signals the end of everything in existence. Remember, that while stirring up passions it is essential that you remain dispassionate. Your mind must be like still water even in the midst of the chaos which is of your own making, for it is the only way you will be able to stop the near madness you have triggered and not be pulled down by it yourself. Without you, there is no way out for anyone else either, which is why it is so important that you find a way to stay afloat—no matter where the tides of time take you or however many times they bash you against the rocks.

This is why I thought it fitting to let you know that as my beloved devotee, you ought to realize that all the paths you choose to take or the ones you have no choice but to take, will inevitably lead you back to me. I know that this simple fact has always eluded you—but the moment you begin to understand it, when you come to believe it with every fibre of your being, is precisely the moment that you will be liberated from the morass of your own making, holding you prisoner against your will.'

Kama rose to his feet and joined his hands as if in prayer, 'How can I not believe the words you have uttered yourself? Shiva himself christened you Hari, for you are the very embodiment of truth and your words cannot be false. I was a fool all this time and the gift of sight notwithstanding, blindness has been my greatest vice. But you have restored my vision and given me the gift of faith. I can ask for nothing else, for the knowledge you have given me today is everything! Give me your blessings Lord, and with your permission, I will depart and devote myself to carrying out your will, now and forever more!'

With the blessings of Vishnu and Goddess Lakshmi still ringing in his ears, Kama returned to Amaravathi and Rati, his transformation complete and him wholly at peace with the past, present and future. As he shook himself out of his reverie now and rejoined his companions, he noticed that Indra was teasing Rambha, mockingly commiserating with her for the horrors she had lived through. Looking at this familiar scene fondly, Kama thought—not for the first time—that he was fortunate to have friends like these who had supported him in the aftermath of the sage's curse and had found it in their hearts to love Purnakala almost as much as he did and to treat her with so much respect.

Perhaps realizing that his dear friend was back in their midst once again, Indra picked up the threads of the conversation and addressed Rati, 'Regarding your reference to Ahalya, perhaps I should explain. In a former age, Brahma created a remarkably beautiful damsel named Ahalya who was absolutely flawless in every regard. I noticed her from the heavens, for it is hard to overlook a woman of such uncommon good looks, and felt a keen desire to make her my own. And so I approached Brahma with due humility...'

At this point, Indra's narration was rudely interrupted by disbelieving laughter which he ignored with magnificent disdain before proceeding, 'I informed the Creator that only the best would do for a woman like her and as I am the best among the Gods, she should be given to me!

But in a fit of contrariness, not to mention extreme ill-judgement, he said that my arrogance would bring about my downfall someday and placed her in the care of the sage Gautama. The sage, renowned for his great nobility, welcomed her into his humble household and raised her in the manner of Bhikshuhanis to keep her safe from the likes of me, no doubt. Pleased with the restraint Gautama had shown, Brahma decided that he was the ideal mate for Ahalya and married her to Gautama. This was despite the fact that I myself had approached him for her hand yet again and shown equal restraint in not carrying her away and ravishing her myself, or, alternatively, pounding Gautama's pious face to pulp.

So it came to pass that Ahalya found herself in Gautama's ashram leading the simple life and she seemed to be thriving on it, for the next time I saw her she looked even more beautiful than I remembered. It had been long years since I had lost my heart to her and my patience had worn thin. It was a habit of mine to spy on the ashram and watch her without anyone getting wise to my presence, but these little sips of her beauty, which only my eyes could fully enjoy, served to give me a maddening thirst for all of her.

Determined to make her mine, I approached her in the ashram at an opportune moment and told her of my feelings for her. Given her upbringing, she was an innocent soul (unlike the minxes I am acquainted with) and blushed with chagrin when I poured out my heart to her. Refusing to even look at me, she declined my invitation to become lovers. But by forcing her chin up and looking into the limpid pools that were her eyes, I realized that she was flattered and, more importantly, that there was a definite flash of desire there though she did her best to conceal it. Letting my hands linger on her face, I told her that it hurt me a lot, but I would respect her decision—and to my delight, this time there was disappointment stamped all over her lovely features. It was almost as if she wished dearly for me to break the barricades she had erected around herself with brute force.

Smiling to myself for having almost won her over, I retreated and made my plans. In the guise of her odious husband and in a place of concealment, I waited patiently, till Gautama made himself scarce. Then I approached her and bade her do her wifely duty by me. Ahalya knew instantly that something was amiss for Gautama was not the sort of man who would leave home to perform his pujas for the day—only to return almost immediately, inebriated by desire for her.

Sensing that it was a stranger who was bedding her, she was still unable to extricate herself from my embrace for it had awoken feelings that had long remained dormant within her. An appreciation of the erotic was not usually encouraged or even acknowledged in the cloistered atmosphere of her ashram, which venerated purity of thought above all else. When the floodgates of her desire were thus shattered open by the expertise of my loving, she was sucked under into a whirlpool of exquisite pleasure. And she welcomed every one of my caresses with two of her own, knowing full well that it was not her husband who was suddenly introducing her to a previously undiscovered world of ecstasy, but a God whom she did not have the will or the power to rebuff.

Blissfully entwined in a languorous embrace of mutual lust, our senses tingling with the danger of our impending discovery, we carried on with our lovemaking—all the time wishing that time would stand still so that we could remain in that happy state forever. But alas! It was not meant to be, for Gautama sensed our transgressions from a mile away and he turned his steps homeward, molten anger lending wings to his feet in order to put an end to our happiness.

Throwing open the door to his room which had become our pleasure chamber, he rushed in. It would have done me a little credit if I had responded to the situation with the dignity befitting my status, but it is hard for one caught naked with another man's wife to muster up any kind of decency. So I transformed myself into a cat and tried to flee but he saw through my deception in a trice and, with the contempt of the righteous wounded, he kicked me against the wall where I lay crouching, with my tail between my legs, mortified more than I care to recall. Then he cursed me saying that since lust was my vice it was only fitting that decent folks be warned of my sex-crazed nature and declared that my body would be covered by a thousand vulvas. To my eternal shame, his words took effect immediately.

At this point, he turned on Ahalya who was trying unsuccessfully to cover her own nakedness, quailing in terror at what sort of punishment he would mete out to her. Accusing her of being a harlot who had brought disgrace to her house and an ungrateful wife for having betrayed the man who took her into his home and heart, he declared that she will turn into a stone.

Unable to withstand his stinging contempt, I fled from the ashram even as Ahalya started hardening into stone. As I ran from the scene of my shame, I could hear her pleading with Gautama but it was more effort than I could muster to stay and find out her fate, so I never looked back. It was Brahma who let me know the rest. Perhaps because Gautama had also loved her as much as I did, he relented slightly in the last moments left to her and agreed to modify his curse. Gautama decreed that the curse will be lifted when Vishnu takes a human avatar and moves among men as the noble Rama and touches her with his feet.

As for me, with a little help from Brahma—who intervened with Gautama on my behalf—my vulvas mercifully became eyes when Vishwakarma created Tilotama for the purpose of bringing about the destruction of the Asura brothers, Sunda and Upasunda. He showed off his exquisite creation—made entirely from all the beautiful things that he had gathered from the Three Worlds—to the Gods, and I was determined not to ogle her like the other Gods who had forgotten themselves completely. As a result of this decision, my body obliged by providing me with extra eyes, so that whenever I needed to gaze upon a beauteous maiden, I would not have to turn my head this way and that. Ahalya is still a rock, but it is only a matter of time before she is also rescued, thanks to the benevolence of Vishnu.

Rati may be angered with the injustice that seems extant in the world where a woman's fate is concerned, but the fact is that the nature of sin and punishment is beyond the comprehension of even the Gods and rests solely in the hands of fate, that mysterious device which keeps the wheels of the universe churning. So it would never do to rave and rant against hapless males!'

Having waited politely for Indra to finish, Rati replied, 'I think it is far too simplistic to blame fate for the excesses of egoistic males who are given to trampling upon the natural rights of the female of any species. Perhaps the time has come to redistribute the balance of power in the Three Worlds, so that the ladies are given a chance to redress the wrongs done by their worse halves which has resulted in so much senseless destruction!'

Indra replied in a carefully moderate tone, 'There is absolutely no precedent in history when the male relinquished power to the female—for the simple reason that the weaker sex is just that! They are thoroughly unfit to either wield power or cope with the harsh demands of the job. Even you champions of feminity will have to admit that the bitchiness, which is such an integral component of the fairer sex, has resulted in the reality of females being their own worst enemies. It is well known that women do a far more thorough job than men of destroying each other, and the worst offenders against ladies are not 'bloody males' but other ladies even taking into account the most brutal rapists, squalid pimps or women killers out there. This particular attribute of females renders them completely unsuitable for the great responsibilities which are the traditional and rightful domain of the males—who, by the way, get more than their fair share of criticism simply for doing a darn good job!'

In the same tone, Rati replied, 'I hope you will not take offence, but it is my firm belief that we ought to set some new precedents whereby power need not be relinquished to anybody but merely re-distributed so that women are given a fair share and both sexes can work as a team with one making up for the deficits of the other. Males are ruthless and headstrong, tending to rely on brute strength to dominate, whereas, despite their so-called bitchiness, females are mothers, born to nurture and nourish—infinitely gentler than their male counterparts and filled with compassion. The will of women have been subjugated for ages, as men like to hog power—and consequently, all life forms have suffered. The world is a violent place and rivers of blood have been shed by men just so they can hold on to something that they have jealously hoarded for themselves.

You are not wrong either when you point out that females are more adept at dragging down their own kind. But this is only because it is harder for a woman to survive in a world created by men for men. Sooner or later, a hardy woman comes to realize that the only way to ensure her own well-being is to secure a place for herself in the heart of a male who has the strength to keep her safe from harm. Which is why females compete with each other for the favours of the wielders of power and it is hardly a matter of choice. This makes it imperative that we become the harbingers of change, so that men don't grow addicted to what they consider to be theirs and engage in increasingly brutal practices and senseless savagery to hold on to power, which results in women becoming victimized, panic-stricken and desperate, forcing them to turn on each other. The battle of the sexes is futile as such a fight can have no winners, but merely an abundance of losers.'

Sensing the agitation that was robbing his wife of her

equanimity, Kama placed his hands over Rati's. She quieted down somewhat and even as Kama stayed silent for long moments she relaxed visibly, finding comfort in his touch. And when he finally spoke, she leaned against his chest so that she could be closer to him, 'I had a role to play in the fates of Purnakala and Rambha. Their transformation into stone made me feel directly responsible and I was consumed by guilt on both occasions. It is easy to understand the strong feelings of persecution that Rambha and Rati are currently harbouring, but unlike Rati, I don't think a redistribution of power is called for because there already is a balance which, though not always discernible, is present nevertheless.

Indra argued that the male of any species has always been and will continue to be the wielders of power and I am inclined to agree, but it is my belief that this is only at an overt level and without women who operate covertly, the efforts of the former would totally go to waste. When Indra himself had to pay the price for killing a Brahmin—by losing his powers and having to leave his kingdom which he had become too weak to protect—it was his wife, Sachidevi who rescued the Devas from the clutches of king Nahusha. The said monarch had been chosen to replace Indra since he had the reputation of being an able and just ruler.

However, though Nahusha was originally a good man, power corrupted him completely and he became a terrible tyrant. Even Indra's worst detractors had to finally admit that he had done a great job as king, and not just by comparison to the new arrogant despot. It was Sachi who found the courage to resist the villain who had usurped her husband's throne. She had the resourcefulness to do what was needed to restore her Lord to his rightful place, even while he did nothing more than conceal himself in the stalk of a lotus plant. And if this were not enough, she also discovered how he could atone for the heinous crime of killing a Brahmin and regain his formidable strength. I have no doubt that she would back you up against Indra, Rati!

Moreover, I don't think the weaker sex is weak at all and they are capable of being far deadlier than their male counterparts when the occasion calls for it. It was Goddess Durga who slew the demon Mahishasura when he won a boon from the Creator according to which no male could bring about his death. He was sanguine in the belief that he had become immortal as it was his misguided belief that no mere female could hope to equal his prodigious strength—and since the God of Death is male, he believed that Yama would never be able to claim his life thanks to the boon. And so he grew complacent, until the fierce Goddess proved to him that she was a mighty warrior despite her sex or even in spite of it, and she certainly had no qualms about decapitating him and cutting out his heart. Even the Gods go to her for protection, knowing that she will always be there to help and lend her services to those who need her protection against the forces of evil. History is littered with such examples of the brilliance of women when men were tested and found wanting.

I must also confess that without Rati's quiet strength or the core of steel that is hidden by her delicate appearance, it would be impossible for me to function to the best of my abilities. She and Priti stood by me when I was lost to myself and it was their love and devotion that saw me through those dark times. In fact, even Shiva is incomplete without Sati by his side. Indra is also devoted to Sachi, though he is fond of getting women rattled by putting forward the impression that he is a misogynist and a chauvinistic pig. He is fully aware of the tremendous worth of not just his wife but women everywhere.

I understand the point Rati raised about males resorting to savagery in order to hold on to their power and the fact that it simply reduces females to the position of slaves who are expected to carry out the will of their masters. However, I believe it came about simply because most were misguided enough to adopt the most expeditious way that they came across in order to keep their ladies safe from harm, and then stuck to it with typical bullishness. Women are considered the most precious and valuable beings in all of creation; therefore, it is a man's sacred duty to make sure she is happy always and protected from danger. The Gods bless the home of a happy woman who is treated with respect and honour, whereas they shun the abode where she is ill-used and miserable—and no amount of sacrifice can redress the situation. The sinners who fail in this foremost of their duties (that of keeping a woman happy) are thrice cursed, and so it became imperative that men devise means to go about performing this particular task.

Certain wise men then came up with a set of rules designed to enable men to protect their women folk better. Ladies would start out their journey under the care of their fathers whose responsibility it would be to raise the child well, protect her from danger, and when the time was right, find a suitable groom for her. As the woman enters this stage of her life, the husband becomes responsible for her well-being. In the final stages of her life, it is the son who is bound by duty to care for his mother and cater to her every need, in order to earn the favour of the Gods. Freedom was considered a commodity most unsuitable for women as it put them in harm's way and the prevalent belief then was that women would do excellently without it.

As is usually the case, some ideas sound perfect in theory and even when executed start out well enough, but time and the combination of many variables have exposed the flaws in this concept—for what was intended to guarantee happiness for the ladies has increasingly become a factor in bringing them untold grief. Rati was right in calling for change. But there is a certain natural order for these things and they happen only gradually. This is why it is imperative for members of both sexes to resolve their differences without drawing battle lines and hurting each other. I think we can all agree that I have said the last word on the subject. We should simply admit that we love each other even when we hate each other and leave it at that!'

Rati hugged Kama, and Rambha and Indra clapped their hands in unison. On that day, at least there were no losers in the battle of the sexes. Kama looked around at these people who were amongst those whom he loved best in the world and was almost content. It had been a tremendous ordeal that he had been through, but he had survived and taken his rightful place among the Gods. Ideally, he should have been happy. But what he felt was apprehension and there was no shaking the feeling that he had been tempered with fire to prepare him solely for what lay ahead.

The Burning

*K*ama was feeding treats to his parrot when Vasanta walked in on him, and the latter immediately felt the uncharacteristic chill emanating from his friend. 'Indra wants to see me…' Kama replied to the unvoiced query, 'It sounded urgent. I expect him to drop in shortly.' Vasanta nodded wordlessly and made ready to depart, for, though Indra had always been courteous to him, the Lord of Heaven expected to have Kama to himself whenever he honoured them with a visit. The God of Spring did not mind too much for even Rati or the other Apsaras were not entirely welcome when the duo had their little meetings. This time, however, he was strangely reluctant to leave Kama and he could not shake the feeling that he ought to be protecting Kama from he knew not what. His eyes met Rati's on the way out and he saw the same unease mirrored there as they nodded to each other in tacit understanding.

Meanwhile, Indra had appeared in Kama's chambers. Not bothering with pleasantries he collapsed on a luxurious couch before he began, 'We are in deep shit! Sit down by my side and listen to what I have to say. For it is clear to me that without you, we are doomed.'

'Has Narada paid you a visit again?' said Kama.

'Yes, he came by…only this time, it was not his usual nonsense about petty squabbles or gossip regarding who is banging whom. We have a serious threat looming ahead of us. I am not sure if you are familiar with the details about how we secured the nectar of immortality?'

'Narada told the story to Rati and me shortly after we were wedded and on our way to Amaravathi.'

'Good! Then you will remember that the Asuras had been vanquished by the Devas in the epic clash after we had churned the ocean of milk to procure the nectar of immortality. With Vishnu's help we got our hands on the Amrita first and inflicted a humiliating defeat on our half-brothers—who had no choice but to flee. Banished to the bowels of the living world, they bided their time with black vengeance helping them survive against the odds, so that they could return at some point to screw things up for me.

According to Narada, king Akhirsen was one of the survivors of the fateful war. He had a daughter named Maya who was a sorceress of tremendous power. She had been conceived at a moment when her father had been blinded by rage and anguish. Having lost the power, prestige and possessions of his ancestors, he had been forced to survive in a dank cave in the underbelly of Mother Earth. Where once he had been a lion among his lot, he was now reduced to the level of an ignoble rat that had to live among its own droppings and forage for a living from the scraps discarded by its betters. The former demon king pumped his frustration into his poor wife and it was from the heat of his anger that Maya came into being.

Akhirsen was fiercely proud of his daughter. Every time he reminisced about their fall—Maya listened carefully with an expression harsher than death and vowed to redress the wrongs done to them. The Asura king told her how they had been promised an equal share of the Amrita and the Devas had played them false.

Narada relayed the rest of the conversation between Akhirsen and Maya with his usual irritating dramatic effects but I will recount it to you: "Those self-righteous Devas go around masquerading as the embodiments of virtue and nobility, and yet they were not above lying through their teeth. Those puny bastards had their arses whipped in fair battle and were on the brink of extinction. Pathetic inbred rodents! They scurried to Vishnu for help and together they hatched the nefarious scheme that proved so tragic for us.

The sons of Aditi did not even have the courage or the physical prowess needed to churn the Ocean of Milk by themselves so they came crawling to us for help. After kissing every Asura's arse they could find like the glorified whores that they are, they told us in good faith, that since we were both sons of Sage Kashyap, born to Aditi and mother Diti, we were also entitled to a fair share of the divine nectar. The duplicitous prick, Indra looked us in the eye and said that we should suspend our hostilities and embark on this endeavour for the greater good—and fools that we were, we decided to accept. Little did we suspect that the treacherous snakes with their pretty smiles were planning to plunge a dagger into our backs.

Having done the lion's share of the task, which saw so many valiant Asuras sacrifice their lives for a noble cause, the nectar was handed over to us by the divine physician, Danvantri. We were rightly adjudged the worthy recipients of the Amrita by Danvantri since he knew that the Devas had done nothing worthy of deserving it and had merely sat on their backsides as spectators, while we carried Mount Mandara to the Ocean and churned it while enduring the poisonous fumes of Vasuki.

The Amrita was in our hands and we had come achingly close to achieving the immortality which we had always longed for. But Vishnu tricked us out of our right by taking the form of the enchantress Mohini and trapping us in her web of malfeasance. While she cast her evil spell on us, the Devas poured the nectar down their gullets and discovering to their surprise that they had finally grown a pair, they butchered us with none of the mercy or compassion that they are supposed to be oh-so-famous-for.

Trust me when I say that they are the real monsters, and in

that accursed war they proved it as much. Asuras were slaughtered in droves for no Asura worth his name would ever surrender or ask for quarter to anybody, let alone a treacherous foe. It is to our great pride that though we were betrayed and found ourselves fighting a hopelessly uneven battle, they still could not outfight us and bring about our complete extermination. We survived and one day, we will take back everything that was taken from us!"'

Indra continued: 'Maya grew up listening to these grossly inaccurate tales about what villains we had been. I am sure Akhirsen was not above accusing us of having violated every "virtuous Asura maiden or maid" we encountered and Maya must have believed his fabricated nonsense.

Father and daughter wept tears of fierce pride and anger every time they relived their tragedy. Maya apparently would always promise her father that she would make the Devas pay for their crimes. The old king would be ridiculously happy on hearing her words and would sigh in satisfaction imagining the proud Devas dragged down from their lofty homes and left to wallow in the dirt, stripped of everything they held dear.

Long years passed in this way and Maya became adept in the science of sorcery. One day, she came to her father in a fever of excitement, for she had somehow discovered the means to destroy us. It involved Lord Shiva for we had pissed him off royally on one unfortunate occasion...'

Kama interrupted: 'Did it involve Sati? I had been meaning to ask you about the events that led to her death. Vishnu referred to the incident once. He told me that Shiva was devastated after her passing and will not be fully healed until he is reunited with her.'

Indra sighed again and looked troubled as he gathered his thoughts about those tragic events of long ago. 'Watching the Destroyer at the height of his misery and rage is not something any of us are likely to forget. You can count yourself fortunate for not being around at the time for nothing can prepare you for what it means to bear the brunt of his killing fury.' Involuntarily, Indra shuddered as he relived those memories and failed to see the mute horror and despair that flared momentarily in his friend's eyes.

Indra resumed his narration, 'Sati, daughter of Daksha, desired to make Shiva her husband. In order to win the affections of the ascetic God, she devoted thousands of years to the performance of penances and succeeded in securing him as her husband. Daksha was not too thrilled with her choice of husband or the efforts she underwent on his behalf—as he found Shiva thoroughly repulsive. It was his firm belief that anyone who did not bother to wash himself at least once in a few thousand years, voluntarily opted to wear the skins of slaughtered animals, and actually chose to inhabit the realms of the dead, did not deserve his respect and certainly not his worship. Since his daughter had obdurately given herself in marriage to an uncouth, unwashed ascetic who reeked of corpses, blood and decay, Daksha decided that he simply did not care what became of her and it was immaterial to him whether she lived or died—provided he never had the misfortune of seeing her face again after the mandatory wedding festivities the other Gods and I had insisted he participate in.

He took further umbrage when Shiva refused to prostrate himself at his feet as befitting a respectful son-in-law. Shiva was merely being thoughtful for, as the greatest of the Gods, if he were to lower himself and pay homage to an inferior (even if the said individual be a father-in-law) that action would result in calamity. Daksha refused to see it that way and decided to nurse a grudge instead, which had tragic consequences for all of us. Daksha decided to perform the grandest yagna ever conducted by the Gods and he deliberately left out his offending offspring and her husband from the invitation list. Sati had believed all along that her dear father had objected to the marriage only because he did not wish his darling daughter to suffer any kind of hardship by dedicating her life to the performance of tapas. When she failed to receive an invitation to the yagna, she convinced herself that it was merely an oversight and begged Shiva to let her go and attend the grand event.

Shiva tried to dissuade her, for, unlike his naïve wife, he knew exactly where he stood with his father-in-law. Try as he might though, he could not convince her and decided to let her have her way as her happiness was paramount to him. Shiva relented and told her that though he himself could not accompany her on account of being uninvited, she was free to go with Nandi to attend on her own.

Sati's initial excitement faded when she reached the venue. The chilling reception she got from her father convinced her that her Lord had indeed been slighted and grievously so. She was furious with her father for daring to disrespect her beloved Shiva so. She was determined to take him to task, but mindful of the occasion, she prostrated herself at his feet to pay her respects—and then, the wife of the Destroyer was ready to say her piece. She rounded on her father and upbraided him for the blatant manner in which he had insulted Shiva. When she was done with him, Sati told off the rest of us as well. Even Vishnu and Brahma were not spared and she chastised them severely for tolerating this affront to Shiva and warning us that nothing good would come off this grievous lapse on our part.

Daksha had not been very happy to see his uninvited guest or her unsightly attendants—who, with the bull at their head, certainly did not complement the ornate décor of the yagna. That she had actualy dared to give him and all his privileged invitees such a dressing down enraged him no end, and he raised his hand as if to strike her. However, sensing that it was not the smartest thing to do, he allowed his hand to drop by his side with a harsh slap. Sati heard the sound and her eyes grew wide with shock when she realized that her beloved father had actually intended to cause her bodily harm.

They grew wider still, first with tears and later with molten rage, when Daksha now opened his mouth and fired off a stream of invectives at her which conveyed in no uncertain terms the depth of his contempt for Shiva. He made no bones about the fact that he thought of Shiva as a polluted skull-bearer who had no business participating in such an auspicious occasion. We all realized that he had gone too far and forgotten that his daughter was a powerful Goddess, but there was little any of us could do to stop the situation from spiralling out of control. Having run out of steam, and with a belated instinct to avoid self-destruction, Daksha allowed the abuse to dry up.

Sati stayed silent for long moments, unable to believe the humiliation that had been meted out to her and the terrible insults that had been hurled at Shiva. The Destroyer's consort did not rave and rant, tear out her hair or shriek in fury—but the power of her anger was a palpable thing and even I'll admit that I was scared senseless at that point. She allowed her eyes to travel over all of us and her gaze warned us of the retribution that would follow. Turning to Nandi, she told him that she had no wish to live with the knowledge that she had been born to a base creature like Daksha who was blind to the merits of her Lord. Asking him to tell Shiva that she loved him and would return to him soon, Sati walked into the sacrificial flames before anyone could stop her. The flames consumed her, even as we watched helplessly in ungodly terror, as Shiva's beloved wife was charred beyond recognition.

Nandi and his attendants got over their initial grief and attacked the guests with savage fury, but they were driven away by the might of the Devas aided by Vishnu and the warlike creatures that the sages conjured up from the sacrificial flames. We had no choice but to retaliate, for Shiva's forces had gone completely berserk. We could not simply stand by and watch as they tore Daksha limb from limb, since he was our host and we owed him protection. They fled to Shiva and told him all that had transpired. When the

Destroyer was informed of the loss he had suffered, his divine fury threatened to engulf all of creation. He tore out a hefty chunk of his matted hair and dashed it against the ground splitting it in half. Two fearsome creatures—Veerabhadra and Mahakali emerged from the halves. Eerie shrieks rented the air, as they incessantly bayed for our blood and from the sounds that now wafted around, more and more hordes of unearthly beings emerged to help them satisfy their bloodlust.

Shiva commanded them to despoil the yagna and to relieve Daksha of his head. Veerabhadra and Mahakali hastened to do his bidding. They poured out of the lofty heights of Kailasha and descended on the gathering like a pestilential waterfall. All who dared to stand in their way were torn to pieces. Flying body parts and geysers of blood festooned the holy site making it an abomination and a place of eternal damnation. The Gods fled en masse from the place for I had ordered a retreat and even Vishnu knew better than to impede the wrath of the Destroyer. The sages, who had formerly conjured up an army, were captured, stripped and hung up by their heels from the branch of a tree—and trust me when I say they suffered the kindest fate. The paltry defence put up by what was left of the celestial army was snuffed out with ease as Veerabhadra and Mahakali made short work of them. Shiva's hordes then desecrated the altar by relieving themselves, defecating on it and committing every possible atrocity they could come up with. I saw everything from the clouds above and it still sickens me to speak of it, despite being a veteran of many unholy wars.

Veerabhadra looked at the scene of unspeakable carnage and was pleased. His savage satisfaction was heightened when he saw Daksha on his knees, weeping at the sight of his despoiled yagna. With grim purpose, he thundered towards him and with one blow of his hefty battle-axe decapitated him cleanly. Flinging the head into the smoking pyre, he raised his hand to signify victory and was joined by Mahakali and the rest of that nightmarish horde.

Led by Vishnu—who was the only one brave enough among the lot of us—we went to Kailasha to face the Destroyer and to beg his help. If it had not been for Vishnu, who somehow managed to reach across the abyss of grief that separated him from us, we would have all been burnt to death. Vishnu reminded Shiva of Sati's last words and promised him that they would be reunited again. I remember weeping myself when I came across Shiva standing tall and howling his misery for the Three Worlds to hear. Vishnu dropped to his knees and hugged Shiva's feet, shedding tears of his own. He begged Shiva to control his emotions for our sake, for he was our father and if we lost him to this tragedy, we would become orphans.

Miraculously, Shiva listened to Hari's poignant words and they seemed to have a soothing effect on him. He calmed down sufficiently at that point and acceded to Brahma's request that the yagna be completed and Daksha revived in the interest of creation, for he was a Prajapati. Recalling his troops, Shiva ordered them to hunt down the sacrificial goat which had run free and to use its head to restore Daksha to life. Grudgingly, he gave his blessing for the ill-fated yagna to be completed. And finally, he told Vishnu that he wanted us to get lost for he wished nothing but solitude for himself.'

Kama was deeply moved on hearing this story and he found himself grieving for Shiva's loss. He hated for lovers to lose each other and he was sorrier than he could say for what the Destroyer must be going through. Even a dreaded enemy did not deserve such a fate, he decided, and a wave of sadness washed over him when he realized that Rati had been marked for exactly the same kind of bereavement. Refusing to dwell on it, for it would tempt him to run away with her and seek refuge in the remotest corner of the cosmos, he forced himself to return to the conversation, 'It is hard to believe that even Shiva is not spared the slings and arrows of fate, not to mention the pain of separation. But what has all this got to do with the old demon king and his sorceress daughter? Shiva is completely detached from the happenings of the world. I refuse to believe him capable of attaching blame to you and the rest of the Devas and bringing about your downfall.'

Indra groaned in frustration, 'You will understand it in a minute. Akhirsen also wanted to know how the tragic tale of Shiva and Sati would work to their advantage. Narada relayed to me exactly what Maya said to enlighten him: "I visited the sacrificial site after the yagna, which went so badly for all involved. Thanks to my skill as a sorceress, I was able to see clearly even that which was obscured to the Gods. Shiva had allowed the yagna to be concluded, but there was no altering the fact that its outcome was tainted with the Destroyer's fury. The corrosive emotions that had been vented on that day—supplemented by the atrocities perpetuated by Shiva's hordes—had left a thick fog of ill-fortune hovering about the place. This, despite the fact that the sages had performed various kinds of purification rituals. Using my powers, I siphoned away every wisp of this maleficent miasma into my womb.

With a little help from a certain sage who has repeatedly proved his seed to be of the most potent kind (having fathered entire races like the Asuras, Devas, Gandharvas and Apsaras in addition to whole species of animals, snakes and birds), I will conceive and raise mighty sons who will be the weapons that will direct the thwarted fury of the Destroyer on the Gods. Brahma, Indra and even Vishnu will be brought crashing down from their exalted positions and we will have our revenge!"

Narada continued: 'True to her word, Maya went to the sage Kashyap. Having no illusions about the likely outcome of her attempting to seduce the great man, she went to him in humble supplication. When asked about the possible reasons that could have brought an attractive maiden like herself to his far from handsome and wrinkled self, Maya was truthful and admitted that she wanted nothing more than the mighty sons their union would produce.

Kashyap was impressed with her honesty and charm. He accepted Maya as his wife and blessed her with three sons—Soorapadman, Simhamukha and Taraka, who he assured her, were born to fulfil the dictates of her lioness heart and make her proud.

Having done his duty by her, Kashyap bade his sons to look after Maya and instructed them to do whatever she asked of them, before leaving his family to take up his meditation again. Maya raised her boys to become fierce warriors and instilled in them a desire to win back their former glory, power and prestige—while also punishing the Gods for supposedly cheating them out of the nectar of immortality.

On her advice, Soorapadman, Simhamukha and Taraka renounced the pleasures of youth in the interest of furthering their cause. Repairing to a secluded spot in the snow-covered heights of the Himalayas, the brothers devoted themselves body, mind and soul towards winning the favour of the Gods. Garbed in next to nothing, they braved the harsh cold that cut like a knife, subsisting solely on fruits, roots and water. Soon the brothers gave up even that, existing solely on the strength of prayer. I did not consider them a threat at the time, for their penances did not seem to be truly effective. When the brothers realized that they had failed to appease the Gods after the passage of a thousand years, Soorapadman decided to sacrifice his physical form as well. He built a huge fire and prepared to jump into it, when Brahma arrived on the scene to stop him.

The three fell at his feet and the Creator declared himself pleased with their penances and offered them a boon. The gift of immortality was asked of Brahma who informed them that it was not something that he could bestow on them as it was beyond his powers. However, he offered a compromise and declared that they would be invincible as all others would have to bow to them—with the exception of the son of Shiva.

Maya had anticipated something like this, and the brothers

were delighted, for it was well known that Shiva had gone nearly demented with grief after the death of Sati. He has immersed himself in his ascetic avatar and seems to have no interest or inclination to re-emerge from his yogic trance. The odds of his having a son anytime in the near future are even less than infinitesimal. Maya's brood in the meantime, after years of enduring extreme privation, have rediscovered their feral appetite for food, drink, sex and power. They are on the rampage and it is only a matter of time before they turn up here with their army of bloodthirsty brutes who have in all probability been raised on fantastic lies about how we raped their ugly mothers when in reality we would have rather coupled with rabid dogs.'

Indra's face was suffused with indignation as he concluded his diatribe and Kama tried to steer him away from the favour he knew would be asked of him, 'What do we know about Soorapadman, Simhamukha and Taraka?'

Indra replied: 'Shiva's son will have his task cut out for him with those three! They are all extraordinarily strong but Taraka is the toughest as he is believed to possess the strength of a thousand war elephants and is faster than the wind. From what I hear, he is an army unto himself. Soora will be relying on him to make piecemeal of whatever resistance we can muster against him.

Simhamukha, in the words of Narada, has the biggest heart among that trio, but given that his entire race is heartless, I am going to assume that his is slightly smaller than a flea's. Even so, we have to hope that Simhamukha can somehow curtail the excesses his brothers are predisposed towards. If we are forced into the ignoble position of conducting negotiations with them—and I am afraid it seems highly probable at this point—we might need Simhamukha to sway his brothers into doing the right thing by us. Too bad he is not the eldest!

Finally, Soora himself is believed to be endowed with every vice that is characteristic of the greatest villains we have encountered thus far. Fearless, arrogant, reckless, bad-tempered, sadistic, ruthless, hot-blooded killer—are some of the many epithets used to describe him. He has united the various Asura clans and they are willing to follow him wherever he goes hoping for a taste of the good life that has been promised to them and a chance to rough up their oppressors. For some reason, Soora holds me responsible for the wrongs done to the Asuras (whatever they may be) and word is that he has sworn to humble my pride, after depriving me of my throne. In that demented mind of his, I am sure he genuinely believes that it is my fault he wet his bed and got spanked by his mother!'

Kama nodded thoughtfully, 'Soora and his brothers sound no better or worse than other enemies faced and crushed by the Devas. They may have been granted a boon of power, thanks to the stupidity of my father, but the fact remains that the nectar of immortality is still in your possession. While you have the Amrita, you are indestructible! So much so, that perhaps you can send them packing by strength of arms!'

'Don't be obtuse, Kama!' said Indra impatiently, 'We have always had Vishnu on our side which is mostly how we managed to prevail over our worst adversaries. This time, he has been neutralized thanks to the boon. As for the Amrita, we can't rely on it every time we are in trouble, for nothing is forever! The nectar serves to delay the inevitable that is all. It is not an inexhaustible resource and we can partake of it only sparingly. Sometimes, I am left with dark suspicions that it is nothing but a placebo conjured up by Vishnu to give us a psychological edge over the Asuras.

Let us say they are not able to kill us, thanks to the Amrita. Even so, they still have the power to defeat us in battle and take us captive, leaving us to rot in a festering dungeon while they burn down our cities, pillage our precious possessions and make off with our women. Many will die but it will be so much worse for the humans. Without us to protect them, they will be lost. Men, children, the old and infirm will be taken into slavery or quickly disposed off, and the women will be captured to be used as the personal playthings of the Asuras. And if that kind of treatment does not finish them off, the subsequent slavery certainly will. Our very existence has been jeopardized.

You are hard on your father as ever, but I talked to him before coming here and he was practically in tears. He loves his work dearly and every little thing he has created is precious to him. Brahma told me that he had no choice but to grant Soorapadman his wish, as otherwise Simhamukha and Taraka would have used their store of ascetic merit bolstered by their brother's sacrifice to annihilate all of creation. Of course, your father could not have allowed that to happen. I think he was hoping that I would repeat it to you and perhaps you could forgive him.

At the time, I was not really concerned about assuaging his guilt, so I simply asked him to give me advice on the best course of action for us to pursue. Fortunately, he held out a modicum of hope—Sati has taken rebirth as Parvati, the daughter of Himavan. Even as a child she seems to have been very fond of Shiva and is his most ardent devotee. She is a grown woman now and ideally suited for him in every way. Almost as if answering my prayers, Parvati has taken up the ascetic way of life to win Shiva's heart and hand in marriage. She is currently employed in taking care of his every need and spends her days at his feet in prayer and service. They say her beauty is remarkable and lights up Shiva's abode—but for all the response she has thus far gotten out of the three-eyed God, she might as well have been the ugliest, most slovenly and irreverent hag that ever lived.

It is my belief that with the tiniest bit of help from the God of Desire whom none can withstand, we can help speed along things. For, otherwise it would be a lamentably long journey towards the conception of the heir in whose hands lies our only chance against those dastardly bastards. Brahma himself decreed that even

Shiva will have to bow before your might so you are the key to resolving this irksome situation. The Devas look to you for the hope of salvation and I am absolutely certain that with you on hand, we will be able to safely steer past this crisis!'

Kama smiled sadly at Indra who genuinely and foolishly believed that he had it all figured out, and explained, 'You are the Lord of Heaven and would be well within your rights to simply order me to go to Shiva and entice him to marry Parvati—which is why I really appreciate you coming over and discussing the issue with me. I will do all in my power to help the Devas survive the difficult times ahead, even if it means taking on the Destroyer. Entertain no doubts on that score...

However, I feel it is only fair to warn you, that your strategy will not work. Please hear me out before you vent your outrage. Fate has ordained that Sati will be reunited with Shiva. Therefore it is a sure thing and it is simply a matter of time before they are wedded. Why not let nature run its course? Shiva is not a regular old male who thinks with his "linga"! He will not be swayed by a pretty face with a body made for sin. We could parade our most sensuous Apsaras in front of him in all their naked glory and he will not turn a hair or even blink. His detachment from earthly affairs and mortal desires is complete, for he needs to exercise such control in order to preserve balance in the world which draws sustenance from his divine essence.

Parvati is famed for her exquisite looks and virtuous nature—you said as much yourself. Yet it behoves her to earn her rightful place by the side of Shiva, as a Goddess like Sati herself did before her. It will take time and effort on her part but I have no doubt that she will succeed, for she is an incarnation of the Mother Goddess Gauri, with her aspirations tied to a great cause and she will never let us down. You would do well to place your trust in her hands, not mine. For me to attempt to hasten the process of their love story will be tantamount to throwing a spanner into the works by disrupting the progression of events that have already been foreordained. Forcing Shiva's hand is never a good idea and will be entirely counter-productive—for the happy ending that you so desire will suffer a setback that will only cause further delay to your carefully laid plans.

The Devas as the possessors of the nectar of Amrita have been in power for too long. The wheel of fortune is turning and it is time for the Asuras to ascend for better or worse. I do not deny that terrible times are ahead for all of us, for they will certainly make us pay dearly for the wrongs they believe have been done to them. We have no choice but to weather this storm as best as we can, till the prophesy is fulfilled and Shiva's son rises to deliver us!'

To Kama's dismay, Indra's face had grown redder and redder during his speech, but he continued speaking till he had said all he possibly could to dissuade Indra from his monumental folly. His words did not have the desired impact and he could almost feel the anger uncoiling from the pit of Indra's stomach, as the latter burst out: 'Let me get this straight… You are suggesting that we sit back and do nothing while the demon hordes swoop down on us and devour us? Or should we cower in hiding like despicable cowards while they burn down Amaravathi, steal our stuff and gang rape our wives? Perhaps I should listen to your wise council…maybe send emissaries to welcome them here, then get down on my knees and pry open my butt cheeks to allow them easier access? Is that what you had in mind? For shame!'

Kama shook his head tiredly, 'You know very well that is not what I had in mind so I will not bother with a clarification, your Majesty!' Indra winced at that respectful form of address which had deliberately been stripped off that sentiment but Kama continued, 'I thought we were friends and as a friend, I have always given you my honest council. If you want an ingratiating sycophant who fawns over you, shaking his head in agreement every time you open your mouth, while loudly proclaiming that the sun shines out of your arse, then you should have visited one of your toadies and left me alone.

It is not my intention to pick a fight with you, given that you are under duress at present. In fact, I officially accede to your request and will certainly take on the Destroyer for that has also been preordained, but it is my duty to warn you that your strategy will not have the desired outcome. Be prepared for the worst, my Lord!'

Somewhat mollified, Indra replied: 'I have no wish to fight with you either and I depend on your honest council. Ordinarily it would make sense to stay out of Shiva's affairs but unfortunately, time is growing scarce even as we speak. Soorapadman will be gathering his forces and he will come at us hard and fast. My war council has been summoned and we will do everything in our power to fight them off or at least delay the inevitable, but our efforts will be futile for we cannot muster sufficient forces to take them on in a head-to-head battle. We have no choice but to spread out our defenses and slow them down, till Shiva's son rises and takes command of our armies. Shiva and Parvati will bless him with weapons and fresh troops and these will fill out our depleted ranks. Unless you do something about it, these events are too far off in the future, and perhaps by the time our champion emerges there will be nothing left for him to fight for.

I do not expect you to leave immediately for Kailasha, but it is my command that you do so at the earliest! Make arrangements for the safety of your family for you may have to join me in hiding till Shiva's son is mature enough to command our forces. Hopefully, the worst will be over soon. With your help, I am confident we can defeat Soora and send him howling to his vengeful mother at the earliest! Then this nightmare will be finished, we can give thanks, go back to rebuilding our lives and move on.'

Kama bowed his head in acceptance, 'It will be as you wish. Thank you for the confidence you have shown in me. And believe me when I say that the Devas will survive this calamity and emerge stronger than ever before.'

Indra left Kama then to make preparations for the war ahead, wildly hoping that perhaps the brothers would fight amongst themselves and kill each other. But it was wishful thinking. Soora marched out with his army and proved beyond a shadow of a doubt that he was going to conquer the known worlds and there was precious little anybody could do about it.

Soora named himself the supreme commander and his brothers were proclaimed as his generals. Together, they decided to take down the Lokapalas and subdue Vishnu and Brahma—thereby stripping Indra of his external defenses—before capturing Amaravathi and humbling his pride. The Lokapalas fortified their fortresses and put up a spirited defence against Soorapadman but it did them no good for his advance could not be halted. Kubera's exquisite city of Alagapuri was the first to fall. The Asura army was simply too numerous and vicious for him to defeat in battle so he was forced to throw open the gates and surrender to them in the hope of appeasing them and saving his subjects. He acceded to their demands for complete access to his enormous wealth with a bleeding heart, but even that was not sufficient to stop them from razing his city to the ground or putting his people to the sword. Kubera wept as Alagapuri burned, and he promised Soorapadman that he would get the comeuppance he deserved for being a heartless bastard. Naturally his comments saw him clapped in chains and dragged away to Soorapadman's dungeons.

The remaining Lokapalas were heartbroken when they heard about Kubera and they were determined to stop Soorapadman and rescue their fellow celestial. Agni fought with fire and Vayu with gale storms and fierce winds that could take a man's head off; Varuna rose from the seas and conjured up tidal waves to swallow up the demons and suffocate them in its embrace; Yama sent his dreaded danda into their midst and rode into the Asura ranks spreading death everywhere. Surya and Soma supplemented their efforts wherever they could, but it was all in vain, for the Asuras were protected by not just Brahma's boon but the misdirected rage of Shiva as well, which just as Maya had predicted, proved impossible for the Devas to fight against. The Lokapalas were rounded up and captured, their homes smashed to bits and their subjects taken into slavery.

Vishwakarma, the architect of the Devas, was commandeered by Soora to build him a beautiful city which was to be named Mahendrapuri. Simhamukha was asked to govern the kingdom and take care of the day-to-day running of Soora's empire, while Taraka was assigned the task of capturing the remaining worlds and bringing them under Soora's yoke. At the head of his vast host, he headed out to subdue all resistance to their rule.

With a chariot driven by a thousand horses, Taraka rode to Vaikunta. Vishnu was waiting for him mounted on Garuda. A bloody battle ensued and Vishnu was effective in keeping the Asuras at bay but he knew that he could not hold out for long as the Destroyer's essence had been distilled within the Asura brothers and hovered protectively over them. Having depleted all his weapons on Taraka, Vishnu flung his infallible Sudharshana chakra at him but instead of beheading him cleanly, it reposed against his neck like an ornament.

It was the last thing the ferocious Taraka himself had expected and despite himself, he was flabbergasted. The enormity of what he had just achieved struck him almost as if he had been dealt a bodily blow. Then, something even more unexpected took place—Vishnu burst out laughing! Taraka could only stare at him in astonishment, while his army also fell silent trying to work out if their general had gained the upper hand or no. Controlling his irrepressible mirth, Vishnu finally addressed Taraka, 'I can't pretend that has happened before, but it was almost worth it to see the look on your face! It has to be admitted that your courage is inspiring for even as you saw death hurtle towards you, you did not flinch and chose to meet it headlong, completely unafraid to die for your brother and the cause you undertook with him. That is truly impressive. Now the Three Worlds will know that contrary to reports, you are far more than a ravening monster with a taste for blood.

The chakra was given to me as a gift by Shiva in a bygone age, and it recognizes his tincture within you even if I myself chose not to acknowledge it to my detriment. It is the reason you are standing alive in my presence and we are having this conversation. My apologies for rising up in arms when his aura protects you!

Do take good care of my chakra, Taraka, in the brief time you will be allowed to hold on to it. Try not to allow your animalistic passions to get out of hand, for my chakra has assisted me too often in protecting the innocent, and will continue to do so even when wielded by someone like you. I am sure you noticed that it has a mind of its own even though it is bound to me, so it would be judicious on your part to tread with caution—for it would never do for your admirable height to be suddenly truncated, would it?

Now that we have gotten the unpleasantness out of the way and successfully avoided further bloodshed, perhaps you will accompany me into Vaikunta as an honoured guest? My wife would love to meet you I am sure, although she was cowering in fright behind Shesha moments ago. But do not take that to heart, for it is only because Tarakasura cuts a fearsome figure, one the Goddess cannot abide. But now that this is over, we can reassure her that you are not the villain we all imagined you to be—one who would use his great strength to trample upon the lives of those who are not similarly blessed.'

At the conclusion of this speech, Taraka raised his hand to touch the whirling chakra at his neck, but, changing his mind, he strode purposefully towards Vishnu instead. Garuda bristled and shrieked a warning at him. The terrifying rakshasa ignored him and approached Vishnu. Then, a miraculous thing happened. Taraka slowly knelt down before Vishnu, touching his forehead to his feet. Then he got on his knees and folded his palms together, 'I could die happy at this moment, for you said yourself that my courage is inspirational. It would be a rare privilege to accept your invitation to visit your abode as a guest and to meet the Goddess of Prosperity, but I must respectfully decline, for at this point, even a slightly higher life form than a ravening monster such as myself must admit that I am simply not worthy of the honour.

Soora is my brother and the God I worship above all else and will continue to do so while there is life left to me. Implicit obedience is my gift to him, which is why I will do whatever he commands me to for better or worse, and if that makes me a despicable villain, then so be it. But for the kindness you have shown me today and your magnanimity in granting me this victory, I will repay you by protecting those weaker than I to the best of my ability. It will be the first step taken by me towards increasing my worth so that someday I will be able to accept your invitation without Goddess Lakshmi shrinking back in loathing or wishing me dead.'

After receiving Vishnu's blessings, Taraka continued on his conquest. His followers had at first been flummoxed by his behaviour but recovered quickly on discovering that he had not lost his warlike tendencies. True to his word, however, he instilled discipline among his hordes and prevented them from committing the dreaded atrocities of war, even though they were triumphant in every battle they fought. Thanks to his efforts, the entire universe came under the authority of his brother. It was his fervent hope that the vanquished would not tell their children stories about the violent excesses of the formidable Tarakasura, for he knew from sad experience that this would plant the seeds of vengeance in their young minds. Soon, they would develop a hankering for revenge which would suck them into a bottomless void of senseless bloodletting, never letting them know a moment's peace—for the sounds of the dying would rob them of it forever.

When Kama heard about Taraka's encounter with Vishnu, he knew that he could tarry no longer. He had already told Rati and Priti about Indra's command. Vasanta had been entrusted with the task of keeping them safe when Amaravathi came under Soorapadman's sway. All was in readiness for him to make his departure. Kama would have liked to feel calm acceptance, for he knew that was what Vishnu would have wanted of him, but he felt only a curious buoyancy of the spirit which made him want to laugh a little. He had to assure himself that it was not the symptoms of hysteria he was feeling as he went to say his goodbyes.

Remembering what the Goddess Gauri had said about fond farewells, Kama was tempted to pick up his bow and arrows and simply walk out. But he settled on a compromise and decided to wish only Rati, Priti and Vasanta before leaving, if only to prevent Rati from chasing him across the nether regions with the lotus stalks she used to hit him with when she was displeased with his behaviour.

The mental image made him smile but it vanished when he saw the three people he loved best waiting for him, having reached a decision he inevitably was going to hate. Rati acting as their spokesperson was the first to speak up, 'Our minds are made up and it will do you no good to argue. Vasanta and I will accompany you on this perilous mission Indra has slapped you with. We were created with the intention of serving as your apprentices and it makes absolutely no sense for you to go alone. Shiva is not some rigid rishi wrestling with his repressed sexuality in the pursuit of ascetic achievement; you will have need of us, if you hope to succeed in breaking his concentration. Too much is at stake here for you to be so annoyingly magnanimous and sacrificing.

Don't bother pointing out the issue of Priti's safety. She was a princess before she married you and more than up to the task of taking care of the little world we have created, in our absence. With the help of the Apsaras, she will make sure that there is plenty of entertainment for the Asuras, and—in gratitude for the avenues of pleasure she opens up for them who had formerly been trapped within their unimaginative sex lives—they are likely to sacrifice their own lives to keep this place safe.

If you still feel inclined to argue, we will be pleased to knock some sense into your head. And we will be inclined to substitute broomsticks for lotus stalks!'

Kama felt the desire to laugh build again but he swallowed the giggles that rose unbidden in his throat before kissing Priti gently on the forehead and making her promise that she would stay safe. Then he spanked Rati gently on the bottom for defying him and punched Vasanta in the arm to show his displeasure for going along with his headstrong wife, since he could not find the words to thank them for tagging along with him. He knew that they were doing this so that he would not be alone as he headed out on what was possibly his final journey

Spurred on by the need of the Devas as they had been completely overrun by the Asuras, Kama and his companions made haste towards Kailasha. As they traversed the heights of the Himalayas, the maras gathered en masse around Kama to lend him all the support they could in the impossible quest he had taken on. Sensing death on all sides, Rati shuddered and cursed them, feeling sure that their presence was not auspicious, 'I still can't understand the need for these creatures. Why do these harbingers of death always remain so close to you? I find it most vexing.'

Vasanta answered first, 'The maras are more effective than me for one thing. My job amounts simply to creating the right atmosphere for Kama to work his magic. But the maras are a far more pervasive presence. They annihilate all thoughts, save desire, and somehow imbue that feeling with an urgency that is simply impossible to suppress.'

Kama nodded in agreement, 'Vishnu would have told you that they are by my side to preserve the all important balance in the cosmos, using his typically obscure terminology and not to mention, his ridiculously complicated ideologies. To answer your question as succinctly as possible, life and death have to exist side by side, because for one to gain the upper hand spells the end of all creation. This is why every time a baby is conceived and delivered, a part of the mother dies. A father cannot be called upon to make this sacrifice and find the generosity of spirit to nourish and nurture the child to whom he loses a part of himself, which is why women hold the key to creation. It is also why a woman deserves to be revered and cherished in return for the great service she performs and the tremendous sacrifice she makes.'

While his companions lapsed into silence, thoughts on sacrifice and service circulated aimlessly in Kama's mind as he trudged towards his destination. He came to the irrefutable conclusion that the task Indra had assigned him was moronic in the extreme and doomed from the beginning. It did not make him feel heroic in the least but merely gave him an unwanted insight into the helplessness experienced by a sacrificial goat. Kama had no taste for glory and he did not want the poets to compose lengthy encomiums on his valour. At that moment he wanted nothing more than to be the divine pimp who played with his bow and arrow to various effects, cohabited with his two wives, messed around with the Apsaras and got drunk with Indra and Vasanta listening to bawdy tales of tawdry amour, without ever giving a damn about the greater good.

Trying to get rid of his dejection, he forced himself to think of something else. His thoughts delved deeper into his psyche seeking a perspective that he could stomach and see him through to the fag end. He wondered what Purnakala must have felt when she was transformed into a rock by Harita and then locked into it by Vishnu when he declared that her sacrifice would benefit mankind. Had she been the cynical sort, she would probably have been infuriated with Vishnu for decreeing that *she* be forced to remain a stupid stone just so that folks could find a cure for their disabilities and enjoy their extra-marital dalliances without difficulty, while Kama was given his freedom. If she were inclined to view the unhappy incident from a different angle, she might have derived a certain macabre sense of satisfaction from the fact that spending an eternity in a composite of hard minerals could hardly be worse than life itself which had proved to be such a bitch. Perhaps she had taken an emotional view and cussed at men in general, and Kama in particular. It was equally likely that she had no time to even think, for the curse had taken effect immediately and once her transformation was complete, further thought would have been impossible—since to the best of Kama's knowledge, aggregate masses of solid were incapable of rational thought.

The possibilities were infinite in number and his mind dwelt obsessively on them—drifting, sifting and discarding the fragments and doing it over and over in an exercise in futility. While pleasantly engaged thus, an image of a dog chasing its tail popped up rudely, disrupting his chain of thought. Scrambling to banish the intrusive presence and bring Purnakala back into focus, he remembered the dignity in her mien when she looked at him one last time before she was lost to him, and he rediscovered himself and felt calmer.

Looking ahead he saw that his journey was almost at an end and he was thankful that it would not be long now. Kama was awed by the wild beauty of Shiva's abode and he decided that even Amaravathi with all its charms paled in comparison to the natural finery and spiritual tranquillity of the home of the Destroyer.

Shiva was fully submerged in a state of Samadhi and he was lost to the world. Kama, Rati and Vasanta watched him from a distance and approached his presence stealthily—though Kama doubted that Shiva would have been affected even if they had charged him on war elephants with drums to signal their appearance. As they drew closer, Kama saw Parvati kneeling at his feet, almost as lost to the world as he was, the only difference being that she seemed content to submerge herself in his presence, and simply be by his side. The beauty of the princess who had traded a kingdom, an abundance of suitors and every comfort imaginable without hesitation, simply for the privilege of being Shiva's maid, took Kama's breath away. It was a lovely tableau and a wonderful sculpture in progress. Parvati's great love seemed to wrap Shiva protectively, as though to keep him safe from baleful influences and mischief mongers such as himself.

Kama looked at Vasanta in despair, for he simply saw no way for them to penetrate the complete absorption of Shiva. Rati caught the glance and, responding to his need, placed her small hand in his, holding it with childlike trust. That small gesture gave him the epiphany he had prayed for and he finally had his answers. Signaling to Rati and Vasanta to step back, Kama prepared himself. He notched his arrow and tensed in concentration but did not let the arrow fly.

Instead he closed his eye and dwelt on love and loss. He remembered the terrible grief he had felt when Purnakala was taken away from him. But even that paled into insignificance when he thought of his impending separation from Rati. A terrible sense of loss flooded his senses, and not knowing when or if they would ever be together again, his heart broke into a million pieces. At that moment Kama knew with dread certainty that even his impending death would be far less excruciating.

As his mind unravelled with grief that almost bordered on madness, Kama forced himself to dwell on his sorrow, till that welcome moment when Shiva recognized a kindred spirit in the vicinity and opened his mind to him in an outpouring of sympathy and empathy. Their spirits were conjoined in their combined misery and Kama felt Shiva's deep-rooted loss as if it were his own. Precious memories of a happier time with the gentle Goddess who had loved him so, the apprehension he had snuffed out when he had allowed Sati to attend her father's yagna, and the all-encompassing guilt he felt over her subsequent fate, were all revealed in their nakedness to Kama—so much so that he almost recoiled as the white hot anguish scotched him with its throbbing intensity.

Aching for Shiva even more than he did for himself, Kama insinuated himself further into the core of the Destroyer, desperate to help him and bring him out of that pall of suffering. Ever so gently, he held out the tender promise of hope, sensing that the Destroyer's loneliness was profound. Kama now proceeded to flood Shiva's mind with the images of a reality that he had not embraced yet—whispering to him of the long-lost Sati who had come back to him in another form. With delicate strokes, the story of Parvati of the fawn eyes and the kind heart was painted. Kama missed out nothing—the yearning she had felt for Shiva since her youngest days, the hardships she had endured for his sake, the dedication of her young life towards caring for him—all were laid bare before the mind's eye of the three-eyed God.

Miraculously, the sparks of hope Kama had ignited using the Destroyer's flinty yearning caught fire and filled him with an alien happiness. Eager to see the miracle for himself, Shiva brushed away the trappings of his ascetic fervour and opened his eyes in sudden heady anticipation to see Parvati on her knees before him, head bowed in silent prayer. As he gazed at her with naked longing, Parvati felt it in the manner of an intimate touch, and she blushed red, although she refused coyly to raise her eyes to meet his. Something within Shiva stirred slowly to life and at that moment, Kama fired five arrows into his exposed heart in quick succession.

For one glorious moment, all was well with the world, for Shiva believed that he had got his Sati back. Parvati dared to meet his gaze then and the spell was shattered for it was a stranger's eyes Shiva saw. He realized with a dreadful pang of fresh anguish that he had been cheated and the Sati he loved was never coming back. Fate was merely offering him a replacement and he rejected her outright. It was like losing his Sati all over again and Shiva tottered on the brink of madness as the devastating grief threatened to tear him into pieces. His fierce survival instincts kicked in as primordial rage coursed through him, drowning out all other emotions in the rush, searching for the interloper who had dared trespass on the innermost reaches of his mind with voyeuristic abandon before freely tampering with his heart.

Shiva's eyes locked into Kama's for a split second. The magnitude of his wrath should have reduced Kama to a limp mass of terror—for there was death writ large in those eyes—but Kama stood erect and refused to flinch. In the eyes of his victim, Shiva saw nothing but understanding and pity. It was more than he could stand and the tenuous restraints holding his rage in check snapped. He opened his dreaded third eye and the offending individual who had dared feel sorry for the mighty Destroyer was reduced to ash.

Rati's Lament

*R*ati had been suffering from an acute case of the shivers from the moment Indra had turned up in their home with dire tidings. Owing to her closeness with Kama, and the uncanny intuition that is so peculiar to the female of the species she had always been troubled by the presence of death that seemed to hover over him. Mostly Rati would tell herself that she was acting exactly like a mortal female whose hormones had gone berserk and laugh off the incessant fear but on bad days, she would fret about it endlessly, wondering if there was not something she could do to keep her husband safe and by her side always. These clammy apprehensions that were the only cloud in an otherwise perfect existence, Rati discussed with no one—not even Kama. She voiced aloud her darkest suspicions only once, and to her surprise, it was to Goddess Saraswati with whom she shared an uneasy relationship at best.

Brahma's consort had wanted to see the wonders of their palace of crystal and white marble that had become the highest authority on love, desire and pleasure. Kama had been most welcoming and given her a personal tour. Initially, on seeing the legendary beauty of her husband's stepmother, Rati had felt the slightest twinge of hostility—which was why she tried to make up for it by being thoroughly charming and warm to her. Conducting a quick comparison in the many, many mirrors that she had had erected all over their house so that she may better feast on the beauty of Kama and herself, she quickly gauged that despite her ethereal beauty, the freshness of youth was lacking in her husband's stepmother—and Rati was ridiculously pleased. At that moment when self-doubt had been sufficiently dispelled, she decided that Saraswati was not bad at all and it made perfect sense that Kama got along so well with her.

Sensing the thaw in the other woman's animosity, Saraswati had become pleasantly chatty. She told Rati about how Vasanta had come into Kama's life and her own role in the story. Playfully, Rati had declared that she now knew who to blame for her biggest competitor over Kama's affections, adding that the God of Spring followed him everywhere, like death. The two women had stopped laughing then, for Rati's careless utterance carried with it the weight of her terror and left her too choked up to go on.

Saraswati had taken the woman destined for widowhood in her arms then and told her about the maras. The Goddess told her Brahma's words about the purpose they were intended to serve in Kama's life and assured her that they would never harm him. She told her about the first time she had seen them scattered around the God of Desire and the chill that had penetrated her being at that moment. Saraswati told Rati that the maras could have that effect and she should simply ignore them. The conversation had eased some of the anxiety that Rati bore—though not entirely. She sensed that though Saraswati had not intended to deceive, portions of the truth were nevertheless being kept from her. Even so she fretted less, and the unease she felt on account of Kama faded—until the time of Indra's visit when her trepidation returned in full measure.

Rati had insisted on accompanying Kama for she could not bear to lose sight of his dear face. When death brushed close to him, en route to Shiva's lonely abode, she felt the chill that had settled in his heart and grew cold herself. She cursed Indra for dragging Kama into his affairs, Kama for not refusing Indra point blank and herself for not dissuading him from his foolhardiness. Soorapadman, his vengeful mother and brothers, sage Kashyap, Brahma and even Shiva did not escape her baleful thoughts. It may have been a little selfish of her, but she saw no reason why Kama should be risking life and limb just because the Devas and Brahma between themselves had fouled up on such a gargantuan scale. Shiva was also to blame for their predicament, she decided. For if it were not for his ceaseless and self-indulgent grieving, he would have married Parvati and sired a dozen sons who would have easily taken care of Maya's brats.

Worried that her despondency might affect Kama, Rati tried to control her wayward thoughts. She brightened when they reached their destination and saw Parvati. Rati could always tell when her husband found another woman beautiful and this was one of those times. His confidence was momentarily boosted and Rati felt good about their chances, for she was sure that Shiva would not be able to stay immune to such a flawless beauty blessed with a spiritual resplendence comparable to his own.

Lulled into a false sense of hope, Rati waited with a confidence that would not waver even when she sensed Kama's despair. Taking his sensitive hands into her own, she willed him to succeed for all their sakes. She had been feeling sanguine about her efforts when Kama beat back his despair and ordered them to stand back, determination writ large on his exquisite features.

Rati had begun to smell victory for her own Lord when Shiva opened his eyes and looked at Parvati with desire, an emotion she was far too familiar with to mistake. Rati had been about to run to Kama and wrap him in a congratulatory hug—when he simply vanished from her sight. For long moments Rati did not comprehend what had happened as she stood there staring into the space that had once been her husband. In a dazed stupor, her mind began to reel furiously, painfully—as she realized that that husband was no more—and she collapsed in a heap, praying that the black abyss into which she had fallen would swallow her up and never spit her out into a world without Kama.

Struggling unsuccessfully against the current that simply refused to let her be swept away, Rati found her consciousness returning. Vasanta had been holding her head in his lap and she recoiled from him in fury for having dared to touch the body that belonged solely to Kama. Turning to the pile of ashes that was all that was left of her husband, Rati began sifting through it purposefully, determined to recover at least a small fragment of that which she had lost. The tears that spilled out of her eyes blinded her completely, but still she persisted in her hopeless pursuit, wiping the phlegm running down her nose with ash-streaked arms and stifling the sobs that ceaselessly escaped from her throat.

Watching her futile search, Vasanta wept for her and the friend he had lost. On and on she searched through the ashes, still fighting the sobbing fits as though determined to keep them at bay. Vasanta wished she would leave the ashes alone and simply cry, for if she stubbornly refused to allow the tidal wave of misery inside her an outlet, it would implode within her and she would die too. 'It is stupid of me to cry,' she told the little mounds of ash surrounding her, finally desisting from her search as the persistent tears kept getting the better of her, 'I know that if there is one thing you simply cannot bear, it is the sound of crying. The sight of me dissolving in a salty flood of tears and blubbering like a baby is likely to be distasteful to you. Initially, I thought you found it to be a turn off since crying makes even the loveliest ladies look hideous, but I should have known better. You simply could not stand for me to be unhappy and liked nothing better than the sight of my smile.

Ever since I realized that, I promised myself that there will be no more tears in our marriage and devoted all the effort possible towards making it happen. It was not an easy thing to pull off, for jealous fits would get me into a snit and the temptation to cry was strong, but I desisted for your sake. I continue to do so, Kama, for wherever you are, it is my wish that you will have no cause to grieve on my account.

The jealous Gods have taken you away from me, but they will not keep us apart for too long, I will never allow it. It is a promise sweetheart... I know that it may seem impossible to you right now, but somehow, I know in my heart that we will be together again. And until that time, I will stay here with you in this very spot where the Destroyer saw fit to claim the life of the best among the Gods!'

Vasanta wept fresh tears when he saw her addressing the ashes thus, hugging them to her bosom and trying to somehow merge with the remnants of Kama. Turning to the weeping God of Spring, Rati spoke with the patient indulgence of a mother who was not too pleased with the behaviour of her offspring but was willing to overlook it, 'It is time for you to leave me, Vasanta. And do try not to cry so, for Kama believed in spreading happiness wherever he went. Your misery over the loss of a beloved friend would act like a toxic cloud that will afflict everyone who happens to be in the vicinity. For the sake of him, whom we both love, exercise a little restraint. Go back to Priti and tell her that there is no need for her to weep either. Kama is not dead. He simply cannot be dead for Brahma has blessed him with formidable powers that cannot be taken away by anyone, not even Shiva! And while his powers endure, so must he.

Moreover, you will not have cause to grieve for too long, for I am going to bring Kama back. I am fully aware by the way you are looking at me right now, that you truly believe that I am a demented woman in the final stages of hysteria but you can spare me the disbelief and pity for they are wasted. I will not fail. My mind is made up; I will do whatever it takes to bring him back. It was wrong of Shiva to take his life, and I will not budge from this spot till the Destroyer is made to account for his mistake.'

Turning away from Vasanta as though she had already forgotten about him, Rati arranged her limbs in the padmasana position, right there among the ashes, and she began her personal odyssey to track down Shiva, force a confrontation with him and bring Kama back. The God of Spring left her there like that. He did not know what to make of her decision but he was confident that if there was the remotest chance of bringing Kama back to the land of the living, Rati would find it.

Rati sat transfixed in the spot where Kama had breathed his last. Devoting every ounce of her body, mind and soul towards achieving the impossible, she directed her comingled grief and rage towards the Destroyer. Refusing to be a supplicant who would urge him to come to her aid by dint of prayer and devotion, she summoned him to her presence demanding that he make amends for the terrible injustice he had done.

In the sanctum of her mind, she would chain the Destroyer to her will, using ropes of rage. There she would hold him captive within the walls of her subconscious. Then she would rave, rant, and rail at him to her heart's content. Her fury in itself would be the equivalent of a billion lashings and she would scourge him with her terrible thoughts, till the point that she gave him as much pain and suffering as he had given her. In the end she would bleed and plead with him, finding solace in their combined suffering.

Rati asked Shiva the umpteen questions for which she herself could find no satisfactory explanation. She would probe him relentlessly for answers with the questions that never stopped. 'How could YOU do this to me?' she raged at him, 'You lost the love of your life. You know exactly how it feels… How could you inflict this fate on someone else? You who are the mightiest, noblest and most compassionate of the Gods? Is this your idea of mercy? I would not wish this on my worst enemy. Even the most loathsome of creatures, should not be made to suffer like this! Why did you do this to me who has harmed no one?

How could you do this to Kama? He is the best among the celestials and was Brahma's greatest gift to the Gods and mankind. Did you hold him in contempt, believing him to be nothing more than the wielder of a toy bow who went around messing with people's minds or merely getting their sexuality revved up? Then you are no different from some of the pettier Gods who used to make fun of him, dismissing him as a pretty boy who was no man, for he was not a warrior. They were all bloody fools for Kama was stronger than all of them put together. He was built like a bull and was tremendously strong. When we trained together in the martial arts there were none who could overpower him. Why, even Yama with his fearsome danda, who can loosen the bowels of the Gods and men alike merely by showing up on his black buffalo, had to give ground to Kama. For even death cannot hope to prevail over true love. He had a gift with weapons of all kinds but he abstained from using this particular skill, for it gave him no satisfaction to destroy things—unlike the rest of the so-called alpha males who cannot seem to get by without tearing down walls, pulling entire cities to the ground, despoiling priceless works of art, carelessly snuffing out the lives of the innocent and indulging in senseless rapine—just so they can prove that their pricks are not vestigial organs.

It would have been easy for my husband to show off his machismo to these fools who believed that being a man meant nothing more than bulging biceps, a marked tendency for brutality, pissing contests and having an insurmountable ego, but he never bothered. He chose to refrain from hurting others no matter what the cause or provocation. It was his personal choice not to get into stupid fistfights or testosterone-fuelled brawls just so the poets could write about him and further add to the stereotypes of inordinate male pride. He was man enough to be gentle, considerate and thoughtful, yet strong enough to protect his own. How many men do you know who can claim the same?

Kama was so selfless, he put the needs of his fellow celestials ahead of his own when he accepted Indra's dangerous assignation. Did you know that he had been reluctant to use his powers on you? He told Indra that no good would ever come of his meddling. I believe that he sensed death coming for him, since Yama is no stranger to him, but he refused to fear for his own safety. The Gods needed his help for Soora and his brothers with their demon hordes have overrun all of creation and are ruling with an iron fist. Only a son born to you can deliver the Devas from this evil—but by selfishly refusing to shed your seed, you are prolonging the misery of all those besieged souls. Kama was not like that! He made the ultimate sacrifice and threw away his life.

There is no precedent in all of history for injustice of this magnitude. It is your fault that he is dead so it is up to you to bring him back. Lord Shiva! Can't you hear me? Why are you not making recompense for your hastiness and cruelty? What are you waiting for?

I cannot believe that you repaid the great favour he did you, by killing him. If not for him, you would have spent the rest of eternity bewailing the death of Sati who is lost to you. Instead of a barren future filled with nothing but emptiness he has blessed you with a brand new beginning with a loving consort by your side. Together, you can find the happiness and peace that has eluded you. Instead of tears, anger, asceticism and an empty bed you will have laughter, pleasure and wonderful children with Parvati. He has given you the gift of love which a lot of people will kill for or spend all of their existence searching futilely for that which only a lucky few will ever find and even fewer live long enough to enjoy. Instead of falling at his feet in gratitude you killed him, thinking yourself above him and his proffered gift, beneath you. It was a horrible thing to do and I need you to admit that you behaved despicably!'

Exhausted from her fiery attacks on the Destroyer, Rati would struggle with bouts of depression. Tantalizingly, she could sense Kama's presence around her and in an agony of anticipation she would reach out into the nothingness, feeling for him, her fingers always closing around the empty air. Then her heart would break again and she would contemplate ending her own life. Gradually Rati came to realize that her late husband's spirit was strong only in certain things—the mango blossoms that had been his favorites, in honey and wine, the silvery moonlight which was beloved by lovers everywhere, the heady scent of roses, in the song of birds and the black bees which had composed his bowstring, and in the season of spring which was most redolent of his presence.

With a pang of horror, it dawned on her that Shiva had diluted the powers of her Lord and spread them among his own preferred tools, cleverly averting the catastrophic consequences that had followed when Harita had cursed Kama with leprosy and deprived him of his essence. Shiva had found a means to channelize the fabled powers of her Lord—without which the worlds would cease to function—into suitable conduits, so that life could go on even though Kama himself was no more.

Utterly desolate, Rati contemplated the implications of Shiva's trickery. Fighting off her melancholy which was a constant menace, she rounded on the Destroyer in an apoplectic fit, 'You are responsible for this diabolical diaspora of my husband's person and powers! It was most clever of you, but it will not work, simply because power of any kind is only as strong as its wielder. This dispersion which you have engineered will not be effective in the least. For Kama can be replaced by nobody and all the worlds with their creatures need him! Thinking that a lousy mango or a bloody rose is substitute enough for the God of Desire is the same as reposing faith in a corpse to do the Destroyer's work!'

When not composing such diatribes of bitter anger in her head, she would adopt a more conciliatory tone, 'Please don't get angry with me or think that I hate you and want to summon you to my presence only to pound better sense into your head. I am sure you understand what it is about bereavement that makes us all do crazy things. Kama's favourite was Vishnu but since the Protector is your greatest devotee, he has always loved and respected you too.

Unlike my husband, my faith is not implicit for I have too many questions for the Gods and no answers have been forthcoming. It has been my choice to treat the Gods with the fondness and affection one usually reserves for friends, because in my opinion, and I am sure you will agree, that is far superior to blind devotion, ignorant reverence or superstitious dread. There was never any disrespect on my part, not even when divine will decreed that Purnakala remain a rock for the rest of time and I was tempted to yell myself hoarse at Vishnu for allowing this travesty of justice to take place. Despite your faults and my deep-rooted disapproval of you for having killed Kama, I do love and respect you but I will love and respect you even more if you come to me, apologize for your crime and bring him back to me.

I am beseeching you to do the right thing by everyone—marry Parvati, have valiant sons with her and restore Kama to life. This heart-rending story, which has stretched on far too long anyway, will have a happy ending and we can all quit mourning and griping.'

On and on Rati alternately cursed and coaxed the Destroyer, relentless in her quest to get justice for Kama and herself. Parvati was similarly engaged, although conversely she did not hate Shiva but loved him to pieces. On the fateful day when Kama had fallen victim to her lover's third eye, she had also felt incinerated. Shiva had looked at her with love but that had changed to disappointment when he realized that she was not Sati. Unable to handle the rejection as well as the violence in him—which had vented itself with such tragic consequences on the gentle God of Desire who had only tried to bring them together—she had fled, but with a resolve that was stronger than ever. She promised herself that she would cure the blindness that beset her chosen Lord, which was preventing him from accepting her, to his and everybody else's detriment.

Parvati knew that Shiva needed her as badly as she needed him, and spurred on by her conviction she poured all her efforts into drawing the Destroyer to her side so that she could rescue him from the nightmare in which he had trapped himself. In her eyes, he was not just the best of the Gods, the mightiest in the pantheon, the terrifying Destroyer or the highest echelon of manhood, but a lovable and extremely sensitive soul who by rights belonged in her arms where she could kiss away the pain. Retreating into a yogic trance that transcended his own, Parvati begged him to accept her love and take her as his wife so that she could cure him of the malaise of spirit that was destroying him.

Shiva was thus buffeted on all sides by the tempestuous emotions of two spirited women who needed two very different things from him. They broke into his forced tranquillity with their incessant demands on his attention. He found his defences being stripped away by their combined onslaught and found himself actually welcoming it, for they were both a blessed relief from his self-imposed exile of loneliness. Parvati's love soothed him, nourished him and repaired his injured spirit. Rati was like a recalcitrant daughter whom he had grown to love all the more for having wronged her. The tantrums she was throwing and the emotional berating she was giving him brought out the doting father in him and he went to her first, keen to make up with her.

Rati had begun to believe that she was destined to spend an eternity in pursuit of Shiva, who would never allow himself to be pinned down in reality, not even for a moment. This was why she was caught completely unawares when the unfamiliar sound of a chortle interrupted a particularly vivid mental session in which she was envisioning herself shaking the Destroyer by the shoulder, forcing him to acknowledge that she was right about everything and he had erred most grievously. Prying open her eyelids, which had been glued shut by a mixture of ash and tears, she found herself looking up at the three-eyed God with whom she had so desperately sought an audience.

For the longest time, Rati had enacted dozens of scenarios of their encounter and she had been cool, composed, righteously indignant and dripping with attitude in all of them. But when she found herself dwarfed by the formidable form of Shiva looming over her, she was paralyzed by stupefaction and forgot every one of the clever quips she had prepared especially for the great showdown.

Shiva held his silence and looked at her for long moments without a hint of the amusement he had evinced earlier. Finally, Rati got enough of a handle on her emotions to address him, albeit in a tone that was thick with confusion, 'I was wavering over which would be more satisfying: to hit you really hard, or to fall at your feet and beg for mercy. The decision is out of my hands. However, as my performance of intensive tapas in the lotus position has ensured that my limbs are locked in place, and I can do neither.'

Rati began crying despite her promise that she would not debase herself by bawling her eyes out in front of Shiva, 'It is impossible for me to go on for even a second without Kama! I cannot do it and it is not my intent to be dramatic. Give him back to me, that is all I ask of you. And if you cannot do that, help me get on my feet so that I may strike you really hard! Perhaps then you will open your third eye and kill me as well so I can follow him down whatever path you sent him on without me...'

To her secret relief, Shiva did not seem angered and when he squatted down next to her in the ashes, Rati was dumbstruck with wonder. When he spoke, his voice was gravelly but so kind that Rati wanted to cry some more. However, this time she prevailed over her emotions and listened to him as sedately as she could, 'If it makes you feel any better, you don't look half as ugly as you think you do when you are bawling your eyes out. Well...just a tad crumpled, if I may say so…' Seeing that his words had elicited a tiny smile, Shiva seemed pleased and went on, 'I believe you beseeched me to grant you the blessed release of death, if I cannot or will not bring Kama back to you. Since we seem to be making stupid, pointless wishes here, I think it behoves me to do the same.

It is the fondest desire of my heart to have Sati come back to me as well… I could give my temper its head and go on a killing rampage and burn down all of creation—or I could discard feelings entirely and lose myself in meditation, but no matter what I do and despite the depth of my need for her, she is never coming back. The truly wise —who are equally likely to be the biggest fools—will recommend that I deal with this crisis with calm acceptance and emotional detachment. They would want me to move on, marry Parvati and beget a mighty son with her, who will rid the world of the current Asura crisis and then they can all breathe easy till they screw things up even worse than before. But I am going to ignore them with their attendant follies and listen only to you. Why don't you tell me exactly what it is you think I should do?'

Never one to shy away from expressing an opinion, Rati spoke up with fresh confidence, 'I can help you! The wise guys or the fools, if you prefer, were right. You said that Sati is never coming back but that is not entirely true, is it? Her last words were that she loved you and would return to you. It seems to me that you have lost your faith in her and that is the reason for your suffering. But she has stayed true to her word and taken rebirth as Parvati. They may not look the same but Sati's spirit is safely ensconced within Parvati and if you would stop being so obstinate you would see it for yourself.

Perhaps you feel that you are being unfaithful to your first wife by allowing yourself to respond to Parvati's love and reciprocate her feelings? But you should know better than that! It does not matter that you can never stop loving Sati or ever forget her. Loving Parvati is not going to change your feelings for Sati and I am sure they both love you enough to understand. Kama fell in love with Priti and Purnakala as well, but that did not mean that his love for me diminished in any capacity. In fact, he perfectly understood when he got to know about the small crushes I had on you, on some of the other celestials—and even the odd mortal as well. He took it simply at its face value: that I happened to like men with really great facial hair, or those with dangerous edges to them! There was nothing more and nothing less than that. There was never any question of infidelity involved and he knew it.

It is perfectly acceptable for you to fall in love and marry Parvati. Sati would have understood for sure, especially since she has taken rebirth in order to be reunited with you. It is the best thing for you. I realize now that you might be inclined to balk at the prospect of falling in love and finally being blissfully happy, for fear that it may all be snatched away again but you can rest easy for I have heard tell that lightening does not strike twice.'

Shiva heard her out patiently and nodded in agreement, 'You have spelt it out very clearly and I promise to take your words into serious consideration. The important thing is that you are no longer being a morbid little fool who asks for the boon of death. For I come bearing glad tidings! Vishnu will be taking an avatar and living among mortals to relieve Bhoomi Devi of her burden, as is his wont. Kama is destined to be reborn as his son. Needless to say, he will be a lion among men and will aid his father in ridding the world of evil. You were not just his wife but able assistant as well and soon he will have need of your aid, for his term on earth will be fraught with difficulties and numerous vested interests will be working against him. It will take all of your resources to steer him safely past the treacherous tides of fate. And when he has successfully accomplished what he was born to do, he will be reunited with you.'

Rati was elated when she heard his words and impulsively she hugged Shiva. 'I cannot find the words to thank you!' she said.

'Your magnanimity is unparalleled! Kama would love nothing better than to be born as Vishnu's son. I will go to him and raise him to be the mightiest warrior of all time. He will go on to achieve great feats of valour that will never be forgotten by the Gods and man. Thank you so much!'

Releasing Shiva from her embrace, Rati spoke again, 'What about Parvati? Will you go to her now?'

Shiva shook his head with a mischievous twinkle, 'I have acceded to the demands of one headstrong and temperamental virago. The sensible thing for me to do at this juncture is to allow sufficient time to elapse before taking on another one. Everything will happen in its own good time. Besides, the wise men as well as the fools are inclined to agree that love lightly won does not last long, so it won't hurt Parvati to take some more time to truly make up her mind that she wants me and no other. Loving me and living with me is no easy feat, I am forced to admit. However, even you will agree that I am worth the wait, will you not?'

Pleased with her vigorous nod of agreement, Shiva kissed her gently on her forehead, counselled her to be patient and left her to enjoy the newfound hope and happiness that he had given her. He fondly hoped that it would be the last time he irked her to this extent. Delirious excitement filled Rati as she contemplated her reunion with Kama. She rose from the ashes and turned her steps homeward to make her preparations for a future amongst mortals. As she walked away, a pall of unease assailed her suddenly and she paused. Shiva had told her that Kama was to be reborn on earth, that he would have need of her before he went on to cover himself with glory, and that having achieved what he was born to do, they would be reunited. But he had not specified what would become of them when their mortal life had run its course. The nameless dread descended on her again but Rati shook it off fiercely for she had decided to place her faith in the Destroyer and wait for time to untie the knots of fate.

Rati had lived in fear and doubt for too long to return to that hopeless state again. She changed direction abruptly and returned to the spot where Kama was taken away from her and which was also the scene of her blessed encounter with Shiva. Refusing to take a moment to think, she built a roaring fire and walked into it. To her amazement, there was no pain as the flames consumed her greedily; only hope.

The Demon's Bride and the Prophecy

*I*t was Mayawati's wedding night. Bedecked in bridal finery, she awaited the coming of her husband with the air of a chicken which knew for a doleful fact that its neck was about to be well and truly wrung. She was at the royal bedchambers in a grim palace of stone. In fact, her husband, Shambara's entire kingdom was grim, desolate and barren. His numerous conquests had seen the accumulation of priceless works of art, which the king had ordered to be installed in suitable places across the land. Which was why Maya found herself gazing at beautiful sculptures placed in odd corners of her room where they stood looking incongruous but managing to make everything around them look even uglier than they were. Maya had grown up in this land but that did not stop her from hating it. In fact, she identified with the alien sculptures more.

From the time her mother had informed her about her groom, she had been hoping that the wedding would be called off on account of his untimely death. But no such luck for her, she thought bitterly. Her husband was a powerful Asura king and the general consensus was that he was invincible. It had been prophesized that Krishna's (believed to be an avatar of Vishnu) son alone could kill him and Maya had difficulty understanding why this process could not be sped up, sparing her the joys of convivial bliss with the king who would never rule over her heart.

In the unlikely event that the poor child escaped Shambara's murderous clutches, it would be long years before he would be ready to face the mighty demon king who was believed to possess the strength of a thousand elephants and the craftiness of a thousand shysters. If that were not enough, he was the most skilled illusionist alive and even the Gandharvas balked at his prowess in what was essentially their specialty.

Maya had done everything in her power to prevent the wedding from taking place, short of eloping with another man, and the proof of it could be found on her person. Her mother had been horrified that a child of hers would actually turn down a match with a king, citing the fact that he was a ruthless killer and a known rapist. She had actually driven home her displeasure by taking a pair of hot irons to her ankles, just to give her a live demonstration of the pain, humiliation and ill treatment that was the lot of women evincing extremely poor judgement.

Shambara himself had been something of a surprise. From what she had heard, Maya expected a hirsute and thickset demon, with a penchant for every vice imaginable, metaphorically and literally bloated up with gas, who would in all probability arrive in her presence gnawing at an infant's limb and quaffing from a goblet of blood. She was taken aback by the imposing figure striding imperiously towards her. Shambara was impossibly tall, darker than coal, and heavyset, but without an ounce of flab. His hair was fine to look upon and soft to the touch. She had been forced to admit to herself that he was an attractive man and it was with guilty pleasure that she dwelt on the fact that she would be the envy of women everywhere for having snagged a wealthy, powerful and good looking husband, who loved her. After all, he had personally chosen her, the daughter of one of his lowly courtiers, to be his wife.

In his inimitable animalistic way, Shambara seemed to really care for her. When he had come to see her for the very first time, he had come bearing gifts as befits a king. But what had really moved her was the amount of thought that had gone into each gift. He had brought the traditional presents of fine cloth, jewellery, flowers, fruits, and livestock—but they had been personalized just for her and clearly, his underlings had been put to work to ferret out every little bit of information they could find about the tastes of their future queen.

Green was Maya's favourite colour and her suitor had gifted her with bales of an exceedingly rare green silk and fine gold and diamond jewellery encrusted liberally with precious emeralds to go with it. Her weakness for mangoes was well known and Shambara's assistants came in bearing baskets groaning under the weight of the delectable fruit. These were followed by more baskets which contained every sweet and savoury delicacy ever prepared with mangoes from the farthest reaches of the universe.

Maya had always had a phobia for anything on four legs that was capable of movement and possessed of teeth and claws. Which was why to the amazement of all present, instead of the customary heads of cattle or hunting dogs, Shambara's attendants carried in glass bowls of exotic fishes with iridescent hues that took the breath away. Informed about her fondness for music, he had summoned the finest singers and musicians in his realm to perform for her. His men even constructed a large aviary—made entirely of the purest ivory that they had appropriated from the Devas—just outside her room and filled it with the most beautiful birds in all of creation, so that their sweet voices were the first thing she heard on waking.

There were other gifts, too numerous and rich for her to take in immediately, but what caught her eye was the fabled Parijatha flowers from Indra's own garden which had been procured just for her. Maya noted that it was a charming gesture since the flowers were known to keep spouses from straying into the arms of other women. As a mighty ruler he was entitled to take as many wives and concubines as he pleased, and he had done so—therefore this promise of fealty was truly touching. Although, it remained to be seen, she thought cynically to herself, whether Shambara would uphold this fine sentiment once he had taken his pleasure with her and come to discover that she was one filly who would never ever be broken to his will.

The bride's mother had seldom understood her daughter, mainly because she could not have cared less about the fevered thoughts of a stripling. But she did have a nose for dissent and she shot her daughter a warning glare to convey the message that she would throttle her to death with her bare hands if she dared to disrupt the proceedings that were going on so smoothly. Noting with relief that her irksome, thoroughly noncompliant daughter had affected a demeanour of extreme coyness for the moment at least, she relaxed and basked in her reflected glory, patting herself on the back yet again for passing on her own flawless beauty to her offspring, which had allowed their family to rise swiftly to prominence. She hoped Shambara and her daughter would produce a strong son together, so that their future would be fully assured.

Maya had pushed down her rebellious thoughts to a place where they were less readily apparent. The truth was that she was charmed but also a little alarmed with the favour shown her by her monarch and groom. During subsequent interactions with him she continued to experience mixed feelings. She had become well aware of the fact that he loved her. His eagerness to be with her and his tendency to reorganize his schedule just so that he could get close to her, was a constant source of amazement to her and all those around him. Maya had grown up listening to her mother constantly telling her that she was not good enough, but in Shambara's eyes, she was the most flawless specimen of womanhood in the Three Worlds and the knowledge made her feel special for the first time in her life. It was for this reason alone that Maya had changed her mind about killing him herself and instead sat brooding on their wedding night, fighting the impulse to flee and alternatively to give in to her rising hysteria which was demanding that she scream her trepidations for the Three Worlds to hear.

Maya loved the fact that a king loved her so truly, but she knew that it would be impossible for her to love him back the same way. For, Maya's earliest recollections of her life included a quest to find her soul mate. Even as a child she remembered having felt incredibly blessed just to be alive, for she knew that there was something special out there in her future. Growing older she had not entirely understood the yearning and happy anticipation she had felt or the fits of melancholy she experienced over having lost something that had been precious to her. Endlessly, she found herself searching or alternately waiting for she knew not what, drawing comfort from the unshakeable, deep-rooted belief that somehow her heart's longing would be fulfilled, feeling certain that although she could not for the life of her tell how it could be so, it was a promise made to her which could never be broken.

Which was why when her parents consented to a match with Shambara with alacrity, she was hugely disappointed for she knew deep within that he was not the one who was a permanent fixture in her dreams but rather, an impediment to their realization. She nearly despaired but hope fiercely refused to die and promised her satisfaction—if only she would safeguard the core of her being from Shambara's aggressive attentions, which she could and did. And so it was on their wedding night, as in the times they had been together previously, that Maya held the most precious and intimate parts of her being carefully hidden away where Shambara may never access them.

Shambara sensed this and his frustration grew to maddening levels. At first, he assumed that Maya was just shy and it made him love her even more, for there was something about this woman who refused to throw herself at him, that he found absolutely irresistible. But gradually, he found himself looking into her eyes, heart, mind and soul and discovered that they were forever barred to him and worse, perhaps reserved for another. It was certainly not something he was used to and definitely more than he could bear, which was why he handled her lack of feelings for him with the most powerful defence mechanisms he could summon to his aid—denial and aggression. Shambara told himself repeatedly that Maya did indeed love him, ignoring his battle-honed instincts, and like so many fools in love he chose instead to believe that his love was reciprocated or would be eventually. And so he continued to chase after her determined to posses her completely. Yet, the more he pursued her the faster she ran, putting up impregnable walls around her that he could never hope to breach.

Maya also disabused him of his romantic notions, mostly because she wanted to be fair to him and alleviate the senseless guilt she often felt. During one of their chats which was never entirely enjoyable for either, Shambara asked her if she had wanted to marry him. Rather uncharacteristically, he seemed a little awkward and tried to make up for his unseemly hesitation by bragging about the number of women who had professed their undying love for him and begged him to marry them or even take them as his concubines. She had crushed him rather casually with her reply, 'I had no intention of getting married. It was my plan to run away from home and join the Gandharvas. The Apsaras seem like such blithe and fun-spirited characters from what I have heard of them. If they had allowed me to join their ranks, I would have mastered their arts and become the most talented and famous of them all without ever being tied down with a husband and children.

At one point, I also toyed with the idea of dressing up like a man and joining whichever army would have me. It seemed like a good idea to travel the world, make my fortune and cover myself in glory. Men always have more fun, don't they? But mother caught me trying on the stable boy's clothes and she beat me bloody which was...'

Before Maya could complete her sentence, Shambara had struck her across the face so hard that he split her lip and sent her crashing to the floor. She was still reeling from the unexpected force of the blow, too stunned to check the tears that ran unhindered down her cheeks, when the man who loved her grabbed a big chunk of her hair and yanked her around to face him, 'Don't get me wrong...' he told her with dangerous calm, 'There is nothing wrong with being a spirited little bitch, for the sons I have by one are more likely to be warlike as befitting heirs of mine. But I will not tolerate disrespect or immorality. The next time you talk about taking up whoring or playing perverted games with the hired help—make no mistake, I will cut your throat and feed your carcass to my dogs!' Flinging her aside, Shambara stormed out.

Maya hated Shambara mostly because she found herself in the somewhat ignominious position of having to kowtow to her survival instincts which warned her repeatedly not to provoke her Asura lord—that is, not unless she wanted her head put through a stone wall. But it was hard not to taunt him when she hated him so. To her perpetual shame, she found she was terrified of him even when he was being tender, for she could never respond with similar ardour. This in turn would invariably get his goat, and bring out his inner jerk. She resented him for being so presumptuous as to believe that by loving her he was entitled to claim sole ownership of her, and deprive her of precious freedoms. Mostly though, what Maya hated about their troubled relationship was that she did not despise him entirely—but despite everything, had actually come to care for him a little.

Shambara had a disconcerting way of making her change her mind about him every time she was fully convinced that he was the biggest ass that ever lived. She would have mouthed off at him and he would have struck her and humiliated her, leaving her seething with fury, wishing that he would die already. It was always around this time that he would do something to rock her world. Once he summoned the best drama troupes and dancers in his kingdom to distract her while she was suffering from a particularly wicked bout of menstrual cramps, because he had found her writhing in pain. She had refused to allow his physicians to see her, dismissing them as concocters of nasty potions which she loathed even more than acute pain. Shambara had seemed a little uncomfortable when she had gotten started on her pet peeve about how the uterus was the actual villain in a woman's life and left in a big hurry, much to her annoyance. When the troupe of entertainers turned up to take her mind off her troubles, she realized that he genuinely hated to see her in pain even if he inflicted more hurt on her than anybody else in her life.

There were more contradictory aspects to Shambara's persona. Despite being the scourge of the Three Worlds and one of the fiercest warriors alive, he loved children and animals. Folklore had it that he dined on infants, but in reality he could not resist a little tyke and could play goofy games with them for hours on end. Little boys worshipped him and little girls fell in love with him and one adorable little moppet even told him to ditch Maya and marry her! Watching him build mud houses for his little buddies or personally comforting a colic-afflicted horse, Maya was almost sorry for having promised herself never to bear his children.

Of course, the fact that she herself could not stand children may have also been a causal factor. The sound of a wailing brat was guaranteed to send her up the wall and it was certainly among her least favourite things in the world. Consequently, she saw no reason to sacrifice her perky breasts, toned buttocks, narrow waist and normal sized privates in order to push out the 'warlike sons' Shambara so desired. The world had no need for more Shambaras and she was doing Godkind and mankind a big favour, she told herself virtuously. And so she willed herself not to get pregnant, and dutifully gulped down the potions she had her maids brew for her, so that any errant sperms that had foolishly fought their way into her sanctum sanctorum were successfully expunged. Maya was careful to keep her exertions in this department the best-kept secret in the kingdom, for if Shambara ever found out, he would certainly kill her, or worse, force her to have his baby.

As she envisioned a series of shattering images of accelerated violence which would become inevitable if Shambara were ever to discover her hanky-panky, Maya thought for the umpteenth time how hard it was to reconcile the many faces of Shambara. It boggled the mind that a despicable wife-beater and a borderline psychopath with rage issues, could have so many redeeming qualities. At this junction, she would be forced to admit that he hardly qualified as a wife-beater since he just struck her on the odd occasion and she never had to endure a sustained beating which among her people, steeped in violence as they were, made him out to be the embodiment of gentleness! Her own mother had not been as fortunate and had often been badly beaten—although at the time, Maya had often felt that she had brought it all on herself by undermining her husband with her tongue. In all honesty, she knew that the same could be said for her. Yet she would often lecture Shambara about how there was never any justification for a man to assault a woman who was physically weaker than him. She had called him a coward for doing so, and had received a back-handed slap as a response.

On the best of days, their marriage was a troubled one and the tempestuous relationship had left her drained. There was the inescapable feeling that she had been trapped like an animal in a cage and there simply was no way to escape. She wanted desperately to be rescued but there seemed little hope for that now. This was why she often found herself wishing for Shambara's heart to simply stop beating. Inexplicably, though she nursed such murderous designs on her husband, through strange presentiment she realized that she wanted this cruel fate for him only to spare him from a death that was even worse. These thoughts baffled her and left her more miserable than ever.

Despite the rocky state of their marriage and the fits of depression it engendered, Maya had to concede that life as a queen was not entirely shorn of benefits. It was wonderful to have more money, power and prestige than one knew what to do with. The decadent lifestyle suited Maya and helped take the edge off her unhappiness and anxiety.

When not obsessing about whether or not Maya loved him, Shambara could be nice. He cured her of her phobia for animals by taking her horse-riding or hunting with him. Maya adored these outings for it was a refreshing change from her otherwise sheltered life and they made her feel wonderfully alive. Her only grouse was that Shambara always accompanied her and would not hear of her taking off on a hunting expedition by herself. Seeing the rebellious spark in her eyes, he gave specific orders to her guards that their heads would be served up to his hounds if they ever allowed her to leave the palace grounds on foot or astride a horse.

Maya had been furious with him but forgave him as she reasoned that supervised excursions were better than none. Seeing that she was enjoying herself by his side, Shambara would talk to her of his battle campaigns against the Devas and even explained to her why they needed to be put in their place, although he had never in his life felt the need to justify or even discuss his actions with anybody else. 'The diabolical propaganda engineered by the Devas and their professional panegyrists against their half-brothers has led to so many stupid misconceptions and imbecilic stereotypes about the Asuras. My personal favourite is that the Devas represent everything that is good, noble and pure in the Three Worlds! As they are purportedly the beacons of supreme virtue, lit up from within by their innate morality and righteousness, they are commonly visualized by moronic mortals as creatures of great physical beauty who tirelessly roam the cosmos protecting the weak and innocent and keeping them safe from the likes of us. When not saving the universe, word is that they sip from golden chalices filled to the brim with the nectar of immortality—so that they may shit nothing but pure gold in order to ensure prosperity for mankind and spare themselves the nuisance of wiping their arses.

On the other hand, the Asuras are supposed to be ugly, stupid, brutish creatures with a taste for fresh blood and virgins, young mothers, pregnant women, old crones and even pretty boys and ugly old men alike. We are supposed to be predators who constantly feed on the hearts of the unwary and cold-blooded killers who are known to thrive on death, destruction and disruption of the natural order. Brahmins swear that we ruin their sacrifices by attacking them in large numbers when the rites and rituals are being performed, killing the holy men, smashing their sacrificial paraphernalia and defecating on their sacred fires, so great is our dislike for all things sacred and pure. I have heard tell that we Asuras copulate with hyenas and jackals to imbibe the worst traits of those beasts and keep it alive in our bloodlines so that we can stay mean and animalistic.

If people had the sense to sift through this rigmarole of rubbish, they would recognize the simple truth, which is, that in reality the Devas and Asuras are not too different from each other, excepting the overall appearance, personality and an often-conflicting belief system! I firmly believe that they are superior to us in only one significant way—and that is they are far more united.

Indra somehow managed to unite them all under his suzerainty, and for reasons unknown to me, his brothers have continued to remain loyal to him despite the fact that he has gotten them into more scrapes than any Asura ever has! The bloody bugger has shamelessly manipulated, cheated, lied, killed and done just about everything diabolical, short of pimping out his mother and wife, and yet he is hailed as the champion of the virtuous! Trishiras and Vritra are among those whom he killed using the most deceitful and cowardly ways imaginable. He threw his thunderbolt at an unarmed Trishiras while he was lost in meditation, all because he perceived him to be a threat to his sovereignty. As for Vritra, Indra brokered a peace with him when he realized that his rival was stronger, and falsely promised him that he would be safe from the malice of the Devas—before proceeding to murder him in cold blood. Even so, his fellow celestials will have none other for a king and their ability to ignore his loathsome nature, even as much as to look the other way when he is banging one of their wives, has paid off in rich dividends for them.

On the other hand, there has been far too much infighting among the Asuras, and we have had more rulers than anybody can count, for we have always had issues with authority figures. Even now we hardly present a united front. Not all the Asura chiefs accept my suzerainty, and many have only submitted because I have proved myself the mightiest amongst them."

Maya interjected at this point: 'That is fine, but what is truly interesting is that you think we are not too different from our sworn enemies. Mother always maintained that the Devas were unscrupulous brutes and the real villains. She said that she knew tales of their debauchery and perversions that would make a rock blush. I asked her to tell me more but she chose to be infuriating and said that such prurient tales were not meant for the ears of a young girl. I have always been curious... What can you tell me about the sexual shenanigans of the Devas? Do they really share their wives around?'

'If I were you, I would rein in that wicked imagination before it lands you in a world of trouble,' her Asura husband pointed out. 'Besides, I am afraid, your mother was right. There is plenty I could tell you over a roaring campfire and a good strong drink about what those fellows get up to in their pleasure dens, but it is simply not suitable for the ears of a young impressionable girl who knows nothing about sex but what her husband has taught her."

Shambara was interrupted when his wife attacked him with her riding crop. Her gently rounded arms could not muster up the strength to do the damage her fiery spirit demanded and merely incited him to gales of laughter which only made her angrier. But finally she grinned as well and sensing that Shambara was starting to get seriously aroused, she hurriedly carried on with their conversation.

'Tell me more about your half-brothers... I have been told that the Devas are the sons of sage Kashyap born to his wife, Aditi, and the Asuras are also his sons born to Diti, and the two have been embroiled in ugly conflict for as long as anyone can remember. But can you tell me what the cause of this incessant warfare is? Did they rob you of your rightful share of your mother's milk or something? Who is in the right here?'

Shambara replied: 'Mother Diti would have cheerfully killed herself before suckling a Deva. Did you know that she once tried to avenge us after the debacle that was the churning of the ocean of milk? She asked father to impregnate her with a son who would bring Indra and his brothers to their knees. Father agreed but stipulated that during the gestational period (which was to last a thousand years), she must perform the sternest penances and remain absolutely pure in accordance with the the scriptures. An ordinary woman would have balked but mother persisted for nine hundred and ninety years and would have succeeded if it had not been for that cur, Indra. He inveigled his way into her retreat by pretending to accept his fate and promising to serve her in the course of her arduous task. On a particularly evil day, when mother had her guard down, he switched the hard rock she was using for a pillow with the stick that had been placed for her to rest her feet on, with the result that her purity was besmirched as she had placed her head in the proper place for her feet. Her great sacrifice was rendered moot and Indra triumphed...'

'What? I am not sure I understand... How can the purity of

a person be affected by something this stupid? Surely placing one's head on the wrong side can hardly be such a big fat deal? Perhaps an incorrect version of the story has been circulated among the Asuras to spare them the gory details of the terrible truth. Indra usually sends his Apsaras to distract sages into paying more attention to the demands made south of their navel when he suspects them of an unhealthy interest in the accruement of power by performing intense tapas. Perhaps he sent the Gandharvas to Diti and they in turn seduced her or something. At the very least, she may have pleasured herself on coming across their well-sculpted bodies, so as to rebel against the pundits of purity who are always telling women to practise abstinence...' Maya stopped abruptly, for she had just sensed the dangerous shift in Shambara's mood on hearing her take on mother Diti's supposed moral transgressions, and she hurried to do some damage control, 'I was just suggesting that this is exactly the kind of scurrilous nonsense the Devas would conjure up to make us look bad. But you are yet to answer my question: how did the sons of sage Kashyap's two wives decide to spend an eternity trying to kill each other?'

Shambara had no wish to fight with his wife either and he decided to let the implied slur on mother Diti slide, 'I would like to blame the Devas, but in truth, there are no good guys or bad guys as such, nor a right or wrong in this situation. Neither side can, in all fairness, be said to represent good or evil in its entirety. When you take two factions, there will always be good folks, bad ones, some morally ambiguous souls, brave guys, cowards, thieves, saints, potential murderers and sexual deviants on either side. Unfortunately, as is almost always the case, there is no noble cause worth fighting and dying for but only a whole bunch of petty nonsense. Both the Devas and Asuras have been jostling for power from the earliest days when they discovered that they hated sharing their food, toys or even a father with each other! There is no lofty purpose here worth putting into song, for we continue to behave like spoilt brats to this day, fighting over paltry possessions we hardly care about! The Devas, however, have chosen to glorify this senseless struggle and their poets have composed a lot of flowery, nauseating pap about the great battle they have been fighting to ensure that good always triumphs in the Three Worlds, and similar garbage!'

Maya said: 'I have always known it. Men refuse to grow up! They are nothing more than silly children with big egos and have far too much muscle power for their undeveloped brain cells! They like nothing better than good food and drink, plenty of bloodshed, and action between the sheets—though not always in that order. Thanks to the foolishness of men, the Three Worlds are in a state of complete shambles with no redemption in sight!'

'Women, on the other hand, become wiser in direct proportion to the speed at which their hair turns white...' Shambara began, but feigning false alarm as she raised her riding crop, he carried on with his discourse, 'Tragically, death makes no distinction between Deva and Asura. Everybody is fair game, which is why whenever we go to war, both sides lose and only death ever makes a killing. This war between us will never end for we are too alike and too evenly matched. We have both inflicted wounds on each other that will never stop bleeding. The Amrita was supposed to give them an edge and result in us being destroyed, but as you know, we survived. Our preceptor, the noble Sukracharya, knows the Sanjeevani craft and can bring the dead back to life. Therefore, their advantage over us has been nullified and we continue to go hammer and tongs at each other. It is a Golden age for the Asuras as we have gained the upper hand, but it will not be for long. We will be forced to pay a price in exchange for this period of grace and death will be it. Soon we will all be gone and there is little solace to be had from the fact that we shall leave a legacy behind, since it is well-known that history is written by the victors and I can't see Indra's scribes being too kind to us. Unfortunately, the fiction that they are the champions of good and we the minions of evil will continue to thrive, and mothers will continue to tell fabricated stories about us to their children hoping to terrify them into submission.

Consequently, they will always come across smelling of roses and people will wrinkle their noses or cower in fear while talking or even thinking about us. Sometimes I think that if mother Diti had been as fair-complexioned as Aditi it may not have been so darned easy to pigeonhole us. Bloody mortals have always had too much regard for everything that is white and shiny even if it is rotten to the core. We, on the other hand, unlike the Devas, are dusky and that naturally makes us black devils.

Traditionally, the Asuras have been associated with the Godless and the heathen. We have been accused of having no respect for the sacrosanct. If folklore is to be believed, we dabble in the dark arts and are raised on sorcery and black magic in place of breast milk. It has been said that many Asuras forbid the worship of the Gods and do everything possible to hinder the worship of holy men. There may be a few grains of truth to these assertions since no Asura worth the name can put up with the pontificating, proselytizing ways of the self-proclaimed guardians of morality with their excessive facial hair. Be that as it may, the fact is that Asuras have as much or as little faith as the Devas, though they have little patience with endless rites and rituals that call for abstinence from the good things in life, such as meat, wine and sex!'

'I agree completely,' Maya piped up eagerly, 'it is stupid to have to give up good things in order to be considered truly virtuous. Self-inflicted deprivation is the root cause of misery in this world, if you ask me. To do good for your fellow-beings, one must be happy. And one cannot truly be happy if one has not feasted, gotten drunk to a stage of stupor or done the nasty on a fairly regular basis. It is hard to believe that there are those who would give up these things to sit through a boring yagna or something equally mind-numbing. My maids told me that some of these grand affairs can last for many years and I could not help thinking that those who go through these things must have either enormous amounts of patience, or a severe case of masochism. Personally, I believe these yagnas must be exceedingly hard on the buttocks and no extravagant promise of wish-fulfilment could ever induce me to sit through one!'

'Perhaps, out of respect to tender heinies everywhere, I should declare a blanket ban on such rituals and immortalize myself in the history books as a protector of backsides if not the true faith!' said Shambara. Maya had collapsed in a fit of giggles and Shambara gazed at her fondly, thinking that there was nothing he loved better than the sound of her laughter. He had achieved so much by himself but nothing gave him the same satisfaction as listening to the musical sound of his wife's happiness, especially when he himself had caused it.

Shaking his head a little, Shambara continued, 'As I was saying, the Asuras are not without faith. We just believe that there is no need for unnecessary middlemen to be appended to our personal relationship with the Supreme Being. Not surprisingly, the Devas and Brahmins disapprove of this kind of overly familiar behaviour with the Gods, though interestingly enough, the truly powerful Gods—the ones that count—have always understood and stood by us. They have freely accepted that we have chosen not to spend our life on our knees, bowing, scrapping and genuflecting before them or seeking their opinion as to the most auspicious time to eat, drink, take a dump or fornicate.

Vishnu and Shiva are wrongly believed to love the Devas more and support their cause. In fact, they have always made sure that power is evenly distributed among us and have prevented both the Devas and Asuras from gaining sole ascendancy. This is why we remain with our horns locked in place probably for the rest of time.'

Maya looked a little troubled when she spoke again, 'You said there is no end to this war and there is no exalted motive for any of you being in it. Why then have you chosen to be a part of it if it is nothing but errant nonsense?'

'I was born a warrior and a ruler. Nothing can change that, not even my beliefs which may or may not be at odds with what I do. We were talking about faith and I have as much faith as the next man, only I have chosen to place that belief in myself. And that is the way of it for me. I fight because I will not be anybody's bitch—and that is about as honourable as I can be.'

'You said death awaits you for that is the price that will be extracted for all you have achieved,' said Maya. 'Does it not scare you? What about the prophecy? People are always whispering about it behind your back...everyone believes that Krishna and Rukmini's son will take your life...' Her voice shook when she said that, for at that particular moment she realized that no matter how much she had always wished him gone, she didn't actually want him to die at all—leave alone face a violent end!

'I am familiar with the terms of the prophecy and all I can say is that I refuse to fret over something that I cannot hope to control. Let Krishna's son grow a pair first and come for me. I will meet him sword in hand or perhaps a rattle will suffice. Beyond that there is nothing I can do. Death does not scare me...' he replied, looking directly into her eyes and possessing every inch of her without even touching her, as she shrank back in sudden fear, 'only the thought of losing you!' They rode back in silence, neither fully understanding the inexplicable wave of sadness that had engulfed them.

Maya remembered that day, when Narada paid her husband a visit in their private chambers. The famous messenger of the Gods arrived without fanfare, in his trademark saffron robes, long hair neatly knotted above his head and the veena which he was never seen without, since it was a gift from Vishnu and therein contained a portion of his divine essence. Narada had requested a private audience with the king and Maya left them together after seeking the blessings of the great man and personally serving him refreshments. As she left them together, she could not shake the feeling that she knew him from somewhere other than folklore but for the life of her, she could not place him. Filled with misgivings, Maya walked away without looking back and she could feel Narada's eyes boring into her back. She recalled the anxiety which had seized her about her husband's safety when she and Shambara had ridden out on that memorable day in the woods, and she wondered why Narada's visit should remind her of it.

Shambara turned politely to his revered guest and enquired about the purpose of his visit, eager to be rid of the troublemaker extraordinaire—before he left his kingdom a smoking ruin and himself, minus his head. 'Surely you must have some inkling as to why I am here?' Narada asked placidly. He sensed the other's impatience and hostility but was in no hurry to get to the point, thoroughly enjoying the growing discomfiture of his host.

'If I were to hazard a wild guess, it would appear that you are here because Rukmini has finally whelped Krishna's brat and my enemies have wet themselves in uncontrolled ecstasy since this child was born with the express purpose of finishing me off! My spies brought me the glad tidings immediately after the birth as you are well aware, so it would not be wild conjecture on my part to say that you did not honour me with your exalted presence, simply to inform me that my bloody murder is in the offing. Which begs the question as to why exactly you are here? Though I must confess, I do not really want to know, since it is obvious that my longevity and continued well-being is hardly on your agenda?'

Narada smiled benevolently and infuriatingly at him before replying, 'That little speech almost had me convinced that you are longing to swat me like you would a particularly irksome fly. But I set great store by your powers of judgement to be confident about the safety of my person. There are many who would swear that

I traverse the length and breadth of the cosmos not to promote spiritual enlightenment and bring people closer to God, but rather to spread mischief and leave a world of trouble in my wake! In truth, they could not be more wrong for I nurse no ill-will towards anybody and I am but a humble servant of my faith and fate. Every time I set in motion a chain of events that has an Asura losing his life—even when he hasn't been guilty of any misdeeds—I am wrongly blamed for doing the Asuras great harm, when that simply isn't true! One fails to see how I actually procure for them, in the process, an enviable position at the lotus feet of the Preserver, Lord Vishnu, which none but a few are lucky to occupy. Surely I am entitled to a little gratitude? And if not, perhaps I should at least be spared the vilification or unnecessary sarcasm?'

'You try my patience severely, sage!' Shambara said, growing increasingly rattled as the sage forced him to wade through his swampy verbiage. 'Why don't you just come out and say what it is you are here for? I know that it was you who convinced Kamsa with your evil tongue to kill every one of Devaki's children befuddling him into thinking that they posed a threat to his life. As a result, Kamsa will be reviled for all eternity as the most monstrous of killers who picked up newborn babies by their heels and dashed their brains out. It was thanks to your remarkable capacity to leak confidential matters into the wrong ears, that he sent the demon Putana to kill even more infants with her poisoned teats. I am sure he enjoys listening to every mother curse his name while he reclines against the 'lotus feet of the Lord' and has nothing but words of praise for your righteous actions which plunged him into such a damnable fate!'

'The Lord works in mysterious ways and it is not our place to question why it was decreed that those newborns had to lose their lives so brutally at Kamsa's hands,' replied Narada. 'All I know is that Kamsa was chosen specially to play a role in accentuating the full glory of Krishna. To the best of my knowledge, complex philosophy is incomprehensible to formidable warriors such as yourself who have been blessed with brute strength but cursed with an inferior intellect. Hence I will put it in simplistic terms for your benefit: Krishna, being the greatest hero the Three Worlds have ever seen, needed—like all heroes before him—an antithesis to vanquish in order to enhance his own stature in the eyes of his followers for the rest of time.

Kamsa served this purpose admirably and as a reward was allowed to advance in the consciousness of the Supreme Being. Having achieved such an exalted position he could not care less about the nattering of foolish mortals who utter all kinds of nonsense in their abject ignorance. The dead babies were rescued by Vishnu himself and he released them from the circle of rebirths, helping them achieve moksha which is the ultimate aim of every soul. You can trust me when I say that they also have no cause for complaint and have achieved transcendental bliss. Incidentally, if it were not for the fact that I am such a humble soul, I would have added that all this came to pass due to my timely intervention.'

Shambara smirked. 'That is so fascinating! I would love nothing better than to spend the rest of my life listening to your intellectually stimulating discourses on why it makes perfect sense to kill babies fresh out of their mother's wombs, just so that they may avoid being born as dungbeetles in subsequent lives! I am afraid there are far more pressing matters demanding my attention, so excuse me for not rushing off to kill a helpless newborn and further besmirching the already tarnished legacy of the Asuras! I hope your laudable efforts in pimping for the fates is successful and you procure suitable bitches to be used in the games of the Gods—but I guarantee that you will find nothing of the sort you are looking for here. And you were wrong about my judgement; if I had an ounce of sense, I would have personally flayed the skin off your back for daring to comment on my mental capabilities!'

'It is truly unfortunate and extremely hurtful that you should hold me in such low esteem and treat me with such disrespect, for I only wished to be a benefactor to you. In fact, your attitude to the prophecy has been very inspiring. Kamsa reacted with uncharacteristic fear and panicked, which led to the horrifying consequences you so graphically outlined. Yet you remain undaunted at the prospect of impending death. I merely wished to convey my admiration for your courage and offer you the benefit of my superior knowledge. In my possession are certain facts which will be of invaluable use to you in the days ahead where you are destined to withstand more than your fair share of trouble and danger. All your life you have struggled against the odds and triumphed in spite of them because of your great self-belief, bravery and perseverance, but I am afraid that this time around even you will not be able to beat the odds. I felt it was my duty to place before you all the facts regarding this unique situation so that when the time comes, you will be able to make an informed decision.'

'If I am going to die anyway, of what use is your information to me? I suggest you stuff it back down your throat before you are tempted to voice them and gall me more than you already have. Perhaps you will choke on your foul words and I won't have to listen to your incessant prattling which is likely to bore me to death long before Krishna's brat can come to finish me off!'

'You make light of death claiming that your life is of little value to you—but surely there is someone in it, for whom you might spare a thought? A real person who will have to cope with the sorrow and turbulence of your passing? How about your lovely wife? Have you ever wondered about her fate? She will make an attractive widow, don't you think? And surely you are aware that the victor of any battle is entitled to his spoils...' Narada observed the anger and anxiety that flickered for a heartbeat in the depths of Shambara's eyes and pressed his advantage relentlessly, 'You love Mayawati don't you? You love her and will gladly destroy the Three Worlds for her. I can feel the effect she has had on you... Don't you want to make sure that nothing untoward happens to her?'

Narada watched with curious detachment as the mighty warrior who had laughed without the least regard for his own life and yielded not an inch when the superior might of his enemies were unleashed on him, blanch ever so slightly with the first real hint of fear. As a brahmacharin for whom celibacy had become second nature, he simply could not find it in him to comprehend why a perfectly sane man would throw away everything, including his life, for a woman who did not even love him back or do her duty to her husband by bearing him at least one son. Narada felt smugly superior at that moment, for he had mastered his senses and was immune to the charms of females everywhere who could drive a man to distraction and send the unwary hurtling to their deaths.

Having completed his brief rumination on men who allowed their male organs to rule over good sense, Narada was ready to resume the conversation but Shambara spoke first, 'Do not talk to me in bloody riddles... Are you saying that Maya's life is in danger? Make no mistake; I'll personally raze the Three Worlds to the ground before I allow Krishna's demon spawn to harm her in any way or even think of forcing himself upon her!'

'Such agitation does not behove you, Shambara! As if a son of Krishna would ever harm a woman or feel the need to use force to have his way with her! The very idea is laughable. Pradyumna, for that is the name of Lord Krishna's son, wouldn't dream of hurting her, for your earlier assertion that he was born for the express purpose of ridding the world of you was somewhat incorrect. Killing you would not be at the top of his priorities for all he seeks is to be reunited with his better half and the great love of his life, whom he had lost in another birth. Their love for each other was legendary but sadly for them, what they had was so special that one too many people envied the sacred bond they shared and cast a baleful net fraught with malevolence over their heads, which even their love could not withstand. So it came to be that the lovers were cruelly separated with only the slightest hope of reunion.

In a former life, Pradyumna was the God of Desire, also known as Kamadeva, and Rati was his consort. When he sought to help the Gods get rid of Soorapadman by exerting his powers over the great ascetic God and foolishly attempting to hasten the union of Shiva and Parvati, he was punished and burnt to ashes when the Destroyer opened his third eye and allowed his divine fury to consume him. Rati was heartbroken. A lesser woman would have been driven to madness by despair and the hopelessness of the situation, for Shiva's actions cannot be undone and the Gods were already referring to the deceased Kama as Ananga or the bodiless one. Why, his powers had already been scattered among his preferred implements! But Rati refused to give up hope of Kama's resuscitation, and by great self-denial, sheer tenacity and unmatched devotion she lodged a successful appeal with Shiva and earned his favour and high regard. The three-eyed God promised her that Kama would be reborn as Krishna's son and they would be reunited...'

Shambara laughed loudly at that and took his time to bring his mirth under control. 'It is good to know that my would-be-killer is the wielder of a sugarcane bow and flower-tipped arrows, renowned in the Three Worlds for being the prettiest in Indra's harem. I suppose he will lure me into the arms of some whore afflicted with an unmentionable disease and who will have her way with me, before leaving me to die in my own excreta, drooling like an imbecile, with my genitals in the final stages of decay. It is hardly the death I would have chosen for myself but I suppose there are worse ways to go!'

Narada abandoned his beatific smile then for a more solemn mien—as befitted the bearer of the worst of tidings, 'Since you are determined to persist with your tom-foolery, I will stop trying to obfuscate the facts and lay them bare for you to sample... Earlier, you were worried that Pradyumna would force himself on your wife, and I replied that there will be no need for Krishna's son to resort to such extreme measures to have his way with women—and this is particularly true of your wife, the enchanting Mayawati...' The sage would have elaborated but was interrupted by a heavy golden goblet soaring scarily close to his head and smashing into the wall behind him. A drop of blood red wine trickled gently down the contours of his forehead before plunging into his ear. If dignity had allowed it, Narada would have immediately probed into the depths of his ear with his index finger—but he had mastered all senses and simply waited for the tickling sensation to subside. All the while he continued to lend his other ear to his host who was letting loose a stream of invective about the dubious morality of his mother. If he had been allowed to get a word in edgewise, Narada would have been happy to set the record straight and inform him about his true origin as a mind born son of Brahma, but he doubted Shambara would care for particulars.

'...don't you stand there looking at me as if I am the one who farted and stank up the room. I have half a mind to take a leaf out of Indra's book and kill you, despite the fact that you are unarmed and a Brahmin. How dare you slander my wife and liken her to be the whore your own mother undoubtedly was? I demand an apology or you will be crying for the bitch that birthed you before I am done with you!'

'Stop it, Shambara! I certainly did not cast aspersions on Mayawati's character. You should have just waited for me to finish before throwing things at my head and testing my great forbearance, for any other prickly Brahmin would have cursed you into oblivion by now. I was merely trying to tell you that your wife is not your wife at all. She always has and always will belong, body, mind and soul, to another. Rati immolated herself to join her beloved in the world of mortals and was reborn as Mayawati. Kama and Rati discovered each other on the day they came into being and not even death can do them part.

Don't interrupt me Shambara...and don't bother insulting the mother I never had. It is offensive to women everywhere when they are attacked over their offspring's numerous real and imagined wrongs. You know that I am speaking the truth about Mayawati's true origins. Think about it and the blindness you seek refuge in will be dispelled and your eyes will grow accustomed to the naked truth.

Using your position as her king, you were the one who forced himself on a girl whose heart has never belonged to you. It was you who chose to ignore the truth reflected in her eyes when they searched endlessly for that which had been taken away from her. Did you not sense the yearning in her soul which cries out in memory of its twin? What about the distance she keeps forcing between the two of you which you have been unable to bridge despite your use of brute force? Why did you refuse to acknowledge the simple fact that she does not love you, never has and never ever will because Kama, in whatever form, is the only man for her? By persisting in your obstinate stupidity you have brought your own ruin upon yourself.

The Gods may not be overly thrilled with lovers who lavish all their feelings on each other (instead of offering it to the Supreme Being) but they like those who get in the way of true love even less! If you knew what is best for yourself, you will walk away from Mayawati now...' The sage paused in his harangue when he caught the expression on the demon king's face and sighed with displeasure, as if Shambara had proved himself intractable and was refusing to respond on cue to the buttons being pushed.

'Don't play me for a fool, sage! The most loathsome aspect of this conversation is your elaborate pretence that you want to do the best thing by me and spare me the death which supposedly lies in the cherubic hands of Krishna's son—who, in turn, is allegedly some namby-pamby God reborn. I would have respected you more and paid a little bit more heed to your words if you had been upfront from the beginning. All you want is for me to try and kill the son of Krishna, so as to transform myself into a villain worth killing. Of course, I'll fail and the brat will have good cause to hunt me down and kill me.

You have made your move and unfortunately for you, I have seen right through your pathetic little ploy despite my so-called inferior intellect. Now why don't you go cry on Krishna's lap and encourage him to conjure up more evil plots that masquerade as 'universal truths' or some such jazz? I am half inclined to follow in the footsteps of the mighty God of Thunder, Indra, and kill a Brahmin.'

Narada bowed deeply before deigning to reply, 'I will pray for you Shambara and your soul. Convey my sincerest regards to Rati, won't you, and tell her to follow her heart always, for it will lead her to that which she has fought so long and hard to recover!' And with those parting words, he vanished from sight, and the second goblet of wine that Shambara flung at his head, missed its mark by a mile.

Shambara swore to himself that he was going to pretend that the accursed sage had never visited him in his life and their conversation had never actually taken place, till the self-deception became an actual fact. Despite his laudable resolve he found himself unable to stop thinking about Narada's damnable utterances. He tried not to imagine his wife with another man—albeit in another life—but he could not stop his treacherous mind from conjuring up images of Maya with a stranger who was a dead ringer for Krishna, engaged in a series of acts that could only be described as pornographic. His diseased mind would induce in him a rage that he found almost impossible to control.

The Asura king tried drinking himself into a stupor, but the booze gave a visceral edge to the erotic images of his wife, that was even more disturbing. He could not shake the dreaded thought that Narada was right about everything. Even though he had sensed that Maya had been concerned for him when Narada had asked to be left alone with the king, she had not bothered to visit him since then. He tried to remember a single instance when she had ever come to him of her own accord instead of merely answering his summons, and he came up short.

Not for the first time, he pondered over the fact that she seemed happiest when away from his presence. Her eyes would light up over umpteen trivial things but never over him. She could become intensely animated in that strange way of hers over a new dance step she had learned or over a piece of music that had sent her into a tizzy. A pigeon roasted to perfection or a 'sinfully delicious dessert' as she put it could make her positively orgasmic, but as for Shambara himself, she reacted with a mixture of fear, unease, guilt—perhaps sometimes with genuine affection, but never love. The anger subsided slowly, leaving a pall of dense depression in its wake. Like a blind man, he made his way to Maya's chambers, hoping for the comfort of her embrace and the slightest semblance of reassurance.

Maya was not alone. She was having a meal with a few ladies whom he recognized as the ones she found less intolerable than the others and they were twittering away and giggling in the way only women can, even though they could barely stand each other. When they noticed their king, the cackling dried up, and sensing his black mood with unerring instinct, they hastily paid their respects and departed. Maya was not happy to see them go and she had no wish to abandon the chef's confection as it seemed. 'Your sense of timing is impeccable as always. It is just too bad that you always expect me to put my life on hold and give you my undivided attention as though you have a monopoly over me or something. And if you are horny, you certainly picked the wrong time of the month for a booty call...' He realized he had picked up her plate with its pink cake and ooze of cream and smashed it against the wall, only the second after he had done it.

Maya's eyes had gone wide with shock and a touch of temper. 'What is wrong with you? Get out! I want you to leave!' she said. His skull pounded with the force of the blood that was rushing to his head, drowning out all reason and leaving only the sound of her voice that was shrilly demanding that he leave her. Shambara kicked her to the ground and did not stop kicking the woman he loved, who was curled up in the foetal position to brace herself from the impact of his feet, till he became cognizant of the fact that she was a couple more kicks away from certain death. He left her then but he could not block out her sobs which sounded less like evidence of pain than of supreme loathing.

It had been six days since the birth of Krishna's son and Narada's ill-omened entry into his life. In the darkest hours of the night, Shambara stole into Maya's bed and cuddled her to his chest. She pulled back even in slumber but he held her close and her feeble resistance vanished. He kissed her forehead gently and told her he was sorry. When Maya woke up a few moments later, there was no one in the room and there was no sign of anyone having been in her bed save the telltale moisture that had dampened her cheek and woken her up. She realized that this was Shambara's idea of an apology and muttering angrily that he could go burn in hell, she tried to go back to sleep, though it would elude her that night.

By then, Shambara was far away. He had decided to fly to Dwaraka, the fabled city that Krishna had dredged up from the sea, just to have a look at the baby who had been born to take his wife away from him. The enchanted city was supposed to be impregnable but Shambara had no trouble breaching the security and making his way towards Krishna's palace. He could not explain it, but he seemed to know exactly where to go, and within seconds he was flying through an open window and peering into a cradle of gold that shone with splendour even at that hour. A beautiful woman slumbered peacefully on a bed close to the crib, and Shambara wondered to himself how he could have thought of her as beautiful when it was far too dark to make out her features. He reasoned that all mothers who truly cared for their little ones were beautiful. Similarly there was nothing in the Three Worlds as ugly as the mother who preyed on her own young ones, he continued his inner monologue.

The pampered infant sleeping within, needless to say, outshone his extravagant bedding arrangements in splendour. Its flawless beauty, adorable curls and heart-warming smile melting the nonexistent heart of the black-hearted villain who had stolen into his chamber with murder in his heart...or so the thrice damned poets will sing, Shambara thought to himself, suppressing the urge to laugh loudly.

The hero-to-be looked no different than other babies. He was a shrivelled thing and looked like a miniature version of the wizened, ancient beggars who squatted outside grand temples with their saggy balls, scraggly remains of hair, and creased skin. In fact, a monkey could have birthed him and nobody would have been wiser. Shambara suppressed the urge to laugh, yet again. The baby was awake and Shambara willed him to cry, thereby forcing his hand and prompting him to smash his would-be-killer's skull against his fancy gold cradle. But the baby did not cry and merely sucked on his comforter, hoping for a midnight drink. Shambara crooked his index finger and held it against the corner of the lad's mouth. With surprising speed, the little ruffian wrapped his lips around it and began to suck with gusto. Shambara's heart contracted then with surprising warmth and this feeling which spread all the way to his toes decided him. If Shambara himself could feel this way about the ugly baby, he dared not imagine how Maya would respond.

Not allowing himself room to think, Shambara scooped up the infant and flew out the window, which had conveniently been left open for him. He had no idea how long he flew or how far, and he wondered why he had not dashed his killer's brains out and altered the course of his destiny then and there. It seemed unimportant at the time and not worth dwelling upon. Shambara simply wanted the baby to be somewhere where he would not have to endure looking at the infant's hideous visage.

The Asura king flew on, till he heard the sound of waves. Looking down he saw nothing but an inky-black expanse of water. It looked beautiful in the moonlight and Indra's poets would no doubt work themselves into conniptions of excitement attempting to describe its fatal beauty. Shambara had been holding Krishna's son tightly, but he may have been mistaken for one moment, the creature was nuzzling against his chest in the vain hope of discovering a milk engorged nipple and in the next moment he had wriggled away from his embrace and dropped like a stone into the milky depths that awaited him below.

Shambara half-expected to see the wonder baby swim for shore, but there was no sign of any such miraculous escape. It all felt strangely anti-climactic, he mused, as he flew back in the general direction of his own kingdom, uncaring that the tears ran unchecked down his hoary cheek.

The Estrangement and
the Reunion

For the longest time, after the mysterious nocturnal disappearance of Krishna and Rukmini's seven-day-old son, Pradyumna, the details of this tragedy were all people could talk about in the Three Worlds. The Yadavas were distraught and the entire kingdom was plunged into deep mourning. They treated the heartbroken Rukmini's loss as their own and the soldiers, as well as every able-bodied man and woman who had volunteered to somehow unearth his whereabouts, scoured their own land as well as neighbouring kingdoms trying to ferret out his location. The nonexistent trail left them heartsick and weary, but still they searched, refusing to give up. The Gods were flooded with prayers to repatriate their beloved prince whom they had grown to love as much as their beloved Krishna, but their prayers went unanswered. Their efforts were utterly and inexplicably to no avail, and finally, having learned nothing more than when they had started out with, the searchers returned to the kingdom to deal with the tragedy.

It defied the laws of logic that a scion of the noble Yadu clan could simply vanish from a heavily guarded palace in the impregnable fortress city that was Dwaraka. Krishna had raised the city (which was said to be ninety-six miles long) from the bottom of the sea and transferred his people from Mathura to this magic safehold with his yogic powers, to keep them safe from the mighty

Emperor Jarasandha. The ruler of Magadha had a personal axe to grind with Krishna who had killed Kamsa and left his darling daughters, Asti and Prapti widowed. Seventeen times, Jarasandha declared war on the Yadavas and seventeen times, his army was annihilated to the last man and only the Emperor himself left standing by Krishna, for reasons best known to him.

The stubborn monarch returned for the eighteenth time but on this occasion, the Yadus also had to deal with Kalayavana, one of the most fearsome warriors of the age. Unwilling to sacrifice a single one of his beloved subjects to either of the predators who circled them relentlessly, Krishna had conjured up Dwaraka to protect his people and take them out of Jarasandha's grasp forever, leaving him free to deal with the threat posed by his enemies.

The Yadus told and retold this story to each other, feeling that their city had somehow let them down by failing to protect their prince. It was unbearable that cruel fate had outsmarted Krishna and deprived him of the son who had been gifted to him by Shiva himself. The God who walked among men, and his wife Rukmini, had gone long years without the blessing of children.

Rukmini, believed to be the incarnation of Vishnu's consort, Lakshmi, never complained for she had always believed that with Krishna by her side she would never ever have cause to be anything but happy. It was this that had prompted the hitherto docile and obedient princess to chuck caution out the window and follow her heart. Even as a child, she had decided that she would marry none but him. Her brother, Rukmi, a protégé of Jarasandha, shared the emperor's dislike for Krishna and had arranged her marriage to Shishupala, Jarasandha's nephew, aka the Bull of Chedi.

Rukmini overheard the conversation between Rukmi and her parents as they discussed her marriage and was angered that they wished her to wed someone whom she found thoroughly repellent. The 'Rutting Bull' of Chedi, as Rukmini referred to him, was a coarse and fleshy man with permanently bloodshot eyes indicative of his excessive fondness for drink and other nocturnal activities that were generally frowned upon. He sweated freely, had chunky arms—with thick curling hair that could easily be worn as braids—and owned a pair of man boobs that rested comfortably against his bulging belly.

The excessive personal details about his corpulent person had been forced on her by Shishupala himself. He had a wicked case of frotteurism, and never missed an opportunity to rub his grotesque self against her. Having no wish to spend the rest of her life with a man who made her vomit, Rukmini defied her parents and brother by liaising with her family priest and urging him to carry an epistle she had penned for Krishna—in which she had poured out her feelings and begged him to carry her away and wed her. Gallant as ever, Krishna had come for her and fought off her brother's as well as the emperor's men to carry her away. In the deliriously happy years that followed, Rukmini had never had any reason to regret her decision since Krishna was everything she had dreamed he would be and so much more. If there was the tiniest cloud in her existence, it was her unfulfilled desire to bear Krishna's children.

Sensing the profound longing in her heart, in that way of his where he seemed to know everything about everything, Krishna took his mount Garuda to Shiva's abode and beseeched him on their behalf. The three-eyed God graciously answered their prayers and blessed them with a son. Rukmini had fallen in love then, for only the second time in her life, with the baby who looked so much like Krishna and who, unlike her husband, would belong solely to her—till he became a man and took a wife.

While it was true that Rukmini had never actually resented Krishna's other women (she refused to think of them as his wives)—for she was an inordinately confident woman, secure in the knowledge of her Lord's love—she would have been lying if she had said that it did not bother her in the least that Satyabhama, Jambavati, Mitravinda, Kalinda, Nagnajiti, Bhadra, Lakshana and every one of the 16,000 women who had formerly belonged to Narahasura's harem walked around with the exact same smug expression as herself, sanguine in the belief that Krishna loved them best of all. Rukmini assured herself that her conviction was the only one that was warranted, since the facts spoke for themselves. She was his first wife and unlike the others she had the most romantic back story, which would be told, retold and kept alive long after they were both gone. As for women like the haughty Satyabama—who insisted on accompanying him when he went off to make war with Narahasura in the kingdom of Pragjyotishapura, or demanded the Parijatha flowers that had been gifted to Rukmini by none other than Indra—they were certainly not worth putting into song.

Despite her commendable high-mindedness in the matter, Pradyumna's birth had made Rukmini realize that she was not overly fond of sharing the men in her life, even if she had kept this well under wraps in her relationship with Krishna. She adored having a piece of Krishna all to herself and she could not bear to be parted from him for even a second. It was why she had insisted on doing every little thing for her child even though there were more than enough people on hand for the task. She fed him, burped him, massaged him, bathed him, powdered him, changed his diapers and loved every aspect of her new job. The queen had also made it a habit to sleep next to the baby, so that she may tend to him at all times.

She had heard a lot of mothers complain about how nobody had warned them regarding the harsh realities of caring for a baby. That there was nothing magical about a baby's poop or upchuck; that the odour had a life of its own and could attach itself to you and send your husband rushing headlong into the arms of the first woman to cross his path. Thankfully, it had not been too bad with her own son.

The new mother in fact loved his baby smell and discovered

that even his poop did not smell too bad! Tickled to think that her baby was a cut above the other babies, she said as much to an ancient ayah who had probably been present at the birthing of every prince since the beginning of their line. The old woman had smiled her grotesque toothless grin at her and informed her that her baby's excreta did not smell too bad since his diet consisted solely of breast milk, and she would love to see if the queen insisted on performing diaper duties herself once he started consuming solids and began ejecting them in copious bursts of noxiousness. Rukmini had suggested that she take a month-long vacation, and the ancient had shuffled out muttering something about how all mothers were alike be they queens or pigs when it came to thinking that their sons were the best and smelled the rosiest.

On that terrible day, when Pradyumna was discovered missing, Rukmini woke up screaming at first light from a troubled sleep which had been plagued with nightmares. She had been naked and running in stark terror across a road paved with shards of broken glass that tore her feet into bloody ribbons. Her little one was still cradled against her breasts and was slippery to the touch. Yet Rukmini held him tightly, as she continued to run in her nightmare. Suddenly, she could run no more for her feet were gone and nothing but shapeless stumps remained where they ought to have been. To her horror, she was completely immobile, unable to get away from the darkness that was approaching them. She hugged him close to her, to keep him safe for as long as she could. But he was no longer in her arms and she opened her mouth to scream for help, that would not be forthcoming.

Rukmini was balanced precariously on the stone ledge of a building with the wind mauling her, tearing at her hair and clothes, screaming murder in her ears, threatening to force her off her feet and send her hurtling to the death that waited impatiently below. She gritted her teeth and defied it, trying to clamber up to the roof. Finally, her hands found purchase and attempted to haul the rest of her body which had grown heavy. As she hung suspended, with the wind fighting her every inch of the way, her eyes alighted on Krishna who stood on the edge of the roof, a little distance from her. He did not hear her cries for help for he was busy tossing her baby high into the air and scooping him out of the abyss, moments before he seemed fated to disappear into it. She screamed for him to stop but he was unaware of her presence and he continued to play his game. On and on they played, while Rukmini's arms grew increasingly tired. Krishna seemed to be tiring too, though usually he could go on forever. But weary he had become, and he simply dropped the child over the side of the roof, just as the wind prevailed over Rukmini and dragged her down to the depths below.

The vicious cycle of nightmares went on and on, and Rukmini cried in her sleep wanting nothing more than to awaken—but she couldn't. The maids heard her cry out and they rushed to her side. They added their screams to hers when they found Pradyumna missing from his golden crib. Rukmini rushed to Krishna promising herself that he would allow no harm to come to their son and he would rescue him from whatever evil had befallen the prince and return him to his mother. Her husband held her close to his chest and soothed her. In his arms she searched for solace but for the first time in their married life, there was none to be found. Krishna's infinite calm from which she had often drawn sustenance was galling to her on this occasion. When he counselled her to be patient, she knew that he was trying to imbue her being with his own strength, but it was not enough. She fled from him before he could see the disappointment and anger in her eyes.

It was believed that Rukmini would not be able to survive the bereavement of her son—for such pain was too much for a mortal to bear—and the Yadus believed that Krishna would somehow bring back his son, to save her life. After all, he had wrought great miracles when he was but a baby himself. The people recalled how he had killed Putana, saved them from the terrible serpent, Kaliya, held up Mount Govardhana on his little finger, and overthrown Kamsa after prevailing over his murderous wrestlers. Surely, they reasoned, it would not be beyond him to find his own son and bring him back to life. For rumour had it that the evil Shambara had stolen the sleeping child and tossed him into the sea. The moon God, Soma, had borne witness to this crime against the Gods and humanity and somehow everyone in the Three Worlds had become privy to this bit of divine gossip.

Days rolled into months and much to the bewilderment of the Yadus, the precious baby did not make a miraculous comeback into the world of the living and Krishna seemed perfectly content to let the matter rest. It had been expected that he would summon Garuda and fly off to do battle with Shambara and make him answer for his sins—not unlike the manner in which he had vanquished Narahasura. But that did not happen either. Gradually, through a series of such anti-climactic moments, the Yadus began to feel a tad ill-disposed towards Krishna; they were looking to him for answers which he seemed unwilling to provide.

Things came to a head one fateful day, when Balarama, Krishna's half-brother and the reincarnation of Sesha, Vishnu's faithful serpent, picked up a plate of food that had been served him in the royal banquet hall and flung it to the ground in a fury of impotent frustration. He turned to his infuriating brother, who continued eating as if he had not a care in the world and addressed him hotly, 'We cannot let this matter rest. I will not be able to rest unless I have avenged the dear boy whom we all loved so much and who was taken away from us by that cowardly son of a bitch, Shambara. What amazes me is that you have not lifted a finger to find him, or bring his killer to justice... You have not even comforted Rukmini, who is dying even as we speak. Hardly any food or water has passed her lips since she has lost her son and you insist on seeking refuge in denial, pretending that nothing of note has happened in our lives, and everything is exactly as it should be!'

'Everything is exactly as it should be, Balarama...' Krishna replied serenely. Balarama banged his fist on the table. He was relieved to note that his younger brother had at least stopped eating, or he would have lost control, picked up the offending utensil and smashed it over his head. The prevalent mood, ever since the disappearance of the little prince, had been one of unbearable grief and abject despair; but Balarama's little imbroglio with Krishna saw a subtle shift of mood, and there was definite hostility, and more than a little anger in the air. The aged monarch, Ugrasena and Krishna's father, Vasudeva, were distracted from their own sadness out of concern for Krishna, but he himself seemed unperturbed.

'We have to do something! I refuse to let Shambara get away with the murder of our prince. I will know no peace until I have bludgeoned his worthless skull with my plough and our men have destroyed his armies and burned his kingdom to the ground. Who is with me?' Balarama roared at the gathered chieftains. With the sole exception of Satyaki, Krishna's dear friend, they all rose to their feet, crying out their approval for Balarama's plan of action.

King Ugrasena spoke up then in a voice that quavered with age but had lost none of its dignity, 'The Yadavas have always obeyed me, their king, and I know that you will all continue to do so. It is my belief that Krishna does nothing without the best of reasons and even though I am as confounded and unhappy about this situation as the rest of you, it is my wish that you all do nothing if that is what he feels is our best course of action. He has never led us astray and we owe him our continued respect, loyalty and faith. I am sure that there is not a man among you who will deny that he has earned it. Moreover, I feel you all need a gentle reminder that great though our loss is, Krishna's loss is even greater. Don't forget that Pradyumna is his firstborn and Shiva's boon to him. The gifts of the Destroyer cannot be taken away that easily—not even by the Destroyer himself. So if he counsels patience, I second it!' Vasudeva and Satyaki and most of the dignitaries gathered applauded his words. Balarama remained standing, however.

'I have more faith in Krishna than the rest of you put together and I will kill the man who says otherwise. Krishna knows this better than any of you!' Balarama's voice cracked with strong emotion as he continued, 'All I want are some answers that I can live with. What has happened to the little prince Krishna? Why won't you set our fears at rest? What will happen to the blameless Rukmini? Is our boy dead, Krishna? Are we to...'

'My son is not dead!' Rukmini had just stepped into the hall. All present turned to gape at her, for she had not left Pradyumna's room since he had been lost. She was dressed simply, in clothes that were too big for her, as she had withered away to a near skeletal frame. But she was dry-eyed as she made her way towards Krishna, who in turn rose and went to meet her halfway. Before all those gathered, she fell at her husband's feet and begged his forgiveness.

Even as Krishna tried to raise her to his feet, she spoke in a voice that rang with the strength of her newly discovered faith, 'Pradyumna is not dead! He cannot be... He is Krishna's son, the gift of Shiva and the child of a prophecy. My baby boy was born to achieve greatness and he will. At this moment, he is simply following his father's footsteps. You will all remember how Krishna himself as a baby was carried by Lord Vasudeva from Mathura to Vrindavan to save him from the evil Kamsa. The river Yamuna parted to offer him safe passage. His mother, Devaki, wept for long years but Krishna was returned to her and the people of Mathura. The odious Shambara may have taken my baby away from me. But he will be returned to us in good time. I know all of this because I know it to be the truth and I am more certain of it than everything else in my life, including Krishna.

It was wrong of me to doubt my husband and you are all

making the same mistake. If he says everything is as it should be, then everything is as it should be. Pradyumna has been taken from us so that he can fulfil his destiny and he will come back to me and to all of us when he has done what he was born to do. In the meantime, let us wait for him in patience and pray for his success and cry no more... Why should we waste our tears? It is Shambara and his people who should be wailing. For, my son will make them pay for the sorrow he has caused all of us!'

Thunderous applause burst out at the conclusion of Rukmini's little speech and even Ugrasena was on his feet clapping his hands to convey his approbation over her words. Krishna hugged his wife to his chest. Balarama engulfed the couple who were the reincarnation of Vishnu and Lakshmi in a bear hug and nearly lifted them off their feet. He then bodily carried Rukmini to the table and filling a plate, he personally began feeding her and insisted that she eat till her stomach was fit to bursting. It was only when she had been fed to his satisfaction, did he stand up again to address the gathering, 'We are the mighty Yadavas, of the lunar dynasty, and the direct descendents of Brahma himself! Krishna belongs to our race and will always be there for us. We can ask for no more! Shambara, the despicable coward, was so terrified of a scion of our race, that he believed his best chance of prevailing against a Yadava hero was to try and murder him while he was still a defenceless baby. For shame! Shambara is the most accursed creature in all of creation and I spit on his name. One day, he will have to answer for his heinous sin and on that day his life will be forfeit at the hands of Pradyumna, who proved too much for him even as a baby and SURVIVED!'

Balarama's roar was taken up by a thousand voices and as the sound reached a towering crescendo, Rukmini felt the final dregs of her grief slipping away—even as rage rushed into the vacuum. At that moment, she abhorred the Asura king with a supreme passion that bordered on madness. He had robbed her of her one dear son and she wanted him to pay a terrible price for it. She wanted him to know pain; she wanted him to be robbed of something that was similarly precious to him. She wanted him to die—a terrible, humiliating, excruciating death that was entirely bereft of glory. As she allowed her hatred and fury to engulf her, unwittingly, her hands clenched Krishna's. She turned and looked into his eyes, and to her surprise she saw her feelings mirrored there. Krishna had suffered as much as she had, if not more, she noted with amazement and now, even her anger paled in comparison to his. With satisfaction, she realized that Shambara was indeed a cursed man, in addition to being a dead one.

Meanwhile, the object of their combined derision and universal scorn was safely back in his kingdom. His subjects rallied behind him loyally and the general consensus was that he had been well within his rights to forcibly remove a threat that had endangered him. After all, you can't point out a man's killer to him and expect him to bounce said killer on his knee. In fact, Krishna himself had justified the killing of his uncle Kamsa, by saying that since the dawn of time the wise men had decreed that it was morally justified, to kill one man if he threatens the welfare of the family; one family, if it threatens the welfare of the village; one village, if it threatens the welfare of the kingdom, and the very kingdom if the immortal soul is imperilled. Shambara represented their kingdom, was in fact, their kingdom and by this same logic it made sense that he kill the child who threatened his as well as the kingdom's welfare.

Having successfully convoluted the laws of Dharma to appease their collective conscience, the followers of Shambara returned to their routines, doing their best to ignore the apprehension that lingered. Killing babies was one thing but everyone tacitly understood that killing Krishna's firstborn was entirely different. After all, he had proved his superiority in the art of killing even when he was but an infant himself; and with the monstrous mount,

Garuda, as well as his wheel of destruction, the Sudharshana chakra, he was perfectly capable of turning their own kingdom into a vast rubbish heap. But such unpalatable thoughts were impossible to live with and were best forgotten in the interests of their mental peace.

Shambara's wife Mayawati, however, took an entirely different view of the matter. At first, she refused to believe that Shambara had just upped and flown out of the kingdom in the dead of the night, made his way into Dwaraka, simply picked up the prince while Rukmini slept next to him and dumped him into the sea. It sounded ridiculous and it was annoying that everyone in the Three Worlds seemed to be buying it—as if in addition to stealing the baby, Shambara had robbed them of their wits as well. The whole thing had the makings of yet another infamous plot by the Devas to undermine an Asura king and vilify him.

Maya was all too familiar with the many shortcomings in her husband's character—his penchant for violence, stubbornness, his impatience and tyrannical behaviour when the world and its inhabitants refused to kowtow to his every whim. There had been several singularly ugly fights when he had simply struck her and walked away. At such points she had often fantasized about killing him...so great was her anger and hatred for him in those moments. But even as she had lain sprawled on the floor, clutching a bruised cheek or limb, feeling for blood or assessing the extent to which an injured body part had swelled, she had inexplicably never doubted that deep down he was as decent and principled a husband and ruler as one could find. The Shambara she knew may be a brute and a pig but it was not in him to kill a baby.

Having exonerated her husband in her mind, Maya eagerly waited for him to visit so that they could discuss this latest ploy on the part of the Devas to discredit their race. To her surprise, Shambara did not show up at her chambers—even when she had taken the trouble to have her ladies-in-waiting drape her sari most alluringly, in the manner that he found completely irresistible.

This was highly unusual, since he could never bear to be parted from her for long. And yet a full month had passed since their last ill-fated encounter when he had interrupted her at dinner with her friends. Usually, he would come to her after a beating, pretending that nothing had happened and listen with half an ear to her lecture on the divine retribution that awaited the moral deviants who hit their wives. He would then murmur a miserable excuse for an apology, refuse to take accountability for his actions (saying instead that she had provoked him)— and just when she was getting worked up again, would calm her down with a hug, promise never to hurt her ever again and pamper her with an indecently ostentatious piece of jewellery. But this time around, he did none of those things.

Initially, Maya was flummoxed at this unprecedented behaviour. Later, however, her bewilderment was replaced with anger and to her horror, hurt. 'All men are nothing but giant pricks...' she fumed to herself, for, outwardly, she continued to maintain a façade of not caring whether Shambara came to her or not. 'How dare that moron swear that I am the only one he has ever loved and then run off into the arms of the first bitch who would sleep with him! I do hope he returns to me so that I can ignore him and tell him to bugger off!'

Just when Maya thought that Shambara had forgotten all about her and that she would have to endure a lifetime of snide remarks from her enemies who were already overjoyed by her predicament, the king of the Asuras came to her bearing gifts that were his most wildly extravagant yet. Maya was genuinely happy to see him and she hugged him on an impulse. Shambara hugged her back fiercely and to her surprise he seemed wildly relieved as though the weight of the entire world had been lifted off his shoulders. She pulled back a little and punched him lightly on the arm, 'I thought you were busy with some nymphomaniac or the other and could not be bothered to visit the one you claim is your true love.' She then hastened to add, 'Not that I am complaining.'

'You are jealous! Why, this is the first time you have been insecure about me! Usually, you are always volunteering to buy me women so that, in your words, I can bother them as much as I like and leave you alone. But you have missed me! I realized it when you swooned as soon as I walked in and sensed it in that lusty embrace you gave me, a few moments ago. Let me assure you, my tender-hearted one, that knowing how my absence hurts you, I won't do it again.'

Maya went red with embarrassment and outrage, 'Aren't you the pompous ass, your highness! Don't flatter yourself! I only missed all the presents that you had become increasingly lackadaisical about sending...' Anxious to change the topic, Maya rambled on, 'So how about those rumours, huh? Isn't it something the way everybody seems to believe that you kidnapped Krishna's son, bashed his brains out with a rock, and tossed his remains into the sea! The gossipy old crows in Indra's court have outdone themselves this time. I am surprised they forgot to mention how you raped the mother of the child even as your hands were still wet with his blood. I thought that little touch would have made you an even more abhorrent symbol of iniquity!'

Shambara's smile vanished and he turned away from her, 'I did not bash his brains out with a rock! The notion that I would rape his mother is monstrous! Even my shadow did not touch her and that is the truth. Why would you even say such a thing?'

'Surely you can tell that I was only making a joke? Granted that it was in bad taste, but it is hardly any reason for you to get your underwear in a bunch! I was merely telling you about the outlandish gossip that has been doing the rounds, because I was sure your sycophantic courtiers would never have the guts to tell you.

As I was saying, people can talk about nothing but the disappearance of Krishna's baby and your alleged role in it. Apparently, Soma saw you drop the baby into the sea. They are saying that Narada told you about that tired old prophecy which we all have known about for donkey's years now, with the result that you worked yourself up into a state of frothy fear and took off like a quintessential Asura to murder the little baby. My theory is that Indra himself spirited away the child with Krishna's consent to make you look bad! I am sure they will bring him out of wherever they have hidden him and brazenly declare that they had simply done all this to protect him from your murderous intentions.

Maya stopped talking then, partly because her hilarious quips did not seem to be going down well with her husband, and partly because, she could have sworn that Shambara was getting increasingly agitated—and in her experience that was almost always a precursor to a beating. How she could tell this by gazing upon his expressionless back she could not explain, even though she knew it for a fact. When it was clear that she was not going to get roughed up, Maya expected to feel a sense of relief; but instead, a cold dread grew inside her, as the truth suddenly hit her.

'You said that you did not bash in his little head and that you did not rape his mother. But those were merely the embellishments I threw in!' said Maya. 'You did not deny kidnapping and drowning him. Please look at me and tell me that you did not go out and kill a baby? You can't do that, can you? Is this because Narada somehow managed to get to you, the way he did to Kamsa, and made a monster out of you? I had a bad feeling from the start about his visit...

I realize now that it is my ill-fortune to be married to an abomination who murders babies, but I simply cannot comprehend why it is so. Once, you told me that you were unafraid of death, that you will meet the child of the prophecy with a sword in hand after he has grown a pair. I was proud of you that day. What happened to your fine words? What could have possibly made you forget yourself and go after a baby who has no defence against the mighty Shambara?

Explain it to me... Help me understand, before the revulsion I feel for you overwhelms me—before it makes me cock a snook at that bloody prophecy and kill you myself.'

'Don't you dare talk to me like that woman!' Shambara snarled at her. As always, since he was unused to anyone hitting him with such derisive contempt directly to his face, he bristled up and buried his conscience under his aggression and massive ego, refusing to consider the possibility that he might just be in the wrong, preferring to pretend that the blame for such egregious conduct on his part could not rightfully be laid at his own door. He had always used this defence mechanism when she confronted him for hitting her, and if she had not been so frustrated with him she would have been amused that he resorted to this even after being accused of killing a baby. 'I am your king and have the right to your respect. And you will treat me with the respect that you owe me for I have earned it. There is absolutely no need for me to justify my actions to you, questionable though they may seem to a stupid bitch like you. Suffice it to say, that it had to be done and I did it. And I would do it again, if I had to. He had to die. He just had to!'

The fury in his voice and the madness in his eyes ought to have terrified her, but she felt her own long dormant rage surge to meet his, 'You can call me every execrable name you can think of...but remember, the term has not yet been invented to describe someone as despicable as you. Calling you a son of a bitch would be apropos because no woman could ever give birth to you! The true dishonour must lie with a female of the canine species. The she hyena, which was no doubt the only creature in the Three Worlds that could have lain with your father to produce you, should have gobbled you up at birth instead of inficting you on us! Your actions will result in the name of the Asuras being blackened forever. You have betrayed your people, especially those who have been associated with you and come to care for you.

And don't you talk to me of respect! How dare you expect it from me? You pretend to be a great warrior of unmatched courage, but in reality you probably hid in the baggage train while your armies did all the grunt work and coasted from victory to victory on the strength of your minions' arms. You have some nerve staking claim to respect given that you freely assault women and children—while turning tail and fleeing from anyone your own size.

This is not the first time that I have wanted you dead. Every time you left me battered and blubbering like a pathetic fool, I would pray for your death with every fibre of my being. It would be my dearest wish in those moments for your heart to stop beating, for you to be set upon by deadly assassins and murdered, for you to be mauled by wild animals that would gore you to death while you were out hunting. I even hoped fervently for the prophecy to be fulfilled so that you would die and I would finally be rid of you. But if at that time my heartfelt wishes had been granted, I would have felt terrible grief and sorrow—for despite everything, it was my belief that you were essentially good and decent.

All that has changed now and I really want you dead. If there is justice in the world, you deserve the most painful and excruciating death there is. The sight of your dead body will bring me great joy and the inhabitants of the Three Worlds will celebrate the demise of the wickedest and vilest organism that has ever been created. Take my word for it, that day will come soon for your capacity for wrongdoing is matched only by your abysmal stupidity. Your victim was Krishna's firstborn and as you know, he does not suffer murderers gladly. Hopefully, he will come up with a punishment that fits the crime and I will be there to see you get your comeuppance.'

Shambara would have hit her when she had gotten started on his origins, but he had simply watched her mesmerized as she railed against him. He had never seen her this angry before and he was transfixed by it. It was only when she began prattling about his impending destruction that he roused himself once again, 'What kind of wife would want her husband dead? You ungrateful little bitch! I dragged you out of the gutters and the brothels where you were headed. Your father had nothing to his name and was planning on fobbing you off to the first beggar who was willing to take you. I rescued you from that fate, and since then I have spared no effort to make you happy. Nobody knows the great lengths I have gone to for your sake, the unspeakable things I have done, the magnitude of the sacrifice I have made. But it was never enough for you. Nothing I did was ever good enough, for your greed would not let you settle for anyone, even a king. There is no satisfying a parasite like you, for you insist on sucking the life out of a man while giving nothing back.

You knew that I wanted children but you disregarded your wifely duties and opted to wallow in your barrenness instead! I forgave you for that as well, but now you want me dead...It was a mistake on my part to love a stone-hearted bitch like you, who would choose widowhood over the longevity of the man who loved her truly!'

'Of course, I could not even consider having your children...' Maya replied sweetly, 'if it had been a boy, you would have listened to the first moron who warned you that he was a threat to your throne, and drowned him! Finally, don't you dare say that I gave nothing back to you, when you've given me so much to fondly remember you by!' At the conclusion of her speech, Maya removed her thaali, mangalsutra, of solid gold and flung it at his head.

Her vicious gesture had the intended effect. He lunged for her and grabbed the throat, he so loved to kiss, in a chokehold. As her feet struggled to find purchase on empty air, Maya was fighting to stay conscious. Yet she managed to choke out two words, 'Kill me!' Shambara loosened his fingers with a start, almost as if he had no idea how they had got there in the first place and Maya fell to the floor. 'You should have killed me. It would have been the smart thing to do, because somehow, someway, I am going to find a way to kill you!'

Shambara recoiled from her hatred of him. His enemies had hurled deadlier things at him on the battlefield and he had not flinched. But with Maya, he had neither the defences nor the strength to take the worst beating of his life. As he walked slowly to the doorway, the fight drained out of him. He turned back for just another look at his wife but his vision was blurred, 'Apparently, I am unable to deny you anything, even now. You will have your wish soon enough. Death is not too far off for me and when it does claim me, despite everything you said, you will be sorry I am gone!' And just like that, he walked out of her life.

Maya became something of a pariah after that, especially when the news of their almighty altercation got out. Apparently it was unforgiveable of her to condemn the killing of week-old babies, since the perpetrator of the crime was none other than her king and husband. She had also flouted the code of conduct governing wifehood, since it behoved a wife to love her husband unconditionally—even if he were to suddenly announce his decision to devote his life towards hunting and killing babies. Her actions in the matter were construed to be the equivalent of sleeping with the enemy, and she was reviled for it. The general outpouring of hostility made life hard for Maya, but fortunately, it was not unbearable. Shambara had always made it clear that while he had every right to ill-treat his wife, he would brook no incivility to her from others. Many had paid the price for their bad judgement in this matter and nobody was willing to push him.

Those were difficult times for Maya and she had never felt more alone. Even her mother would have been a comfort—though Maya knew for certain that she would have ruptured a spleen over the fact that her daughter had thrown away her exalted position out of a misplaced sense of morality. After all, what good has that ever done anybody? But both her parents had passed away in quick succession, so there was no help forthcoming from there. In fact, the only good thing about her situation was that she did not see too much of Shambara and there was comfort to be had in her newfound solitude. She kept herself busy and waited for her purpose in life to be revealed.

There was no way she could have known it at the time, but it was out of this marital strife that Maya found the perfect happiness she had always searched for. It was Narada of all people who presented it to her on a golden platter. He had sneaked into her room, on a day Maya would never forget, holding a heavily wrapped object in one hand and his veena in the other.

Under the circumstances, Maya felt it was perfectly alright to dispense with civility, 'What are you doing here, old man? Have the fates sent their humble servant to inveigle me into doing something dastardly in the interest of the greater good? What is it you have been asked to bamboozle me into doing? You have already made my husband offer proof (as if any were needed) that he is the stupidest creature in all of creation, by talking him into drowning Krishna and Rukmini's son. Even as we speak, the bereaved parents are probably hard at work churning out kids by the thousands to avenge their loss and soon we'll have the Yadu forces at our doorstep. I shall hate to be around for that bloodbath which is sure to be our due, thanks to Shambara's monumental folly and your infernal meddling.

What is it you would have me do? Am I expected to take out Rukmini with a meat-cleaver before she gives birth to anymore divinely anointed Asura killers? Or would you prefer me to fornicate with a donkey, so that the masses can be suitably shocked by the sexual peccadilloes of the queen of the Asuras?'

Narada smiled serenely at her and placed his palm on her head as though she had placed her palms together in salutation instead of just verbally attacking him. He deposited his bundle gingerly on her divan and sat down beside her on her favourite settee, before wriggling his backside to make sure it was satisfactorily ensconced. It was only only then that he was ready to address himself to Maya, who had been watching him open-mouthed, 'It is too bad you were not paying attention when your mother schooled you on the social graces. If it were not for your complete lack of manners, you would have been a perfect specimen of womanhood! But I am not here to discuss decorum, as you have rightfully surmised. It is my honour to request your assistance in a matter that is of paramount importance to the Three Worlds. I can also assure you that it does not involve copulation with beasts of burden.'

'I am so grateful!' Maya retorted dryly, 'However, surely you realize that you are in no position to demand favours of me after what you did to Shambara? Out of the goodness of my heart, however, I will consider it, if you tell me what it was that you told Shambara that made him do what he did.'

'Come now! Surely you won't insist that I tell you all my secrets just so that I can cajole a favour from you which in actuality is a favour I am actually doing you? Be that as if may, I will answer your question out of the goodness of my own heart—I told Shambara the truth and nothing but the truth, and he made of it what he did and acted in the way he did to his own detriment, if not your own.

When I went to meet Shambara, he received me with even greater hostility than you are displaying right now—although in all fairness, even if he may have been justified in treating me the way he did, you certainly aren't. It is unfair of you to blame me for what Shambara did. One would think that I borrowed Garuda from Lord Vishnu and drove him at beak point to Dwaraka and forced him to rip Pradyumna from Rukmini's breast and consign him to a watery grave. In another life the two of us were very good friends and whether you realize it or not, I still am and always will be one to you.'

'That is good to know. And it was lovely of you to oblige me by explaining so clearly the exact reasons for Shambara's madness that prompted him to murder a baby. It all makes perfect sense to me now. Thank you very much for that.

Despite what you said earlier, I am not lacking entirely in manners. Allow me to apologize for my rudeness. And you are right, Shambara should have known better. I cannot think of a single thing that you could have possibly said that would even come close to justifying what he did. However, for your part, you cannot blame me for being suspicious about your intentions, especially since we both know that it was you who nudged him ever so gently to take the dark path that he had avoided, despite his natural inclinations all his life. With one fell stroke he has erased everything noble he had once stood for. He will for evermore be remembered as one of the sickest creeps in the history of the world. But I suppose what is done is done and there is no rewriting the past or gainsaying you. Now please let me know how I may assist you so that I can reject you and we can both get on with our lives.'

'Oh! You will not be rejecting me, of that I am sure. I come bearing a gift that you will treasure forever. In fact, I can hardly wait for you to see it. Before that, however, I would like to convey my approbation for the way you stood up to Shambara and refused to support him in his evil ways. It has come to my attention that you reprimanded Shambara most strongly for his insupportable conduct in abducting a baby and dumping him into the sea. So great was your condemnation that you apparently accused him of being a coward, born to a hyena, and who deserved the death he had coming to him. In response, your husband almost killed you, but then mercifully, got a hold of himself and walked out—resulting in your current estrangement.

Believe it or not, Shambara's monumental folly, which you rightly inferred me to have brought about, is the best thing that could have happened to you...and you can roll your eyes all you want, for aside from making you look positively demented, it establishes little else. As I was saying, as far as you are concerned, this rift is a blessing since it allows you to play a vital part towards ensuring that good triumphs over evil. You have been chosen to redress a great wrong and to restore balance in a world that has been teetering on the brink of complete destruction, ever since the toadies of darkness gained the upper hand...'

'Toadies of darkness? Did you know that you have the worst case of verbal diarrhoea that I have ever known?' Maya told him, though not unkindly, 'You claim that the thing you want of me is of earth-shattering importance, but if are going to be this voluble, the world will end long before you get to the point.' She was inclined to laugh a little but suddenly became distracted when the little bundle on the divan moved. With an effort, she tore her gaze away and turned to Narada who was watching her eagerly.

'He is not dead, is he?' Maya whispered. 'I should have known that Krishna's son cannot die so easily. The child of the prophecy has survived! In fact, I should have figured it out the second you came in holding what looked like your own dirty laundry. How is this even possible?'

'Of course the dear boy survived!' Narada laughed! 'And he is the reason I am here. It has fallen to you to take Krishna's son into your care and keep him safe from harm. More specifically, it will be your job to make sure that Shambara does not find out his true identity till the time is right. If you can protect him till he grows to manhood, the great favour you would have done for the Gods and man will be repaid many times over and you will reap the benefits in this life and more importantly in the afterlife as well! What say you?'

'But I do not understand...if he is alive it means Shambara could not have killed him. Maybe I wronged him after all. Is this the result of your scheming? You could have easily taken him away and laid the blame at Shambara's door.'

'Shambara did kidnap Pradyumna, make no mistake about

that,' said Narada. 'Yes, it was hugely heart-warming of him not to emulate Kamsa and dash the baby's brains out—but that does not mean he tossed him into the sea thinking it was a cushy little waterbed. He knew full well what he was doing; for despite his dim intelligence, even he knew that a newborn baby couldn't swim to shore. Shambara's intent to cold-bloodedly murder the baby seems painfully obvious to me, and in your heart, you are aware that I speak the truth for you *did* see murder in his eyes, did you not?

You made excuses for him when he assaulted you as if you were a lowly cur, and not the love of his life—as he proclaimed. It is time for you to open your eyes to the incontrovertible fact that he is a killer who needs to be put down before he can do even more harm. Which is why, I cannot stress enough the importance of concealing Pradyumna's true identity from Shambara. In fact, I must insist upon it. If he were to discover the baby he tried so hard to kill, is in his beloved wife's arms, nothing could possibly assuage his rage, save your combined deaths. If such a thing were to happen to Krishna's son, he will destroy this very world in his anger and grief and not even Shiva will be able to stop him.'

Maya had tears in her eyes when she replied, 'How is it you know things of which I have spoken to no one? It is terrifying and humiliating at the same time and I must beg you to say no more of Shambara and myself. Let us simply talk about Pradyumna, whom you brought into my life. I wept for this baby after discovering what Shambara had done. It gives me great happiness to know that he lives and that, it is to me that the responsibility of caring for him has been assigned. No harm will ever come to him, while there is life left to me. I accept the charge you have given me and I am grateful to you for it.'

Even as she spoke, Maya had been inching closer and closer to the baby, wonderment writ large on her features, suffusing them with a glow that rivalled the lustre of the sun—till she finally got within sight of the baby. The latter had, meanwhile, wriggled out of his makeshift bedding, looking around expectantly for someone to attend to him. He seemed to like Maya, for he gurgled merrily and smiled his toothless smile at her. Narada noted with contentment that she was lost at that moment. She gasped a little, because he had literally taken her breath away, and she lifted him and held him gently in her arms, terrified that Narada or somebody else would take him away from her. Nothing in the world could have prepared her for the sudden onslaught of powerful emotions that flooded her being and she was shaken to the core, yet happier than she had ever been in her life.

Narada handed her a sparkling feeding bottle made entirely of precious stones, and soon the young prince was contentedly sipping from it, well-satisfied with the comfort of her lap. As she rocked him gently on her lap, Narada told her about the feeding bottle: 'Vishwakarma made it for him, especially at the request of the Goddess Lakshmi, who in her mercy, understood the grief that is ravaging Rukmini and wanted to do something special for her lost child. Needless to say, it is a special bottle that will never run out of milk as long as Pradyumna needs it. Kamadhenu, the cow of plenty, has blessed it with her bounty. And don't worry, to the naked eye, it will look like he is sucking on a nondescript toy.'

Maya had been a little embarrassed with her unabashed display of mawkish sentiment, given that the sage had an unnerving way of stripping her very soul naked and laying it bare, and now she spoke with all the flippancy she could muster, 'I love it! I was worried that you were going to say that a fallow breast is not a full breast or something and burden me with the so-called gift of lactation. This way is so much better since I won't have to suffer the evil that is cracked nipples or hire a mulch cow for him. Please convey my heartfelt gratitude to the Goddess and the divine architect. My manners are improving wouldn't you say?' Without waiting for his reply, Maya rushed on: 'I am beside myself with curiosity. Do tell me how he managed to escape from the sea, for after all, as you said, he could not possibly have swum to shore, and clearly he did not track you down of his own accord so that you may deliver him to me.'

Narada shrugged elegantly, 'Is it really important? Why is it that you people are forever on an impossible quest to unravel the mysterious workings of the universe? Perhaps a fish swallowed him and he was discovered in its belly when a fisherman trapped him and slit open its belly. Or, if you find that story a little hard to swallow, we can always say that Varuna, the reigning deity of the water bodies and one of the guardians of the universe, kept him safe and handed him over to me. If you are inclined to be fanciful, we could swear that a fantastical sea monster, possessed of none of the vulpine instincts of Shambara, plucked him out of the depths with a tentacle and catapulted him to the heavens—just as I happened to be passing by. It does not matter. What matters is that he came to my possession and I have brought him over to you as it was the will of the Gods—which I personally ascertained when I presented him to Lord Vishnu and his consort. All the Gods flocked to Vaikunta to feast their eyes on this precious child and to bestow upon him their blessings. It was the general consensus that he is even more winsome than Krishna was at the age and all agreed that he was born to accomplish mighty things.'

'Yes, indeed!' Maya exclaimed. 'He is going to be amazing. Ordinarily, babies are more than a little boring but somehow this one is different. You will probably laugh at me for being overly fanciful but I feel a deep connection with this little kid. He has only just come into my life and already it feels as though I have known him forever and I don't want to be parted from him even for a second.'

'I don't think you are being fanciful at all. It is normal for new mothers to feel as you do and in your case...' Narada trailed.

'I have never been and I never will be a mother. Children have a horrible tendency to suck out your very life essence like the little parasites they are and leave nothing but a wrinkled horrid shell. In keeping with my beliefs, I have chosen not to become a mother.'

Narada responded: 'The wise have often declared that a woman is bound by duty and her sex to be fruitful and bring forth children. In fact, Svetaketu, the great sage, pronounced that a woman who refused to bear children would be incurring a very grave sin. Nobody said it is easy to be a mother. Every time a woman gives life to a child, she herself dies a little and is revived only if God be willing. It is a tremendous sacrifice to bring new life into the world and raise it to adulthood. Which is why a mother is deserving of so much respect and it is something all women should aspire to.'

'I respectfully disagree! Don't get me wrong. Good mothers are entitled to all the admiration and appreciation in the Three Worlds, but I genuinely believe that not everybody has what it takes to be a good mother. And bad mothers are the equivalent of some in the animal kingdom who feed on their young. Those are the criminal offenders and I think one would do better not to be a mother if one does not have the aptitude or inclination for it. It is simply silly to give in to societal pressure and transform oneself into a brood mare, even though one is extremely unsuitable for such a pursuit.

As for that garbage about those who choose not to have children incurring grave sin, surely it must have been spewed forth by some bloody male who had precious little chance of getting laid, and wanted to lure some desperate woman with fading looks and a ticking body clock, into his bed. And you are hardly one to talk about the merits of motherhood, as you have opted to steer clear of the householder's way of life. You have ingeniously avoided the cares of nagging wives, wailing brats and demanding mistresses, trading it in for a chance to gambol around the Three Worlds to your heart's content and to be in the thick of action wherever it unfolds. Don't even bother telling me that the laws governing mortals don't apply to you—Shiva and Vishnu themselves have taken wives, so why must you alone be exempt? Not that I am censuring you, it is perfectly understandable that you have chosen this way of life. Personally, sometimes I dream of running away from here and seeing the Three Worlds all by myself so that I may discover the secrets that underlie the mystical workings of the universe. However, I have been caged all my life and at this time, it is highly unlikely that I'll know enough to flee from the cage even if the door is thrown open to me.

Getting back to the procreation issue, I am doing the world a favour by refusing to breed. If all the men and women in the world make it their life's business to pop out their brats by the dozen, the world will soon be overrun and there will be no resources left. People will turn to cannibalism for sustenance! Mother Earth will be devastated by the horror of it all and then the Gods will unleash cataclysmic calamities in the form of floods, earthquakes, and plagues to deplete the population. But it will not be enough. Wars will be fought and more people will die, be they good, bad or ugly. Even that will not be enough and what then? I don't even want to think about it. Right now you all favour indiscriminate procreation to ensure the survival of the species but soon there will be laws formulated and endless propaganda to stop people from creating more people. Like I said, it is in the best interests of the world for me not to have more children.'

'It gladdens my heart to be in the presence of a great visionary who will go to such lengths to justify her somewhat selfish tendencies,' said Narada. 'But given your professed dislike for children how come you are willing to take in this one?'

'There are many reasons. I owe it to him because Shambara is responsible for his plight. He seems like a good kid. We get along just fine. He drank his milk, burped and went right back to sleep. I have maids who will take care of him when he gets really disgusting and soothe him if he were to have a crying fit. Like you said, he is even more winsome than Krishna and it will be diverting for me to have him around. When he gets to be that age when boys are naughty, destructive and downright maddening, I'll pack him off to Sukracharya's Gurukula and nobody will dare to go after a ward of the great Sukra. And he will be released only when he reaches manhood, by which time he will be ready to take on Shambara. Finally, he is not like the other kids because he is mine. And don't say I sound like a mother because the greatest thing about this situation is that I get to be a mother without actually being a mother and that is the only way to be a mother in my opinion.'

'And to think that I was accused of having verbal diarrhoea! I approve of your plan; Sukracharya with his yogic vision will not stand in the way of fate and will definitely accept him as his pupil. Be that as it may, I am happy that you have accepted the charge and now it is time for us to part as friends. If you have need of me, you won't even have to call for me, for I will be there of my own accord.'

'You are a friend,' said Maya, placing Pradyumna on her settee, arranging her cushions around him in a protective circle, before falling down at Narada's feet to seek his blessings in an impetuous gesture of reverence. Narada smiled in satisfaction and was grateful that she had finally come around to his way of thinking. He blessed her and made ready to leave. As he walked away he congratulated himself for his unparalleled ability to carry out even the most notoriously difficult assignments handed to him by the treacherous whim of fate.

Maya watched Narada depart before she curled up next to the baby. Her mind was whirling at impossible speeds, and the enormity of the task handed her, struck home. There were a lot of things to be taken care of—arrangements had to be made for the baby and a cover story had to be conjured up accounting for his presence in her life. Maya ran a finger down the baby's soft cheek, and wondered why she was not panicking or pulling out large chunks of her own hair. The answer was simple, her exhilaration kept the fear, anxiety, panic and baby phobia at bay. It was inexplicable how she, who had always gone to such great lengths to avoid the little critters, could experience such delirious happiness with the entry of one into her life. It was most irrational of her, but somehow she knew that life was going to be incredible with him. The thought made her so happy that she began to weep, but silently, so as not to awaken the baby which had become her life.

The Mother and the Lover

*I*t is exceedingly rare, given the fact that life has the well-deserved reputation for being a bitch, but there are occasions when the universe seems perfectly attuned to your innermost desires and everything seems to fall into place in a harmony of synchronization. Suddenly, the world stops stinking to the high heavens and is magically transformed into a canvas of beauty with no unsightly blemishes; an abundance of bright sun, cool breezes, pretty rainbows, prettier butterflies, waterfalls galore and the tinkling sound of merriment everywhere becomes the way of life. In short, Maya was delighted that her life no longer sucked.

One of her loyal maids, who had been ready to serve all the way to her last breath, died conveniently and suddenly on Maya. No doubt it was a lamentable occurrence, but the timing could not have been better. Everyone believed that the poor woman had died of a broken heart, but only after completing the operose three-day labour of delivering her boy which had been born to her of a faithless lover, who ran back to his wife soon after. Word was that Maya had adopted the maid's bastard since Shambara had grown tired of her charms, as a result of which her life had become as empty as her recalcitrant uterus. Maya herself never confirmed or refuted this story, saying simply that she was meant to have the baby. The more mean-spirited souls tended to suggest that perhaps Maya herself had had him on the wrong side of the marital bed, but nobody paid much attention to this version—not because it was entirely lacking in proof but because discussions of this nature pertaining to the queen resulted in severed heads.

A welcome offshoot of the adoption was that suddenly, everybody was inclined to be kinder to the new mother. It had been easy to hate her when she held the top spot in their king's heart and had him catering to her every demand, even though she was failing steadfastly in the duties of a wife by being stubbornly barren. But now that Shambara was giving her a wide berth and she was cutting a sorry figure for having decided to raise the bastard child, Maya had become very likeable indeed.

The more uptight ladies of the royal household had found her endlessly alarming. It was bad enough that she was not establishing her proficiency in the birthing bed, but she did not even have the grace to be devastated about it. Ideally, she ought to have wept her eyes out, sought them out for advice on how best to get knocked up, and performed excruciating penances so that she may be blessed with the gift of babies. But Maya had done none of those things and seemed perfectly content to continue in a state of shocking childlessness. One may even be forgiven for thinking that her exertions on the marital bed were solely for her own pleasure!

However, that was all water under the bridge. Clearly, she had been putting on an act all this while, even though her heart had been bleeding all along over her wretched incapability. Now that she had somehow contrived to enter the ranks of motherhood, thereby signing up for its special joys and torments—the wrinkles, the thickening waistline, the hairfall—Maya had insinuated herself into their midst. More importantly, her bastard had the same chance of sitting on Shambara's throne as did the contents of their chamber pots—considering the army of legitimate sons and blood relatives in line—which meant that nobody minded her lavishing excessive affection on the boy.

As for the lad himself, who was called Munna, the ladies had to admit that he was exceedingly beautiful and a constant delight to them all. He was a resplendent child, blessed with the complexion of the rare blue lotus and the most charming of features. His hair was curly and soft, while his eyes were so huge and beautiful that they could melt a stone. But his most notable feature was his sunny disposition. In all of the kingdom or even the Three Worlds, a happier, more content child could not be found. Everybody fought for the privilege of feeding him, holding him, cuddling him, playing with him, or presenting him with toys, while Maya preened with pride as if he were her own son.

Munna was sitting up when the other babies his age were just turning over, running, when they had learned to crawl and talking when they had just mastered the art of gurgling, cooing, grunting and growling. And he grew better looking by the day. Most importantly, he had the ability to give joy to so many without actually doing anything particularly noteworthy. As Munna grew older he proved himself to be a natural leader and something of a rapscallion. He was forever getting into scrapes with his band of ruffians and getting away with murder only because he had been blessed with more than his fair share of good looks and charm.

Like his biological father, Munna loved dairy products and his particular favourite was seem paal. It was a delicacy prepared from a cow's first milk. What made it special was that it was produced only for the first two weeks after the calf was delivered, thicker than regular milk and more yellowish. The dairy hands would collect this milk carefully and hand it over to the king's head chef, who would then mix it with jaggery (an unrefined brown sugar made from pine sap), whole milk, and a touch of crushed cardamom—before pouring it into moulds and steam cooking it till it achieved the consistency of a flan. The preparation would be allowed to cool and then, this simple dish would truly be a dessert fit for a king.

Munna could never have enough of it. He would assign his band of boys to reconnoitre the stables closely and gather intelligence about the cows, especially those in the advanced stages of pregnancy. And no sooner had the calf been birthed, than the gaggle of pint-sized spies would pass on the intelligence to their counterparts posted near the kitchens, so that they would remain vigilant while the chef put the finishing touches on the yummy treat. Munna himself would lead the stealth operations to secure the seem paal, and these covert operations were carried out with so much finesse and speed that almost always they were accomplished without a hitch—much to the annoyance of the head chef, who would then complain to Maya.

Maya would soothe him and pay him some recompense for his trouble, before summoning Munna to tender an apology. The latter would explain that he had done nothing wrong since the cows were all his friends and they had given him permission to help himself to all the milk he wanted. At that the victim of the purloined paal would grow increasingly red and rush forward to spank the young ruffian across his rascally buttocks—but Munna would stop him in his tracks with a prettily worded speech about how anyone would find irresistible whatever this culinary genius put on the plate! The genuine admiration would make the chef sputter a little with embarrassed gratification, following which he would lead the boy to the kitchen to sample more of his gourmet fare.

Though everybody loved him and vied for his affections, Munna loved best the beautiful lady who had taken him under her wing and who was like a mother to him. Maya hated being addressed as 'mommy', 'amma', 'aunt', 'big sis' and the other warm epithets of filial relations, and hence had insisted that Munna call her simply 'Maya'. Even though his admirers were numerous, he himself always turned to Maya—whether he wanted some tender loving care for a bruised knee, an audience for when he recounted his day's adventures, or simply to sit in companionable silence. Maya loved these moments with Munna because of the special feeling of closeness it gave her, and felt herself to be the luckiest person in the Three Worlds.

They could spend hours making up stories for each other's amusement, singing songs, racing each other in the garden, or playing their silly games. Maya would pack food for them and they would spend the day fishing in one of the streams that could be found on the palace grounds before making an ashy meal over a campfire, both swearing it was the best fish they had ever had. Other days they would go trekking or on picnics.Munna would make her necklaces from flowers or pebbles and she would wear it for days on end. This was their alone time and nobody was allowed to intrude. Maya cherished every one of those precious moments with Munna carefully, savouring the feeling of pure joy she felt when they were together. His presence in her life completed her and made her so happy that she was positively terrified.

The thought of losing Munna could keep her up nights and the panic would leave her paralyzed. It had been that way ever since he had been given to her as a baby. She had loved the feeling of his warm body next to hers and they would sleep together on her bed. The nurses had harrumphed in disapproval at this and told her horror stories about babies who had been accidentally smothered to death by their heavy mothers. Maya had tried putting him to sleep in his crib, but Munna would grow restless and she would give in, letting him sleep next to her and staying up herself so that she did not crush him.

Cooking had never been her forte, but she had insisted on preparing his meals herself and feeding him personally. The nightmare-inducing nurses had been full of anecdotal information about how babies could die from consuming food that hadn't been prepared under sanitary conditions, or if a particularly big morsel got lodged in the windpipe. Apparently toddlers could drown in half-filled buckets of water, under a horse's hoofs, or from a fall. They could even die in their sleep for no discernible reason.It seemed impossible that there were so many ways for a child to die. Maya failed to understand how a child could possibly make it to adulthood without the help of a miracle.

From being an agnostic, she suddenly rediscovered her faith and would spend her sleepless nights praying to Shiva and Vishnu to keep Munna safe. It was oddly comforting and she could have sworn that both of them were actually listening to her and keeping an eye on Munna. For he was so healthy that the nurses said it was positively indecent. He was not one to take to his bed with a runny nose or a temperature when there was a whole world out there awaiting his pleasure. Maya would thank the Gods, shush the nurses and quietly ward off the evil eye from Munna by taking some camphor in her hand and circling her clenched fist all over him, three times before burning it outside. If a younger version of herself had seen her get up to all these shenanigans over a kid, she would have laughed herself silly.

Maya could not trust anybody else with Munna and so she did it all herself. She was the most vigilant and hands-on-mother in the kingdom and—unlike the others—the cares of motherhood left her curiously unmarked and she seemed to have magically rediscovered her youth and beauty. Since she had not actually been through the rigours of a pregnancy and delivery, her youthful figure remained intact and she became even slimmer through the act of running around a hyperactive boy all day. She had also escaped the sordid curse that were stretch marks and much to the irritation of the other women her age, her belly was as smooth and beautiful as ever while theirs looked as though they had been savaged by wild animals. Her breasts had defied gravity and age, both having lost none of their elasticity or shape. Worst of all, though she made absolutely no effort, she looked far more beautiful than she had as a blushing bride (though her charms had been formidable enough to land herself a king even then).

The harridans of the harem noted her devotion to the baby with mixed feelings and said that it was a classic case of overcompensation.

As for her blossoming beauty they held her entirely responsible for the lapse. They swore that she had no business looking so damned good when her husband had shunned her. It was simply disgraceful, they agreed, how amazing she looked. Maya herself was so lost in Munna that she had mostly forgotten about herself. She was content that everybody loved him and more importantly, that he loved her back exactly the same way she did.

Even Shambara did not hate him entirely, though admittedly he came close enough. Maya may have made it clear that she wished to have nothing more to do with him, but Shambara would still drop in to see her once in a while, which was still far too often for Maya's liking. He just wanted to make sure that she was doing alright, he told himself, and not because he missed her. Moreover, he was curious about her new hobby or whatever the hell it was that had prompted her to raise someone else's grave mistake. When he espied Munna, playing on her bed, the Asura king was a little nettled. He was appalled at himself, but he found himself resenting the little man who had so unceremoniously usurped his position in Maya's life and he wound up addressing the tyke a little more gruffly than he had intended, 'And who might you be?'

Munna leaped to the ground and took his time appraising him, before replying with courtly dignity: 'My name is Munna. You must be the king. I can't say you look like a king because I have never seen one before and you don't look that different from the other Asuras, just a lot older. As for your question, I have no idea who my real parents are but that is exciting because I can make up new stories everyday about my origins.

Sometimes, I am the child of a valiant Asura lord and a beautiful Deva princess or vice versa and sometimes, I am a maid's bastard or the twenty-second kid of a poor fisherman and his flower-seller wife who were unable to feed an extra mouth with yet another on the way, but today I am the product of a forbidden union between an Apsara and a Kshatriya king. Or perhaps, I am Maya's gift from the Gods—or she is my gift from the Gods. I live with Maya now and she is my everything. When I grow big, it is my intention to marry her and take her away with me so that we can explore the Three Worlds together.'

The child pointed to Maya as he made this lofty declaration and Shambara turned to look at her as she walked in. He drew in his breath sharply and heard his heart pounding like an adolescent boy who was having his first awakening to the charms of women. After all these years, she could still make him feel that way. To his irritation, he saw that Maya could not entirely mask her pleasure at those words and her husband half wished that this Munna person had been an illicit lover in bed with his wife, so that he could kill him without further ado and usher him out of her life.

With an effort he shoved the unworthy thoughts out of his head before addressing himself to his wife's adopted son, 'I am her husband and her king. Why would she leave me and marry a runt such as you and a bastard at that?'

'It is simple...' came the grave answer, 'She likes me more than you.' Shambara could have said a lot of things at the time about up jumped bastards or given in to rash impulse and belted him one, but Maya intervened smoothly and sent Munna from their presence. The imp fled to the kitchens pausing only to give Shambara his most fierce look, and as he sped along the winding pathway, he signalled for his usual suspects to join him since he had already decided to consume every dish in the royal household, so as to leave nothing but gruel for the king's dinner.

'I hope all is well with you my Lord,' Maya intoned politely.

'All is well, dear wife! It is most kind of you to enquire about my well-being,' Shambara replied in the same tone, although it sounded deliberately affected to Maya's ear, 'I just wanted to make sure that a brahmarakshasa has not taken possession of you and robbed you of your wits for it has come to my attention that you, who to the best of my knowledge has always been something of a baby-hater, has suddenly discovered the full strength of hitherto dormant maternal instincts and is lavishing them all on a bastard whose origins remain mysterious.

It was curiosity that prompted me to pay a visit and see with mine own eyes the heart-warming sight of you playing at being a mother—especially since I tried so hard to get you to do the same for us and you repulsed my every effort.'

'If you are here to beat me up for it, I suggest you leave at once and return to the pox-addled whore you were lying with before coming here. Her stink is all over you and I don't want you polluting the pleasant atmosphere here!' Maya had meant to be dignified and proper but her hackles were up in response to his rising anger and she could not resist a few jabs at her husband.

'I am not sure whether you are acting jealous or defensive although I am inclined to believe it is a little of both. It is funny you should get in a snit over the fact that I enjoy the company of women who don't loathe the sight of me. Don't you think you are being a tad selfish—not to mention unreasonable? After all, it was you who spurned me... I know you wanted me dead, but did you also want me to be absolutely miserable and spend my days pining for you, so that my enemies may laugh at how big a fool in love I was?'

'Frankly, I don't give a damn about what you get up to, provided you just leave me alone. You are free to enjoy the company of all the ladies of the night you want. Why are you even here? Do you really want to know why I am playing at being a mother like you called it? Well, it is because unlike some who find succour in the arms of prostitutes, after cruelly kidnapping and drowning babies, I have a conscience and did not want to stand by and let another infant die if it could be helped. Hopefully, I have satisfied your curiosity!' Maya finished defiantly, and met his gaze squarely even as it bored holes into her, refusing to swallow the lump that was lodged in her throat.

'Of course! You are trying to make amends for your husband's sins the way a good wife should', said Shambara. As if there was ever any doubt! It gladdens my heart no end to see you mothering a child who must be the same age as the one I supposedly murdered! They tell me that you are a good little mother and the bastard is quite the loveable and remarkable creature with his fine array of talents, leadership qualities and a marked taste for what by rights ought to belong solely on my plate. I am sure you will do a fine job with him and he will be a credit to you in future. Perhaps he will even make up for every disappointment you have ever had with the males in your life and give you the happiness they could not. Whichever way it goes, I wish you well and contrary to what you think, I have always wanted you to be happy and I will never wish otherwise for you.

Now I am afraid, it is time for me to bid you farewell, Maya. I have a kingdom to run and you have a bastard to keep safe from the vagaries and vicissitudes of cruel fate. Now, why don't you kiss your husband goodbye?' Without waiting for her acquiescence, he pressed his lips to her mouth—which was as cold as death—and he was gone.

Maya stood rooted to the spot for a long time before her legs gave out and she collapsed on to a chair nearest to her. There she remained, trying to gauge exactly how much he knew and if his sagacity was real or imagined on her part. Maya was still trembling—when the warmest hands, smelling of paal payasam, wrapped themselves around her shoulder and a little body pressed up against her, causing her anxiety to melt away. 'I did not like him at all!' piped up the little imp, 'What were you thinking when you married him? He is ugly and has red piggy eyes! And I bet he is mean...why else would he make you so upset? But don't worry about him, I have just the thing to help you get the taste of him out of your mouth.'

Munna then showed her the booty he had won from his latest

raid. It was a grubby dish containing the paal paayasam that had been prepared for Shambara's dinner. He fed it to Maya with his hands and explained its particular merits, while slurping some of it himself. 'Did you know? The chef lets the boiled rice, milk and sugar simmer for hoooooours with the most exotic spices like cardamom and saffron, tossing in some almonds, cashews and raisins as well, till the entire thing just melts in your mouth! It seems almost a pity to eat it because you know that it will be out in your chamber pot by morning.' And when Maya burst out laughing, Munna was well-satisfied with both the paal payasam and himself.

Far too soon for Maya's liking, it was time for Munna to put himself under the tutelage of a guru. The obvious choice was the renowned preceptor of the asuras, Sukra who was respectfully addressed as Sukracharya. The great man was the son of Bhrigu and by all accounts he was a genius whose voracious thirst for knowledge had led to his uncovering of a vast number of universal secrets, in addition to having a complete mastery of science and magic. His was a fiery personality and he had dared to incur the wrath of Shiva by making off with Kubera's wealth. As punishment for his audacity, Shiva had pinned him down with his trident, before raising him to his lips and swallowing him whole. While burning in the fires of his stomach, Sukra had not panicked but merely called to mind the most potent incantations for pleasing the Destroyer and begun reciting them in earnest. Sure enough, Shiva had forgiven him and released him through his penis. This rebirth from the linga enhanced his already formidable powers. He was an extraordinary man with enormous appetites, yet conversely he was also capable of enduring great privations.

Sukra had been with his father, Bhrigu, whilst the latter was fully absorbed in the performance of hardcore tapas. Bored into a state of moral torpor, he had seen the heavenly nymph, Vishvaci, and become enamoured with her. Quickly realizing that pursuing her would be a lot more rewarding than sitting by his father's side for a few dreary centuries, he left his body behind and pursued her all the way to heaven—where he succeeded in wooing and winning her in Indra's sabha.

Conjuring up thick clouds of darkness to conceal them, he had spirited her away to a cosy den where they made love for hundreds of years. Having willingly sacrificed his ascetic merit on the raging flames of his lust, he fell from heaven where he no longer belonged and was reborn on earth which was deemed better suited for the lascivious. Vishvaci was reborn as a lamb and the heat of their passion brought them together again, scarring their souls and condemning them to an endless cycle of rebirths from which Sukra would not have been released at all, had it not been for the timely intervention of his father. Bhrigu, on returning to the world of the living, was shocked to find a desiccated corpse in place of his son. He pulled up Yama, the God of death, for having the gall to take possession of his son's soul. And by threatening to curse him, Bhrigu coerced Yama into giving life back to his son.

Thankful to have been rescued from endless lifetimes enslaved by his baser instincts, Sukra acquired a fresh perspective and stepped into a new role as preceptor of the Asuras. Wishing to do his best by them, he decided to undertake the harshest of penances to win Shiva's favour. He suspended himself upside down with his feet tied up with thorns and his head hanging, inhaling the smoke from constantly burning chaff while performing austerities, to please Shiva. For a thousand years he had remained thus, until Shiva himself appeared before him and released him from his self-imposed bondage. The three-eyed God granted him all the desires of his heart—which included great stores of ascetic merit for having successfully pulled of a feat that none before had even attempted and which none could hope to emulate. In addition to this, he was given the gifts of wisdom, knowledge, and all the precious stones in the Three Worlds. Perhaps the most notable of his acquisitions was the sanjivani craft which was the art of bringing the dead back to life. Shiva himself taught the mantra to him, demonstrating the great esteem he had for Sukra.

Indra had watched the progress made by the preceptor of his sworn enemies with great unease. He realized that he could not possibly send his Apsaras to lure the great Sukra away from his grandiose purpose. Having thought the matter over carefully, he assigned his own daughter, Jayanthi, to the task and not being the worst of fathers, he gave her strict instructions to merely serve the acharya with a pure heart without attempting to seduce him. When the time was right, she was to ask Sukra to marry her and insist he spend ten years with her. Rightly surmising that Sukra would never refuse a maiden such as her, especially after the torments of the flesh he had put himself through, Indra figured that the borrowed time would give him and Brihaspati ample time to undo the effects of the fruits of Sukra's labour in the cause of the Asuras.

Exactly as Indra had anticipated, Sukra could not resist the sweet maiden who had forsaken the privileges that her status as Indra's daughter had given her, in order to devote herself entirely to his needs, which included scraping off dried faecal matter from his suspended body. He acceded to her request and married her, before wrapping Jayanthi and himself in a web of invisibility so that they may enjoy the privacy which was so dear to him and to better devote themselves to each other without the bother of the demands on his time by his clingy disciples. In the interim, Brihaspati presented himself to the Asuras having taken Sukra's form and began his instruction with none of them suspecting the deception.

When Sukra finally returned, having enjoyed a surfeit of carnal pleasures, his disciples were confounded and cleaved to Brihaspati in their confusion, believing him to be their preceptor—with the result that Sukra cursed them by promising them defeat in the great battle against the Devas and a complete loss of their intellect. It was Prahlada, the then king of the Asuras who assuaged Sukra's anger and begged him to take up his role as their guru once again, after the curse had run its due course. Sukra had agreed and returned to them, after his words had come true and the Devas had succeeded in trouncing them in battle. Since then, he had continued in his capacity as their benefactor. He had served many generations of great Asura kings and had been instrumental in bringing about every towering achievement the Asuras could lay claim to.

Maya knew that there was none better suited to undertake the formal education of Munna, and remembering Narada's words, she was confident that Sukra would take him in. Unlike the others, he would surely know the truth about Munna, but Maya was confident that he would not turn him over to Shambara. Narada had told her that the Yadavas were the direct descendents of Yadu, who was the son of the Kshatriya king, Yayati and Devayani, a Brahmin maiden who had been Sukra's beloved daughter and the light of his life. With the gift of his yogic vision, Sukra would surely divine his origin and would love him the better for it. Moreover, according to Narada, someone of his stature would know better than to mess with the workings of fate.

It was the accepted practice for a child to be sent to his guru's ashram between the ages of four and seven, and there he would remain for the duration of twelve years, or till his master was satisfied that his charge was fit to be released into the outside world. The impending separation filled Maya with sorrow, but she knew that it was for the best. She was determined not to become mawkish about the whole thing. Everybody who was anybody in their cloistered world would be watching her reaction closely on the day of Munna's departure and if she so much as shed a tear, they would all clamour and gossip over how she felt the need to show excessive maternal affection since she wasn't *really his mother*.

Munna himself was excited by the idea of studying under Sukra, since the Asuras held him in high esteem and he had heard all the stories. 'I can't wait to ask him if all the stories are true... Do you really think Shiva pissed him out? I wonder if he remembers what it was like to mate with a goat. Some of my friends told me that he may not accept me as his disciple because I am base born but I think he will, don't you?'

'Of course, he will,' replied Maya. 'Sukra has the most brilliant mind in the Three Worlds and he will not be foolish enough to reject you. He will know that he is fortunate to be given the chance to work with someone as wonderful and talented as you.'

'Why can't you come along? You are wonderful and talented as well.'

'Unfortunately, I will not be able to accompany you, Munna. This is a journey you will have to undertake on your own. My thoughts alone will go with you. Finish your education and then return to me. I will always be waiting for you. But you know that already, don't you?'

'Yes, you have told me that many times. And you know that I am going to come back and marry you. Be sure to remind Shambara of that. He did not seem to understand when I told him that the last time we met.'

'I'll remember...' Maya promised and sent him on his way with minimal fanfare. Her seeming lack of emotion on such a poignant occasion set the tongues wagging and her detractors tsked a little, and said that one could not expect the stone-hearted woman, who had spurned her own husband, to fall prey to the child's tender emotions. The criticism, however, was lost on Maya, who was too embroiled in her personal grief. At the time, she wished fervently that she had been born as one of his band of boys. Then she could have been with him in Sukra's ashram and they could have grown up sharing the same experiences together. Maya sighed. It was just too bad that women were expected to spend the better part of their lives waiting for men who may or may not return to them. It was torture, but Munna had promised to come back to her and she could do naught but hold on to what amounted to little more than childish sentiment—since all boys wanted to marry their mothers anyway, and she was the closest he had to one.

Exactly as Maya had anticipated, Sukra was only too happy to accept as a pupil, a scion of the Yadava race, even though he appeared before him as a humble supplicant and a lowly bastard. There was no mistaking the fact that he carried in his veins the blood of his beloved daughter, Devayani, whom he had once loved above all else and for whose sake he had given away the secret of the sanjivani mantra to Brihaspati's scheming son, Kacha. He never had cause to regret taking in Pradyumna—or Munna as he was known then—for he would go on to become one of his most distinguished pupils and bring much pride to Sukra's name.

The simple life in the ashram suited Munna very well indeed. He had liked Sukra from the beginning, as the skinny, dark sage garbed all in white had quite a protuberant belly that clearly indicated that he had a weakness for good food. A long time ago, an excessive consumption of wine had been Sukra's biggest vice and it had done him and his own great harm. He had foresworn all intoxicants since then, but had given himself leave to indulge his prodigious appetite where food was concerned. This was why, unlike any other ashram where the fare was simple and nourishing, Sukra's disciples had plenty of good things to eat.

Munna ate well but it was his thirst for knowledge that demanded constant quenching and Sukra enjoyed moulding his keen mind so that someday it would blossom into something comparable to his own. In addition to the Vedas and Vedangas, Munna was taught arithmetic, astronomy, history, science, warfare and a host of survival skills. Not surprisingly, given the lineage where he had sprang from, Munna turned out to be a natural in the science of arms, and under the expert eye of Sukra, his skills burgeoned considerably, leaving his contemporaries far behind.

Sukra was pleased with the rapid strides Munna made in every aspect of his education. Even though he was superior to the other, more illustrious, students in every possible way, there was never any sign of vanity or arrogance in Munna. He was always willing to help his fellow students grow as proficient as himself. No chore was too mundane for him, and in his company the other boys found even cleaning latrines a fun thing to do. On the surface he was irritatingly perfect, except that it would never reflect on his personality, and he remained as endearing as ever. What with the fabled good looks of the legendary Kamadeva, coupled with the irresistible personality of Krishna, it was no wonder that Munna was as close to the ideal male as one could get.

Munna was soon being singled out for extra lessons, better suited to his remarkable talents, and Sukra began schooling him in the science of illusion. He explained to his young protégé that Shambara was the reigning master in the discipline and he himself had taught it to him. Just as he had expected, Munna applied himself with more than his usual diligence and was determined never to desist from his labours till he heard from Sukra's own lips that he was second to none in that esoteric art. His guru was very pleased with the level of dedication of his pupil who was proving so adept at tuning into the quicksilver movements of the mind, which was by far the most confoundedly complicated entity in all of Brahma's creations. He began tutoring him in Mahamaya, which was the most advanced level of the power of illusion, so that he would be rendered immune to evil spells created from black sorcery as well as other types of enchantments.

Sukra explained to him the importance of stripping away artifice, which came in millions of appealing guises that were designed to beguile, confuse and ultimately seduce a man into forgetting himself, in order to get to the very heart of truth. He demonstrated how deception could be employed to use a man's fears, anxieties and phobias to manipulate him. Munna was told never to take refuge in delusion, even if it held out the delicious promise of pleasure or a surcease from suffering. Over and over he drilled into his student the need to seek out the naked truth in all its bloody glory, even if it meant subjecting oneself to a laceration of the mind, for therein lay the hope for self-discovery. Sukra taught him to welcome the truth into his being, allowing it to hold him in its thorny embrace, permitting it to claw its way inside, scouring out all the falsehoods, thereby cleansing him entirely and leaving him impervious to the assaults of illusion.

Munna made rapid strides into the realms of the mystical with Sukra's guidance. In the process he delved inwards and began the exploration of his own psyche since he had been taught that true understanding began only with an intimate knowledge of the self. It was at this juncture that the going got tough for Munna, and it was up to his guru to help him navigate his way past the notoriously difficult terrain, with gentle humour and infinite compassion, 'I did not think you would have any problems in this regard. After all, you are something of an exhibitionist and seem to have no qualms showing off your physical charms to the ladies who come to bathe in the river. Think of your mind the same way and remember that despite all its blemishes, it is an exquisite thing.'

'At the risk of sounding immodest, it must be said that my mind does not seem to be able to match the perfection of my butt! Sometimes it is wild and tends to get away from me. With a will of its own, it insists on chasing after the impossible.'

'Your mind is far more succulent than your backside and I am not just saying that! It is my belief that the mind would have you accede to your heart's desires instead of shying away from it and soon you will discover that it is by far the wiser course.'

Sukra was careful not to rush his student along the path to self-awareness. Rather, he nudged him along by barring his own heart and soul to the pupil whom he could not help treating as a beloved grandson. Ordinarily, gurus would maintain an aura of mystique in front of their charges and avoid too much intimacy to prevent the appearance of cracks in the foundation of respect that was so integral to the relationship between a teacher and his pupil. Sukra relaxed his guard a little with Munna, on account of their shared blood ties as well as a firm commitment towards ensuring that he triumphed over his enemies and went on to have a glorious future. The duo would go on long walks and take immense pleasure and satisfaction from their shared conversations.

On one such occasion, Sukra laughed out loud when questioned about his famed encounters with Shiva and the lamb, feeling proud that none but the get of his own indomitably spirited daughter, would dare to broach such a topic with him, 'That was such a long time ago! My sensual excesses brought me a great deal of censure, and that pleased me so—for the guardians of morality are usually juiceless creatures who grudge others the pleasure that they themselves cannot have. Wouldn't you agree that it is better to be envied than pitied?

My critics, like the sainted Brihaspati, point out the excesses in my nature to be a huge flaw and hold it out as an example to their pupils on how not to piss away the ascetic merit they have earned. But I myself don't see it that way and am heartily proud of every mistake I have ever made and would certainly have no hesitation about doing them all over again. As far as I am concerned, regret is the poison which destroys the spirit and my disciples are taught never to waste time bemoaning things from the past which they ought to have done differently—when it is so much simpler to extract all that was good about any unfortunate occurrence and leave everything else behind as they amount to nothing more than unnecessary encumbrances that serve no useful purpose but bend the spine before ultimately breaking it if one does not have the good sense to dump it.

I have always found that there is something in the nature of man and beast alike that thrives on danger, even actively seeking out high-risk situations to gratify this primeval instinct. Yet, strangely enough, it is only while dancing with death that one can feel truly alive,, precariously balanced on the knife edge where it is possible to defy one's demise and embrace it concurrently.

I never felt more alive than when I was burning up in Shiva's digestive juices. Just the memory of that level of arousal was sufficient to give me a high that sustained me for thousands of years. As for the lamb, you referred to; I cannot possibly explain it to you. With Vishvaci, I experienced something rare and exquisite and a billion lifetimes were insufficient for us to enjoy each other to either of our satisfaction. The feelings we shared were so powerful, that they chased us across entire lifetimes and subsequent rebirths which is why it made sense at the time to pursue an inter-species relationship with so much ardour! Had she been born as a porcupine or a particularly smelly sow or even a venomous serpent, it would still not have served to deter my passion.

You look a little sceptical, so perhaps I should mention that at the time of my infamous affair, there was no knowledge of a previous life to guide or even dictate my actions. All I had were the demands of my heart that would brook no denial. In retrospect, I am grateful that I somehow found the courage to indulge my innermost desires at the risk of allowing future generations to revile my actions which could be deemed prurient, for a heart that is true to its owner will lay its desires bare and not mire it in a treacherous swamp of confusion that will surely deprive one of any chance for happiness.

I have proved myself to be somewhat garrulous no doubt, but it is my hope that you never forget what I have told you today, but hang on to it for dear life and steer yourself towards the happiness that is well within your reach. Listen to your heart and follow its dictates the way a blind man would his stick and you will find that it will never lead you astray. So-called civilization and even science is not without its merits, but never allow yourself to become enslaved by their iron laws that worship slavishly at the altar of logic and rationale—for ultimately, faith alone holds the key to salvation.'

Sukra need not have bothered with the injunction to listen because Munna hung onto every word his guru uttered as though his very life depended on it, and engraved it firmly in his heart. Later, he would go over them again and again in the inner recesses of his mind, etching them firmly in his memory. He felt honoured that Sukra was sharing the wealth of his experience with him, but on this particular occasion he got the feeling that his preceptor was trying to convey something that had an especial relevance for him. Holding on to that thought he addressed his guru, 'You are omniscient! I have not discussed my dreams with anybody and yet you seem to be fully cognizant of them. They have been robbing me of my peace of mind and I was just toying with the idea of raising the issue when you yourself not only brought it up but in your generosity, you have imparted valuable counsel as well!'

Sukra smiled knowingly, encouraging Munna to continue. 'My dreams are haunted by a wondrous woman,' said Munna. 'I have loved her all my life. Even as a child, I had made up my mind to marry her. She never realized how serious I was. The years spent apart from her have only made me more determined and come what may she will be my wife.'

'If I might hazard a guess, it is the redoubtable Mayawati we are talking about here, aren't we? Shambara's wife, who raised you from when you were a pup... You could not have made a more controversial choice if you tried. There would be many objections against such a match but I won't insult your intelligence by pointing them out to you.'

'Yes guruji, I know them well enough. It would be said that she is my mother, which I know that she is not. Others will dwell on the fact that she is another man's wife, which she is. All I can say to that is in her heart and mind she never gave herself to him and that is enough for me. Not many know this, for Maya is full of bravado, but the strongest emotion she feels for her loutish husband is fear. Even as a child, I could smell her terror every time he forced us to endure his company and it would make me furious that my fingers lacked the strength to wrap themselves around his thick neck and choke the life out of him. With me, however, Maya feels happy and safe. As far as I am concerned, we were meant to be together and that is all there is to it.

Some would accuse me of treason against my king. To them, if I were inclined to give an explanation which I most certainly am not, it would be that blind loyalty is one of the stupidest traits and if I cannot respect the fellow, then I certainly cannot accept him as my king. As to the age factor, the best I can say is that it is highly irrelevant to me and opinions contrary to mine are worth less than nothing to me.'

'I find it admirable that you are willing to acknowledge what is in your heart,' said Sukra. 'But for a man who knows exactly what he wants and has made it abundantly clear that he will not rest till he has achieved his objective, I sense unseemly hesitation in you and it provokes my curiosity greatly; for a more self-confident and bolder soul I am yet to meet in the Three Worlds.'

'I think you know exactly what it is that is giving me cause to pause, but even so you enjoy making me formulate the most difficult of thoughts into words.' Munna said teasingly before continuing, 'I fear nothing in the Three Worlds and yet the thought of losing Maya, even before winning her, is enough for me to get a bad case of the jitters. She loves me the same way I love her, there can be no doubt about that, but she is a faithful wife and my biggest fear is that she won't leave her loser husband for me even if it is out of misplaced concern for my safety or out of a misguided sense of loyalty to the brute who has left so many scars on her mind and body. Unreasonable doubts plague me both as I sleep and as I wake. Some days, I have half a mind to give up my studies to go chasing after her and make her mine. It is the weirdest feeling to know that the universe conspired to bring us together, given that nobody seems to know my true origins. Some say that a fisherman discovered me in the belly of a giant fish, others say I am a maid's bastard. Maya has never discussed it with me, and I never asked. I was content to have her and know that we belonged to each other. Through the strangest, most mysterious circumstances, Maya and I came together. But I am loath to trust in the perverse fates, for before giving me to her, they sentenced Maya to life imprisonment with a monster.

It is as you said—this unseemly hesitation and anxiety is alien to my personality, yet somehow, it feels justified. I have loved her all my life and my heart tells me that we were meant for each other. Yet somehow, that lousy bastard got his grubby paws on her first. The feeling that she has been taken away from me, has the unmistakable ring of déjà vu... as though I have lived through it before, and it leaves me shaken, with tears in my eyes and ice in my heart. Fear cuts through me like a knife, but the feeling passes and I am left with iron resolve—she will be mine in this life and forever more. Of that I am certain!'

'As am I... For in the face of your resolve, nothing in the Three Worlds is impossible. She is as good as yours! Besides, women simply can't resist self-assurance in a man even if he has a false heart.' Sukra told him with fierce pride in his eyes and a smile on his lips.

'Unless Shambara has put her off men for good and she has decided to embrace lesbianism.' Munna added wryly, a tad embarrassed with his emotional outburst a few moments ago. He had always had the ability to find joy in everything and spread laughter wherever he went. The intensity of his feelings for Maya and the dark passions she had unearthed took even him by surprise and he fell back on humour for his comfort.

Be that as it may, Munna smashed the inner barriers he had thrown up within himself and made rapid progress in his studies. Almost too soon, Sukra pronounced him as the greatest practitioner of the science of illusion, and both were fully satisfied with their respective efforts. At the age of seventeen, Munna was deemed fit to leave the gurukula and return to the world outside. He fell at Sukra's feet and asked his master what he would like as a gurudakshina. In reply his Guru said, 'Make Maya yours and let nothing, not even her inhibitions, stand in the way. Take what is rightfully yours and allow nothing take it away—not fate, the Gods or even intervening lifetimes. That is all I ask of you as my gurudakshina.' He then blessed him and kissed his beloved disciple on the forehead. Munna had tears in his eyes, for this particular demand from his guru was designed not to take but to bestow and as a result, it was the most powerful blessing in the Three Worlds.

Sukra watched Munna leave with his friends and his thoughts turned to the three-eyed God. He smiled a little for he did so love a tussle with him and was positive the Destroyer had got his message.

A Time for Love and Death

*M*unna and his friends traipsed back to their homes, delighted with the idea that their whole lives stretched ahead of them with such promise and nary a clue about the back-breaking responsibility, mind-numbing tedium and crushed dreams that adulthood usually entailed. But young hearts, bubbling over with confidence and hope, can hardly be expected to be pragmatic. Most of the freshly-minted erudite were swearing that from that point onwards, all kinds of mundane domestic chores like sweeping, scrubbing, washing clothes, cooking, dusting etc., would be firmly relegated to the women in their lives. Pleased with their resolve on such a matter of tantamount importance, the talk turned to their plans for the future.

Many among them would be recruited into the army and they would have grand adventures. Others would take up more scholarly pursuits and hope to attain the eminence of a Sukra. But before that their families would arrange suitable matches for them so that they may partake of the pleasures of a householder's life before being called upon to perform their duties to their king and people. While his friends were discussing the qualities they expected from their wives (which mostly amounted to a big heart housed within a commodious bosom), Munna himself made little effort to participate in the conversation. He liked his friends well enough, but he had always felt far removed from them and on their way home, his thoughts were solely on Maya.

The object of his thoughts, inexplicably, somehow knew that she was featuring prominently in them and her heart soared with intense gratification. Most would have scoffed, but Maya had always been able to hone in on Munna's every mood. Even while he was at Sukra's ashram and great distance had separated them, Maya had known that her temperament always mirrored his. As he drew closer to her, she could feel his longing and was startled by her fervent excitement in response to his need.

Word about Munna's arrival preceded him and the ladies of the palace found vantage spots where they could steal glimpses of him and swoon to their hearts' content—for Munna was extraordinarily beautiful. Unlike his biological father who was renowned for his deft ways with women, Munna was far more reserved in his manner, but it was his polite charm and courtly manner that made him irresistible. Maya watched the women swarming over him and she was amused at the pride she felt over just how good-looking he was.

Polite as ever, Munna talked to everyone who accosted him, enquiring about their well-being and making polite conversation. At snail's pace, he wound his way to Maya's chambers where he knew she would be waiting with his supper. She had always loved to feed him and he was already looking forward to the feast she would have readied for him with all his favourite dishes. Typically, she had not come out to meet him. Munna was not disappointed since he knew that she was not big on having fond reunions that involved tears, arcane rituals like the taking of aarathi, and bucket loads of sentiment. Besides, like her, he preferred to catch up in private, away from prying eyes and wagging tongues.

Maya greeted him warmly with the biggest hug ever, although after much deliberation she had decided on a warm but non-committal kiss on the forehead. Neither of them broke away for a long time, till Maya finally took the reluctant step backwards before she would begin to believe that she really was as sex-starved as the other ladies in the palace made her out to be. It was a sobering thought and Munna's mischievous grin left her feeling even more like a prepubescent teen.

Neither was particularly hungry but they sat together to tuck into the scrumptious feast she had laid out for him. The awkwardness melted away, thanks to the efforts of the chef who had remembered fully well Munna's eloquent praise of his talents, and had put together a lavish repast that included meat kebabs, lamb biriyani, onion raita, vegetable pakoras, and rice pudding. Soon they were chatting together like the best friends they were. Munna told her stories about his experiences in the ashram and had her in splits with renditions of his escapades. Maya listened with rapt attention allowing herself to be drawn deeply into his world. She had been chaffing badly, tethered to a claustrophobic existence with Shambara's women, and relished the sense of freedom she always felt with her Munna.

'It is so good to have you back. I missed you a lot. When you left all those years ago, I wished with all my heart that I were a little boy as well so that we could be together. It is infuriating to be a woman, sometimes...there is always too much waiting around it seems!'

'You say the oddest things! Sukra would have loved to have you in the ashram. He enjoyed nothing better than a keenly contested debate. Personally, I am glad you are not a man. In fact there is nothing I would change about you. Why mess with perfection?'

'Oh stop it! You always did have a way with words and could probably talk Yama into keeping his gift of death to himself!' Maya teased him, cherishing the compliment nevertheless. 'I would love to be about half my real age, single and absolutely free to do as I please without having to deal with moral outrage from every imaginable quarter.'

'You know what they say about youth being wasted on the young. Age is a just a stupid number and it would stay that way if you keep it that way without giving it undue importance. The same goes for your marital status. A marriage that is a marriage only in name, is not the real thing. Finally, you don't seem to be aware of it, but the truth is you are absolutely free to do as you please. You fight with the desperation of a cornered animal to free yourself from the chains that are holding you down, without ever realizing that they are entirely of your own making. Personal freedom means so much to you but you are terrified to take it, though it lies well-within your grasp, for you do not trust yourself with it. It holds the key to your happiness but you are afraid to seize it, for you cannot stop yourself from wondering if too heavy a price will be exacted from you. As a safeguard you lock yourself away in a cage, holding out for your idea of perfection, unwilling to settle for anything less, yet refusing to believe that perfection could possibly exist.

To compound matters, you can't forgive yourself for making every decision in your life guided by the nameless fear that has you so much in thrall and which you fight so unsuccessfully. Your heart cries out to be rescued but if anyone were to reach out, your guard is up at once and you morph into the equivalent of a drowning person who tries to drag the rescuer down under. Fortunately for you, I can be patient and it is my firm belief that eventually, I'll wear you down and help you get away from yourself.'

Maya drank deeply from her goblet so that Munna would not be able to see the delirious joy one felt on finding complete understanding and acceptance from a loved one. Even so, she fought the treacherous hope which was threatening to flood her, since it had a track record for letting her down. When she replied, her tone was deceptively flippant, 'Clearly Sukra has been filling your head with a whole lot of psychobabble. Such talk of chains and cages and drowning people! Anyway, before I forget...have you heard from the army as yet? Word of your talents has filtered back to us and I have no doubt that you will be recruited immediately.'

'Shambara would love to send me to the front, I am sure, and hope that a messy and ignominious death awaits me there. But I am not in a tearing hurry to disappoint him nor am I going to put my talents at his disposal. For now, it is my intention to make up for lost time and be with you as much as I possibly can.'

'That suits me just fine. But I can't keep you all to myself. People will start talking. You will want to take a wife, I expect. Perhaps you already have someone in mind?'

'As a matter of fact, I do...' Munna was pleased to note the crack in her coolly nonchalant veneer as he pressed on. 'You will be happy to know that I have decided to marry someone exactly like you for it would be impossible for me to love any other!'

'That is nice but I am one of a kind!' Maya informed him loftily, though her heart trilled on hearing him say he could love no other. She had to be dreaming, for people who had been away for so long, did not simply return, seem to gauge your innermost desires and propose love and marriage in the most casual of ways! Munna had started to speak, so she tuned in hastily.

'Then what are we waiting for? Let us wed in the Gandharva style and be done with it. Clearly we are meant to be together, so let us get married and consummate our union without further ado. The enforced celibacy in Sukra's ashram has not done me any favours and I am bored to death with Mistress Palm and her five daughters.'

'Hush, Munna! I can't believe you feel this is appropriate talk at supper!' said Maya, choking a little and refusing to meet his eyes as a flush crept up her neck which Munna was observing closely. 'If you keep this up, we will be providing unnecessary fodder for the gossip mills and there will be a whole lot of unsavoury talk about us. They will say that I am undersexed and have raised you to fill my empty bed. Then your future will be ruined and no father worth the name will be willing to give his daughter in marriage to you, and you might as well get betrothed to Mistress Palm and her get!'

'Who cares about foolish talk or a commitment to love of the self in perpetuity when there are so many better options? Words are just wind and they can hardly hurt anybody. Why should we take that kind of irrelevant nonsense into account while planning for our future?

My time with Sukra was most fulfilling but I missed you so much that there were days when I wanted to throw it all away, kill Shambara, make you mine and tell the rest of the world to go straight to hell! There is no way I'll allow anybody or anything to come between us ever again and certainly not a gaggle of gossipy old crones!'

'It is easy for you to talk!' said Maya. 'The male of the species can do as they please and get away with just a lousy slap on the wrist—even if they take up whoring, gambling, boozing or dedicate their very lives to depravity. A woman does not have it that easy. Her reputation is her armour. And if that is stripped away, she is lucky if she is stoned to death, for the alternative almost invariably is gang rape and murder—in that order, if she is particularly unlucky! But it is not *my* honour that I am most concerned about, it is *you*. I cannot stop thinking about what the king and his men will do to you if they find out about us! They will kill us both but not before torturing us to the point where we will be begging for Yama to come get us!'

'Aren't you a ray of sunshine, though?' Munna replied, looking at her with deep affection. 'As if I would allow such a thing to ever happen to you! And the very idea that Shambara's pet poodles could manage to get within a mile of me without losing control of their bladders is laughable. Your problem is that you have lost your confidence because you got stuck with that old fart! Now all you have to do is hold my hand, close your eyes, trust in me implicitly and take one gigantic leap of faith!'

'Please, Munna! You really must be more careful about what you say! There are spies everywhere. Talk like this will be construed as treason and retribution will be sudden, swift and fatal!'

'I am not scared of him, Maya, and neither should you be!' Munna said with a sudden burst of intensity. 'He is a lousy coward for daring to strike a woman who cannot hold her own against brute strength. Don't look so surprised; it was not too difficult to figure out the reason behind the haunted look in your eyes! I am going to make him pay for what he did to you and then you will be rid of him forever.'

Maya tried to talk, but the tears were flowing thick and fast. Munna ran to her side and held her gently in his arms, stroking her hair and murmuring soothingly into her ears till the wracking sobs ceased. She shoved him away then and muttered, 'See what you have done? Weeping makes me look so hideous! My eyes get puffy and red, my skin gets blotchy, my nose starts running and since I rarely have a hanky on me, the sniffling begins and there is no creature in the Three Worlds uglier than me. Don't you dare deny it! And I can't believe the sight of my tears makes you want to laugh! You are such a pig!' Maya had intended to punch him but they would up simply putting their hands around each other's shoulders, and plonking down right there on the floor.

Munna settled her head comfortably against his shoulder before speaking, 'For the record, I think you look lovely when you have a wicked case of the weepies. Now I need you to explain to me why you won't dump Shambara and come away with me... In all likelihood, it is possible that you like him even less than I do. Despite the nonsense you spouted about a woman's reputation being her armour, I know you don't really care about wagging tongues. As for me, thanks for the touching concern, but I am perfectly capable of taking care of myself and my woman. You know that, don't you? Yet, I sense this frustrating barrier in you which I just can't seem to get around. What is it? Why do I get the bad feeling that you know something I don't?'

Maya did not answer for a bit. She was thinking about Narada's visit and the secrets that had been given to her for safekeeping. Now might just be as good a time as any to tell Munna the truth about his origins. It had long been a sore point with him, though perhaps he would be able to make the best of a bad thing, as he usually did. He already hated Shambara and if he found out how he had been robbed of the privilege of being raised by Krishna and Rukmini and forced to hide behind the guise of a lowly birth, though he was a prince of the mighty Yadava clan, his blood would be up and he would know no satisfaction till he had put an end to Shambara's existence. It was what he had been born to do and from what she had heard, Sukra had moulded him into a fine warrior. Yet, Maya hesitated.

Narada had told her to keep the secret till the time was right and she had no way of knowing when that would be. Life would be simpler if divine voices from heaven called out instructions or at least cued in suitable music at key moments to help people navigate their way past uncertainty, Maya thought to herself. And where was the irksome Narada when you wanted him? Instinct told her that she should simply go with the flow and keep her mouth shut, until told otherwise by divine messengers or divine musicians.

Since Munna was still waiting for her reply, she tried to put her scrambling thoughts into some semblance of order, 'I just think it would be imprudent to pack up my bags and run away with you just right now. Why, it seems like yesterday when you came barely up to my knees and enjoyed wiping your nose on my sari! Suddenly after twelve long years, you have just returned admittedly taller and cuter than ever before and already you are talking about eloping with the closest thing you had to a mother! I am a lot of things Munna, but I don't fancy myself as an adulterous whore. Shambara and I have lived separate lives for a long time now and he was never my soulmate. But we are still married and I don't want to be unfaithful. Tawdry affairs hardly make for great love stories and it is just the sort of thing that provokes the Gods and fates into springing terrible tragedies on those who have dared to veer too far away from the straight and narrow.

There is no need for you to look so hurt. Some of these things have to be said. But I am not holding back out of a sense of propriety. If it were not for the fact that I hate stating the obvious, you would have heard no end of 'I Love Yous' from me. In fact, the years apart from you nearly drove me into the madhouse. I did nothing but fantasize about you returning to me before my hair turned white, my teeth rotted and fell out and every drop of juice from my body was sweated out. My favourite fantasy was of me convincing Sukra that I was a lad of noble birth and getting taken in as a pupil. Then I would seduce the man you had become and we would spend every waking moment in each other's arms. We have waited so long to be together and we should not do anything rash to jeopardize our situation. Let us just wait for a little bit longer and come up with a plan that guarantees a happily-ever-after, as opposed to a violent end that does not preclude the possibility of one or both of us getting sodomized before having our throats cut out!'

That should have been that, for as far as arguments went, it was a reasonably good one. Maya had shown admirable restraint, as had Munna, and both aspired to take the moral high road. Except that it was incredibly short-lived, for they became illicit lovers sooner than Maya would later care to admit.

The truth was that on seeing each other after twelve years, they felt like victims of starvation, who after years of denial, had been magically plopped in front of a heavily laden buffet table, with every thought driven out of their heads—except for one which was that they gorge till they were fully satiated. Neither had any wish to be parted from the other for even a moment and Munna refused to leave her side. They would stay up talking late into the night, and foolishly believing that words were all they would need. Maya made a half-hearted suggestion that he bunk with a friend since it would be looked at askance if a fully-grown man spent his nights in the anthapuram, which was the traditional domain of women and children. But Munna argued that there was nothing wrong with him wanting to stay in his childhood bedroom and his argument carried the day.

Munna and Maya pretended not to remember that even as a kid he had preferred sleeping next to her, and no matter how many times she carried him after he was asleep and tucked him into his own bed, he would still find his way back to her. This was how they later surmised he had turned up in her bed, since they were not sure how exactly their grand odyssey of love began, except that it did. All they remembered was that a lover's tender demands had been made and assent provided. Maya was positive she had put up quite a fight but in the end, she gave in, the way she always had to him, because somehow, resisting him felt so wrong.

Having discovered each other after what felt like eons, Munna and Maya were determined never to let go. The intensity of their passion for each other seared them with its heat and both were shaken, a little frightened but deliriously happy, for they possessed the secret knowledge that they had just been initiated into a secret garden of pleasure where only a chosen few ever got access.

Recklessly they threw caution to the winds and refused to get out of bed for days on end. Maya told her maids that she had taken ill and had no wish to entertain visitors or be disturbed. Their world shrank to the intimate space under her bedcovers and in their minds it was a matchless existence that lacked for nothing. Munna told her that if he could tear himself away from her, he would perform the most insanely difficult penances like Sukra, to win Shiva's favour and ask that time be suspended in their snug little world for two, so that they could stay there forever, without worrying about the past, future, responsibilities, duties, the madding crowd and the real world out there which was such a hostile place for lovers.

Mostly, they would make love and coo sweet nothings into each other's ears, but occasionally, Maya would grow a little troubled and she would attempt to seek out the cause of her anxiety. She sensed that snug little worlds for two seldom lasted, because they were held in place by gossamer threads that could snap with a sigh. Her unease would grow and she would confide in Munna, 'You will think me stupid and something of an ingrate but I can't help thinking that though what we have is perfection, it has all come together in the most imperfect way imaginable. Here we are in Shambara's kingdom, you are banging his wife, who sort of adopted you, and we are pretending that we are all alone in some sort of enchanted Neverland, cut off from everything else in creation. At this exact moment Shambara's spies could be on their way here with orders to hack us into little bloody pieces for the crows to feed on. If we were to stop and really focus on the hard facts of life, then we would admit that even multiple orgasms pale into insignificance in the face of an imminent and unpleasant death. I always wanted to go away gently into the good night and not have my naked body, or what is left of it, handed over to Yama in a smelly sack!'

'Why am I not surprised that you somehow managed to find the seedy underbelly of our paradise? But moving on, it is a tad insulting, though one wouldn't know it from our "banging" as you call it, that a part of you still sees me as the kid who you mothered. I thought you said that word of my talents filtered back here? If that were true you would have known that Shambara's dogs would have crawled back to him minus their heads if they were stupid enough to think they could prevail over me. Hopefully that will allay your unnecessary fears about us being hastened to Yama's abode against our will.

As for the niggling imperfections you talk of, Sukra would say that it is merely the universe balancing itself through the minutiae of its microcosm which is our relationship. He would say we should disregard it the way we would a particularly foul-smelling fart that is a necessary, but evil price to pay for having consumed a rich and thoroughly satisfying meal.'

'And you thought it unjustified that a part of me still sees you as a kid!' said Maya. 'Speaking of Sukra, did you ever get down to asking him if he did it with a deer? Did he not find the antlers to be something of an encumbrance?'

Munna smiled. 'As a matter of fact, I did and it was a lamb not a deer. Actually, I thought it was a charming story. He said that the lamb was his lover from a former life for whose sake he had willingly given up the ascetic merit that had opened the doors of heaven to him. Sukra said he had traded it all in a heartbeat, for access to the kind of ecstasy that trumped all the joys that heaven had to offer. He added that he does not regret it in the least.'

Munna paused and continued: 'Perhaps we were also lovers from another time and you so scandalized the masters of the universe with your excessive sexual antics, that they booted us out of heaven straight into the midst of the Asuras to sober us up! But clearly, you have not changed one bit and perhaps the Gods, who are missing the voyeuristic satisfaction we provided them, are eagerly figuring out ways to get us back!'

Maya laughed at his absurdity but was grateful to him for making her feel light-hearted and giddy again. 'Actually, I would love for us to have a story like that,' she said. 'But even if we did have one and I sparked off moral outrage with my sexual excesses, it is my belief that it would largely be irrelevant to our current situation—if only because we have no memories of what might have transpired in another lifetime! It is mostly the now which matters for it may have some bearing on our subsequent futures. Just so we are clear, if you are reborn as a crocodile, be warned that I will certainly kick you out of my bed and have the archer shoot you down.'

Thus they loved, laughed and lived in the little bubble they had created for themselves. At the time, they foolishly believed that it just might last forever if they willed it to be so. Munna believed that if you wanted something with every ounce of your being, the universe conspired to give it to you. His better half, however, who was a great one for bursting bubbles, believed that even if you got what you wanted and your life became as magical as you always dreamed it would be, such a perfect state was not meant to last and it always came with an expiry date. And once your time is up, not only do you have the misfortune to see your paradise crumble before your very eyes, but you also find that having been given a taste of such sublime bliss it is impossible to give it up for abhorrent reality. If that were not bad enough it would now be accompanied by the insupportable tang of pain and grief for that which was found and lost.

Maya said none of these things aloud, however, choosing instead to still the treacherous murmurs that sprang from her doubt. Yet, her uncertainty continued to lurk in the darkest caverns of her mind, cowed when she was lost in the caresses of her lover but not for long, confident that sooner or later they could feast upon her fear.

For Maya had neither Munna's faith nor his steady confidence. Even so, she wanted desperately to believe and tried her hardest to do so. For the briefest time she almost did and just when tentative faith raised its head, their little bubble which had proved to be so remarkably resilient, exploded, yielding to the inescapable reality that even Munna could not get away with—sleeping with Shambara's wife under his very nose. And certainly not forever as he and Maya had been hoping.

Shambara did not send his men to haul them in chains before him with the intention of venting his rage upon them at his leisure. Instead he came for them himself, in the dead of the night. The affair his wife was having with her son was hardly a secret and people were talking about it barely a couple of days in; yet the illicit lovers had got away with it for a few weeks only because nobody had the courage to tell their king that his wife had put the cuckold's horns on him,and subjected him to ridicule and humiliation. Of course, his loyal subjects were far too scared to even think of chuckling over his misfortune or even being scornful unless of course they had indulged in one tipple too many. The excessive booze would bring out the laughs and contempt in spades. Much was made, in the colourful language of the taverns, over the failings of a king who was not man enough to keep his wife in his own bed, and most wondered what it would feel like to bang a queen who had proved herself to be such a whore.

The women in the kingdom, from the highest to the basest born, did not think it was a laughing matter. They made it out to be a tragedy of epic proportions and reserved their excoriation solely for the whore (in this regard at least they were in perfect agreement with the loutish men in their lives) who could not be faithful to the man who had been generous enough to raise a lowly courtier's daughter to the status of his queen. The women could not get over the fact that not only was Maya guilty of adultery but had chosen to sin with her own son! Surely she deserved to be tortured for the rest of time and then some!!

The ladies turned on one of their own, with the raptorial instincts of creatures that eat their young, and dwelt obsessively on what exactly mother and son were up to, shacked up in their den of inequity. The more rabid of the moralizers made relentless attempts to 'visit' but it would have well been simpler to request the Devas for a sample of the nectar of immorality, for they were all told that Maya was suffering from a contagious illness. Denied the opportunity to upbraid her in the strongest possible language and wound her with words, they would leave with malicious remarks on how they hoped her moral laxity wasn't catching.

Munna got off lightly in comparison, for too many were enamoured of him and it was opined by the ladies of the royal household that he was as much a victim as Shambara, for Maya had surely raised him for the express purpose of warming her bed, which no other self-respecting male would care to inhabit. Maya had preyed on his natural affection for one who had raised him, and distorted it into something so hideous that it did not bear talking about. They waited eagerly for the guilty couple to be dragged out naked and in chains to face trial and punishment for their crimes of an unnatural, lewd and lascivious nature. But there was no wish-fulfilment for the longest time, which only fuelled the hostility against the lovers with most clamouring for their heads on a plate.

Shambara was the last person in the kingdom to be made privy to the details about his wife's affair. Given a choice, he would have preferred to have gone to his grave without ever being told about Maya's betrayal, but the murmurs were too many and too poisonous for denial to be a viable defence mechanism. He waited for the rage to explode within him but to his dismay, it was not anger but a tidal wave of grief that engulfed him. Good sense warned him to have his best men take care of them both quickly and quietly, but he so wanted the rumours to be proved false that he did not wish to countenance a course of action that would justify them.

No proof was needed of Maya's treachery, for in his heart he had always known that she was not his, and the affair confirmed his worst fears. They had been separated for long years and she had made it clear that he was not welcome in her heart, home or bed. As king he could claim his right to enter her life whenever he wished and would periodically force his way into her bed. But while he had made her submit to his advances—which she endured by lying like a corpse under him—she could and had effectively locked him out of her heart. Towards the end, her resistance had proved impregnable and Shambara's visits had dwindled. Even so nothing could have prepared him for the emotional devastation that accompanied the knowledge that she was lost to him.

More often than he cared to remember, he had himself

called her a whore but he had known that the foul epithet was not deserved—because in the past, despite their insurmountable differences, she had been true to him. However, now that his subjects had started calling her a 'harlot from hell', he had a good mind to have the tongues ripped out from every fetid mouth which dared to say so. But the order was not issued. Instead Shambara decided to see the truth of it for himself, for a part of him stubbornly refused to believe that Maya had left him forever and chosen her adopted son whom he had foolishly allowed her to raise.

On a fell night, when the seed of self-destruction that Narada had so assiduously planted had reached full bloom, Shambara made a final trip to complete the odyssey of suffering that he had embarked upon since that night when he had made the foolhardy decision to kidnap and drown a baby. The spectre of that brat had come between him and his wife and now it seemed had driven her into the arms of a child-man with laughing eyes, a silver tongue and a black heart, who had no qualms about stealing that which rightfully belonged to his king. Summoning his magic he flew into Maya's bedroom, deciding he wanted to find out the truth for himself.

Shambara saw them curled up in bed, fast asleep in each other's arms. Perhaps he had expected to find them rutting away like dogs in heat and stinking of sin, thus provoking him to wring their bloody necks when they were at their most vulnerable. But in repose, they looked sweet like little children. He could not see Munna's face, just his arm cradling his wife's breasts in an embrace that was both possessive and protective. Maya was curled up in the foetal position and pressed up against his chest, as if she was trying to melt away into him. She looked warm, comfortable, and very much at peace with the world.

He suddenly remembered the wariness in her eyes every time he approached her with happy anticipation in his. One would have thought he was a wild animal come to rip her throat out. The pain he had experienced on being rejected thus, felt fresh as he relived it. Following Narada's visit, their already troubled marriage had come apart at the seams, but that had not stopped him from wanting or needing her. Conversely, his wife seemed much happier having kicked him out of her life and knowledge of the fact had hurt a lot. He had taken a bevy of beauties into his bed over the years and showered them with riches, hoping there would be one among them who would make him forget Maya. But it never happened and his loving wife had been singularly relieved that he had his distractions and she would not have to endure his embrace. Needless to say this would infuriate him and he would insist on claiming his rights as a husband—which she would concede with as much ill-grace as she could get away with.

Looking at her again, he was reminded of the many occasions when he had reached out to her after making love, wanting to comfort her, knowing that she felt violated; but she had shrunk away from him as if she wanted nothing better than to disappear. Suddenly, he felt more lachrymose than he ever had in his entire life and it was this mental image of himself kneeling down beside the bed where he had caught his wife in flagrante delicto with another man, weeping his eyes out, that finally got his dander and awakened his wrath.

The rage was directed at the woman who had brought him to this ignoble position, and his heart hardened with hatred for her—whom he had always loved far too much for his own good. But he hated himself even more, for even then, all he wanted was for Munna not to have her if he himself couldn't. He howled his misery at them, rudely awakening them, just as he picked up a heavy goblet and smashed it on Munna's head with a satisfying crunch. He grabbed hold of Maya's hair and ripped her from Munna's embrace, hurling her unceremoniously into the wall behind him. Munna raised himself up just in time for Shambara's foot to find purchase on his chest and send him hurtling from the bed. This time, the corner of a little table laden with sweetmeats for the lovers, found the back of Munna's head and Shambara gloated when he saw a splash of blood.

Maya screamed in horror and the concern Shambara heard in her voice for Munna drove him right over the edge. He turned on her then and began raining blows on her unprotected naked form with fists that were honed to physical perfection from a hundred battles. Grabbing her slender throat, he began to bash her head against the hard stone floor again and again, hating her so much that he realized no matter how many times he killed her, it would be insufficient to quell the black misery she had wrought on him. He was so far gone that he did not even feel the dagger that was punched into the back of his throat by the child from the prophecy, whom he had tried so unsuccessfully to kill.

It was a mortal blow and Shambara was a dead man. But his fingers would not unloose from Maya's throat and as the inky black blood spilled out on her, they mingled with her tears and Shambara was filled with savage satisfaction when he saw the guilt and sorrow in her eyes in response to the hatred in his. In his last conscious moments he tried to draw comfort from the fact that he had also destroyed her, the way she had destroyed him. And he wished the bastard from the blasted prophecy, the joy of her—she, who was nothing more than a piece of damaged goods now.

Picking Up the Pieces

*I*t had all happened way too fast to register properly. One moment they had been blissfully asleep, and suddenly they had awoken into a nightmare where the monsters were real. Years into the future, Munna and Maya would never be able to discuss the events of that night for their individual reasons. The former wished that his first kill had been a cleaner one. Sukra had honed Munna's skills and made him a fine warrior, but he thought ruefully that this perhaps was not what he had been trained to do. He had somehow managed to swallow the bitter pill with rationalization but nevertheless did not care to bring it up again and fill his mouth with its acrid taste. The latter never managed to overcome the corrosive guilt that assailed her and could not forgive herself for betraying her husband or bringing about his death, though she did learn to live with it.

At the time, Munna was hopping mad because he knew that Shambara had almost killed Maya and himself and that for a few seconds he had been completely powerless. He cursed himself for having been caught completely off guard and for his arrogant complacency which had nearly cost them dear. Never again, he swore to himself and immediately switched into damage control mode.

Shambara's dead weight was crushing Maya's naked body underneath and Munna cursed again under his breath as he dragged the carcass of his rival off her, kicking it unceremoniously to one side. He caught the expression on her face and it nearly knocked the wind out of him. Tenderly he hugged her and the shell-shocked lovers mourned the loss of the most magical moments in their life for one brief moment. He draped a sheet gently around her as Maya's maids who had been incessantly warding off the evil eye from the duo during their time together rushed in to attend to their injuries. They took care of the gash in Munna's head and the swelling in Maya's, as well as the numerous bruises that pockmarked her body before hastily helping them to dress. All their lives hung in the balance and Munna was urging Maya's maids to flee at once but they had been with their mistress from when she was a baby and all they cared about was helping her escape with her lover.

They had helped lower them down from a window into the courtyard below, when the guards barged in. They found the dead body of their king and they flew for the window to stop his killers. Finding their way barred they cut down the obstructers and sounded the alarm. Munna had a chariot waiting for just such an emergency loaded with weapons and provisions needed for a long journey. It was tucked some distance away from the vast palace grounds and with Maya dead on her feet, they stood little chance of making it. Shambara's loyal guards poured in from all directions determined to give them a taste of their vengeance. They had failed their king and as compensation they wanted to perform his last rites with the blood of his killers.

Munna mowed down the first wave of attackers, snatching a sword from the first guard he had killed, by bodily hurling him to the ground and smashing his spine. Armed thus he became an implacable whirlwind meting out death in all directions as he ploughed his way forward, with Maya trudging on behind him. He knew that he had come dangerously close to losing her on that night and he knew that he would tear down the Three Worlds with all its creatures before allowing such a thing to happen again. As the tide of soldiers came for him in relentless waves, he used the magic taught him by Sukra to shield her from them and devoted his entire attention to slaughtering them with his arsenal of celestial weapons against which the common soldiers had no defense. Munna could not care less, for Maya's safety was paramount and he would have slit the throat of a blind old woman if she had been in his way.

On that night, Munna was terror incarnate and he stood poised to rip Shambara's entire army into pieces and annihilate the entire kingdom if need be. He transformed himself into a ravenous beast of prey, and to the eyes of the royal guard and the elite armed forces, he appeared to be a gigantic winged monster corded with muscle, claws and teeth that tore into their midst killing them faster than was logically possible. Rising up into the air, he rained down fire upon his enemies burning them whole, ignoring their screams for mercy. The fires spread faster than thought, fuelled by his unstoppable anger and desperation. He rose higher and higher into the heavens as the conflagration he had sparked blazed on. Maya was in his arms and she seemed to be unconscious. The gash behind his head had opened up and his blood spilled on the flames causing them to flare up in a macabre dance of devilish destruction. Munna was weakening rapidly and he knew not how to save himself or his beloved. That was when he espied his chariot which loomed invitingly before him, an island amidst the burning wreckage and Munna swooped down towards it, somehow knowing that he would be safe once he got into it.

The chariot seemed to rise to meet him, and gathering its precious burden, rose into the heavens and sped off into the cool night. Munna would have liked to know where he was going but he was also losing consciousness fast and he made sure that he was still holding on to Maya. When he looked up for a brief moment, he saw a face. It was a beautiful one and though it was alien to him, Munna felt that he knew the owner of the face, which was so like his own. He wanted to thank the apparition for the timely help but he knew it was not necessary as he blacked out.

When they came to a little later, they had not reached their

destination wherever that may be. Munna was relieved to note that
Maya was also up. She appeared wan but at least she was not at
death's door. Their miraculous escape had not exactly cheered her
up but she seemed eager to speak, 'I have something to tell you
Munna... It is important and so I must beg you not to interrupt
until I have had my say. We are on our way to Dwaraka, for
there is only one in the Three Worlds who could have intervened
on our behalf and saved us from an army of murderous Asuras.
The time has come for you to know the secret of your birth. You
belong to the noble Yadava race and were born to Krishna and
Rukmini. As you know, Krishna is believed to be an incarnation
of the divine Protector and Rukmini is an avatar of his consort,
Lakshmi. You are their firstborn son, the Yadu prince they lovingly
named Pradyumna. It had been prophesized that Shambara would
meet his death at the hands of this special child.

Shambara knew about this prophecy but he did not seem too
perturbed about it. That changed when Narada paid him a little
visit shortly after you were born. To this day, I do not know what
exactly the muni told him but one night, Shambara transported
himself to Dwaraka, abducted you and dumped you into the sea.
Everybody thought that Shambara had killed the baby but you
survived. Narada paid me a visit after that and placed you in my
care. He told me that I had to keep you safe from Shambara and
instructed me that under no circumstances was I to let on what
I knew until you had accomplished what you had been born to
do. It has been an honour to carry out the divine task assigned
to me, and I have been rewarded richly for my efforts. Whatever
I did was to further your interests and it was never my intention
to deceive you. Narada stressed that I was to hold my tongue and
not meddle in the natural order of things. Please forgive me if you
feel that I have wronged you in any way...'

Munna was relieved to see her old spirit flicker briefly in her
eyes even as he was trying to recover from the sucker punch she

had just dealt him. He knew that Shambara had killed a part of her that night and he was determined to restore her to her old self, no matter what it took. 'There is nothing to forgive. Offhand, I can think of quite a few things to discuss with that moronic muni you mentioned, but let us forget him for the moment. There is nobody in the Three Worlds who is unfamiliar with the glory of Krishna and the great deeds he has accomplished. Why, my favourite bedtime stories were the ones you told me about him! I am truly blessed to claim him as my father. No doubt it would have been amazing to have been raised by him but it is pointless to dwell on what might have been.

My childhood was a happy one and you made it so... You were so fiercely protective of me! Do you remember that tall, mean kid who used to bully me? He told me that my mother was a slut and wanted to know what it felt like to have been conceived in a drunken orgy. Though I had no idea what an orgy was, I still made sure that his nasty head was sufficiently doused in a bucket of cow dung! When I told you about it, you were so furious, that you tracked him down, hauled him up by the scruff of his neck and warned him that you would cut off his tongue, if he dared to speak that way to me again! He believed you and was scared senseless—which effectively ended his bullying days.

You are still the same and you feel the need to protect me from the big, bad world outside. I was more than capable of taking care of myself as a kid and now, even more so, but it feels nice to know that someone always has your back. As for the prophecy, it reeks of bullshit to me. I refuse to believe that the sole purpose of my existence was to kill that piece of scum—even if he did deserve to go out the way he did for ill-treating you and for robbing my mother of her newborn son. Even so, the accursed events of tonight will not validate my life. As far as I am concerned, I was born because I needed to find you and it is for this alone that my being is precious beyond measure. Nothing will alter this reality for me, and I know you feel the same way. Enough said!

Don't beat yourself up over any of this, okay? I know that twisted little mind of yours... Sometimes shit happens and it is nobody's fault. Shambara should have had the sense not to listen to the Naradas of the world and go off the deep end in the middle of the night. He should not have attempted to kill you either, leaving me free to plunge a dagger into his throat. It will be useless to ask you to forget the whole damn thing but do me a favour and try not to dwell on this anymore, for obsessing over how things could have happened differently is not going to change anything.'

They lapsed into silence after that, each sifting through their own thoughts as they headed into a future neither had a clue about. Munna's thoughts were with his birth mother and father. After enduring years of being ridiculed as a lowly bastard, he would now be claimed by the illustrious Yadava clan as one of their own. Sukra must have known this truth, for he had instructed him at length on his lineage and told him many tales about Krishna. Munna should have been deliriously happy but he felt nothing in particular. He remembered the face he had seen when the world around him was going to hell and wondered why it was that it felt like déjà vu. All roads lead to the owner of that face—a fragmentary thought with no apparent context interspersed itself into his consciousness—and he felt a wonderful sense of calm. Maya, however, was far from calm, he knew. She seemed to be pulling back from him and the harder he held on, the quicker she seemed to be slipping away like grains of sand from a tightly clenched fist.

Maya's thoughts were indeed far more dolorous. She was happy that Munna would be reuniting with his birth parents soon. It was impossible to even begin to imagine what Rukmini would have gone through when Shambara stole her baby. If Munna had been taken from her, she would have offered herself up as a meal for Agni rather than go on in a world without him. Rukmini must be a very brave and virtuous woman and she deserved to have her son back. But Maya was not too sure about the reception she herself would get as the former queen of the Asuras and wife of Shambara. Moreover, she had committed adultery, helped kill her own husband, and to top it off, she was famously barren. Munna would be beloved by his people, she had no doubt, but she had to wonder whether the proud Yadus would accept her as his wife. Not liking the direction her thoughts were taking, she brushed them aside fiercely. It was Munna's day of glory—he had taken on the mighty Shambara, though still a mere slip of a youth and she had no wish to cast a pall over the joyous occasion of his triumphant homecoming with her own gloom.

The famous city of Dwaraka took their breath away when they landed. Munna was exuberant and Maya found herself caught up in his excitement. Thanks to the grace of his divine father, their injuries were all gone and they made a very handsome couple. The inhabitants of the city were struck by the beauty of the duo and remarked that the ridiculously good looking youth was a dead ringer for Krishna and surely the gorgeous woman with him had to be a Goddess. Dare they hope that the Gods had been kind and their long lost prince was returning to them? They directed the two in the direction of the palace after welcoming them with flowers and hearty cheers of greeting. Before long, the royal guard arrived to escort them to the palace where the Yadava elders had congregated to meet with them.

Krishna and Rukmini were waiting for them as was King Ugrasena, Vasudeva and Balarama. Also present was Narada. Rukmini stood up first and for a second she just stood there staring at her son. Not a day had elapsed where her thoughts had not revolved around the beautiful baby who she had not had the good fortune to raise with her own hands. Then she ran to him, and as mother and son hugged, the entire gathering brought their hands together in applause, for her profound happiness was a beautiful thing to behold. 'I knew you would come back to me! My faith has been rewarded. My boy was always destined for greatness, and though still a lad, you have done the Yadus proud by getting rid of the evil Shambara! It is my honour and privilege to have given birth to you and to call you my son!'

Munna was overwhelmed and he knew not what to say to the beautiful woman who was his mother and whose love he now knew had protected him and served as a talisman against misfortune. He hugged her back before paying respectful obeisance to the family elders who were also weeping openly. One look at the dear face of Krishna, his father, and he had to fight back tears. Without a word being exchanged he realized that his father had always been there for him, watched over him and helped him realize his destiny. Respectfully, he prostrated himself at the feet of his father who was also the God he had prayed to since he was old enough to do so. His father's brother, Balarama, hugged him as well and clapped him on the shoulder, before remarking: 'Why, you are a spitting image of Krishna! And twice as handsome, I must say! It is good to have you back among us lad, and we can expect great things from you in the future as well, I am sure.'

With a woman's unerring instinct, it was Rukmini who noticed Maya, standing as unobtrusively as possible in the background of the charming family tableau that was unfolding in front of her, 'Who is this beautiful woman who accompanies you? Is she a Goddess? What is her relationship to you might I ask?'

It was Narada who replied, 'She is a Goddess! Though known to this world as Mayawati, her name is Rati. Her husband was the God of Desire, Kamadeva, whom Shiva unfortunately burnt to ashes when his meditation was disturbed by the gentle God, who was merely helping out the Devas by trying to hasten the union of the Destroyer and Parvati. Rati performed penances to win her Lord back and succeeded in winning the grace of Shiva who promised her that Kama would be reborn as Krishna's son and she herself as Mayawati.

As Mayawati, this remarkable lady has had to endure a life of great hardship and privation. It is to her credit that she somehow managed to take in the baby, who was all but lost to you, and kept him safe from Shambara, known for his violent temper and abusive ways—at great risk to her own personal safety. She watched over Pradyumna and helped him add to his repertoire of natural skills so that he might prevail over Shambara in their epic clash which was preordained, and which Shambara had so foolishly attempted to avoid.

It was she who revealed to Pradyumna how Shambara had stolen him from a loving mother's embrace and tried to kill him, condemning them to long years of painful separation. When Pradyumna heard about how his mother had grieved for him, not knowing his fate and fretting endlessly over her firstborn son, spending the days and nights praying to the Gods to keep him safe from evil, he was provoked to great anger. Only the worst sort of monster would do that to a good woman who has harmed nobody, and Pradyumna was determined to put the creature down. He challenged Shambara, forcing him to own up to his foul deeds, and vanquished him in the legendary duel that followed, which was surely one for the ages. For as they fought, the old maestro of mahamaya had to yield before the new champion, trained by the great Sukracharya and in whose veins run the blood of Krishna himself. Having defeated Shambara in combat, Pradyumna had to deal with his armed forces who tried to capture and kill Mayawati for the role she had played in bringing about the death of their king. With unmatched valour Pradyumna fought his way past the demon hordes and has returned to us, having covered the family name with glory and proving himself a credit to his family and race!'

There was not a single dry eye in that large gathering when Narada concluded his gripping tale. Even Munna and Maya were spellbound as they listened to that magnificent story which they were also hearing for the first time, though it was theirs for all intents and purposes. Munna, who had been nursing the most uncharitable thoughts about the muni—who had brought about so much mischief in so many lives—found his attitude softening towards Narada. He saw the gratitude in Maya's eyes and she looked as though she wanted to hug Narada, though he knew that in the past she had definitely been less kindly disposed to him. The favour Narada had done them by outlining their story with such an almighty dose of poetic license was enormous, for it bestowed great glory upon the lovers as opposed to their being treated with universal scorn by the highly principled Yadavas. This truth was not lost on Munna and he was grateful for Maya's sake as well as his mother's. Anyway, he reasoned to himself, the stories that get told are almost as good as the ones that actually happen and it all depended on the perspective you chose to take. He glanced at his father for confirmation and was rewarded with a wink from the great man who seemed fully to concur.

As for the revelation that he had been the God of Desire in a former life, truly it had blown his mind. Sukra must have known this as well for he had told him Kama's tragic tale so many times that Munna had finally said that he could not care less about a stupid schmuck who had played pimp for the Gods with a ridiculous toy bow and who had clearly deserved to be blown apart, for meddling with matters of the heart when there more more important things to do. His guru had nearly died of laughter and at the time Munna had patted himself on the back for his wonderfully irreverent sense of humour. Needless to say, he was now mortified at the memory but could not wait to discuss it with his father—whom he already thought the world of—and Maya.

Rukmini wiped the tears from her eyes and hugged Maya, formally welcoming her into their home and addressing her fondly as a beloved daughter. 'If I am your daughter and Munna is your son, does that make him my brother? I suppose sleeping with a brother is preferable to having sex with a son,' Maya thought in the privacy of her mind and quashed a hysterical urge to giggle madly. A garbled sound emerged from her throat as she hugged her new mother back, which Rukmini chose graciously to ignore. 'Entire lifetimes would be insufficient to repay you for the tremendous service you have done the Yadavas,' said Rukmini. 'My son is blessed to have someone like you in his life. It is truly miraculous that your love for each other is so great that it has managed to survive the three-eyed God's wrath. Your coming to the land of the Yadavas is a blessing, for surely it is a harbinger of great prosperity and good fortune and I welcome you with all my heart.'

Maya touched her feet and received her blessings. All present could feel the palpable warmth between the two women brought together by their great love for their prince and were moved to tears. The Goddess Rati, who had known herself only as Mayawati, felt as though the ground under her feet had given way on hearing Narada's tale. It all made sense to her now—the long years of despair, the interminable waiting and the peace she had found in Munna's arms. Listening to Narada's revelations made her feel as though she had been granted absolution for all her sins and life was beginning afresh for her. In gratitude she sought the blessings of every one of the Yadu elders as well. When she stood in front of Krishna, she hugged his knees and wept. The dark Lord comforted her, and calling Munna to him, formally declared them to be man and wife as the congregation got to their feet in thunderous applause.

Munna heaved a sigh of relief. He had not known it but for some reason he had been dreading the meeting between his mother and wife. All things considered everything had gone smoothly and the two women had actually embraced, and his secret fears had been unfounded. Munna smiled to himself and vaguely wondered why Krishna who seemed so attuned to his thoughts was looking pityingly at him. As for Maya, she sensed her lover's satisfaction and mentally shook her head at his naiveté and his unrealistic expectations that the women in his life were going to love each other to pieces and get along just fine.

Munna settled into the Yadu way of life as if he had been raised in it. Blessed with the natural charm of his father, he had no trouble getting along with his people and his extended family which included more aunts, uncles, siblings, cousins and relatives than he could count. As Sukra's foremost student there was no dearth of demand for his talents and soon he was making himself useful in every department of governance. In addition to the day-to-day demands of running the kingdom under the guidance of Krishna, he also began training young boys in the science of warfare and students began flocking to him from far-flung lands. Everyone wanted a little piece of him and he was happy to oblige. But he was happiest when he was making up for lost time with Krishna. The two of them made it a habit to take off all by themselves whenever it was possible, and Munna grew to love those excursions.

Krishna continued his education which Sukra had begun and Munna found it most stimulating. He felt blessed to receive such divine knowledge from the man who was believed to be a God and who just happened to be his father. Munna would have been happy to kill Shambara all over again for robbing him of a childhood with such a special father. But he was glad that they had been reunited and was determined to make the most of it. The two of them grew very close and Munna found he could talk to him about anything, even the things which he had shared with none, not even Maya.

The killing of Shambara had been weighing heavily on his conscience and he unburdened himself to Krishna when they were resting after an invigorating session of swordplay. 'It is unfortunate but all pointy things, even this most magnificent of swords, remind me of the time I stuck a dagger into the back of Shambara's throat. It must be admitted that no man deserved it more, but even so it bothers me a little. If only I had known the truth about my origins, I would have openly challenged him to a duel and dealt with him honourably. Then there would have been no need for Narada to spin his fine yarn which was calculated to save not just his sorry behind but also spare Maya and me from disgrace!'

Krishna spoke: 'What disgrace is that? The fact that Maya chose to be with her lover and husband, whom she had performed penances to win back instead of bowing and scraping to convention? Or your timely actions in saving her from the brute who was going to kill her just after the two of you had been reunited and discovered the happiness that had been lost to you?

Don't waste your time with regret or second-guessing your actions from the past. They are pointless pursuits which will keep you mired in the past even as the promising present and future languish for want of wholehearted attention. Shambara would have been just as dead even if you had taken great pains to hand him an honourable death whatever that may be. Death is death and there is nothing to render it more dignified, honourable or palatably pretty. It is as final for the man who meets it with a sword or a woman's breast in his hand as it is for the man who has to yield to it while voiding his bowels or scratching his balls. You can imbue your life with beauty, meaning and purpose, but death is far less glamorous. It is simplest to focus on living right because life offers you a modicum of choice and at least the illusion of control which death certainly doesn't.'

'I suppose you are right! Already, I feel less like a piece of dog turd! And seeing how you mentioned death, there is this other thing which has been bothering me a little... I am no stranger to death, am I? As Kama I was a victim of Shiva's anger and it would seem that I have been given a new lease of life. I am grateful for it is a good one but do you know what the future has in store for us? Sooner or later we are all going to die... What is going to happen next? What will become of Maya, mother and you? Will we meet again?'

'You did not just stop with wondering about the future, did

you? It seems to me that you have already made up your mind about it or at the very least figured out a way to live with your doubts and uncertainties...'

'As a matter of fact, I have, but how come you prefer to let me, your favourite son, figure out stuff for myself whereas when Arjuna, your loving cousin and self-proclaimed best friend, comes to you with his dumb self-indulgent queries, you launch into lengthy sermons that will in all likelihood have future generations poring over pages and pages of philosophical, pleonastic gobbledegook that will easily take entire lifetimes to comprehend, if at all? Wait! Don't answer; I will work it out for myself... It is only because Arjuna represents the dumbest segment of humanity who possess more brawn than brain, and need to be spoon-fed the simplest matters of life!

Anyway, forget him! As I was saying, on most days it is very clear to me what the future will be about. It is a vast canvas that is filled with endless possibility. While it is true that in a former life Maya and I were the star-crossed lovers, Rati and Kama who lost each other and everything they had built together—the fact remains that we traded in that existence for a fresh one, where I am blessed with a father who does not seem inclined to curse me, a loving mother, relatives, friends, students and of course, Maya who is the best among wives and also the best amongst lovers or friends. I am well aware that this life will also be taken away from me, but I am confident that the people and the things I care about the most will never be lost to me forever. I believe this with every fibre of my being!'

Krishna patted him gently on the shoulder, 'It is good that you believe such stuff, because otherwise you are likely to go stark, raving mad and I am being succinct here given that you seem ill-disposed towards tautology. As for the reason I don't launch into lengthy sermons with you, it is because as my own flesh and blood, a part of me is within you, and therefore, all you have to do is look within for all the answers and philosophical discourses you could wish for!'

'But of course! I did wonder why it is so easy for me to put myself to sleep!' said Pradyumna. 'And for the record you are not fooling me by telling me what I want to hear. You consider just about everything in creation to be your children and therefore you are present in everyone and everything which makes me no more special than, say, a pillar!'

While Munna bonded with his father, got pampered by his mother, and took thoroughly to his new life, Maya had a harder time of it. Never the most sociable of creatures, she found it difficult to adjust to her new world. Rukmini was never overtly hostile and was cloyingly sweet to her. Maya responded in kind. The other ladies of the royal household tended to treat her with pointed deference which made it clear that they might be willing to tolerate her presence but they had no wish to befriend her. Munna was also spreading himself too thin and moreover, his mother seemed determined to monopolize him during the precious spare time he had.

Never one to allow minor irritants to get the better of her, Maya took steps to carve a life for herself in this strange land. Since she was not a huge fan of Munna's mother, she made it a point to befriend Krishna. Then with her father-in-law's blessing, she bought a string of ponies and began giving riding lessons to the younger girls. It was ironical that a skill her first husband had taught her would prove so instrumental in giving her life with her second husband some purpose, but there it was.

Needless to say, her young students loved her for helping them break away from the boring norms of accepted ladyhood—which included sewing, embroidery, singing and dancing and forcefully excluded fun stuff like swinging a sword, stringing a bow or learning to ride a horse or an elephant. Maya opened for them the doors to a whole new world of freedom and her charges worshipped the ground she walked on just for that.

Their mothers were hostile at first and muttered darkly about demon-born harlots, bereft of modesty, who thought nothing of flashing their privates to the entire world while getting astride a horse, but they warmed to her when she offered to teach them to ride as well. The more timorous ones were content to simply sit behind her as she cantered along, feeling wonderfully wild and alive, while the bolder ones summoned the courage to mount a horse and some even managed to gallop across the sprawling palace grounds while the men looked on in slack-jawed disapproval which only made the pastime even more fun. Maya organized many such rides and picnics. These enjoyable excursions made her a great favourite with the ladies. Soon they had all taken to her and were rushing to her for advice on a wide range of issues from the quickest way to get rid of a pimple to how best they might enhance their sex lives. Maya helped them all and soon she was almost as beloved as Munna.

Munna may have become very busy but even so he reserved all his nights for her and she would joke that he was merely using her for sex while he would retort that it was hardly cause for complaint. A brief few months into their new lives saw Munna and Maya thoroughly content with how everything had panned out for them. It was around that time that Rukmini decided to give her precious son a gift.

She summoned her son to her and told him that she wished to do something special for him, hushing him up when he started to say there was no need. Like loving mothers everywhere, she had found a suitable bride for him. The girl's name was Rukmavathi and she was the daughter of her own brother, Rukmi. Rukmini assured her son that the new daughter-in-law possessed all the qualities men prized in their wives. Maya wondered uncharitably if her mother-in-law meant Rukmavathi was hypermammiferous or possessed of an exceptional rear. As for Munna, surprisingly, he did not seem too upset about his impending marriage to a stranger—especially one who purportedly possessed all the qualities a man could wish for in a wife. 'You know I cannot refuse you mother!' was all he said and Maya wished men would someday find the gumption to make a clean break from the umbilical cord which they insisted on clinging to with both hands for the rest of their natural lives.

'Frankly, I am a little surprised at your choice, mother,' she said aloud, 'from what I have heard, there is some bad blood between Krishna and Rukmi, who still insists that you were kidnapped by the dark Lord whom he openly derides as a coward and lowly cowherd though everybody knows that you fell in love with him and plotted to elope with him. Did your brother not swear to defeat Krishna and bring you back, failing which he would not return to his kingdome of Vidharba? If my facts are correct, Krishna not only crushed him but was so annoyed with the stream of imprecations he was uttering, hoping to bring down calamity on the heads of his sister and so-called abductor, that he tonsured him and rid him of his facial hairs as well. Father-in-law would have humiliated him further if Lord Balarama had not intervened and urged him to desist, if only for your sake.

Rukmi does not strike me as the sort of man who would have the generosity of spirit to forgive a hated enemy and magnanimously let bygones be bygones having realized the error of his ways. The man has made no secret of his desire to be avenged upon the pair of you and has prayed to Shiva to help him in his nefarious designs. The Destroyer obliged by gifting him with many boons—one of which included a special bow that rendered him invincible. It was his hope to destroy Krishna with this weapon but he had not reckoned with Shiva putting paid to his plans by saying that the bow will return to him if it were used against his dear Vishnu, no matter what form he was in. They say Rukmi's disappointment was profound and he channelled his anger into winning kingdom after kingdom with his bow and is now a force to be reckoned with.

I could be wrong but it does not seem right to welcome a man with such black vengeance in his heart, into our family, where he could work all manner of mischief. For all we know, he could have raised his lovely daughter to hate the Yadavas and instilled in her a desire to hurt its members. Pardon me if I speak out of turn, but it seems to me, that it is but common sense not to embrace a fanged serpent and its hatchling!'

Maya knew she had gone too far when she saw the look of dismay on Munna's face but defiantly she held her ground. She would be damned if she allowed Rukmini to force some ugly relative with ulterior motives and murderous intent on Munna. Rukmini had gone deadly white with outrage. Before her marriage, she herself had complained no end about her arrogant and obnoxious brother who had tried to get her married to his creepy friend. She remembered how she had quailed in the face of his anger when Rukmi had caught up with them and been defeated by Krishna. So great was his hatred for her that he had looked her in the eye and called her a whore with a taste for all that is putrid and baseborn. Those stinging words which had brought tears to her eyes had provoked Krishna into teaching him a much-needed lesson, but she could not bear for others—not even her own husband—to malign her elder brother.

Rukmini was certainly not going to allow a jumped-up chippy like Maya, who had quite a chequered past of her own, to get away with judging her own noble family, 'It is very sweet of you to express so much concern for the well-being of this husband at least...' Rukmini purred and watched with supreme satisfaction as her barb found its mark, before continuing, 'But I don't think there is cause for worry since nobody could possibly care more about Pradyumna or his safety than I do. It is monstrous to suggest that Rukmi or his daughter would even consider hurting me or my family over an elopement that is ancient history. Rukmi even commiserated with me when Pradyumna was taken from me and offered comfort the way a good brother should.

Rukmavathi is a good girl blessed with abundant beauty, charm and a loving heart. She will be an exceptional wife and an asset to my son. I have known her since she was a baby and a sweeter child I have not had the privilege of seeing, with the exception of my own firstborn. They were made for each other—Pradyumna and Rukmavathi. Besides, everybody says she takes after me in spirit and flesh. More importantly, if her wide hips are any indication, I am positive that we will have strong heirs very soon. If my words are proved false, I will cheerfully cut off my tongue and give up my life!'

Munna thought it prudent to keep his thoughts to himself, though he was upset with all the talk about pulling out tongues and dying. His wife seethed but thankfully, she held her peace because she was reflecting on how nauseating it was that her mother-in-law genuinely thought it fitting that a clone of herself, spawned from the same gene pool, was the ideal vessel for her son to pour his seed into in order to ensure the family line remained unbroken. The emotional blackmail was the final straw and Maya was determined to make her dear mother-in-law follow through on her empty threat when her brother's brat turned out to be the bane of Munna's existence.

Krishna had been silent all along but he winked at Maya (cheering her up immeasurably with this little show of support), and gently blocking the gruesome vision she was having of Rukmini in her death throes, before gently chiding his wife, 'You know that Maya did not mean to insult you. Even you have to admit that you are overreacting a little and behaving exactly like the obsessive mother you swore you would never become. Maya was merely recalling that the Yadus do not hold your brother in high esteem, especially after he cast his lot with our enemy, Jarasandha, and his cronies. In fact, I myself told Maya about the little altercation the two of us had on the day he hoped to marry you off to the odious

Shishupala and it is hardly surprising that she went off the deep end, when you suggested that her husband marry Rukmi's daughter.

My better half, Rukmini is not just the most beautiful woman in the Three Worlds but the wisest as well. Do you remember the many tantrums Satyabhama has thrown because she was sick with jealousy of my great love and regard for you? You always treated her with great magnanimity and kindness because you were able to understand her feelings and you sympathized with her. I know that she has irked you ever so slightly with her competitive spirit and little games to prove to herself that I love her best among my wives. But out of the goodness of your heart, you chose to be indulgent and treat her the way you would a precocious infant or an annoying younger sister. It was because you know that I will always have enough room in my heart for those who choose to shelter in it, and that the place you hold there will never come under threat even if I am always making room for others as well. You have been content and our marriage has been perfect because of it.

Maya is also our daughter now and I was hoping that you would give her the benefit of your great wisdom. Instead you, who have always been clear-sighted even when forced to share your husband with more women than you care for, are finding it notoriously difficult to share your son with another. If you think about it, it is so ridiculous that it is funny!'

Everybody smiled at that, even Rukmini, for Krishna's glee was too infectious to resist. Rukmini and Maya both felt abashed for giving way to pure spite the way they had. They knew themelves to be good women who had simply brought out an ugly side in each other, which they had no desire to nurture any further. The former was the first to speak. 'I owe you an apology... You saved my son and kept him safe when he was all but lost to me and I loved you for it but I also hated you a little because you had usurped my place in his earliest memories and well, because you are his world. The two of you don't even realize it, but you complete each other to such an extent that the rest of us feel as though there is no room on your isolated, self-sufficient island for anyone else. It was not at all nice on my part to be so resentful of your happiness!'

'You need not apologize!' said Maya. 'I am to blame for trying to keep Munna all to myself. And it was wrong of me to have said all those awful things to you. Krishna was right about you, there is no woman in the Three Worlds more worthy of emulation! Please forgive me!'

Rukmini hugged her in response and the two women found their hearts were considerably lighter as they had mutually disposed off the heavy burden of angst. The elder woman then graciously explained herself to the younger one, 'Rukmavathi fell in love with Pradyumna when she came here to visit me and decided that she would marry none else. Her father arranged a swayamvara for her and she rejected all the suitors present, declaring that she had already given her heart to Pradyumna. My brother was not entirely pleased, it has to be admitted, but Rukmavathi appealed to me for help, and I gave Rukmi a stern talking to. We agreed that father and mother would have wanted our two families to get along and this was a good opportunity to forge new bonds of familial affection. I have given my word that Rukmavathi will be wed to Pradyumna and all that remains to be done is for us to go to my brother's newly formed kingdom of Bhojakata and bring her home formally.'

It was all that remained to be done. The Yadavas began preparations on a grand scale for the impending nuptials. Due to the munificence of Krishna, Dwaraka was famed for being the city of plenty. Its citizens dined on plates of gold and lived in palaces with bejewelled pillars that outshone the sun. Nothing would do for the wedding of their prince but the very best. When the Yadus set out for Rukmi's kingdom of Bhojakata, they were weighed down by baggage trains packed to bursting with ornaments, garments, and other assorted treasures for the bride-to-be. Passersby swore that the opulence on display would have put Kubera to shame. Rukmi, of course, would not be outdone and he had arranged an extravagant ceremony for his daughter.

Rukmavathi was a gorgeous bride. She did not possess the fabled beauty of Rukmini or Maya but mercifully, she looked nothing like her father. Pretty, but not overwhelmingly so, and corpulent in a pleasing sort of way, her biggest assets were her bouncing curly locks and her smile which was on full display during the rituals for obvious reasons. She had won the man of her heart and there was not a happier soul in the Three Worlds.

Munna took an instant liking to her and he said as much to Maya, 'You can tell just by looking at her that she will be an absolute delight. I was worried I'll wind up with a Bhama and will have to devote the rest of my life towards making sure that my wives don't kill each other!'

Maya agreed, 'Your mother was right. She does possess a certain quality that men value above all else in their wives—the ability to love her husband unconditionally, worship him on a daily basis, and treat his grossest bodily fluids as if it were the blessed nectar of immortality—even if he turns out to be the biggest son-of-a-bitch that ever lived. You could have been a rapist and murderer of children and she would still go to her grave insisting that you are a hero and champion of the masses who deserves to rule the universe in place of the Gods.'

'Life is going to be interesting with my two wives, to be sure. One would drink the nectar of immortality and call it piss, the other would drink piss and thank the Gods. But I can hardly complain, for sugar and spice will always balance each other beautifully!'

'I am the sugar and spice in your life, never forget that!' piped Maya. 'But I am not going to ruin the moment for you. Rukmini has chosen wisely because this girl seems very sweet and she is going to make you very happy. And as you said I will be there to make sure that you don't overdose on sugar and go off into a coma. I am going to congratulate your mother on her choice and also to ask her to find me a hot young stud of a groom and if she refuses, I can always threaten to go after her handsome husband instead.'

Wisely, Munna chose to ignore her parting shot, as well as the fact that she clearly had the hots for his father. But then again, who didn't? And so it was that Munna met his new bride with laughter in his eyes and deep affection in his heart. The wedding festivities went on for months and to Rukmini's great relief, her brother was on his best behaviour. Even Krishna was amenable to her suggestion that he refrain from provoking her hot-headed brother into an ugly brawl that would mar the auspicious occasion, and that he keep an eye on the short-tempered Balarama as well.

Krishna not only listened to her but took Maya under his wing as well. She had made her peace with the fact that she would not be the only queen of her husband's heart, but Krishna sensed that she could use a shoulder to lean on and rose to the occasion. He told her stories about Kama and his two consorts knowing that it would make her feel better. Maya was pleased to note that it was Rati—not Priti—reborn as Maya who had found Kama reborn as Pradyumna.

'I have decided to be happy for him...' Maya told Krishna, 'and for myself as well. We have been through too much together and the time for misery is well and truly over. I have had my fair share of grouses with this life. Ideally, I should never have been married to Shambara or forced to play a role in his death. In a perfect world, Munna would have been mine alone and I wouldn't have to share him with every princess with a crush; but there is no point in lusting after perfection which cannot be had when an imperfect, yet happy, life can be had and enjoyed.

It is my good fortune that Munna and I have found each other after what must have been eons of painful separation. We have much to be thankful for and I am not going to ruin it by dwelling on curvy princesses who have all that stupid men want. Besides, it could have been worse and I could have lost him to booze or drugs or a bereaved, angry God again!'

'Good for you!' Krishna hugged her gently, 'Just be happy and try not to get in your head too much. I know you have been trying unsuccessfully to understand how it came to be that you wound up in Shambara's bed, despite the fact that you had pleased Shiva and successfully solicited his aid. But the time has come for you to let it go. All these things happen for a reason, even if it is not immediately discernible to you. Don't let your tumultuous thoughts get the better of you and drown everything else in your head and heart. Find your inner peace and allow the hand of destiny to guide you.

Remember that there are no happy or sad endings, for the soul has neither a beginning nor an end. It is immortal and will take the course it must, which is beyond anyone's control. When the time comes, you will not forget what I told you today, and hopefully, it will help you stop being stupid and blind.'

Maya might have been offended had anyone else said these words, but she was not and hugged her father-in-law whom she liked even more than Munna at the time. Rukmini noted that the two of them seemed to be spending a lot of time together and might have been mildly annoyed, but at least they were keeping each other out of mischief and she supposed she ought to be grateful for it. Rukmini breathed easier when they all returned to Dwaraka with their limbs and heads intact. Just as she had predicted, Pradyumna had taken to Rukmavathi and they made a charming couple. Even Maya had voiced her approval of her new sister. Rukmini had been appreciative of the compliments about her brother's daughter but she wished Maya had left unsaid a couple of rather tasteless and highly inappropriate jokes, the sum of which she had preferred to forget. All that was left to make her world perfect was an eagerly awaited announcement from her children that she would be a grandmother soon.

Munna and Rukmavathi applied themselves most energetically and enthusiastically towards fulfilling Rukmini's desire. Thanks to their laborious endeavours, before the year was out, Rukmini was cuddling her beautiful grandson who was given the name Aniruddha. The youngster took after his father and grandfather in all respects save one. No divine voices rang out at the time of his birth, heralding him as the slayer of some notorious villain, thereby jeopardizing his safety.

Rukmini was so relieved that she wept with joy and declared that all her prayers had been answered. Maya tended to believe it was simply because that particular story had already been done to death and did not bear recounting, and in fact disagreed with Munna who said that Shambara's fate served as an example to keep potential baby killers at bay. Krishna merely smiled, and said only that the family line would be carried on by the heirs of Aniruddha. His words delighted his family and they lavished their little prince with all the love they could muster, for Aniruddha held in his little hands their combined hopes for a bright future and everlasting life.

A Taste of Blood,
Glory and Romance

The birth of his son fulfilled Munna in ways he had not even dreamed possible. His entire existence revolved around his boy and even Maya said she had fallen in love all over again. In fact, there was not a soul in the entire Yadu household who did not love the little prince. They could easily spend hours discussing how Aniruddha had distinguished himself on a particular day even if the baby had done nothing but sleep, feed, burp, gurgle and eject bodily wastes in an unbroken circle. The days when he raised his head, turned over, began consuming solids, crept, crawled and started walking for the first time, were all celebrated as major occasions.

Dignitaries from other lands were shocked on one particular occasion when the Yadu royals spent the better part of a day analyzing the remarkable manner in which the infant ran. They were informed, with the gravitas befitting a staid administrative meeting, that while running, Aniruddha would clutch his chest with his left hand and propel himself forward with swinging up and down movements of the right hand. It gave him what appeared to be a cute if uneven gait, and the Yadus were convinced their prince could outrun a cheetah and run circles around the finest racing horses in the world.

Arjuna, the famous Pandava warrior and Krishna's best friend arrived from Indraprastha to see the baby, laden with gifts. The citizens of Dwaraka came out in droves to catch a glimpse of the hero they had adopted as their own when he had wed a daughter of the land and Krishna's sister, Princess Subhadra. Arjuna was suitably entranced with Aniruddha and declared that his strong fingers and firm grip indicated that he would be a fine archer. The third Pandava then insisted that he himself would teach the prince the science of Dhanurveda and raise him to be an archer on par with himself. This declaration sent the members of the royal clan into paroxysms of glee. Munna reciprocated by declaring that he himself would take little Abhimanyu, Arjuna's son by Munna's paternal aunt Subhadra, under his wing, and would not rest till he had made him the greatest warrior of all time. The two behemoths then shook hands on their deal, while the extended family looked on.

In addition to seeing the baby, Arjuna had come to invite the Yadus for the Rajasuya yagna which his elder brother, Yudhishtra, was performing. Most members of the royal family including King Ugrasena, Vasudeva, Krishna and Balarama accompanied Arjuna back to his kingdom. As always, Munna felt a tad resentful when his father left with Arjuna and he thought it was a good thing that Abhimanyu took after his mother's side of the family. The Pandava brothers would no doubt keep his father with them as long as possible since they tended to be a whiny bunch and would complain endlessly about how their cousins, the hundred Kauravas led by the eldest, Duryodhana, were forever making life difficult for them. Munna himself thought that the brothers were lucky that Dhritarshtra, the blind old king and Duryodhana's father, had generously agreed to give the Pandavas a separate kingdom. The way Munna saw it, it was Duryodhana and not Yudhishtra, who had a stronger claim to the throne. After all, Pandu who had been Yudhishtra's father had been the younger brother and the only reason he was made king was on account of his brother's blindness. He quickly tired, however, of thinking of all the drama queens in the Kuru clan and only began to wish that his father would return quickly—for truth be told, he missed him already.

Munna's sense of foreboding would prove to be justified, because with his father and uncle gone, it was practically a tradition for some enemy or the other of their clan to turn up at their gates with a big fat army, howling for the blood of the Yadus. Almost as if on cue, Dwaraka came under a deadly attack, mounted by one of Krishna's oldest enemies—Shalva.

King Shalva counted Rukmi and Shishupala among his closest friends. He had been present on the day when the Princess Rukmini had been cruelly abducted by Krishna. He had been among the warriors who had given chase, only to be defeated with embarrassing ease by Krishna. As he lay face down in the mud, watching the retreating wheels of the victor's chariot, Shalva had sworn to avenge his disgrace. In the years that followed, his obsession with Krishna took on a dangerous edge. Everywhere he went people sang the praises of the cowherd and his so-called heroic deeds. Krishna's fame was so widespread that it was said that even the Gods did not enjoy the same popularity. It was outrageous that his enemy, who routinely abducted virgin brides and even other people's wives, should be so revered while Shalva himself seemed destined for obscurity even though he was a hero who had risked his life for friendship's sake. Yet there was not a poet in the world who would sing verses in his praise unless he was willing to pay through his nose or urge them to do so at sword point, which usually resulted in some extremely uninspiring and insipid lines that were not worth hearing or repeating.

Determined to remedy what he found to be an absolutely insupportable state of affairs, Shalva used his madness to fuel the intense tapas he performed for long years. When the three-eyed God came before him, he threw himself at his feet and sought a boon that would help redress the wrong Krishna had done him. Consequently, he became the proud owner of an enchanted chariot, constructed by Vishwakurma, the architect of the Devas, known as Saubha. This splendid vehicle would be completely indestructible and impervious to attacks launched by Gods, men or fierce predators. It would take its master anywhere his heart desired, rain down weapons on foes, and turn invisible so that its victims would not even be able to see what manner of creature had brought about their deaths.

Having received such a wondrous gift from the Destroyer, Shalva could have chosen to see the wonders of the Three Worlds, explore new territories unknown to man, or even take a few ladies to some private wonderland where they could devote their entire attention to the pursuit of amorous sports—but he was a madman on a mission. Armed with his Saubha, and gathering together a large force for good measure, he attacked Dwaraka. He reasoned that it would be best to destroy everything Krishna loved, before killing him in the interest of writing a truly memorable revenge saga.

Without warning, Shalva swooped down on the Yadavas, and it fell to Pradyumna to resist him and save his people. He rose to the challenge like he was born to do. Gathering the scattered forces of the various clans—which had been torn apart by the suddenness and brutality of the attack, he mounted a determined counter-attack, urging the Yadavas to fight for their loved ones and for their beloved city. Drawing on his own considerable resources, painstakingly accrued under the tutelage of Sukra, Munna succeeded in unmasking Shalva who was using his monstrous vehicle to cloak himself in a veil of invisibility.

Freed from the illusion, finally the Yadus knew what they were up against and mercifully, they were no longer sitting ducks. Despite the spirited defence they put up, their combined strength waned against the Saubha which seemed to be an incarnation of the Destroyer himself. All hope seemed lost when Munna took a mace directly to the chest and lost consciousness. His charioteer lost no time in driving him away from the battlefield and the Yadu troops were utterly demoralized. Shalva moved in for the kill, as victory danced achingly close to him.

The mad king had not reckoned with Krishna's mighty son, however, who recovered almost immediately. He was so infuriated with his charioteer for daring to flee from the battlefield and making him look like a coward, that he almost followed through on his threat to chop off his head and hurl it at Shalva. The poor man, who had believed prince Pradyumna dead, was so relieved to see him alive that he took only a moment to salute his master before rushing him back to join the fray.

The sight of their bloodied prince returning to the battlefield like a lion among men, unmindful of the grave injuries he had just received, put fresh heart into the soldiers and they fought with renewed savagery, determined to kill every single one of the damned interlopers.

For twenty-seven days, Munna held off Shalva, refusing to yield even though his arsenal was completely depleted and his strength at its lowest ebb. But he fought on, for the alternative was the inevitable sack and rape of Dwaraka which he refused to let come to pass. He swore to himself over and over again that he would not let his son grow up without a father or a kingdom and he threw every ounce of his formidable spirit into the attack, determined to uphold his promise. Across the legions separating them, he felt the presence of his father urging him on, revitalizing his flagging strength, and constantly encouraging him to hold on—for Krishna would never let down those who had placed their faith in him.

Meanwhile, Yudhishtra had completed his Rajasuya yagna but almost immediately there were inauspicious omens in the sky that heralded the coming of doom. The bull of Chedi, Shishupala, denounced the proceedings in unholy language when the first offerings were bestowed on Krishna, profaning the sanctity of the occasion as he heaped abuse on the dark Lord. Finally, it was the Sudharshana chakra released by Krishna which cut him off for good. As his head rolled on the floor, Krishna quietly told his brother that they were needed post haste by their people and they left as quickly as possible.

The beleaguered Yadava troops were the first to spot Krishna, who swooped down on Shalva mounted on Garuda. The mighty eagle whom legend had it could support the weight of the entire world with just one of its feathers, was never far when his chosen master needed him. The soldiers screamed with joy—but none louder than Munna who still refused to leave the battlefield, though he had sustained serious injuries that were in need of urgent medical attention. But there was no way he was going to miss watching the father he worshipped in action, as he decimated their enemies.

From his vantage position in the sky, Krishna took care of the enemy soldiers first, who had dared to attack his stronghold. As the cheering soldiers watched, Shalva attempted to steer his chariot in Krishna's direction but for some reason, the saubha would not release its weapons on him. He screamed at Krishna mouthing obscenities in a thick stream. The latter, though, was completely unperturbed and using his bow he sent sharp arrows whizzing in his direction. Efficiently they chopped off Shalva's limbs, and as he lay dying, the last thing he saw was the Sudharshana chakra coming for him.

Munna started jumping up and down in his chariot, chanting his father's name as the rest of his people joined in. He was still cheering himself hoarse when he passed out and his charioteer speedily took him to the royal physicians. Later, when he came to, he found Maya cradling his head in her lap, as he reposed on his own bed. She was singing him a song (he refused to think of it as a lullaby) about mighty men who performed glorious feats. Seeing that he was awake, she uttered a little cry of pure relief.

'I am so glad you are finally up!' she babbled excitedly, 'You should have seen yourself when they brought you to me! It was as if you had been chewed up and swallowed by a pack of wild animals that then chose to spit you out! We were all so scared, and that little milquetoast you married started keening thinking you were dead, forcing me to give her a tight slap to shut her up. Krishna came in just then and assured us that you would be fine and just needed to sleep a little, for heroism can be very tiring business indeed. He sat next to you for a bit and you should have seen the expression on his face. He was so proud I thought he was going to explode! We all are.

It was absolutely amazing the way you threw back that bastard! Every single report that trickled back to us was full of the glorious feats you pulled off. We had some of the soldiers who had seen you in action brought to us and they told us that you reminded them of Krishna at his most magnificent. The citizens of this great kingdom have done nothing but sing praises of you and Krishna. Most have assembled at the palace gates to catch a glimpse of you and assure themselves that you are fully healed.

We heard how you were injured when that fiend, Shalva, attacked you from behind and ordered his fire-spewing mounts to kick you in the head. Your charioteer steered you to safety but you were furious that he had taken you away from the battlefield and ordered him to take you back even as you bound up your fractured skull with the hanky I gave you, simply to stop the bleeding so that you could jump right back into the fray. But how come you don't have any head injuries? I suppose Krishna fixed you up with his magic or whatever it is he does... Did you know that I have never found you sexier than I do now? You're just too cute when you fight bad guys to the death!'

Munna grinned as she blathered on, deciding that there was no point in telling her about what had actually happened on the battlefield—especially since he himself was fuzzy on most of the details. He certainly did remember though that the blow he had taken had been to the chest, not the head, and that to the best of his knowledge, there were definitely no fire-spouting horses anywhere in the picture, since the marvellous saubha did not need them. As for the hanky, try as he might for the life of him, he could not remember being given one or what had been its eventual fate. He supposed he must have dropped it and someone would have used it to bind a wound, mop their brows or blow their noses which was definitely not something Maya would appreciate hearing. Rukmavathi peeked in timorously right then and hesitated, worried that Maya may just slap her again for intruding on their privacy but Munna's first wife was feeling expansive and she waved her in.

As the women fawned on him in admiration, Munna thought it felt great to be a hero. Indra who had been following his career on earth with great interest was delighted he felt that way and made up his mind right then and there that he was the man to help him with a certain niggling problem. He said as much to an old friend who was also very fond of Krishna's boy, 'Pradyumna is the most likely candidate to help me out of a potentially dangerous situation. The boy was positively brilliant on the battlefield! He is brave, strong and too bloody good-looking to be true. Just the sort of fellow who can make his way into an impressionable young virgin's heart without even trying...'

'The boy has just escaped death by the skin of his teeth and already you are planning to snatch him away from the loving caresses of his lovely wives! Of course you are thinking of plunging him into one of your perilous missions which generally end with one or more persons being cursed, or dying, or wishing they were dead...' replied his friend who was a little too familiar with Indra's scheming ways.

'Oh, come on! I love Pradyumna like a son and there is no way I would even consider doing something to endanger his safety—not for all the power there is to be had!'

The high-flown sentiment was wasted, for it elicited a disbelieving grunt in reply, 'Of course you cared a lot for his safety when you sent Narada to pay a little visit on Shambara which resulted in the boy being dropped into the sea when he was but a wee one. Everybody knows that being dunked in the sea when you can't even raise your own head, is most beneficial for good health and a long life, right?'

'You should give me a little more credit!' said Indra. 'As if Krishna would have just stood by and allowed his precious firstborn to meet such an end! If my actions had resulted in Pradyumna's untimely death he would have personally destroyed Mother Earth before slicing off my head and Narada's as well. While it is true that the dark Lord is the most evolved of Vishnu's many avatars (in that he is more God than man), the fact remains that there is a very tiny part of him that is human with all the attendant strengths and weaknesses of that lot. Did you know that his only weakness is his precious son? After all, Pradyumna was Shiva's gift to him and he values him highly.

Not many know it, for the general consensus is that he is like the lotus blossom that lives and thrives on water but is entirely detached from it. But when Pradyumna was lost to him he knew grief and it has come to my ears that he went to Shiva seeking comfort. It was the Destroyer who soothed him and sent him on his way by promising him that Pradyumna would lead a long and distinguished life which was nothing more than his destiny. Obviously Krishna knew the truth of these words but even so, he needed to hear it from the lips of Shiva. Sure enough, while still a stripling, Pradyumna proved himself to be quite the hero, which is hardly surprising as he is Kama reborn and Krishna's son. He then proceeded, of course, to seduce Shambara's wife before killing the mighty Asura himself, thereby establishing his credentials as a legendary lover and mighty warrior, second only to Krishna!

Since then, as you know, Pradyumna has taken it upon himself to train the next generation of warriors in the science of Dhanurveda and has earned the respect of all in the Three Worlds for the fine work he has done. After his latest achievement, which has resulted in the world being rid of another madman, it is time for him to enhance his legacy by carrying out an assignation for the noble Devas.'

'So what I have heard is true!' said the friend. 'Apparently, you were paid a visit by your brother from another mother, the Asura King Vajranabha. It is almost fitting that he is named after your beloved thunderbolt! They say that he has grown very powerful ever since he succeeded in hoodwinking Brahma into bestowing boons of power on him. If the legends about him are to be believed, Vajranabha is so strong that he does not need armies to subdue mighty kingdoms and force them to yield to his will. With the entire world at his feet, he has set his sights on your throne, but with unprecedented graciousness, he refrained from giving you and the celestial army the licking which would be but a given. Instead, rather foolishly, he came to you with the hope of making you see the sense of avoiding unnecessary bloodshed. He told you that since you are both sons of Kashyap, he has an equal right to the throne of heaven and since you have held onto it for so long it is only fair that you abdicate in his favour and let him have his turn.

If my sources are to be believed, you looked as though you had been rammed in the rear by a rhino. But to your credit, that remarkable brain of yours switched to high gear and you made a quick recovery. Smiling sweetly at Vajranabha who allowed himself to be suckered in, Indra of the infinite cunning managed to stall successfully for time. Pretending to be thoroughly amenable to his suggestion, you sent for your Apsaras who got into some of their more erotic dance routines and relieved Vajranabha of the little lucidity left to him. While he was lost in the beauties of Urvashi's naked charms, you told him that it would be best to wait until Kashyap finishes his penances so that he may preside over the coronation of the new king of the heavens. The demon king agreed and returned happily to his kingdom.

Meanwhile, since even you wouldn't dare push the dark Lord where the safety of his son is concerned, I am guessing you went humbly to him as a supplicant and enlisted his aid. It is on his suggestion that you are finally ready to act!'

Indra grinned with pleasure, 'You do know me! Just for the record, it is extremely tiresome dealing with my father's excessively ambitious and seemingly endless heirs who have this irksome habit of popping up at the most inopportune moments which forces me to come up with ingenious ways of getting rid of them. They are all ugly, brutal, tyrannical, and uniformly deluded in thinking that they have what it takes to sit on my throne. However, they are also notoriously difficult to kill. A lesser king would give up the exercise completely—for it seems that everytime I have just finished taking out one threat, a new one crops up, and it just goes on and one... But I am not daunted! It is my job to rid the world of such scum and I take it very seriously indeed.

Krishna agrees with me fully on this and he was not in the least angered when I explained the role Pradyumna will be playing. I assured him that his son will find this assignation to be most pleasing. As I said earlier, there is a beautiful young maiden to be had as a reward for the service he is going to do me. The lad has already demonstrated a taste for Asura women who are forbidden to him and it is my belief that he will find Vajranabha's daughter, the enchanting Prabhavati who is already madly in love with him, entirely to his taste!'

'I am not surprised you have already got to the princess. But how did you manage to pull it off? Vajranabha came to his senses once he put suitable distance between himself and your celestial temptresses, and is wary of your intentions. I hear he declared that all entry to his kingdom of Vajranabhapura be restricted until he himself has authorized otherwise. As for his daughter, he is fiercely protective of her and she is not allowed male visitors even if they are ancient, juiceless or sworn to practice celibacy for life. I am curious as to how you circumvented his precautionary measures.'

'It was simple enough. The celestial swans that belong to me are so famed for their beauty and their repute for bringing good fortune, that they are welcome wherever they go. So they roam the

Three Worlds with complete freedom and occasionally I have used them to spy for me. On my instructions, these birds have been frolicking in the pools that dot the palace grounds. Hearing the amazing birds talk about how Vajranabhapura is even more beautiful than Indralokha...' here Indra grunted as if he could not believe the lies people would swallow to feed their egos, 'Vajranabha himself was suitably enraptured and has encouraged them to visit as often as they liked. On my instructions, Suchimukhi, the cleverest of the flock has befriended the princess and has been telling her all about Pradyumna. The thing about over-protective fathers who foolishly try to raise their daughters without allowing them to interact with the opposite sex is that they make their wards excessively curious about the male of the species while facilitating the development of a smouldering sexuality that is rendered all the more powerful because it is repressed.

This is the reason these girls are likely to fall in love with the first male who steps into their lives for whatever reason. Prabhavati turned out to be no different as she is currently madly and recklessly in love with Pradyumna whom she has never seen and though she is fully aware that he belongs to an enemy race. Thanks to me, she has given her heart to one of the greatest heroes of the age and not just any random passerby. She has come to know everything about Pradyumna—from his matchless good looks to the women he has loved and married, and of course his heroic exploits. Prabhavati has displayed a voracious and insatiable appetite for the titbits Suchimukhi has been feeding her and savours every fresh chunk of information with delight. Now she lives for him and will gladly kill for him.

Suchimukhi has given the princess her word that she will contrive to deliver Pradyumna into her hands and Prabhavati is over the moon about it. Now the time is ripe for Suchimukhi to deliver on her promise. Even as we speak she is on her way to speak with Pradyumna about the Asura princess who is pining away for him. Krishna's son has a tender heart and after his recent brush with death, he will be more than game for some romance with the mysterious princess, locked away by her tyrannical father, who is waiting for him to rescue her from her prison. The swans are resourceful enough to help him gain access, especially since I myself have suggested a suitable plan. And if my calculations are right, we will soon be rid of yet another evil Asura and can enjoy a period of peace—till the next tainted fruit from my father's loins ripens to give us grief.'

Exactly as Indra had said, Suchimukhi, the wondrous swan, was indeed conversing with Munna, or at least trying to, as his first wife was present at the time and she did not seem to care very much for talk about yet another princess who had fallen in love with her husband. But Munna seemed intrigued and the swan was encouraged to persevere despite Maya's repeated and unnerving assertions that she had developed a sudden craving for roasted swan. Suchimukhi told Munna that Prabhavati was remarkable to look upon and there were many suitors for her hand but she had refused them all because her heart was set on Munna.

Maya had heard enough, 'All this talk of heady romance is making me nauseous! This winged troublemaker with the glib tongue must have been sent by Indra who is yet to meet an Asura he can walk past without contriving to kill him. It seems clear to me that he wants you to kill this dream girl's father, and the girl is only being offered up as bait to lure you into Vajranabhapura. I can see that you are pathetically smitten already but I still feel that you should know exactly what you are getting into before running off to no-man's land lured by the promise of a pretty face and hot sex!'

'Maya, for the umpteenth time, I am perfectly capable of looking out for myself and you should really stop impressing upon me that one plus one equals two as if I wouldn't be able to figure it out for myself!' Munna told her good-naturedly.

Maya considered telling him that when men started allowing their one-eyed monsters to guide their decision-making process, they tended to become completely ignorant of obvious facts like one plus one equals two. But she swallowed the words, knowing that while he could never get angry with her, there was still no reason to push him into doing so by undermining him in front of relative strangers. Moreover, she could tell that the sly swan had fully sold him on the idea of making the foolhardy attempt to break into a highly guarded palace in order to enjoy the forbidden charms of a willing princess. Men were so infuriating sometimes! Almost as infuriating as women who schemed endlessly to get them into their beds!

She decided to question the swan some more, thinking it might be prudent to gather all the information she could about this new rival, 'You spoke about this woman's incomparable beauty but I noticed that you failed to mention if she is a nice person. Tell us more about her character... Is she really worth all the fuss?'

Suchimukhi considered the question seriously before answering her, 'I can assure you that she has a lovely personality. She is warm, loving and generous to a fault. Everybody loves her because she does not behave like a haughty princess at all. She has a kind word for all who cross her path and can never refuse anyone who is in need of help. Her love for Pradyumna is true, and more importantly, she thinks very highly of you. I told her how you kept him safe from Shambara and she was awestruck.

If my judgement is correct, it is not her intention to unseat you from Pradyumna's heart—if such a thing were indeed possible—but having lost her heart to him, she merely seeks to claim a small piece for herself. You would not deprive your younger sister, would you, or force Pradyumna to spurn her for your sake?'

'It is not in her nature to force people to do what she wants, Suchimukhi!' Pradyumna sprang to her defence, 'She is not above trying to influence my judgement but in the end I make the call and even if she disagrees most strongly, I know that her full-hearted support will be mine.'

Maya smiled at him, amazed at his ability to make her love him all the more even when she was seriously contemplating breaking his neck over his philandering ways. 'Munna has his heart set on marrying Vajranabha's daughter and I will not stand in the way of his happiness. But dearest husband of mine, I pray that in our next life, there will be a much-needed role reversal and I'll be the man to your woman. Then you can wave me off and keep your feelings in check while I sow my wild oats with gay abandon and marry as many women as I feel like.'

Krishna came in just then and Maya, who had been planning to walk out on that note, paused in midstride to seek his blessings. 'Your son is all set to embark on yet another amorous adventure. He stands there pretending to hesitate over my feelings in the matter but the truth is he knows that with me, he can get away with murder and so he takes advantage of my good nature. As always, before giving his full commitment, he awaits your approval. I could have told him that Indra would not have dared involve him in such a risky enterprise without your express approval—but men think they know best and nobody thinks to seek my opinion!' Thoroughly pleased with herself for hitting two high notes in a row, she brought her palms together respectfully before her father-in-law who was smiling fondly at her—and beat a hasty retreat.

Suchimukhi looked at her retreating back admiringly before offering an opinion, 'She is something, isn't she? I have been to every inch of the Three Worlds and nobody, absolutely nobody, has every contemplated eating me, except her! But now that she has given her blessing, perhaps it is time to act!'

'Have the preparations been made Suchimukhi? I don't think it would be advisable for my son to go into Vajranabhapura all by himself. His mother will have my head if I were to let it happen. It is my wish that he be accompanied by some of our crack troops...'

began Krishna.

'Father! You are almost as bad as mother! Do you seriously expect me to take our entire army along for a romantic tryst? Will they be holding lamps and watching over me as I go about my private business?'

'Calm down, Pradyumna! If I did not think you capable of handling Vajranabha, I would have gone with you myself. But it is my belief that you cannot do this on your own. First, we need to get you into Vajranabhapura without detection. Magic and illusions will not fool the demon king. On Indra's suggestion, I have agreed to send you along with some of our best men as part of a travelling troupe of renowned drama artistes led by Bhadra who is the finest actor alive. He has a reputation for bringing our history to life on stage with his colourful and moving performances.

Suchimukhi has already talked to Vajranabha about the brilliance of Bhadra and the demon king, who fancies himself as a connoisseur of the fine arts, has extended an invitation to this troupe to come and entertain his court with their acclaimed portrayal of the Ramayana. You will have the perfect cover to enter the city and Suchimukhi will help you keep your assignation with the princess. When the time is right, you can elope with her after taking care of her father!'

Munna thought it was a good plan and he could not wait to put it into action. In no time at all, he had put together a small but deadly fighting force who then incorporated themselves smoothly into Bhadra's troupe. Their next stop was the kingdom of Vajranabhapura, the gates of which were thrown open to them on the orders of king Vajranabha.

It was a wonderful city, especially when contrasted with Shambara's kingdom of bleak stone. Vajranabha certainly had an eye for beauty and his kingdom sparkled, reflecting the amount of planning that had gone into its making. The royal household was accommodated in a sumptuous palace that was almost a city unto itself. The king had also ordered airy, spacious and tasteful homes to be constructed for his people. He had not stopped there but built roads, hospitals and recreational facilities, so that his citizens may dwell in comfort. Beautiful gardens, parks and limpid pools were also seen in abundance. Peacocks roamed the land freely with regal grace, having adopted Vajranabhapura as their own home.

Munna watched a woman feeding the peacocks that had congregated in her home with grain out of her own hand and he felt a pang of conscience. Already he had fallen in love with the city and he was sorry that he was not entering its warm embrace with goodwill in his heart. Despite the fact that the king had restricted access to his kingdom, the hospitality of the people could not be faulted and the members of the drama troupe were exceedingly well taken care of.

They were presented before the king and his court where they were received with great enthusiasm. With endearing candour, Vajranabha informed them that he was not a big fan of the Ramayana which he felt consisted mostly of one-dimensional characters who seemed too noble to be true or far too wicked to be believable. And though he was not entirely unwilling to suspend disbelief, he simply could not see an army of monkeys defeating the mighty hellions of the legendary Ravana. But his biggest issue with the Ramayana was that he felt it had been cowardly of Rama to abandon his pregnant wife in the forest, after listening to a dumb washer man! He himself would have had the audacious cretin's head for daring to cast slurs on his own queen. And if he had entertained doubts about her chastity he would have had her head as well!

Bhadra's smile had become somewhat stilted by then, but Vajranabha assured him that he was nevertheless looking forward to the performance and would do his best to keep an open mind. Munna could not help thinking that it was always the cads who felt free to judge the noble Rama who, at his worst, was still a better man than the rest of mankind put together.

Vajranabha was not at the forefront of his thoughts, however, for his daughter was monopolizing his entire attention. He was no longer the brash youngster who had once been so impatient in love that he had allowed himself to be caught completely unawares. This time around he would do nothing to endanger the safety of the mysterious princess who had managed to reach across impossible distances to stake her claim on his affections. Munna waited patiently till the day Bhadra and his troupe were ready to perform. Then he waited some more till the play was well underway and the audience were suitably immersed, before planning his getaway. A scene involving the rape of Rambha who was on her way to meet with her lover and betrothed, Nalakubera, when she was intercepted and raped by Ravana, was being portrayed and every single member of the court followed the example of their king and had their eyes glued on the stage. So engrossed were they with the plight of Rambha that Munna and Prabhavati could have pranced naked all around them and none would have noticed.

Munna tranformed himself into a bee and hid among Suchimukhi's feathers as the bird flew to the princess's chambers. Vajranabha had felt that the content of the Ramayana was too adult for his impressionable daughter and had denied her permission to watch the show. Ordinarily she would have sulked but not this time for Suchimukhi had promised her that she would be in Pradyumna's arms. The time had finally arrived when she could live out her dreams in the realms of reality as opposed to one of fantasy, and she could barely keep her excitement and apprehension under wraps.

Prabhavati felt the presence of her lover even before she saw him. Overcome by shyness, the princess stood bashfully before the unbelievably handsome man who stood in her room where no man had ever dared to do so before. As she gazed at his feet which were also beautiful, she realized that on that night there would be no sleep for her and she could not have been happier. Her happiness added an extra dimension to her beauty and Munna thought she was the most alluring woman he had ever met.

Maya had warned him not to let his expectations skyrocket, as otherwise disappointment would become a likely outcome. But she need not have worried for Pradyumna thought that his adorable, blushing lover exceeded his wildest expectations and then some. They wed in the Gandharva style and soon there was no time or need for shyness. As they sported madly through the long hours of the night, communing in the timeless rhythms of love, Munna remembered Maya as they broke apart briefly and he felt a twinge of guilt. Then he remembered that one of her favourite sayings was that good sex was not something to be knocked and she would have agreed that the best sex of his life was hardly something to be censured. And very soon he forgot about her, lost in the enchanting embrace of the princess Prabhavati.

Over the next fortnight, Bhadra held the king captive with his exquisite art while Pradyumna and Prabhavati held each other captive with their love. But the wise would have predicted that such a state of affairs was hardly meant to last. A princess can only do so much to prevent her overzealous attendants from discovering the numerous love bites that adorned her body, before they got wise to the fact that their little girl was now a grown woman.

The news was whispered in Vajranabha's ear and all too soon the lovers were busted. The king's guards burst into their room in the dead of the night to catch them in the act, but this time, Munna was prepared. He had sought the help of Vishwakarma to build a flying chariot for him along the lines of the infamous saubha that had come so close to killing him. He fought off Vajranabha's men, moving at the speed of light, and killing them before their eyes had time to get accustomed to the darkness that was the proven friend of illicit lovers everywhere. With the same speed, he bundled Prabhavati into his chariot—and for a split second it seemed that they might actually be able to make a clean and speedy getaway. In the meantime, his men had opened the city gates and allowed access to the Yadava forces which had been lying in wait. Soon the Yadus were locked in deadly combat with the Asuras, who, taken by surprise were having the worst of it.

Watching his beloved city go up in flames, Vajranabha rose up into the heavens on his own vehicle and went in pursuit of Pradyumna, determined to make him and his wretched daughter answer for their sins. So great was his fury that he succeeded in bringing down Pradyumna's chariot. Prabhavati's father and lover were soon locked in a struggle to the death. Vajranabha's courage and valour on that day could not be denied but he was no match for Krishna's son who soon had him on his knees with a sword to his throat. He would have killed him then but Prabhavati begged him to be merciful and he held his hand.

Vajranabha was having none of it however. 'Kill me!' he snarled at Pradyumna, 'a life handed to me as alms from a whore of a daughter who I no longer claim as my own, means less than nothing to me. You might as well kill me because if you let me live, you will be sorry. I will not rest till my family name and honour is restored and that would be possible only by spilling the blood of this bitch. I slew her mother when I discovered that she had raised such a dishonourable creature who would sacrifice her father and his innocent subjects, just because she is in heat. Make no mistake; there will be no peace for me until I have slain her as well.'

The vanquished king looked at his Kingdom which would soon be razed to the ground and he uttered a howl of anguish that made Munna reel and Prabhavati wail in distress. The sound of her regret infuriated Vajranabha and he turned on her, eyes blazing with hatred, 'The blood of your father and his people are on your hands, accursed daughter of mine! The Yadus have sacked the city which I raised with my own hands, sweat and blood. Alas! That I have lived to see this day! They will not rest till every able-bodied man has been killed or forced into slavery and every woman raped or murdered. Even the old, infirm and children will not be spared. This is the result of your wanton lust and you will pay for it with your blood!'

'Don't you dare blame her for the consequences of your massive ego! It is not a crime to fall in love!' Munna spoke up in her defence. You would have done well to understand your daughter's feelings and chosen to give her hand in marriage to me. But you care only for your false pride and have recklessly endangered the safety of your people.'

'I will not be preached at by a treacherous son-of-a-bitch who killed the noble Shambara whose salt he had partaken of and under whose roof he sought succour! As if that were not despicable enough, you lay with and married your mother!' Vajranabha roared at him, uncaring that the sword had pricked his throat and was weeping blood, 'Coward that you are, you sneaked into my kingdom using false pretences, at the urging of Indra, the greatest villain that ever lived and you dare to tell me what I ought to have done to save my people! It was my ambition that doomed them and I am prepared to die for it, but before that revenge will be mine!'

Munna saw the madness in his eyes as Vajranabha lunged desperately towards Prabhavati who was sobbing as if her heart had broken. The sound pushed him over the edge and with one almighty heave of his sword, he lopped off Vajranabha's head even as he jumped back to avoid the thick stream of blood that was being pumped out by the headless trunk. Hearing a sound, he looked up and he saw his father's mount in the sky coming towards him. Krishna had sent Garuda to make sure his son and new bride were escorted safely back to Dwaraka once their mission was accomplished.

As they flew to Dwaraka on Garuda's back, Munna held his sobbing wife close to his chest, reassuring her that everything would be alright, till she nodded off in his arms. He saw Vajranabhapura blazing in the distance and in his heart he was sorry for the beautiful city that had been home to so many precious memories. The exhilaration that followed a kill had always eluded him and he felt heartsick with misery. From Garuda's back, he had seen firsthand the price so many had paid for two people's happiness.

As Garuda took him far away from the site of his pain, the ache in his heart lessened. In the distance he could see Dwaraka beckoning to him brightly. The two people he loved best in the world were waiting to receive him. And for the first time he believed that everything would be alright as he had promised Prabhavati; if not immediately, at least eventually.

The Road to an Ending

$\mathcal{D}$waraka was abuzz with news. The long simmering conflict between the five Pandava brothers and their hundred cousins, the Kauravas, had finally come to a boil. Not content with conning his cousins out of their kingdom of Indraprastha and sending them into exile in a dicey game of dice, Duryodhana refused to let them have their kingdom back when they returned after the stipulated period of thirteen years. The Pandavas had decided to go to war and both sides had begun preparing furiously for their almighty conflict. Krishna had acted as a peace emissary, but his efforts came to naught and he returned to Dwaraka.

The Pandavas and Kauravas were both related to Krishna, but he was closer to the former as they were the sons of Kunti who was his father, Vasudeva's sister. The third Pandava, Arjuna was his best friend and married to his sister, Subhadra. He had arrived in Dwaraka to formally enlist Krishna's help towards their cause. Duryodhana had also come for the same purpose and the citizens could barely contain their curiosity, since it was a well known fact that Krishna never turned away anybody who came to him for help.

Krishna announced his decision to the warring cousins and both were seen leaving Dwaraka as if they had been delivered the Three Worlds on a silver platter. Munna found out what transpired in the secret meeting and he stormed off to remonstrate with his father. Not for the first time, he thought that Arjuna was one of the most annoying men that ever lived with his incessant demands on Krishna. Personally, he thought that Duryodhana was perfectly justified in not wanting to return their kingdom to them. They would probably piss it away— along with their wives and children— in yet another gambling match. On entering his father's room, he found his uncle Balarama bellowing at his father. Munna knew that he ought not to interrupt, but he was extremely protective of Krishna, and though he agreed with everything his uncle said, he still could not bear to hear his father get yelled at. He walked in with impunity knowing that his presence would serve to take the edge off his uncle's wrath.

'...Sometimes, your actions are too reprehensible for words Krishna! It is bad enough that those idiots have determined to fight among themselves and destroy the better part of an entire generation, but you have made it a hundred times worse. How could you make Arjuna and Duryodhana choose between the Yadava army and yourself? Now the Pandavas will have you on their side while the Kauravas will have our army! Do you think any Yadava worth the illustrious moniker will ever find it in him to lift a finger against you? And if there is one such, I will be perfectly happy to smash his senseless skull with my plough!

Did it escape your attention that I command our forces? Are we to face off against each other? What if I were determined to kill your precious Arjuna and his witless brothers? Would you sever my head with your Sudharshana chakra and weep as my life's blood drenched Mother Earth? Answer me Krishna... Is that what you want?'

Krishna smiled at him as if he had no inkling why his brother was so worked up. 'At the outset, I made it clear to Arjuna and Duryodhana that it was my firm decision not to take part in the actual fighting, nor will I be armed. So the question of whether I will opt to decapitate you with my chakra does not arise. Besides, you could not kill Arjuna if you tried, for only Shiva can check him in battle. As for Arjuna, he will not lift a finger against you because he knows I love you. Are you satisfied now?'

Balarama kicked the back of a chair in frustration. 'Absolutely delighted! It was exactly what I needed to hear. I get to keep my head and you get to shovel horse shit in addition to having a fantastic close-up view of Arjuna mowing our men down. I will not be a part of this accursed war, Krishna! The Pandavas and Kauravas are related to us and I will fight neither for nor against either. As of now, I will formally give up the command of our army. My mind is made up. I will go on a long pilgrimage and wait out this period of madness which has made killers out of good men.' His eyes alighted on Munna and they softened briefly before he rounded on Krishna again, 'Why don't you name Pradyumna commander of the Yadava army? It is only fair that in a war where brother is intent on killing brother, that father and son be forced to turn against each other.' And with those heated words he departed with none of the usual serenity that was characteristic of those who were planning to undertake pilgrimages.

Pradyumna knew that Krishna would not go back on his word no matter how much Balarama screamed at him and would certainly participate in the war. So he merely went and laid his head on his father's lap as was his habit. His main grouse had been that Arjuna had asked his father to be his charioteer, but proximity to Krishna had given him a greater sense of clarity and he knew that Arjuna loved Krishna almost as much as he did and merely wished him to be close to him in the heat of war. Generous and understanding as ever, his father had acquiesced because he in turn loved Arjuna almost as much as his firstborn. Munna decided to let the matter rest.

It was Krishna who spoke first, 'You will not have command of the army. I will need you to look after the kingdom in my absence. There is none better suited to the task than you.' Munna nodded mutely in assent as his father continued, 'Satyaki, my dear friend, will kill himself if I ask him to go to war against me, so

Kritavarman will be given the job. I daresay he will be more than happy to accept!'

'Good for him!' Munna replied finally, 'I am just glad that there will be no part in all this for me since I have had it up to the gills with all the senseless blood-letting than goes on in this world. Ever since the truth of my origins was made known to me, I must admit to feeling a little ashamed knowing that I was the God of Desire reborn, since it is well known that he preferred a toy bow to a real one, and that choice he made, in my eyes at least, somehow made him less of a man. But now I realize that perhaps he had the right idea all along. Violence never makes anything better, and blood is too heavy a price to pay for anything that is worth having. As a lad, I wished for glory on the battlefield. Now it is my wish that the lad I was, had had the sense to wish for something else!'

Krishna's eyes lit up at the mention of Kama, 'I was aware of how you felt but I knew you would come around! Kama is the best among the Gods as you are the best among men. Never forget that! For a minute there, it felt like listening to him talk! It is my fond hope that future generations will learn from the mistakes of their ancestors and have the strength and courage to take the path of non-violence, the way Kama chose to. But that is a long way off and in the meantime we will persist in our stupidity and pay the price for it with blood. This war was meant to happen and fate will have its way, like it or not!'

'I suppose so but it is clear to me that the outcome has already been determined. In recent times I have become omniscient like you, so I know beyond a shadow of doubt that the Pandavas are going to win. Many fools may attribute their victory to the nebulous fact that Arjuna is the greatest warrior of all time, but I am no fool and by my reckoning the war was decided when Arjuna made the cleverest decision he ever has, which was choosing you over the mighty Yadu army.'

Munna was right about the outcome of the battle and Krishna was right about fate always having its way. Munna watched his father leave for battle and uttered a silent prayer to Shiva to keep him safe and grant him success in the tremendous endeavour he had undertaken. Gloom descended on the kingdom like a wet blanket and though Munna kept himself as busy as he possibly could, it would be the longest eighteen days of his life. Messages about the war poured in every single day and there was seldom any happy tidings to be had for sooner or later every family in the kingdom received dire tidings about the death of a loved one.

On the thirteenth day of the battle, the worst imaginable news was brought to the kingdom by a messenger who could barely speak as the tears poured down his face in an endless torrent. Munna was able to decipher the meaning behind the garbled flow of words though—Abhimanyu, Arjuna's son by Subhadra, had been killed. He had seen all of sixteen summers. Munna grabbed the messenger and shook him violently till he had composed himself enough to tell him every single detail.

Dronacharya, the commander in chief of the Kaurava forces had arranged his troops in the dreaded Chakravyuha formation. Only four men alive knew how to penetrate the wheel-shaped arrangement known for its ability to run over everything in its path—Krishna, Arjuna, Abhimanyu and Pradyumna. The Samsaptakas or the suicide squad, deadly warriors who had taken a terrible oath to die rather than yield on the battlefield, had challenged Arjuna to a fight and led him to a remote corner of the battlefield. In the meantime Drona was using the formation to tear apart the Pandava forces and take Yudhishtra captive in order to fulfil his promise to Duryodhana. In desperation, Yudhishtra had asked Abhimanyu to help the family, for at the time it seemed highly probable that the day would end with all their deaths if they could not find a way to stop Drona. The young hero had risen to the occasion and forced a breach, without the slightest care for his own safety.

The rest of the Pandava forces were supposed to follow closely on his heels—since the prince had revealed that he knew the means to penetrate the Chakravyuha but not how to get out from its clutches. However, the plan was foiled when Jayadratha, the king of Sindhu, repaired the breach spurred on by his obsessive hatred of the Pandava brothers—and they could only throw themselves desperately at the unyielding wall of soldiers even as Abhimanyu was hopelessly trapped inside.

Wrapped closely in death's cold embrace, Arjuna's son had been unafraid. He stood poised to end the battle on that very day, as he slaughtered the Kaurava forces in large numbers, even as they converged on him, unable to close on the lone warrior. The Kuru stalwarts had then resorted to foul means to save themselves. On Drona's instructions, Abhimanyu was engaged on all sides though it was against the rules of combat. Karna, Duryodhana's best friend and Arjuna's worst enemy, slew his charioteer, killed his horses and broke his bow from behind—for no man on earth could disarm him in straight combat. Drona severed his sword at the hilt and Karna smashed his shield. But Abhimanyu had fought on, refusing to yield. Picking up a chariot wheel, he had taken the fight to his enemies who circled him relentlessly like birds of prey. When the wheel was also shattered by a cloud of missiles, Abhimanyu had picked up a fallen mace and duelled with Saindhava, the son of Dushasana, the second Kaurava brother. Both men had swooned then and Saindhava was the first to recover. Without giving Abhimanyu time to recover, he had smashed his skull in and killed him at once.

Munna had lost control by then and he was weeping uncontrollably. He screamed for his attendants to bring him his weapons and arrange for a vehicle so that he may depart for Kurukshetra immediately. 'Those bastards killed the peerless Abhimanyu with deceit and treachery! They will pay for it with their blood! He was my favourite cousin, my best student and as dear to me as my beloved father and son. I loved him even more than my wife! Take me to Kurukshetra this very instant! I will cut off Dronacharya's tongue for giving voice to the fell deed that was carried out. I will sever Karna's villainous hands with my own sword, and leave him to bleed to death. Saindhava must die as well for finding it in his black heart to murder that noble child. None of the Kauravas will survive my wrath!

How my father must be grieving over the loss of his favourite nephew! I can't even imagine what my aunt Subhadra and Abhimanyu's young wife, Uttara, must be going through. She was carrying his child—and that poor baby will never know his father!

Where are my weapons? Bring them to me or I will have every single one of your heads. Or forget the damn things! My hands are good enough. I will rip the entire Kaurava army to shreds with them.'

The members of the court were shell-shocked with grief and despair. Abhimanyu had been one of their own and they mourned his loss. Witnessing their beloved prince Pradyumna—whom they had never seen bereft of a smile—scream out in anguish was more than they could bear. Gruff veterans remembered Pradyumna's laughter which had rang out across the battlefield when Shalva had attacked him. They joined their tears to his, even as good-hearted soldiers and courtiers now held him down, forcibly restraining him from carrying out his threat.

Munna grabbed one of the men, holding him down, and dashed him to the ground. More would have followed, but Mayawati entered the assembly in response to his primordial grief. She went straight to her husband and placed his trembling arms around her own shoulders. In soft tones, she begged those present to excuse her husband and she led him away, protective as ever.

Maya led him to her inner apartment so that they may have some privacy. All around them they could hear the sounds of great mourning, for Abhimanyu had spent the better part of his childhood in Dwaraka and had been greatly loved by all who knew him and even those who didn't. The few who had been indifferent to the boy, could not remain so any longer as they heard of his tragic end, and joined in the general pathos. Even after his death, Abhimanyu would manage to win more hearts than he had while alive and would continue to do so over the endless passage of time. Brief though his chapter had been, it was a glorious one and on the strength of it, there would never exist a world which lacked for people who loved him and continued to weep for him.

The sorrowful dirge which seemed to have enveloped the universe nearly drove Munna mad. Maya held him tightly against her chest offering him what comfort she could and lending him her strength till he quieted down. When he began to talk the words poured out in a rush, 'I offered to train the boy in the science of arms when Arjuna said he would do the same for Aniruddha. As it turned out, the Pandavas were exiled when Abhimanyu was still a boy. Krishna brought Subhadra and his nephew home to Dwaraka, for his beloved sister wished to follow her husband into the forest and my father could never allow her to know hardship. I was entrusted with the charge of Abhimanyu and was able to fulfil my promise to make him the finest warrior to have walked the earth. He was so special, Maya! We were so close at the time. I was Sukra's best pupil and my guru lavished great attention upon me. I did the same for Abhimanyu. In my eyes he was as precious to me as my own son.' His voice broke as painful memories flooded his consciousness.

Maya picked up the thread and replied gently, 'I loved him too. Even as a tiny tot he had such a big heart, full of kindness and compassion. I remember thinking that he was every bit as wonderful as you are.'

Munna smiled through his tears, 'Abhimanyu was a better man than I am, Maya. They used to say that the best qualities of the Pandava brothers, Krishna and my own self were combined in that boy. It was not just hype, it was the plain truth. I was never perfect like him. My character has a flaw—in that I have always been mildly resentful of Arjuna. His friendship with my father bothered me no end and I hated the fact that they enjoyed being with each other so much. Sometimes I delude myself into thinking that I have, or ought to have, a monopoly on his attention and affection.

I remember an occasion when Abhimanyu asked me if I knew what he had in common with Krishna, Arjuna and me. After a bit of teasing, I confessed my ignorance. He told me that the four of us belonged to an elite membership, as there was nobody else alive who knew how to break the terrible Chakravyuha formation. Needless to say, I was flabbergasted. It was incredible that someone of his tender years had successfully mastered something that only a few mortals had before him. Abhimanyu was pleased with my reaction and revealed how he had learned the technique while still in his mother's womb. Apparently Arjuna had been talking about it with Subhadra—although, before he could quite finish his discourse, Subhadra had dozed off. As a result, though Abhimanyu knew how to force his way into the deadly formation, he had never been able to learn the secret of how to fight his way out. It was his intention to surprise his father when he returned from exile, by showing him what he had learned from him and to get Arjuna to teach him the rest of it.

In retrospect, I realize that it was most unwise of me to let it go at that. I should have taught him the rest of it then and there. A little knowledge is a dangerous thing and the world will know the truth of this adage, thanks to my extreme stupidity. Perhaps my pride had gotten the better of me and made me a little miffed that he sought to learn the secret craft from his father and not me. Thanks to my hubris, the dear boy is dead and no amount of regret will bring him back. At the very least, I should have done what Satyaki did by casting my lot with the Pandavas. Then there would have been no need for Abhimanyu to have undertaken this suicide mission. Drona, Karna, Dushasana's evil son and the rest of their ilk may not have been responsible for his death after all. His blood is on my hands.'

'Don't say that Munna!' said Maya. 'You can't blame yourself for the actions of the evil Kauravas. How could you have known that such a travesty would come to be? It would be inconceivable for someone with your integrity to break someone's bow from behind or kill an opponent while he is unconscious. You could not have seen this coming. My husband is the noblest among men and I will slap the moron who says otherwise, even if it is you! What do you think Krishna would say if he heard you talking like this? He would have chided you for being every bit as arrogant as Arjuna if you begin to believe that you exercise any control over the mysterious workings of the universe.

Abhimanyu would have hated for all his loved ones to be unhappy on his account. Do not grieve for him. He has achieved more in the sixteen years granted to him than most do over several lifetimes. While still a boy he proved that he is more man than the rest of mankind put together. I know a wise man who is fond of saying that the people he cares for will never be lost to him forever. When he said it, I remember thinking he was full of shit, but I believe him now and I think you should too.'

Soothed thus, Munna came back to his senses slowly. As originally intended, he did go to Kurukshetra that very night. The Pandavas would be absolutely gutted and they would be leaning heavily on Krishna. Worse news had come to Dwaraka. Munna learned that the situation had been compounded by a terrible oath which Arjuna had taken. The third Pandava had sworn to kill Jayadratha, the man who had been the root cause of Abhimanyu's death, by sundown the next day—failing which he would enter the sacred flames and give up his life.

Munna sensed that even the indefatigable Krishna had a little too much on his plate. Abhimanyu had been a great favourite of Krishna's. Knowing his father, he would be bearing the weight of the combined grief of all who had cared for the dead hero. He would also be concerned about keeping Arjuna alive as the Kauravas would put their entire army between him and Jayadratha. They would be slavering over the chance to get rid of Arjuna which would effectively mean the end of the war, and every warrior on their side worth his salt would do everything in his power to make it happen. Munna would not be able to rest without checking on his father and providing what comfort he could for the bereaved, so he hurried to the battlefield.

For Krishna and the Pandavas, Munna's presence was a great comfort. Showing no outward signs of the grief that had almost felled him earlier, Munna cheered them up as much as he could by sharing some of his fondest memories of the pupil he had loved like a son. Following his example, all present told their favourite anecdotes about Abhimanyu, and the session served as a palliative for their pain. Arjuna alone, Munna observed, stayed silent as though carved from stone.

They needed their rest for the big day ahead and Munna did not want to keep them up. He said his farewells and made ready to depart. Before leaving he took Arjuna aside for a brief word. 'With your permission, I would like to take aunt Subhadra and Uttara with me to Dwaraka. The battlefield is no place for a woman in Uttara's condition. Maya and I will do everything in our power to cheer them up and help them deal with their loss.'

'I would like that very much...' replied Arjuna in a carefully controlled voice. Munna would have liked to say a few words of encouragement, offer his support or even reiterate his confidence in the third Pandava's ability to pull off what he had undertaken—but he said nothing. Arjuna was a proud man and he would display no sign of weakness. So Munna simply nodded and turned to

leave, when Arjuna spoke again, 'You have my gratitude, Munna.
It makes me feel easier knowing that my wife and daughter-in-law
are in safe hands. Thank you!'

Still at a loss for words, Munna nodded again and went off
in search of his father. Krishna was talking to his own charioteer,
Daruka, and Munna waited till he was finished before approaching.
He simply stood in silence till his father chose to address him, 'If
Arjuna fails on the morrow, then the entire world will feel my wrath
for I will personally destroy Bhoomi Devi and all her creatures.'

'Arjuna will not fail father... You know it as well as I do. He
feels he let down his son while he was still alive and he will never
allow his death to go unavenged. And with you by his side, he
cannot fail even if he were to try.'

'It was nice of you to come this far, Munna,' said Krishna.
'Arjuna may not have shown it but he appreciates all you have
done. He also knows that you are not to blame for what happened.
I want you to erase such thoughts from your mind and return
to Dwaraka with Subhadra and Uttara. We have turned a corner
now and the end is in sight. I will be with you soon. Now go!'

Obedient as ever, Munna complied with his father's wishes.
Rukmini and Maya took it upon themselves to look after the
bereaved women. Arjuna did manage to fulfil his oath, with Krishna
helping him every step of the way. His astounding triumph put
fresh heart into his troops and the Pandavas succeeded in defeating
the Kauravas. After long years where hardship and toil alone had
been their bosom companions, the five brothers seemed finally to
have regained their kingdom and put the worst of their misfortunes
behind them. Conversely for the Yadavas, trouble was waiting just
around the corner.

Krishna had stayed on after the war, to help the Kauravas bury
their dead and put their affairs in order. Gandhari, the bereaved
and embittered mother of the hundred Kaurava brothers had taken
a very harsh view of the role Krishna had played in the death of

her boys. Years ago, she had taken the decision to forsake the gift of sight when she had been told that her groom was a blind man. Having willingly opted to share his world of darkness, Gandhari had become famous for her noble sacrifice and amassed a sizeable amount of ascetic merit.

The aged queen, who had the respect of all who knew her, was especially angered over the manner in which her firstborn, Duryodhana, had been killed. Bhima, the second Pandava brother, and her son had slugged it out in a massive fight to the death with their maces. This match had particularly high stakes as the winner would get the crown. Bhima's superior strength notwithstanding, Duryodhana's skill in wielding the mace was unmatched in the world. Her son had come within touching distance of victory—when Bhima had smashed his opponent's thighs with his mace inflicting a mortal blow on him, having been prodded into flouting the rules of fair combat by Krishna

When all was over, the Pandavas, accompanied by Krishna, appeared before the blind king Dritarashtra and Gandhari, the parents of the deceased Kauravas, to pay their respects as decorum demanded and to somehow make them feel better about the fact that they had slaughtered every one of their hundred sons. Gandhari's terrible sorrow and endless grief coalesced into a spear point of unreasoning madness which she directed towards the dark Lord, 'Take a good look around you, Krishna! There are bodies as far as the eye can see, floating on a sea of blood. You have painted a portrait of destruction that you should be ashamed of. Your handiwork is unsurpassed as the ultimate artist of doom!

Do you not hear the sound of melancholy in the air? It is the sound of sorrow crashing over the ears in a shattering crescendo and it is more than enough to drown out even the memory of what it was like to be happy. The battle of Kurukshetra has left too many of us as victims to live out our lives in misery and despair. So many lives lost, so many families destroyed, so much blood, and so much misery! YOU orchestrated this massacre Krishna, and the blood of every single one of the dear departed is on your hands.

You could have stopped this, but you allowed this atrocity to unfold and reach its gory conclusion. Don't think you have gotten away with the horrors you have perpetrated. For there is still justice in this world and if I have any say in the matter, you will be made to answer for your crime!'

The old queen was panting for breath as the intensity of her emotions began to overpower her. Frail and weak though she was and nearly prostate with grief, she cut a terrifying figure as she prepared to declare her sentence on the dark Lord whom she fully blamed for the tragedy that had overtaken the mighty Kurus. When she spoke, her voice was a harsh staccato with an unworldly timbre that chilled the bones of those who heard it. 'Exactly thirty-six years from now, this mass madness which engulfed the mighty Kurus and drove them into a killing frenzy which saw the flower of a generation lost forever, will overcome the proud Yadus. They will turn on each other and kill everyone in sight, blindly and senselessly. Your women will know the bereavement we do...they will tear out their hair and beat their breasts, having gone berserk with despair. The very air will reverberate with the sounds of their moaning. You alone will be left standing to see the rotten fruits of your crimes, as the ones you love most in this world will be lying dead at your feet. Unable to bring back the dead and feeling utterly helpless, you will finally succumb to death, and depart this world alone and without glory!'

All present stared at Gandhari in dismay, unable to believe the things she had spoken to the God who walked among men. Arjuna was struck dumb with horror and belatedly he wished he had clamped his hands over her mouth to stop her from giving voice to the curse she had just uttered. Krishna, however, was entirely serene and when he answered, Arjuna was stunned to hear a note of amusement in his voice, 'Your words will certainly come true, Gandhari. The Yadavas are an invincible race and it will take more than the combined powers of God and man to overpower them. Therefore, it was preordained that we meet our ends at our own hands. It is most kind of you to offer us a passage out of this cruel world and you have our gratitude.'

Krishna may have been magnanimous on hearing his death sentence but the rest of the Yadavas certainly did not feel that way. The general view was that Gandhari was a senile old bat who had taken leave of her senses. It was argued that her words could not possibly come true since every ounce of the ascetic merit she had earned had been erased when the abominations that were Duryodhana and his brothers, had been born to her.

The story went that she had been consumed with jealousy when word reached her that Kunti had delivered five strong sons who could lay claim to divine origins. Gandhari could not conceal her impatience because she had been carrying her hundred brats in the womb for long years now and had still not delivered them. She had whipped her belly with a belt to hasten the process and delivered a big lump of flesh. It was Veda Vyasa who had come to her rescue and deemed that she would have her hundred sons if she cut up the shapeless lump into a hundred pieces and kept them in jars of ghee. Surely, the Yadavas argued, a woman who had taken a belt to her unborn children could hardly have a great store of ascetic merit. Krishna had faced worse threats from the time that he was a baby, and surely a cranky old crone with a vitriolic tongue could not possibly bring about the destruction of an entire race!

Munna took an equally dim, if less frivolous, view of the matter. He simply could not believe that Gandhari had spoken so disrespectfully to Krishna and had the unmitigated gall to blame him for the wrongs inflicted on the world by her evil son. In fact, if he had not been such a principled person, he would have certainly snapped her spindly neck in two and left her to croak.

He was sitting with his father when such unworthy thoughts were churning around in his head. Krishna, the omniscient, sensed what he was thinking and spoke: 'Gandhari's words had their roots in emotional turmoil and were entirely bereft of the spirit of Dharma. But that is hardly any reason for a mighty warrior and slayer of the demons Shambara and Vajranabha to contemplate the brutal murder of an old lady. If you think about it without getting worked up, you will become aware of the fact that the two of you are not entirely different. Gandhari cursed me blinded by grief and you are angered by her actions, blinded by your love for me.'

'I hate to be argumentative Father, but Gandhari and I have nothing in common. She is a mean old woman who dared to blame you for a tragedy of epic proportions which was certainly not your doing. And she did us all actual harm with the power of her words.'

Krishna spoke 'From where she stands, Gandhari was not entirely incorrect in her summation of the situation. We both know that my role in the war did not begin and end as Arjuna's charioteer. And she was right to accuse me of having brought about Duryodhana's death. If Aniruddha had been killed in such a manner, you would not have paused to debate the rights and wrongs of the situation but pursued and killed the man responsible without any further ado. You would have felt perfectly justified, for that is the way of the warrior. Gandhari, being a woman, merely used the most potent weapon at her disposal. We should not harbour any ill will towards her. Don't look so gloomy son; it is not the end of the world!'

'Except it is the end of our world as we know it!' said Munna.

'So what if it is? It is hardly a matter to get so mournful about when viewed from the right perspective. If we have served the purpose of our creation, then there is no point in simply hanging around, is there?

Remember the milk sweets you enjoyed as a kid? It was good

only when you consumed it in limited amounts. If you had spent your entire childhood gorging on them ad infinitum, I can assure you that the consequences would have been disastrous not only for you, but for the cleaners of your chamber pot as well. It is the same with life—we are all allotted a brief span of time on Mother Earth and it is up to us to make the most of it. When it is time, we should retire gracefully, instead of clinging stubbornly to life as we know it or think we do, simply because we are terrified of the great beyond!'

Munna grinned suddenly, 'I am not as scared as Maya is. She says that in our former lives we were both devoured by flames, and thanks to the whims of fate, she wound up in Shambara's palace and was forced to change the diapers of her former lover before marrying him. As regards Gandhari's curse, she was of the opinion that it is a good thing our lives have been cut short because she is not getting any younger and she did not want either of us to grow so old that we'll need diapers again! But she is concerned that in yet another life, it may just be our misfortune to be born as a mongoose and serpent or father and son! You know my wife... she went on and on in this vein, citing endless possibilities—until I finally shut her up by saying that I would love her just as much in the next birth, even if she were destined to gobble me up!'

Father and son were consumed with mirth when Rukmini walked in on them. She was pleased to see them in such a good mood. It had been bothering her that Pradyumna had seemed a little pensive in recent times, but he seemed to have recovered his good humour. 'It is good to hear the sound of laughter again. The aftershocks from Kurukshetra have left us all with a bad case of the blues but I feel it is time for us all to move on. A wedding in the family is just the thing to cheer us up!'

'It sounds lovely mother!' said Munna 'I did warn Father, that someday he would try your patience beyond the point of even your endurance, and you might just find yourself a brand new groom from your legion of admirers who continue to worship on the altar of your beauty!'

'Stop teasing your mother, Pradyumna. It is just like her to plan a wedding for me to help take my mind off Gandhari's curse!'

'You are both so cute!' Rukmini retorted with great dignity, though she did appreciate the compliment her son had paid her. 'If you are done with the schoolboy humour, I'll tell you both about it. It is high time Aniruddha was married and I have found the right girl for him... She is my brother Rukmi's granddaughter and her name is Rochana.'

Krishna groaned loudly as though he was in mortal agony and Munna just laughed some more. Rukmini addressed her dear husband who she sometimes found to be a tad aggravating, 'You married Rukmi's sister and to the best of my knowledge, you have no cause for complaint. Pradyumna is married to Rukmavathi, my brother's daughter, and their union has proved a most fortuitous one and has given us Aniruddha. My mind is made up and I will not hear a word against the match. Rochana will be my grandson's wife. She will definitely be an asset to our family.

Pradyumna, I heard your talk of shutting up your first wife, when I entered the room, and it is my suggestion that you work your magic on her. She keeps talking about the fallout from inbreeding which must surely be part of her demon-lore and if I am forced to endure more of her nonsense, I may just lose my mind!'

Rukmini had been right. A wedding was exactly what was needed to lift the spirits of the populace. The ladies enjoyed gearing up for the big event and devoted their entire time and attention in the days leading up to the big day, towards looking their very best. They tested to see if their efforts had paid off by parading prettily past the men folk, hoping to elicit compliments and proposals from them, which ranged anywhere between inappropriate and indecent. The men enjoyed the sight of pretty women everywhere and spent the time eating, drinking, flirting and gambling. Music and dance came into their lives again and the good times seemed to be back. The journey to the kingdom of Bhojakata was like one big picnic and further down the line, many among the Yadus would recall it as including some of the happiest and most memorable moments in their lives.

The wedding festivities went off without a hitch. Aniruddha and Rochana made an adorable couple and family members on both sides got sentimental over babies who grew up too fast and the magic of first love. Unfortunately, there was trouble in the offing. Shortly before the Yadavas were due to return to their kingdom with the newlyweds, all hell broke loose.

The years had not been kind to Rukmi and that certainly had not sweetened his disposition. Most of his friends had been ruthlessly killed by the man his sister had been stupid enough to marry. That old wound still rankled and it galled him to see his adversary go from strength to strength. In addition, he had recently sustained a severe blow to his pride on the eve of the battle of Kurukshetra. Rukmi had been sympathetic to the cause of the Pandavas because they had Dharma on their side. The fact that Duryodhana's ally, the son of a lowly charioteer, Karna, had defeated him in battle, though Rukmi was the possessor of the invincible bow given to him by Shiva, weighed heavily on his mind. He had been forced to accept the suzerainty of Duryodhana as a result, who had also exacted a heavy tribute from him. Yet Rukmi kept telling himself that this was not what had influenced his decision.

In avuncular fashion, Rukmi had told the Pandavas not to be afraid since he was willing to win their kingdom back for them with his own hands. At that, the haughty fool Arjuna had taken umbrage and told him that he certainly had no need of Rukmi's help to fight his own battles. Rukmi was then told he may stay or go as he pleased. Smarting from the humiliating rejection of his magnanimous offer, Rukmi decided to throw in his lot with Duryodhana. But to his chagrin, Duryodhana had been equally hostile and said that it was not his habit to partake of the discarded leavings of the Pandavas. The mighty king of Bhojakata had been forced to sit out the Great War which included the wholehearted participation of the greatest heroes and finest warriors of that golden age determined to earn their place in history. Rukmi was deeply saddened that his own legacy would fail to acquire the lustre it deserved because proud men had rejected his kindly offer of aid.

Though filled with bitterness and regret, Rukmi had agreed to the marriage of his granddaughter to Krishna's grandson for his sister's sake. He could never forgive her for eloping with his enemy but over the years he had become fond of her, because she seemed to be the only person in the world who showed him genuine affection. Rukmini not only honoured him herself but also made it clear to the Yadavas that she would brook no disrespect towards her brother.

One fateful night, Rukmi had been drinking heavily. On the suggestion of some of his relatives, he decided to invite Balarama for a game of dice since Krishna's brother was notorious for his singular lack of skill in the game. Despite heavy lossess, Balarama continued to play and angered by Rukmi's smug satisfaction at his poor run of luck, he raised the stakes to a vulgar amount of gold pieces for one last throw. To everybody's surprise, Balarama won but Rukmi would have none of it, disputing his claim—despite the fact that a divine voice declared in the Yadava's favour. Convinced that the 'divine voice' belonged to Krishna, Rukmi accused Balarama of being a lousy cheating bastard. Krishna's brother was a man with pronounced anger issues and he was not one to take to unjustified name-calling kindly. With a roar of anger, he grabbed an iron pestle and killed Rukmi with one mighty blow.

Needless to say, the journey back to Dwaraka was a sombre one marred by Rukmini's grief. She could not believe that Balarama had killed Rukmi who was her own brother, Rukmavathi's father and Rochana's grandfather on the auspicious occasion of Aniruddha's marriage. Krishna had forcibly held her back when she had tried to run to her brother, but she had heard tell that Rukmi's skull had been smashed open and he had been unrecognizable in death. The pall of bloodshed resulted in tarnishing what should have been a beautiful ceremony, and cast a shadow of uncertainty over the future. Rukmini had a feeling of impending doom and would have lain awake night after night trembling with fear, if Krishna had not taken it upon himself to siphon away her misery and dread so that she could rest easy.

There was worse in store for the Yadavas as the years rolled by. The revered sages, Vishwamitra, Narada and Kanva had paid a visit to Dwaraka. A group of youngsters thought it would be the height of good fun to play a prank on them. They dressed up Sambha, Krishna' son by Jambavathi, as a pregnant woman and displayed her to the sages asking them to reveal the sex of the baby. Infuriated with the blatant disrespect shown them, they spoke as one: 'That is no woman, but Krishna's son, Sambha. But he will deliver a baby of iron and it is this offspring of folly and foolishness that will bring about the destruction of your entire race. Feel free to laugh now, for your joke will be preserved forever in the reeking halls of infamy!'

Sambha was distraught and he fled to his brother, Munna, for advice. Weeping with regret he apologized over and over again, completely oblivious to the presence of Maya who was sitting silently in the room. She watched as Munna cheered up his imbecile of a brother with the kindness that was so characteristic of him, telling him exactly what he needed to hear, 'You are truly fortunate little brother! Ordinarily, when men are stupid they pay in heavy coin for it. But you, on the other hand, have earned direct passage to heaven for your great sacrifice in acting as a vehicle for implacable fate. Gandhari's words will come true through you, and by delivering us from the trials and tribulations of mortal life, you have earned the gratitude of our immortal souls!'

Sambha became calmer as Munna talked thus and even puffed out his chest a little. He was advised bed rest for the duration of his pregnancy and Munna even joked that the ladies would willingly welcome him into their anthappuram, now that he was going to be a proud mother! Maya could have told him that the ladies were more likely to beat him to death with their slippers, but she held her tongue. Sambha was mollified on hearing Munna's words and made his departure. Maya continued to watch her husband in silence His face was completely inscrutable and she thought that he became more and more like Krishna every single day.

He turned and smiled at her then, as though her thoughts pleased him and with a start she realized that it was reminiscent of a peculiar trick of Krishna's where the dark Lord could respond to thoughts which hadn't even been uttered. 'Sambha will deliver his baby around the same time as Rochana. Aniruddha and I had a race to decide who gets to name the child. The little rascal did not think his old man could win but I did and so the honour is mine. Since it is going to be a boy, I have found the perfect name for him. He will be known as Vajra. As you know, Indra's thunderbolt goes by the name and it can also refer to the diamond. My grandson will combine the unstoppable force of a thunderbolt with the indestructibility of a diamond.' Maya agreed it was a wonderful name but she also thought it incredible that he could discuss baby names just after being told that his brother was going to deliver an iron mace that would, in all likelihood, bludgeon them all to death.

Just as predicted, Sambha and Rochana delivered their babies at the same time. The iron mace birthed by the former was presented to King Ugrasena and on his instruction, the grotesque weapon was ground to a fine powder and discarded in the sea along with the sharp tip which stubbornly refused to be pounded. The tide played spoilsport and deposited the powder on the shore where an ugly patch of reeds sprouted up at once. The tip of the mace was swallowed by a fish just before it wound up in a fisherman's net. When its belly was ripped open and the alien object fell out, the fisherman sold it to a hunter by the name of Jara.

Around the time, the Yadavas were in for considerable excitement as their Prince Aniruddha disappeared one night. The prince had last been seen sound asleep in his bed but the morning found him missing along with the bed. It was a matter of grave concern and the entire kingdom feared the worst. They remembered the dreadful years when Pradyumna had been lost to them and they thought it too cruel that he go through the agony of a kidnapped child as well.

Krishna and Munna seemed more relaxed and when Rukmini demanded an explanation for their infuriating attitude, it was Maya who explained, 'It is true that Anirudha is missing but it does not make sense that his kidnapper or kidnappers would take his bed along. Given how good looking the prince is, I am sure it is a delicate situation involving an infatuated young girl. When the colourful love lives of the Yadu men are taken into account, we can safely say that the young woman is an Asura princess and it is more than likely that she has a homicidal maniac blessed with boons of invincibility for a father.'

'This is not a joking matter! "The colourful love lives of the Yadu men", may sound romantic and exciting but there is far too much bloodletting in these stories to my taste. If as you say, there is a young woman involved, who deems it perfectly acceptable to spirit away a married man while he is sleeping, then we really have to wonder if her character is suitably spotless!'

'I am sure her character is just fine!' Krishna replied. 'If she had carried him out in chains after gagging him to stop his kicking and screaming, there would admittedly be a reason to worry. But I am sure this mysterious woman is merely high-spirited with a vivid imagination. We still need to ascertain his whereabouts and I have organized search parties to collect information about the same. Don't worry about him, Rukmini! He is no longer a boy, but a man fully grown, and I am sure he will be able to take care of himself.'

Narada paid the Yadus a visit after a few anxiety-filled months had elapsed with nobody being wiser about the current location of their prince. It was the muni who wandered the Three Worlds, who was able to shed light on the matter, 'The Asura King Banasura of Sonatipura, has a beautiful daughter named Usha. Her father enjoys the protection of Lord Shiva and Parvathi and the divine couple are guardians of the kingdom. Once, Usha accidentally saw Shiva and Parvathi making love to each other, and the intimate acts she witnessed made a deep impression on her. Soon after, her dreams were haunted by a handsome young prince and she fell in love with him.

Usha confided her troubled thoughts in her friend, Chitralekha. Promising to help her fulfil her desires, Chitralekha drew portraits of all the princes she knew—till at last Usha discovered that the man of her dreams was none other than Aniruddha of the Yadava race and the grandson of Krishna. Her friend then brought him to her while he was sleeping in his bed.

Aniruddha and Usha were wed in secret and had been living together, but alas they were discovered! The valiant prince slew the guards who attempted to capture him, but Bana employed his dark magic and incarcerated him with the help of a terrible noose infused with the power of a serpent. He needs your help to free himself and when I found out about his plight, I made haste to let you know!'

Krishna, Balarama and Munna left at once for Sonatipura where Bana awaited them with his army. Shiva was present with his son, Karthikeya, the commander-in-chief of the Devas, to honour his promise to his devotee. A short but furious battle followed where Krishna took on Bana shielded by Shiva, Munna duelled with Karthikeya and Balarama turned his attention to Bana's army led by his able ministers. Munna fought Karthikeya so furiously that he was forced to retreat. Shiva also yielded to Krishna and the latter would have killed Bana had not Shiva personally appealed to him to spare him.

Aniruddha was released and the Yadavas made ready to return home. It was their finest hour as they had proved on that day that neither man nor the Gods could ever hope to prevail over them. A jubilant populace awaited them when the triumphant Yadava army returned with their prince and his new bride, having once again prevailed despite impossible odds. They bragged that even the three-eyed God could not stop Krishna in battle and Gandhari be damned, they were all going to live forever. Their joy had reached its zenith, when Krishna's divine discus, the Sudharshana chakra which had been given to him by Agni, detached itself from his finger, flew up into the sky of its own accord and hovering briefly over his head, disappeared forever into the heavens. The laughter died in their throats and the citizens of Dwaraka returned to their homes in silence.

Munna knew what it all meant, of course. They had turned the final corner. Now nothing but death remained to them. The Sudharshana chakra had returned to its owner, the Protector, Vishnu, because it sensed that Krishna needed it no more. It was a sobering realization. In keeping with his thoughts, evil omens were seen soon after. Thirty-six years had elapsed since Gandhari had pronounced her infamous curse, and the kingdom was rocked by the appearance of evil omens everywhere.

Their sparkling city was invaded by rats the size of pigs. They came out of nowhere in the black of the night. Bold as you please, they gnawed at the exposed limbs, faces and even hair of sleeping men and women, causing them to awake screaming in agony. The furry monsters were said to be so huge that they could easily carry away little babies—which they devoured at leisure. Pregnant women miscarried or they died in labour having given birth to beasts which rend their way out of the womb and fled from the scene of their foul crime. Milk curdled in every home and freshly cooked food turned rotten in their stomachs and was regurgitated as bloody vomit.

The people poured out their complaints to Krishna. Young men in their prime were being afflicted with wasting illnesses or going blind without any discernible cause. Young girls lost their hair and went bald. Feeding mothers suffered from cracked nipples that oozed blood, not milk. Their lifestock had turned ferocious. The sheep laughed like hyenas and their cows attacked them with horns that suddenly seemed longer and sharper.

Krishna listened to them all and declared that the men would leave on a pilgrimage to Prabhasa where they would pray to Lord Shiva to have mercy on them and to save them from their troubles. Preparations were made for the last journey they would all take and the men made ready to leave, listening to last minute admonishments and endearments from their loved ones.

Munna and Maya were not coochie-cooing, however, but engaged in a heated argument. Maya wanted to accompany Munna but he would not hear of it though she uncharacteristically dissolved in tears, begging him not to leave her. Furious with him for making her cry, she ordered him out of her chambers but Munna turned his back on her and went to sleep. Maya spent a restless night, alternately wishing for him to wake up or for her to fall asleep. Finally, she dozed off but it seemed like she had barely shut her eyes when she awoke again. Munna had left her bed.

Maya tried to find him but nobody had seen him. Rochana said that he had stopped by to see Vajra and had played with his grandson for a bit. The little boy had asked him to buy him a flying chariot and Munna had said that he would have one made for him soon. Rukmavathi and Prabhavathi had seen him too and they were both in tears. Maya left at once before they started yammering about their shared loved for Munna.

She had just about resolved to kill him when Munna materialized in front of her out of nowhere. 'I know you hate it when I leave you in bed alone on morning afters, but father wanted me to take care of a few things. You are not mad at me are you? Give me a kiss so that I know you have forgiven me.' He looked so handsome when he puckered his lips that for a second Maya felt like a girl again. Her knees wobbled and her stomach churned but she tried not to show him exactly how much he could still affect her after all the years they had been together. Ignoring his lips, she kissed him gently on the forehead and their eyes locked for just a heartbeat. Maya looked away as her heart started pounding against her chest, fear rising like a tidal wave to drown it. Aniruddha walked into their room just then, 'You lovebirds never give it a rest do you? I hate to interrupt this passionate scene but grandfather wants us to leave immediately and you are to go to him at once!'

Munna gave her hand a final squeeze and left hastily, since he did not want to keep Krishna waiting. Anirudha followed, after giving Maya a quick hug of farewell. Shortly after, as women and children said their goodbyes, a long procession wound its way out of Dwaraka. None of them would return. All alone in her room, Maya was fighting the urge to run behind Munna. She wished she had given him a passionate kiss, just the way he liked it to show him that he had been forgiven. And to tell him that she could never stay mad at him. There was more, so much more to be conveyed. But it would all have to wait.

Epilogue

Beyond the Flames, Ashes and Death

Rati was inconsolable as the scenes of horror she had insisted on witnessing played themselves over and over in her head, till she thought she would go mad. Kama did his best to calm her down, but she could not stop crying and finally, he lifted her on to his lap and gently rocked her, thinking to himself that all this drama could have been avoided if she had only listened to him. 'You knew this would happen, didn't you? It was foretold...' he began, knowing that she needed to discuss the tumultuous events that had such a great bearing on them.

'Of course, I knew it was going to happen. But it was so awful!' said Rati. 'Nothing can prepare you for something like this. I can't get over how Munna and Maya died! It was just too tragic and so unfair! Why couldn't they have died in their sleep together, too old to care about living anymore?'

'In the long run, it does not matter how you die! The purpose of death is to separate the soul from the body and set it free. If you look at it objectively and with detachment, you will realize that there is nothing more or less to death.' Kama said, knowing that cool logic would only make her angrier but he said it anyway because he preferred an angry Rati to a sad one.

'I am sick and tired of all the fuss over the bloody soul!' Rati snapped. 'What is the point of the stupid thing if you can't see it or touch it and barely feel it? And what has become of Munna and Maya's souls? Do you know? I certainly don't. It is not as if the damn things emerged out of their mutilated bodies like golden lights and merged with our bodies or something. Isn't that what is supposed to happen, given that the two of them were us reborn? It is all so confusing! I saw what happened to Krishna as well. The hunter shot his arrow clean through his heel, which is the only vulnerable part of his body, and released him from a mortal's life. They say that his essence became one with Vishnu but I have no idea how such a thing can be ascertained without any discernible proof!'

Kama was pleased to see that the tears had dried up and he decided to keep Rati talking. 'Most things cannot be proved beyond reasonable doubt, but that in itself proves nothing,' said Kama. 'Ultimately it all boils down to faith. And it was my belief that you discovered yours when Shiva brought us back to life and reinstated us in our old positions at heaven. Parvathi did succeed in winning him over with the power of her penances, though some believe that it was my infallible arrows which did the trick, albeit in the manner of a delayed reaction which was unfortunate because it led to a world of tragedy for the both of us.

Be that as it may, Shiva and Parvathi were wed. The Destroyer even parted with his seed and as you know Karthikeya emerged from it. He did battle with Soora and his brothers, managing to rid the world of them and restored Indra to his throne. Once the dictates of destiny were fulfilled, all the Gods—led by Vishnu, the Goddess Gauri and Indra—appealed to Shiva about my fate. Indra told me that the three-eyed God had appeared thoughtful and commented that it had been beyond his own powers to bring Sati back. Vishnu had spoken up then and said that Sati's death had been her choice and Shiva could not thwart free will, but my death was his doing and if he willed it, he could undo it. The Goddess added that when Shiva lost Sati, he would allow none to help him not even himself. It was I alone who managed to get past his formidable fortifications, and it was thanks to my efforts that Sati found her way back to him as Parvathi.

Parvathi also added her appeal and told Shiva that my intentions had not been self-serving like Indra's and I had genuinely tried to help him. Therefore, he must restore me to life in the interest of the Three Worlds in general and for her sake in particular. The Destroyer seemed to concur and long story short, we were back! Shiva thanked me for blessing him with such a wonderful family and he added that the world needed me and my toy bow more than ever. He even jokingly assured me that I could feel free to shoot him with my arrows whenever I liked, promising to keep his third eye shut if I ever did so.'

Rati's tone was impatient when she spoke again, 'That is a wonderful story and you know I love it. But let me stress that if you ever point your arrows in Shiva's direction, you may not have to worry about his third eye but you will certainly have to contend with Parvathi's wrath. Believe me, she is far scarier when angered!

As for my faith, I seem to discover it only to lose it again and again. After what happened to Munna and Maya, it has become hard for me to believe. The blood bath, at the holy spot where the River Sarawati merges into the sea near Prabhasa, has shaken me to the core! I can't believe that the Yadus managed to get stinking drunk while on a pilgrimage! Then Satyaki had to bring up the moral transgressions of Kritavarman during the battle of Kurukshetra. It was bad enough that he did that and got them all embroiled in an inebriated argument, but then he proceeded to chop Kritavarman's head off right in front of his clan members! Kritavarman's relatives then pounced on him, but Munna intervened, trying to save his father's dearest friend, and that murderous mob killed them both.

He was so beautiful, Kama, almost as handsome as you are! Even after he breathed his last, they went on punching him, kicking him and pulverizing the remains until he was reduced to nothing more than a bloody blob. Even Maya would not have been able to recognize him. Seeing the remains of his son, Krishna went on a killing rampage. He grabbed those horrid weeds and they became a formidable mace in his hands. He used it to kill so many of his own kith and kin that I lost count and seeing him like that made me cry some more. Others followed his example and the Yadavas went mad killing each other till there was no one left to kill.

Krishna alone remained standing when his entire clan lay dead at his feet. He dropped the mace and sent word to Arjuna through his charioteer Daruka, before allowing the hunter to take his life. Mercifully, Balarama was not part of the mass killing. He gave up his life voluntarily while meditating on the seashore. I was weeping so hard by then, I could barely see what was going on, but there was worse to come.

Arjuna arrived on the spot and performed the funeral rites for the deceased Yadus. In keeping with Krishna's final instructions, he organized the women, children, the old and infirm that was all that was left of the Yadava clan and led them towards Indraprastha Maya was part of this group. You should have seen her Kama! It looked like she was already dead without her Munna. En route, the group was attacked by bandits. Arjuna tried to defend them but his memory failed him and he could not even string his legendary bow! He could only watch helplessly till the ambush ended as swiftly as it had begun. Heartbroken, he shepherded the survivors to Indraprastha and crowned Munna's grandson, Vajra as the king.

Those ruffians made off with as many women as they could. Maya came to life then. She knew that she would be gang-raped before being sold into slavery so she fought them and forced them to kill her. They knocked out her teeth, tore her clothes and smashed her knee with a mace when she refused to uncross her legs, but still she attacked them like a wildcat till they plunged a dagger into her chest to get her to stop struggling...' Rati was crying again and Kama had just opened his mouth when she burst out, 'Don't you tell me they are in a better place, because I'll lose control and kick you out of here!'

'I wasn't going to say that!' Kama assured her, 'The truth is that I have no idea where they are but unlike you, the way I see it, there is no reason to be so upset. We did not know what would become of us after the burning. Personally, I cannot account for the interim between my infamous encounter with Shiva and my revival and I know it was the same for you. It remains a mysterious black hole in my memory. Indra told me about your penances and Shiva's promise about how we would be reunited in the world of mortals. If it hadn't been for that, I don't think we would have watched over Munna and Maya the way we did...

Like us, they fell in love and had a wonderful life before they had to give it up. But the point is, we are back together despite the fact that neither of us saw it coming. Munna and Maya have an equal chance of reuniting someday in the future... That is comforting is it not?'

'It is hardly comforting!' Rati retorted. 'The whole thing is just too damned arbitrary! All you have done is scare me about our own future! Indra is going to send you off on one of his fool's errands again and you will run afoul of a sage or a God who will blow you up to itty bitty bits and then we will be back exactly where we began. Where does it all end?'

Kama smiled. 'When you talk like this you sound like Maya! Remember how Munna said she could drink the nectar of immortality and still call it piss?'

'Of course Maya tended to sound like me! I am the original product remember? But you have not answered me, what will become of us Kama?'

'I honestly don't know, Rati. It is unlikely we will be around forever, but in the meantime, why worry about it? And don't you think Munna sounded exactly like me when he said that the people you care for will not be lost to you forever? I believe in what we said with every fibre of my being!' Kama was pleased to see that he had finally succeeded in getting her to stop crying. She was rolling her eyes at him over his foolish optimism, but it was still an improvement on tears. Perhaps he should talk to Brahma about creating his next batch of women, sans tear ducts.

Rati was speaking, and Kama tuned in at once, 'I don't believe in any of those things anymore, Kama. But I have always had faith in you and in us. No matter what happens, we will always find our way back to each other. And that is a promise!'

Touched by her words, Kama wrapped his arms around her and nuzzled her neck gently. It had taken a miracle for them to find each other and he still could not know for sure if it was real or just a dream. And even if all this was an impossible fantasy, he wouldn't have cared, for he knew only one thing for sure. After he had been burnt to death, Rati had found a way to reach him past the flames, ashes and whatever lay beyond. That was enough. He was grateful and could ask for no more.

Bibliography

Ascetic Mysticism: Puranic Records of Shiva and Shakthi. Ed. Sadhu Santideva. New Delhi: Cosmo Publications, 2000.

*Benton, Catherine. *God of Desire: Tales of Kamadeva in Sanskrit Story Literature*. Albany: State University of New York Press, 2006.

Bhattacharya, J. N., and Nilanjana Sarkar. Eds. *Encyclopaedic Dictionary of Sanskrit Literature*. 1st ed. Vol 1. Delhi: Global Vision Publishing House, 2004.

Chaturvedi, B.K. *Vishnu Purana*. New Delhi: Diamond Pocket Books, 2006

Danielou, Alain. *The Myths and Gods of India: The Classic Work on Hindu Polytheism*. Rochester: Inner Traditions International, 1991.

Garrett, John. *A Classical Dictionary of India*. Asylum Press, 1871.

Kapoor, Subodh. Ed. *The Indian Encyclopaedia*. New Delhi: Cosmo Publications, 2002.

Kempton, Sally. *Awakening Shakti: The Transformative Power of the Goddess of Yoga*. Boulder, CO: Sounds True, Inc, 2013.

Kennedy, Vans. *Researches into the Nature and Affinity of Hindu Mythology*. London: Longman, Rees, Orme, Brown, and Green, 1831.

Krishna, Nanditha. *The Book of Vishnu*. New Delhi: Penguin Books, 2009.

Leviton, Richard. *The Gods in their Cities: Geomantic Locales of the Ray Masters and Great White Brotherhood, and How to Interact with them.* Lincoln, NE: iUniverse, 2006.

Menon, Ramesh. *Blue God: A Life of Krishna.* Lincoln, NE: Writers Club Press, 2000.

Parmeshwaranand, Swami. *Encyclopaedic Dictionary of Puranas.* 1st ed. 5 vols. New Delhi: Sarup & Sons, 2001.

Encyclopaedia of the Saivism. 1st ed. Vol.1. New Delhi: Sarup & Sons, 2004.

Pattanaik, Devdutt. *Indian Mythology: Tales, Symbols, and Rituals from the Heart of the Subcontinent.* Rochester: Inner Traditions International, 2003.

Rosen, Steven, J. *The Agni and the Ecstasy: Collected Essays of Steven J. Rosen.* Ed. J.B. Morgan. UK: Arktos Media, 2012.

Sivaraman, Akila. *Sri Kandha Puranam.* Chennai: Giri Trading Agency Private Limited, 2006.

The Vishnu Purana: A System of Hindu Mythology and Tradition. Trans. H.H. Wilson. London: John Murray, 1840.

Uberoi, Meera. *The Mahabharata.* New Delhi: Ratna Sagar Pvt. Ltd, 1996.

Verma, Rajeev. *Faith and Philosophy of Hinduism.* New Delhi: Kalpaz Publications, 2009.

Vishnu Purana: English Translation. Trans. M.N. Dutt. Calcutta: Elysium Press, 1896.

Wilkins, William, J. *Hindu Mythology, Vedic and Puranic.* Alexandria: Library of Alexandria, 1975.

Williams, George, M. *Handbook of Hindy Mythology.* New York: Oxford University Press, 2003.

Zimmer, Heinrich. *Philosophies of India.* New York: Bollingen Foundation New York, 1969.